The Unforgiven
Echoes from the Past
Book 3

by Irina Shapiro

Copyright

Table of Contents

Prologue

Narrow shafts of summer sunshine pierced the leafy canopy and lit the murky green water, which sparkled playfully as it lapped against the shore. The world seemed to stand still, nature awaiting the outcome of the human drama playing out on its barren shore. She stared into the barrel of the pistol, unable to believe it was real and had been there all along, ready to be used by the hand of the person who'd harbored such malice for so long. She'd never seen death up close, but it had been her constant companion these past few years. It was death that had led her to this moment, this impasse. Or had it been life?

She took a shuddering breath and met her enemy's gaze, hoping she didn't look as scared as she felt. But she was scared. Terrified, in fact, because everything that had happened had been her fault and she wouldn't allow the person she loved best in this world to take the fall. Could this really be it? Was her life to be cut short when it had only just begun, when she had finally come to understand what it meant to love and want, not as a child, but as a woman? Would this person who was meant to love and care for her be the instrument of her destruction?

When the pistol wavered for just a moment, she thought the danger might be past, but she was mistaken. She lunged for the gun just as the bullet erupted from the pistol's toy-sized barrel, the loud crack startling a flock of cranes. She crumpled to the porch, as if in slow motion, as searing pain tore through her chest. She watched in amazement as a bloody flower bloomed on her camisole, the petals unfolding with unnatural speed. She heard the cry of a child, a sharp intake of breath from her executioner, and then the muted cadence of words, spoken harshly and with great purpose. But most of all, she heard her own ragged breathing and the pounding in her veins, loud in her ears as the lifeblood began to drain from her onto the rough boards.

She lay on her back, her gaze fixed on a gossamer shred of cloud that lazily floated across the sun, momentarily shielding her gaze from the glaring sun. Her heartbeat began to slow as she felt a trickle of blood ooze from the side of her mouth and onto her shoulder. She used the last of her strength to reach out and clasp the hand of the one she'd been trying to save, and then let go. The final thought that passed through her muddled mind just before darkness descended was that she'd never been meant to live in the first place because her very existence had been an affront to God.

Chapter 1

April 2014

New Orleans, Louisiana

Quinn stepped out onto the wrought-iron balcony of her hotel room and was instantly enveloped in the warm embrace of the Louisiana afternoon. Moisture permeated the air, making it feel thick and lush. She'd spent time in hot places before, but this was not the dry, merciless heat of the Middle East or the shimmering haze of the Caribbean. This warmth was fecund and fragrant, and made her feel heavy-limbed and drowsy. It was hard to believe she'd been wearing a winter coat and scarf only that morning when she'd boarded her flight at Heathrow. Both were now stowed in her case, and wouldn't be needed until she returned to cold, rainy England. She did feel tired. It was around eight o'clock in London, and she'd woken up at an ungodly hour to get to the airport on time. Perhaps she could lie down for a bit.

The cool breath of the room's air conditioning made a welcome change from the heat outside. Quinn kicked off her shoes and stretched out on the double bed, but her guilty conscience wasn't about to let her off the hook and allow her to rest. She'd argued with Gabe last night, and the fight weighed heavily on her, making her wish they'd parted on better terms. Gabe had driven her to the airport and helped her with her luggage, but had been cool and distant, even when he kissed her goodbye, still smarting from the night before. He had a right to be cross; Quinn knew that, but she still hoped he'd understand her point of view.

"Quinn, we are getting married next month," Gabe had fumed, willing her to change her mind about going to New Orleans. "Emma is finally settling into her new routine. Your parents are coming from Spain in just over a fortnight. You have Sylvia and your newfound brothers to deal with, *and* you're pregnant. Why must you do this now?" he had demanded. "I promise you, we'll go together in the summer. I'll be able to take time off from work and Emma will be on summer holidays, so she can come with us. What's the bleeding rush?"

But Quinn wouldn't be deterred. She knew Gabe's argument made perfect sense, and he had every right to question her sanity, but she had to do this, and it had to be now. She couldn't get on with her life and plan her future until she put this last piece of the puzzle in its rightful place. She'd found her birth mother after all these years, and now knew the story of her birth and the reason for her abandonment, but somehow, finding Sylvia had generated more questions than answers.

Sylvia wasn't at all what Quinn had expected or hoped for, nor was her explanation of what had led her to leave her newborn in a church pew foolproof, raising the convoluted question of Quinn's paternity. Perhaps she would never truly know if Sylvia had been raped by three men, as she claimed, or had been a willing participant in a drunken Christmas Eve romp that had resulted in Quinn's birth. There had been a fourth candidate as well, a married man Sylvia had enjoyed a brief fling with just before that fateful evening, but he'd proved to be sterile, and had been crossed off the list of possible dads, leaving Quinn with one last candidate, an American——Seth Besson——who had to be responsible for the burden of her strange gift. Quinn's ability to see into the past and step into the lives of people who were long dead had to come from his family, since it hadn't come from Sylvia. Quinn needed to put her questions and fears to rest before she welcomed her child into the world, since her baby might be weighed down with the same ability, if it was genetic.

Quinn sighed and turned onto her side, pulling in her knees and curling into a shrimp-like position. She wished Gabe would call. She couldn't bear that he was angry with her. He knew how important this was to her, but she couldn't feel good about pursuing her birth father without his blessing. She reached over to the nightstand and checked her mobile. There was a text from her mother, one from her cousin and best friend Jill, and several from Phoebe Russell, commander-in-chief of the upcoming wedding. Gabe's mother had embraced her role with relish, planning the ceremony and the reception afterward down to every minor detail. Quinn didn't mind. The only aspect of the wedding planning she'd really enjoyed was choosing her dress. It had to be special, and it had to be unique. She'd visited several bridal boutiques but hadn't found what she was looking for, until she got a call from Jill.

"Quinn, I got it," Jill had cried into the phone. "It's perfect. Exactly what you wanted. Come and see."

Jill's shop now carried more new and trendy merchandise, since she couldn't make a living only from vintage stock, but she still kept a large section of the shop devoted only to vintage pieces, and from time to time she came across a real gem. Jill had been right. The gown was exquisite. It was made of ivory silk and embellished with delicate embroidery picked out in gold and silver thread. The pattern circled the waist and crisscrossed in front before tracing the outline of the deep V-neck and coming down the back, crisscrossing once more before rejoining the embroidery at the waist. The silk fell in delicate folds, giving the gown a Grecian look and conveniently camouflaging Quinn's tiny belly. The baby would probably be moving by the time she actually got to wear the frock, but for now it was still slumbering peacefully inside her womb, its steady heartbeat on the scan the only proof that it was doing well. Quinn splayed her had on her belly. This was her first pregnancy, and she alternated between delight and uncertainty, devouring pregnancy manuals and reading up on every new symptom as it came up.

"I'm doing this for you," she whispered. "For both of us." She hoped that was true. Finding the source of the gift didn't mean she could do anything to turn it off. It wasn't a tap or a light switch, and she wouldn't know for years to come if her child would be able to see into the past like its mother. Quinn hadn't known about her ability until she was nearly ten. But she had to try. At the very least, finding out would appease her deep curiosity about the origin of this strange legacy.

The mobile trilled just as she was beginning to doze off. Gabe.

"Hello," Quinn said, unsure what his mood would be like.

"Sorry I didn't ring earlier. I was stuck in a meeting. Did you get in all right?" Gabe asked, sounding contrite.

"Yes. It's so warm here," she complained. "I should have brought lighter clothes."

"Hopefully, you won't be there long enough to need them. Quinn, just get this done and come home. I'm really not comfortable with you being there alone."

"Gabe, we've been over this. I'll meet the man, ask him for a DNA sample, question him about his family history, and leave. Nothing to worry about. Nothing at all."

"Right. Nothing to worry about," Gabe repeated.

"You're practically oozing sarcasm," Quinn replied with a smile, relieved that he was no longer angry with her.

"Am I? Well, I'm a bit concerned about you walking into some man's office, announcing to him that you are his long-lost daughter, demanding physical proof, and then interrogating him about his psychic relatives. There are some who might not take kindly to that."

"You know, you are becoming a real worrywart, Gabriel Russell. I've never known you to be so over-protective."

"I've never loved anyone this much before," he replied, a catch in his voice. "I'm just worried about you and the baby."

"No need to be. How's Emma? Is she in bed?"

"I just read her a story, tucked her in with Mr. Rabbit, and snuck out before she had a chance to trick me into reading her something the length of the *Iliad*. You know how she hates going to sleep. She keeps asking when you'll be back. She misses you."

"I miss her too. Tell her we'll go shopping for her dress as soon as I get back."

"She can't wait to be a bridesmaid."

"I have a more important role for her, but I want it to be a surprise."

"My lips are sealed."

"Daddy, I can't sleep," came a wail over the line. "Read me one more story."

"Sounds like a call to duty," Quinn said, smiling. She wanted nothing more than to read Emma a story and then curl up next to Gabe in their bed. She'd put on a brave face for Gabe, but she really was worried about meeting Seth Besson, and she wasn't entirely sure whose reaction would be more volatile, hers or his.

Chapter 2

The day was muggy and warm, with abundant sunshine bathing everything in a hazy glow. Quinn stepped out of the taxi and stared up at the sign on the indistinct gray building in front of her. The squat and solid office had small windows prudently covered with shades against the sun. Several lorries of varying sizes were parked in the lot adjacent to the building, their cabs empty of drivers. This part of town was more industrial, and not a little seedy. The sign above the door read 'Besson Trucking LTD.' The lettering must have been a bright red at some point, but had faded to the color of dried blood, a rusty brown that was beginning to flake in places. Quinn took a deep breath and opened the door.

She stepped into a small reception area with a worn gray industrial carpet and several hardback plastic chairs. An older woman, who seemed to think it was still the sixties, sat behind the desk, her beehive hairstyle vibrating as she typed vigorously. The phone rang and she snatched it up, signaling to Quinn with one pink-tipped finger that she would be with her momentarily. Quinn considered taking a seat, but was too nervous, so she remained standing. She supposed it wasn't very important for a lorry company to look smart, but she'd expected something a little more upscale. Perhaps Mr. Besson couldn't afford to renovate, or simply didn't see the need.

The receptionist finished the call and smiled at Quinn, stretching her frosted pink lips in a genuine smile of welcome. "How can I help?"

"Good morning," Quinn began. "I have an appointment with Mr. Besson."

"Oh, right. Of course you do. You're that nice British lady who called yesterday. Well, go right in, darlin'. Just through there," she said, indicating the door directly across from her desk. "He's expecting you."

"Thank you."

Quinn briefly considered walking out and going straight back to the hotel to collect her things before racing to the airport to catch the first flight to whatever hub would offer her a connection to London. This was mad. She didn't belong here. What could she possibly hope to gain from meeting this man, who was as far removed from her own culture and background as he could be? She suddenly wished that Gabe were there, and couldn't recall exactly why she'd been so adamant about doing this alone.

You've come all this way, she reminded herself as she took a hesitant step toward the office. *Just meet him and find out what you can, then run.*

Quinn walked toward the door under the watchful eye of the receptionist. She knocked and a voice from within the office invited her to enter. She sucked in her breath as she pushed open the door, only to exhale it in surprise. The man, or more accurately boy, seated behind the desk couldn't be the right person. He looked to be about eighteen, and had shaggy dark hair and something resembling a goatee, which he had probably tried to grow to hide some of his adolescent spots.

"I was hoping to speak to Mr. Besson," Quinn said as she advanced into the office. Her stomach soured with disappointment. It would seem that she'd come halfway around the world in pursuit of the wrong Seth Besson.

"Yeah, I know. Sorry. I'm Brett Besson, the heir apparent. Dad's out of the office for a few days and I've been roped into looking after things here. As you can see, it's practically a beehive of activity," the young man said, dripping sarcasm. "I'm supposed to be on spring break, hanging out with my friends. Instead I'm stuck here with Sandra Dee."

"Sandra Dee?" Quinn echoed, confused.

"You know, from *Grease*. Oh, right, you're from England. You've probably never seen it."

"Sorry, no, but I've heard of it, of course."

14

"Anyhow, how can I help you? Ms. Allenby, is it?"

"Yes." Quinn looked around, feeling awkward at being expected to stand in front of the desk like an errant pupil before a headmistress.

"Oh, sorry. Please sit down," Brett said.

Quinn sat in a leather armchair facing the desk, unsure what to say to the young man. She could hardly explain her reason for being there without telling him what his father had been up to thirty years ago while doing a semester abroad in Scotland. Whatever anger and resentment she felt toward Seth Besson, she had no right to take out her feelings on his unsuspecting son, so she had to be discreet.

"Local or interstate?" Brett asked.

"Sorry, what?"

"What type of trucking are you interesting in?"

"Actually I need to speak to your father regarding a personal matter. When do you expect him back?"

"He's supposed to be resting till next Monday, but I bet he'll come prancing in here by Thursday, desperate to ream me out for not doing enough in his absence. What kind of personal matter?" Brett asked, his eyes narrowing as he gave Quinn an appraising stare.

"The kind that I can discuss only with him. He's resting, you said?" she asked. Seth Besson would be a few years older than Sylvia, so probably still in his forties, or possibly early fifties. "Is he ill?"

"Dad doesn't want any of his competitors to know, but he's had gallbladder surgery. He thinks admitting to any type of ailment makes him look weak. Not like he's got arthritis or cataracts, or something old people get." Brett shrugged dismissively. "Tell you what. He's bored out of his mind sitting around the house, recuperating. How about I give him a call and tell him there's a pretty British lady here to see him. Let's see what he says." He gave Quinn a conspiratorial wink and reached for the phone.

He hung up after a very brief conversation and scribbled something on a notepad, then tore out the sheet and handed it to her. "Here's the address. He's waiting for you."

"Is it far from here?" Quinn asked as she looked at the address.

"It's in the Garden District. A half-hour ride, at least. I take it you'll need a cab?" Brett buzzed the intercom and spoke to the receptionist. "Hey, Shirley. Call Ms. Allenby a cab, will ya?" He hung up and turned back to Quinn. "The cab should be here in about ten minutes. Good luck with Dad."

"Thanks," Quinn replied and got up to leave. "It was lovely to meet you."

"Eh, likewise, I'm sure," Brett answered with a sly grin. She was sure he was having fun at her expense. "Give my best to the queen," he added, confirming her suspicions. *That little wanker!*

"I'll be sure to do that next time I'm invited for tea," Quinn replied with a forced smile and walked out of the office.

"You can wait in here if you like," Shirley said. "It's getting toasty out there. Lived here all my life, and still can't get used to the infernal heat. And it's only April." She sighed.

"Thank you, but I'll wait outside," Quinn replied. It would be wiser to remain in the air-conditioned office, but she just wanted to leave. A few minutes in the muggy heat wouldn't kill her.

By the time the taxi arrived nearly half an hour later, Quinn was sweating and regretting her decision to wait outside. The air conditioning was barely working, so she rolled down the window and allowed the breeze to caress her face as the car made its leisurely way through congested lunchtime traffic toward the Garden District. She suspected the driver, hearing her accent and realizing she was a foreigner, had decided to take the scenic route since she'd have no idea if he drove in circles for an hour. He finally stopped in front of a brick mansion, its impressive wrought-iron gates, a bronze letter B proudly displayed within a circle of cast-iron leaves. A security camera positioned atop a brick pillar turned its eye on her when she rang the bell.

The gates slid apart silently on well-oiled hinges. Quinn walked up the drive, which was flanked by a lush lawn and flowering shrubs that she thought were azaleas. The three-story house resembled an English manor house, though it looked fairly new.

A small, dark-skinned woman opened the door and invited Quinn to come in. "Mr. Besson is expecting you," she said. "He's out back, on the lanai."

The housekeeper led Quinn down a tiled corridor and through a huge modern kitchen toward a sliding door that led to the back garden. It was an oasis of leafy plants and gurgling water that cascaded from a waterfall into a decorative pond. Quinn saw the white and red glimmer of koi fish as they passed close to the surface, making the water ripple and shimmer in the sunlight. A large in-ground pool just beyond the pond sparkled in the sunshine, and several large umbrellas shaded clusters of empty beach chairs. There was a bar area and a small stand off to the side, which Quinn knew from past experience was reserved for a DJ and his equipment. Seth Besson clearly liked to entertain in style. Quinn looked around, but didn't see anyone.

"He's over there," the housekeeper said. She directed Quinn off to the right, where a shady gazebo housed two deck chairs with a low table between them. A man in a T-shirt and shorts reclined in one of the chairs, a baseball cap pulled low over his eyes. "Ah, Mr. Besson. Your guest is here."

The man jerked awake and sat up, wincing in pain at the sudden movement. He pushed up his cap and smiled at Quinn, making her breath catch in her throat. Was this man really her father?

"Hi. Seth Besson. Please make yourself comfortable. Dolores, bring us something cool to drink. Or would you prefer a pot of tea? I'm afraid I only have Lipton. Not much of a tea drinker, I'm afraid," he added apologetically.

"Something cool would be lovely. Thank you," Quinn replied, rooted to the spot.

"Iced tea? Lemonade? Mineral water?" Seth asked.

"Lemonade, please."

"Dolores, you heard the lady."

The housekeeper scampered off and left Quinn with Seth. Quinn couldn't help but stare. He was a big man—not overweight, but muscular and tall. He had dark hair, dark eyes, and a bronze tan that gave him a Mediterranean appearance. Quinn tried to find something familiar in his blunt features, but saw absolutely no resemblance to herself except the hair color, which she also shared with Sylvia. Seth's hair was cropped close to the scalp, so it was hard to tell if it might curl when allowed to grow longer. Quinn's hair wasn't curly, but had a natural wave, just like Sylvia's, and her eyes were a deep hazel. Neither Sylvia nor Seth had hazel eyes, but Sylvia had once remarked on Quinn's resemblance to her own mother.

Seth took off his cap and looked up at her. "You gonna stand there all day?" he asked with a smile. His teeth looked very white against his tan and he had a nice smile that actually reached his eyes and made Quinn feel a little more comfortable.

She took a seat and faced her host. "I'm sorry to barge in on you like this. Your son said you're recuperating from surgery."

"That little twerp. I told him to keep quiet about that. No one needs to know my private business," he groused. "Trucking is a cutthroat business. My competitors are vultures who'll go after

18

my contracts if they think I might not be paying attention, even for one day."

"I had no idea trucking was so competitive," Quinn replied. She hadn't meant to sound sarcastic, but Seth's grin faded and he cocked his head to the side, watching her with interest.

"Enough about trucking then. Tell me why you're here."

Quinn suddenly wished the ground beneath her would open up and swallow her whole. This man intimidated her even more than Robert Chatham had when she met him in Edinburgh. She knew Chatham's type well, but Seth Besson was an unknown quantity. She looked up and saw his eyes glinting with amusement.

"Come on, doll. I won't bite. Let's hear it."

Quinn could draw out the story and build up to what she'd come to say, but Seth didn't seem like someone who'd appreciate a song and dance. He looked like a man who valued directness and economy of speech.

"I believe you are my biological father," she said and waited for his reaction. He continued to look at her, as if she hadn't spoken. She was just about to ask him if he'd heard her when Dolores appeared with the lemonade.

"Try it. No one makes lemonade like Dolores. She puts in a bit of honey to sweeten it instead of sugar. I drink pitchers of this stuff during the summer," Seth said as he waited for Quinn to taste the drink.

"It's wonderful." Quinn took several sips to fill the awkward silence that sprang up between them. When Dolores finally walked away, Seth continued to watch Quinn with that unfathomable expression.

"Mr. Besson—"

"Call me Seth," he interrupted. "No need to stand on ceremony, especially if you think you sprang from my loins," he added with a chuckle. "So, who's your mother then?"

"Sylvia. Sylvia Moore."

Seth shrugged. "Doesn't ring a bell. Tell me more."

"You met her at the house of your friend Robert Chatham, Christmas Eve of 1982."

"Did I?"

"You did," Quinn replied, resenting his refusal to engage. He was baiting her, making her anxious.

"I'm sorry. I don't remember."

"You don't remember raping a girl at a party?" she demanded, now angry. How cavalier these men were about a girl whose life they'd nearly ruined. Sylvia had been nothing to them, a mere diversion that was forgotten as soon as their hangovers wore off the following morning. Perhaps they had been so pissed they hadn't even recalled the events of the previous evening, thinking they'd just had a bit of fun and stumbled off to bed, getting up with a clear conscience on Christmas morning.

"Sweetheart, I'm hardly a saint, but I can assure you I've never forced my attentions on any girl. They all came willingly enough, and if they weren't interested, there were plenty of other fish in the sea."

"This one didn't," Quinn retorted.

"Look, I don't know what your mother told you, or even who she is for that matter, but I'm pretty sure you're not my spawn. Now, having said that, I will gladly give you a swab or whatever it is you need from me to put your mind at rest. I'm sure there's a lab right here in New Orleans that can expedite the results. I'll even pay for the test out of my own pocket to show you

I bear no ill-will toward you and I have every confidence you are not mine. How 'bout that?"

"That's fine, but I will send it to my own lab, if you have no objection."

"Let's do two. I'll take one to a lab here and you can send yours to whomever you choose. That way we'll know for sure."

"Do you at least remember Robert Chatham?" Quinn asked as she reached for a DNA kit from her handbag.

"Sure. I met him at university. Cocky little bastard. Thought he could use me to gain popularity."

"May I ask you a question?" Quinn said as she handed Seth a swab.

"Go right ahead."

"What made you choose Scotland?"

Seth Besson was so quintessentially American that Quinn simply couldn't imagine him walking the halls of St. Andrews University, or being friends with someone like Robert Chatham. They were polar opposites. The only similarity of note was their arrogance, which grated on Quinn since it was meant to shred her confidence.

Seth laughed and took a sip of lemonade. "Pure idiocy is what it was. I got it into my head that I hated the South and wanted nothing to do with my daddy's trucking business. I wanted to go to Europe and live in the land of knights and kings. Well, my grades were excellent, so I applied to a few programs and got into the Sorbonne and St. Andrews. I don't speak a word of French, other than the language of food, so I chose Scotland. Seemed like a good idea at the time. I was never more miserable. It was cold, wet, and boring. Most other students treated me like I was some sort of curiosity because I was American and spoke the Queen's English with a Southern drawl, so I fell in with Robert and his crew out of desperation. He was a real jackass, to be sure, but at least he invited me to come along when they went to the pub or to a football match. I was his pet American, and he used me to pick up girls, who liked my accent and asked all kinds of ridiculous questions, like if my family owned slaves. Yes, my family owned slaves before the Civil War. I will not apologize for what my ancestors did. Y'all did much worse. Just check the history books."

Quinn glanced away from Seth, annoyed by his belligerence. She wasn't there to compare notes on their countries' histories. Every country had their moments of shame and glory, and England and the United States had more than most, some of those highs and lows forever intertwined and frequently explored in literature, film, and song.

Seth smiled ruefully as he removed his cap, scratched his scalp, and replaced the cap on his head. "Sorry, I digress. Anyway, I lasted one semester, then ran back home with my tail between my legs. And before you ask, I didn't do much dating in Scotland. The girls just weren't my speed."

"Are you saying you were celibate the entire time you were there?" It was a rude question, but she had to ask. Seth Besson was her final candidate. Neither Rhys, Robert, nor Stephen was a DNA match, so if Seth wasn't either, who the hell had fathered her?

"Celibate? Lord, no. I fucked like a bunny, if you pardon my saying so, but I always, *always* used a condom. My mama always said, 'Don't bring nothing into this world that you're not willing to take responsibility for,' and the last thing I wanted was to leave a child of mine in Scotland. I am happily divorced, but I love my son and have been a good father to him. I take that role very seriously, and if you prove to be mine, I will take my responsibility toward you just as seriously. I'm a man of honor."

A little taken aback by his speech, Quinn nodded in understanding. She couldn't fault a grown man for having a sex life, especially with women who were willing. It was none of her business, and she had no right to judge him until she knew the truth. Sylvia had not been entirely honest with her anyway, and had withheld important details that had led to Quinn questioning

22

her motives and her version of events. Rhys Morgan backed Sylvia's story. Robert Chatham swore she'd been willing. And Stephen Kane, who'd had a brief relationship with Sylvia before the ill-fated Christmas party but left her to reconcile with his wife, called Sylvia 'sexually aware' and said she had known what she was about, even at sixteen. Seth Besson was the only candidate left standing, and he couldn't even remember her—or so he said.

Seth scraped the inside of his cheek with two swabs and handed them both to Quinn, who inserted them into plastic tubes and sealed them. She handed one back to Seth and stowed the other in her purse. She'd overnight it to Colin Scott as soon as she left Seth's house and located a FedEx office. Colin would have the results for her by the end of the week, if she were lucky.

"Look, I'm sorry you're disappointed," Seth said. "It's important to know who your parents are, and I can see how it would leave a blank hole in your sense of self, but you've come all this way for nothing. I hope you find what you're searching for."

"Thank you, Seth, and I appreciate you giving me a sample. I won't trouble you again unless I have to."

"No problem. To tell you the truth, you were a welcome diversion. I hate sitting here by my lonesome. I'm an active person by nature. I'm going into the office tomorrow, ready or not. Brett will be thrilled. That boy does nothing but hang out with friends, playing video games and smoking weed. I suppose I can't blame him, I was no better at his age, except I played the guitar instead of video games. We didn't have much in the way of electronic entertainment back then. I got an Atari eventually, but the games were primitive and mind-numbingly boring, not like today's stuff. I play sometimes when Brett's not around. Assassin's Creed; now that's a great game." He smiled guiltily. "Sorry, I didn't mean to ramble on. I just don't enjoy solitude, I guess. I should have thought of that before I cheated on my wife and lost the only woman who was willing to put up with me. Say, would you like to stay for lunch? Dolores makes the best gumbo."

"Are you supposed to be eating that after your surgery?" Quinn asked, vaguely remembering that gumbo was a spicy Cajun dish.

"No. But I'm not one for bland food. God, I hated the food in England. Come, say you'll stay. I hate eating alone."

"Thank you, Seth, but I must get going. It's been a pleasure meeting you, and I wish you a speedy recovery."

"Suit yourself. Safe flight back," he called after Quinn as she walked away.

Chapter 3

Quinn turned up the air conditioning to high, kicked off her shoes, and flung herself on the bed. She'd had a wasted trip, and Gabe had been right all along. She was chasing shadows. What did it matter who her biological father was? She had a great dad who had loved her since the day she'd come into his life thirty years ago. He would be the one to walk her down the aisle next month when she married Gabe, and he would be the one her child would call 'Grandpa,' not some hot-blooded American alpha male who could trace his roots back to the Confederacy and was probably of the opinion that the South should have won the Civil War. They had nothing in common, and for good reason.

Damn you, Sylvia, Quinn thought viciously. *Why can't you just tell me the truth instead of sending me on this wild goose chase? Is there another man in the mix that I don't know about?*

How many more men would she have to accost with her DNA kit? It was embarrassing and frustrating, and it didn't exactly elevate Sylvia in Quinn's eyes or lend credence to her story. Perhaps Gabe was right and Sylvia had manipulated the facts to gain Quinn's forgiveness and understanding. After all, it would be pretty hard to expect sympathy from the daughter she had abandoned if Sylvia admitted to sleeping with half a dozen men around the same time, getting pregnant by one of them, and then dumping her baby in a church pew and walking away without a backward glance.

Quinn wanted to remain angry, but some part of her pitied the woman. Sylvia had been afraid of losing the daughter she'd just found. She was a woman nearing fifty who'd recently lost her husband to cancer and was about to lose her sons. Sylvia had moved to London to be close to Logan, who worked as a nurse at the London Hospital, but Logan had just moved in with his partner, Colin. Jude, whom Quinn had finally met a week before leaving for New Orleans, spent most of his time on tour, playing various clubs and bars across the U.K. with his band. He was excited about having booked their first gig in Dublin, which was sometime in

June and might open doors to other engagements in Ireland. Sylvia was proud of Jude's ambition and success, but was lonely when he was away, since she didn't have many friends in London.

Quinn folded her arms behind her head and considered her newfound family. The jury was still out on Sylvia, especially after the meeting with Seth Besson, but she liked Logan. He was only a few years younger than Quinn and had a carefree nature that made him easy to talk to. The fact that Quinn already knew his partner and had his approval also bridged the gap between them, making it easier to pursue a relationship. Quinn and Logan had exchanged a few phone calls and texts since meeting a month ago and she felt a swell of sisterly love toward him. Given time, they could become great friends and establish a life-long bond.

Jude, on the other hand, was a totally different kettle of fish. Quinn supposed it was his artistic nature that made him moody and silent, but she felt a definite spark of resentment when he leveled his blue-eyed gaze at her. Perhaps he was worried that his mother would somehow love him less now that she'd found a child she'd abandoned years ago, but Sylvia fussed over Jude so much that it was difficult to imagine such a scenario for even a moment. Sylvia went on and on about Jude's upcoming performance in Ireland, and that was the only time Quinn had noticed a spark of excitement or felt any warmth between Jude and Sylvia.

Jude had hardly paid his mother any attention when they finally got together for dinner at Sylvia's, and barely made eye contact with anyone, except Emma, who seemed to amuse him. Both Gabe and Logan tried to engage him in conversation, but Jude replied with monosyllabic answers and gazed at something just beyond everyone's heads. Quinn noticed him pulling at the sleeves of his jersey, as if afraid someone would see his forearms. He wore a black and white kaffieh wound about his neck and nearly bit Sylvia's head off when she asked if he'd like to take it off.

Both Logan and Sylvia tried to compensate for Jude's silence by making conversation and fussing over Emma, who lapped up the attention. She asked if she might call Logan 'Uncle Logan.' He loved the idea, but when Emma turned to Jude with the same request he simply said, "No thanks, kid. Maybe you can bestow that honor on Colin, since he's now a member of this family. Should I be referring to you as my brother-in-law?" he asked, pinning Colin with his hostile gaze.

"Colin and I are not married. Yet," Logan retorted. Colin shifted uncomfortably, but didn't reply, choosing this moment to excuse himself instead.

"You may call me 'Grandma Sylvia,'" Sylvia chimed in. Quinn hadn't expected that and wasn't at all sure she was ready for Sylvia to become a full-fledged grandmother to Emma. After all, Emma wasn't her biological granddaughter, and it seemed too soon to put a label on their relationship.

"But I already have too many grandmothers," Emma protested. "I had my gran who died, and now I have Grandma Phoebe and Grandma Susan. Do I have four grandmothers when everyone else has two?" Emma asked, seeking clarification. At four, she couldn't possibly hope to grasp the complexity of all these relationships, particularly when the adults were still trying to figure them out and find their footing.

"Sweetheart, I only meant that I would like to be your honorary grandma," Sylvia amended.

"I don't understand," Emma said anxiously.

Quinn put an arm around Emma to comfort her. "It's all right, darling. We'll figure this all out. When I was little, I had to do a family tree to learn all about my family. Perhaps we can do that for you. Would you like that?"

Emma nodded enthusiastically, but Gabe frowned in Quinn's direction. Emma was too young to comprehend the connections that made up her current family. A family tree would lead to a lot of awkward questions, such as why Gabe hadn't been married to her mother or why they'd lived in different countries until Jenna was killed in a car accident that led to Emma coming to live with her father. Having to explain Quinn's parentage would be no simpler task, and Gabe didn't know enough to fill in the blanks for Jenna McAllister, whom he hadn't seen since the weekend Emma was conceived.

"Perhaps we can wait until you're a little older," Gabe suggested. "Then we'll be able to add your brother or sister to the family tree. Wouldn't that be fun?"

"Would I get to come first?" Emma demanded. "I'm the oldest."

"Of course you would be first," Gabe assured her.

"Well, that's all right then. We can wait until there's a baby."

Sylvia's face lit up like a lantern. "Are you...?"

"Yes," Quinn replied, blushing furiously. "It's early days yet."

"Congratulations, sis," Logan exclaimed. "I never thought I'd get to be an uncle, and now I get a gorgeous niece and will have another niece or nephew to spoil. What'ya think, Jude?"

"Splendid," Jude snarled. "Can't wait."

"Jude!" Sylvia cried. "What is wrong with you today?"

"Nothing." Jude pushed his chair back with a vicious scrape and got up from the table. "I'm going out." He turned so suddenly that his kaffieh moved aside, revealing purpling bruises on his neck. He quickly adjusted the scarf and fled the room without saying goodbye. Neither Sylvia nor Logan seemed to notice the bruises and carried on as if nothing had happened.

"Well, I think it's time for pudding. What do you say, Emma? What's your favorite?" Sylvia asked as she began clearing the dishes.

"I like ice cream."

"And a lucky thing it is too, because I got ice cream in three different flavors and a sticky toffee pudding as well. Do you like that?"

"Not really. I'd like some ice cream, please," Emma replied, remembering to be polite.

"Ice cream it is then. Coffee, anyone?" Sylvia asked, looking around the table.

"Tea for me," Colin replied.

"Me as well," Quinn added. She liked coffee, but now that she was pregnant, the bitterness gave her terrible indigestion and the caffeine made her jittery. The tea had caffeine as well, of course, but for some reason didn't have the same effect.

Sylvia bustled off to the kitchen with Logan on her heels, and Colin joined them. Quinn turned to look at Gabe over Emma's head, but he shook his head.

"Later," he mouthed.

It wasn't until Emma was safely tucked into bed that Quinn and Gabe finally got a chance to discuss the evening. "Well, that was a bit awkward, wouldn't you say?" she asked him.

"Logan is a great bloke, and I've always liked Colin," Gabe replied, leaving it at that.

"So what did you think of Sylvia now that you've met her in person?"

Gabe shrugged eloquently. "I don't know, Quinn. It's hard for me to trust her, given what I know. I will take my cues from you when it comes to her."

"Fair enough. And Jude? Did you see those bruises?"

"Quinn, don't get involved. Sylvia won't appreciate it."

"What do you mean?"

"I mean that Jude is clearly a drug user. He kept pulling down his sleeves to hide the track marks on his forearms."

"And the bruises on his neck? Do you think he's been in a fight?" Quinn asked.

Gabe shook his head, an expression of pure skepticism on his handsome face. "No, darling. The bruises encircled his neck and were too even to be caused by someone grabbing him by the neck. I think they were left by a leather belt."

"What? Why? Like a dog collar?"

"Maybe. Or more likely erotic asphyxiation. I've seen those types of bruises before. My roommate at uni was very fond of hanging himself off anything that would hold his weight. He said the orgasms were so powerful you could never go back to straight sex."

"Oh, dear," Quinn replied, shocked. "Whatever happened to him? Have I ever met him?"

"He died when he was nineteen. Took it too far one day and asphyxiated himself. I found him hanging off the back of the door, purple-faced, eyes popping out of his head, prick still in hand. Apparently hanging gives one a massive erection, or so the police surgeon said."

"God. How old were you?"

"Eighteen. It was horrible. I couldn't sleep for weeks. Kept seeing his face. I might have saved him had I come back to our room sooner, but I went to the library and was late getting back."

"It wasn't your fault, Gabe."

"No, it wasn't, but I still felt responsible somehow."

"Don't you think we should say something to Sylvia and Logan?" Quinn asked.

"They know," Gabe replied. "Didn't you notice how hard they tried to act normal?"

"But Logan is a nurse. He knows what could happen!"

"Yes, I'm sure he does," Gabe said and pulled Quinn into his arms. "Let's not talk about Jude anymore."

She had let the subject drop, but couldn't stop thinking about what she'd learned. She wished she'd made more of a connection with Jude, but there was time yet. She'd try to speak to Logan about Jude the next time they met. It was too touchy a subject to bring up over the telephone, and anyway, Jude left for Wales the week after their dinner and would be away until the beginning of May.

A text from Gabe startled Quinn from her reverie and brought her back to the present.

Gabe: *Can you talk?*

Quinn called Gabe's mobile. It was so good to hear his voice. "Yes, I can talk," she said.

"Did you meet with Seth Besson?" he asked without preamble.

"I did. He claims not to remember Sylvia or that night at Chatham Manor. He seemed genuine enough."

"Did he give you a swab?"

"Yes. I overnighted it to Colin. Perhaps I should just leave, Gabe." Quinn didn't mean to get emotional but her voice shook as she tried to hold back the tears. "Will I never know the truth? I seem to be going in circles. If Seth isn't a match, which seems a likely outcome, then who the hell is my father?"

"Quinn, come home," Gabe pleaded. "Let this go. It doesn't matter who your father is, and it doesn't matter where you got your psychic ability. You are you, and nothing you discover will change that or give you any answers about our baby. If our

31

child inherits your gift, then we will do our best to help him or her cope with it and learn how to control it."

"I know. You are right, as usual, which is very annoying. I was just hoping to talk to someone who's experienced the same thing, but I reckon that's not to be." She sniffled. "I'm officially giving up."

"No more pursuing strange men?"

She heard the smile in his voice. "No more. I found one of my biological parents; I suppose that'll have to do. And I have two brothers, which is something."

"That's two more brothers than I have," Gabe joked. "Would have been nice to have a sibling. Speaking of which, how's our little mite doing?"

"It's doing well. I don't even feel pregnant. The morning sickness seems to have passed, and now I'm hungry round the clock. I should get something to eat. I haven't had lunch yet. But first, I'll book a return flight."

"I can't wait to see you," Gabe said. "It feels like you've been gone for months."

"Yes, it does. So get off the phone and let me find a flight home," she replied, smiling happily at his eagerness to have her back.

"I love you," Gabe said, his voice so low and velvety it sent shivers down Quinn's spine.

"I love you more."

Chapter 4

Quinn zipped her packing case and checked her watch. She still had an hour until she had to leave for the airport. A long day lay ahead. She had been able to book a flight to London on Virgin Atlantic, but would have a nearly three-hour layover in Atlanta. By the time she arrived in London and cleared customs it would be close to midnight.

There was no point skulking in her room, so Quinn went down to the restaurant. Several people were enjoying breakfast on the patio, and the appetizing smell of their bacon and eggs made Quinn's stomach growl. She ordered breakfast and a pot of tea and tucked in, seeing no reason to ignore the demands of her body. The baby needed nourishment and so did she. She'd lost a few pounds over the past few months, to the dismay of her doctor, but now she would gain them back. Quinn wasn't overly concerned. Her only priority was the health of her baby.

She was buttering a piece of toast when her mobile rang. It was just after noon at home, so it wouldn't be Gabe. He had a meeting scheduled and said he would be tied up until around three. She'd spoken to her parents the night before, and Phoebe wouldn't call her unless she had some urgent wedding business to discuss. Quinn glanced at the caller ID, but the number wasn't familiar. She considered ignoring the call, but changed her mind when she saw the exchange and realized it was a local call.

"Quinn, Seth Besson here," the deep voice informed her.

"Good morning, Seth." Quinn wondered why he was calling her. She hadn't heard from Colin yet, but had decided not to wait around. There seemed little point.

"I have the results of the paternity test," Seth said. "My ex-wife works at a hospital. We're on fairly good terms, so I asked her to pull a few strings and get this expedited. I just wanted to put your mind at rest, and my own."

"Thank you for taking the trouble. I'm actually going home today, so I guess this is goodbye."

"Quinn, we're a match," Seth said, a catch in his voice. He sounded as shocked as she felt. She'd automatically assumed he was calling to confirm the result was negative. She hadn't expected this.

"Are we?"

"Ninety-nine percent."

Quinn reached for her teacup and took a gulp of scalding tea, burning her tongue. "Are you sure?"

"Yes. I'm sorry I dismissed you. I was telling the truth when I said I didn't remember Sylvia. I really didn't, and honestly, I still don't remember anything about her. I called Robert Chatham last night. We haven't spoken in thirty years, but I needed to know if what you suggested was true."

"And is it?"

"Look, Quinn, can we meet and speak in person? Please."

"I'm leaving for the airport in less than an hour," she replied, unsure what to do.

"Please don't go. There's so much we need to talk about. I'd like to get to know you, if that's okay. I'm coming to pick you up. Where're you staying?"

"I'm at the Omni Royal Orleans Hotel."

"I'll be there in twenty minutes."

Quinn set her mobile down on the table and pushed away her plate. The thought of food suddenly turned her stomach. Seth was a match. A ninety-nine percent match. Well, he had to be, given that she had ruled out everyone else, but he'd been so vehement in his denial she'd thought for sure Sylvia had lied to her again. And he'd called Robert Chatham. Quinn briefly wondered if

Chatham had told Seth of their meeting in Edinburgh, but it was irrelevant. She wouldn't apologize for what she'd done. In retrospect, her strategy with Robert Chatham had been misguided, but she'd learned her lesson, and approached Seth Besson openly and honestly, if only to avoid another misunderstanding.

Seth Besson is my father. Quinn wasn't at all sure how she felt about this newfound knowledge. What if the results were a mistake?

She rang Colin. He would have called her if he had the results, but she had to speak to him nevertheless. He was her colleague and friend, and Logan's boyfriend. He would be honest with her. He always was. The call went straight to voicemail and Quinn hung up in frustration. Colin rarely answered the phone when at work. As a pathologist, he was elbow deep in a postmortem most days. In any case, he would have passed her samples on to the lab, which would take at least another day or two, even if he put a rush on it.

Quinn abandoned her breakfast and headed back to her room to cancel her flight. Her hand shook as she booted up her laptop and brought up the Virgin Atlantic website. Despite Seth's revelation she still longed to go home. She'd come to find her father and learn the truth at last, but suddenly she was overcome with an overwhelming sense of unease. The thought of seeing Seth in a few minutes made her mouth go dry with nervousness. Her father. Her actual biological father who might hold the key to her ability to commune with the dead.

Quinn canceled the flight and shut the lid of her laptop before going to the bathroom. She stared at herself in the mirror. She looked pale and anxious, her hazel eyes huge in her face. Her normally wavy hair was curling every which way and frizzing from the constant humidity. Quinn wound her hair and pinned it on top of her head in an artful bun, leaving a few tendrils around her face to soften the look. She applied a bit of lipstick and refreshed her mascara. She still looked haunted, but at least she wouldn't appear like she was the one doing the haunting.

Her mobile, which she'd left on the vanity next to the sink, began to vibrate. Colin.

"Hi, Colin," Quinn began. "I—"

"Quinn, sorry I haven't rung you sooner. A personal crisis, but more on that later. I have the results of your paternity test. I asked Sarita to take it to the lab personally and wait while they processed the samples. Quinn, it's a match. This man is your father. No doubt about it."

"I know."

"How on earth do you know?" Colin demanded, as though annoyed to have been beaten to the punch.

"Seems you're not the only one with useful contacts. He called me this morning."

"Congratulations?" Colin made it more of a question than a statement, and Quinn suddenly felt lighter. She laughed and walked out of the bathroom, ready to face whatever the day brought.

"Yes. Thank you, Colin. Congratulations are in order. Did you say you had a personal crisis?"

"Never mind. It's all sorted. You go and find your roots." Quinn heard the mirth in his voice. "Speak soon."

She hung up and texted Gabe.

Quinn: *Seth is a match. Staying on for a few days. Will keep you posted. Love you.*

**

"How are you feeling?" Quinn asked Seth as he held the car door for her. "You're still recuperating from surgery. I should have taken a taxi to your house instead of having you collect me at the hotel."

36

"Oh, I'm fine. Don't worry about me. I must admit, I'm overwhelmed. A daughter!" Seth said, his voice filled with wonder. "Kathy had a mouthful. That's my ex-wife. Said I'm even more irresponsible than she thought, and wanted to know how many more children I have scattered throughout the world."

He got into the car and pulled away from the curb, heading toward the Garden District. "Look, Quinn, I can only imagine what you must think of me, given the eh…circumstances, but please give me a fair chance. I'm not a violent person, nor am I someone who disrespects women. I have no clear memory of that night, but in my gut, I know I didn't do what you're accusing me of. I obviously had sex with this woman—your very existence proves that—but it had to be consensual. It had to be," he added, his tone desperate.

Quinn had absolutely no reason to trust him, but something in his eyes told her he genuinely believed what he was telling her and he was desperate for Quinn to not think badly of him. "Give me time," she replied.

Seth nodded and looked ahead at the heavy traffic. "Of course. Take all the time you need. I'm not going anywhere." He made a sharp turn into a less congested street. "I've actually prepared a few things for you," he added shyly. "Some photo albums and mementoes. I thought you'd like to see them. You must have a lot of questions. You can ask me anything, you know. Anything at all."

Quinn stole a sideways peek at Seth. Now was as good a time as any, but she dreaded bringing up the topic. He didn't strike her as a spiritual person, so he would probably laugh at her and think her a kook.

"Seth, is anyone in your family gifted with psychic ability?"

"What?" He turned to gape at her and nearly ran a stop sign. "No. No psychics. Sorry. Why would you ask that?" He looked at her again, one hand casually on the wheel. "Are you psychic?" His expression fell somewhere between horror and amusement, much as she'd expected.

Quinn shook her head "No, just curious. I heard there was lots of black magic in Louisiana. Voodoo and all that," she added, feeling foolish in the extreme.

"Sorry, not a witch doctor among us. That kind of stuff came over with the slaves from Africa and the Caribbean. Is that something you're interested in?"

"History is something I'm always interested in, but today, I want to know more about yours."

"I'll be happy to tell you anything you want to know." Seth pulled into his driveway and shut off the engine. He turned and gave Quinn a goofy grin. "I know what the lab report says, but deep inside, I still can't quite believe you are my girl. My God, what a shock to the system! Wait till I tell Brett. I hope Kathy hasn't spilled the beans yet. She'll probably take extreme pleasure in making it all sound as sordid as possible."

"I thought you said you were on good terms."

"We are, for the most part. We keep things civil for Brett, but she's still angry and bitter. Can't say I blame her. If I had to do it over again, I would have appreciated her more. She's a good woman, Kathy. Solid. I was the one who screwed up."

"How do you think Brett will take the news?" Quinn asked, recalling Jude's resentful expression when he'd met her. Brett seemed a lot more easygoing, but then again, he hadn't expected to ever see her again, especially not in the role of long-lost sister.

"Oh, he'll be thrilled. Brett always wanted us to have more children, but Kathy just wasn't on board. Never wanted to have kids. I begged her not to have an abortion when she got pregnant with Brett. Took some convincing. She's a pediatric oncologist. Did I tell you that? Her career always came first. Brett said that other people's children were her first priority, and he wasn't all wrong."

Quinn followed Seth up the steps to the house. Dolores opened the door and invited them to follow her into the dining room.

"I asked Dolores to make us some breakfast. It's always easier to talk over food. Don't you find? I didn't know what you might like," Seth added when Quinn gaped at the abundance of food. There was some sort of egg casserole, hash browns, pancakes, spicy-smelling sausage, and something that looked like fried dough sprinkled with powdered sugar. "Those are beignets. They are my particular weakness. Delicious, but not so good for the old waistline."

Quinn sensed Seth's nervousness and was glad he felt anxious too. This was awkward for them both, and he was trying to make it easier. "They look wonderful."

"I made you a pot of English Breakfast, Miss Quinn," Dolores said as she placed a lovely flowered teapot with a matching cup and saucer in front of Quinn. "Mr. Seth got the tea specially, and the teapot," she added with a smile.

"Thank you. There was no need to trouble yourself," Quinn said as she took a seat. She was touched by the gesture and wondered if Seth had bought the china himself or sent Dolores to the shops.

"He buy it himself," Dolores said, her tone confidential, as if Quinn had asked the question aloud.

"That was very kind, Seth."

Seth blushed and smiled. "It was nothing."

"I serve you?" Dolores asked.

Quinn couldn't refuse, so Dolores piled her plate with eggs, hash browns and several links of sausage.

"You eat savory first, then sweet," she explained. "That's how Mr. Seth like it."

Quinn took a forkful of egg casserole. She had no idea what type of spices Dolores used, but she'd never tasted eggs quite like this before. She'd tried *shakshuka* in Jerusalem, but these flavors were unique to Louisiana. The sausage was spicy, and the hash browns soft on the inside but crunchy on the outside—fried to perfection.

"Beats beans on toast, ha?" Seth asked happily. "Here, try one of these." He slipped a beignet onto her plate.

"My God, this is…" Quinn couldn't find the right word.

"Orgasmic is what it is. Sorry, can I say that to a daughter?" Seth blushed and she laughed at his unexpected prudishness.

"I'm an adult, Seth. You can say anything to me."

"Tell me about yourself. Tell me everything, from the moment you were born until today. Do you have a picture of your mother?" he asked. He clearly had no recollection of Sylvia at all.

"Seth, before I tell you anything, I need to ask you something."

"Shoot."

"I know what you said in the car, and I want to believe you, but I need to know the truth. I promise I won't judge you or refuse to have any dealings with you. I will give you a fair chance based on the man you are today."

Seth nodded. "Go on."

"Did you take advantage of my mother that night? I know she might have been drunk, or drugged, but I'm fairly certain the sex wasn't consensual, not on her part."

Seth's gaze slid away from Quinn, and he set down his fork. "Look, the honest truth is that I don't know. I drank a lot in those days, and Robert wasn't above slipping an E pill into the drinks. That was just the kind of underhanded thing he would do,

40

which was why I never kept in touch with him after I went home. I didn't consider him a friend. I recall waking up at Chatham Manor the next morning with a blinding headache and love bites on my neck. I clearly had unprotected sex with your mother, but I have no recollection of the act itself. If I did anything to hurt her then I'm genuinely sorry. And I'm sorry I wasn't there for you. I would have been, had I known."

Quinn shook her head in dismay. After speaking to four men who'd slept with Sylvia around the time Quinn was conceived, she was no closer to the truth of what had happened that night. She supposed she'd never really know. The only thing she knew for sure was that Sylvia and Seth had made a baby, and it was her.

"I had a good life, Seth, and wonderful adoptive parents who loved me like I was their own. I couldn't have asked for a better mum and dad."

"I'm glad of it. At least we didn't ruin your life, as we so easily could have. My son says at least once a week that I ruined his life," Seth joked and reached for another beignet.

"Seth, tell me about your family. As far back as you can."

Seth pushed away his plate and leaned back in his chair. "I only know what I've been told, and I leafed through the documents when I retrieved them from the safe this morning. My grandfather was big on family history, but I didn't much care, at least not while he was still alive. My father wasn't interested either. He started the trucking company and built it up from two moving vans to a million-dollar concern. Don't be fooled by the shabby office. We own more than two hundred trucks and make deliveries all over the country. Besson Trucking Limited is a very successful business."

Quinn nodded. She had no wish to talk about trucking, but the company was clearly Seth's passion, so she rearranged her face into an expression of polite interest.

"I more than doubled our fleet and brought in some lucrative contracts. Dad welcomed my ideas, and supported me bringing in new technology. Until then everything was recorded manually in the logbooks and everyone paid by check. Now it's all electronic. It's a beautiful thing."

"I'm sure it is."

"Brett wants to go into sports medicine. He doesn't give a rat's ass—pardon my French—about the business. He'll probably sell the lot before the ink dries on my death certificate."

"I'm sorry. Kids rarely want to follow in their parents' footsteps these days."

"Are your parents academics?" Seth asked.

"No. My mum worked as a secretary before I came along, and dad was a civil engineer."

"And Sylvia?"

"Sylvia was a teacher."

Seth nodded. "Well, I tell you, I never had much interest in history, ours or anyone else's. I liked math and science, and majored in business and finance at school. Never even picked up a historical novel, besides the ones I had to read for school. *A Tale of Two Cities*," he said, shaking his head. "What did I care about the French Revolution?"

"Isn't Besson a French name?" Quinn asked, hoping to redirect Seth to the subject of family history.

"Yes, it is."

"So your ancestors came from France?" Quinn prompted. Most likely, they would have been affected by the French Revolution, but Seth didn't seem to see the connection.

"Are you finished?" Seth asked, looking at Quinn's still-full plate.

"Yes. I actually had something at the hotel."

"Let's go in the living room and I'll show you all the information I have. It isn't much. Granddad donated all the documents to the museum, including the family tree. It hangs in the foyer."

"The museum?" Quinn asked.

"Oh, right, you wouldn't know about that. My family used to own a plantation on the River Road before the Civil War. It's been converted to a museum. Most of them were. The house and slave quarters have been restored, and now the whole enterprise brings in a pretty penny, except that we have no claim to the proceeds. Belongs to the Historical Society."

Quinn followed Seth into the living room where papers and photos were piled on the coffee table. Seth pushed aside most of the papers and unrolled a scroll on the table. "This is the draft of our family tree. Granddad put this together. I don't know how accurate it is, or if everyone is on it, but this is the best I can do at the moment. There's a very knowledgeable tour guide at the plantation. Dina Aptekar Hill is her name. You'd do well to speak to her. Her ancestors came to Louisiana when it was nothing more than woods and swampland, and she wrote a book about their journey. She's a great resource."

"I'll definitely look her up," Quinn promised, making a mental note of the name. "Do you know anything about him?" she asked, pointing to the name at the very top of the chart.

"Maurice Besson came over from France at the end of the eighteenth century. He was a farmer from Burgundy. No one knows what made him enlist. Perhaps the farm was failing, or maybe he had a thirst for adventure, but he joined the army and fought under Lafayette during the Revolutionary War. After the war, he settled somewhere near Quebec and became a trapper. He was only about eighteen at the time."

"Quebec?" Quinn asked, surprised. "That's a long way from New Orleans."

"It sure is. I have no idea what brought Maurice to Louisiana, but he must have done well for himself because he bought a good-sized parcel of land on the shore of the Mississippi. There's an original bill of sale at the museum. Take a look. This is a photocopy."

Quinn studied the copy of the certificate. The ink was faded to gray, but she could still make out the signature and date at the bottom. *Maurice Besson, March 18th, 1787.*

"Maurice married his neighbor's daughter, and the two properties were consolidated as soon as his father-in-law passed away, leaving Maurice with a sizeable plantation and over a hundred slaves. He and his bride, Arabella, had a son, Jean, and two daughters, both of whom died in infancy. Jean inherited the plantation."

Quinn traced the line on the paper. The tree didn't have many branches, not even after several generations. The Bessons were not a fruitful family.

"See here," Seth pointed out. "Jean married Sybil and had two sons, Albert and Charles. Albert, being the eldest, inherited, and Charles moved to New Orleans, where he lived until his death in 1858. He didn't have any children. I am descended from Albert Besson, who had one son, George, who also had one son, Brett. Brett became something of a family name. There were several."

"Yes, I see," Quinn replied.

"Actually, there hasn't been a girl in the family since Maurice's two daughters. Until now," Seth added shyly. "You are the first Besson girl to be born in two hundred years." He rifled through the papers and pulled out an ancient sepia photograph. "Check this out. This is a daguerreotype of George's wedding to Amelia. This is the first-ever family photo. They had several copies made, so there's another one at the museum. What'd you think?" he asked, handing the photo to Quinn.

She stared at the photograph, drinking in every detail of the wedding party. There were about twenty people in the photograph, nine on each side of the bridal couple. George was a handsome young man with light-colored hair cut fashionably short at the back with longer locks in front. A forelock fell into his light eyes, which stared into the camera with an air of amusement. Everyone else wore solemn expressions. The bride had dark curls and wore a white gown that must have required yards of lace. Her hoop skirts almost completely blocked her new husband's legs and her veil hung nearly to the ground, making her appear somewhat ghostly. She gazed up at George, a look of adoration on her young face.

"She looks so in love," Quinn said as she handed the photo back to Seth.

"Yes. Granddad said it was a love match."

Quinn glanced at the dates beneath George and Amelia's names and looked away. Amelia had outlived her husband by about ten years, but neither had enjoyed a long life.

"Seth, do you have anything that belonged to any of them?" she asked carefully.

"Such as? You mean letters or diaries?"

"Yes, that would be very helpful, but perhaps an object of some sort, even a button."

"Believe it or not, my granddad actually had Maurice's uniform, and it was intact."

"Where is it now?" Quinn asked, her voice catching with hope.

"On display at the museum."

"Did your grandfather not keep any mementoes of his family?" She could hardly take an object from the museum without permission, and if she asked to borrow something, she'd have to explain why she needed it.

"He did. Granddad kept everything and only gave the museum what he had in duplicate, but after his death, no one much

45

cared. My dad cleared out his house and kept only this box." Seth pointed to the cardboard box from which he'd taken the photograph and several other papers. "Anything larger than a book went to the museum."

"I see," Quinn replied, wondering how to get her hands on something that had belonged to one of the Bessons. She needed a starting point for her investigation, but it seemed there wasn't much left in Seth's possession.

"Wait, there is something," Seth exclaimed. "I forgot all about it. It's in the safety deposit box at the bank with my mother's other valuables. She always admired it, so my grandmother gave it to her on her sixteenth birthday."

"What is it?" Quinn asked, hoping for a piece of jewelry.

"It's an ivory fan. It's quite beautiful, really. It belonged to Amelia, and happens to be the only thing left of her. My grandfather gave the fan to my grandmother when they married. She liked to show it off and refused to part with it when the museum opened. It'll be yours now since my mother no longer has any use for it."

"Is your mother still alive then?" Quinn asked, her breath catching in her throat. Seth's mother would be her biological grandmother.

"Yes. She's in a nursing home. I visit her regularly, but at times she doesn't remember who I am. She has Alzheimer's and it's gotten much worse these past two years."

"Could I possibly meet her?"

"Sure, if you'd like. We can go tomorrow, and I'll ask her about the fan. She'd want you to have it."

"Oh, I couldn't possibly keep it, but I would very much like to see it."

"I'll have it for you tomorrow."

"I can't wait," Quinn replied, and meant it.

Chapter 5

Quinn was a little nervous when Seth picked her up next morning for a visit to the nursing home. He seemed fine at first, but grew agitated as they drew closer to the place. Palm Place Nursing Home was in an upscale part of town and looked like it cost a bomb. The front lawns were exquisitely tended and the building looked more like a resort than a home for the elderly. Seth asked if they might stop at a bakery first and came out with a small box tied with a red ribbon, clearly a gift for his mother.

"Is everything all right?" Quinn asked. "Would you prefer that I remain in the car?"

"No, no, of course not," Seth sputtered. He gave Quinn a faltering smile. "If today is a bad day, none of this will matter, but it it's a good day…" He trailed off, his expression contrite like a little boy who was about to be caught with his hand in the biscuit tin. "My mother will be disappointed in me. She always taught me to do the right thing, the honorable thing. I know it's an old-fashioned concept, but she is an old-fashioned Southern lady. Some things still mean the world to her. But I'm a big boy. I can handle it."

Seth and Quinn walked into the lobby, which was cool and decorated in shades of gray and blue, with pictures of sailboats and scenic beaches on the walls. Potted palms and other plants gave the place a homey atmosphere, unlike some of the cold, utilitarian nursing homes Quinn had seen in England.

"Mr. Besson," a nurse called out from the nurses' station. "Mrs. Besson is on the veranda. It's too nice a day to be indoors. She'll be so happy to see you. Just sign in for me, please. Both of you."

The nurse handed them visitor passes and they made their way toward the door to the veranda, which hugged the entire back wall of the building. It was shady and cool, and faced lush manicured gardens bursting with color. Several elderly people sat in rocking chairs, either alone or with visitors, and nurses hovered discreetly nearby.

A woman of about eighty sat by herself, her gnarled hands folded demurely in her lap. She had short iron-gray curls that looked to have been styled just that morning, and wore a cream sheath dress with a pale yellow cardigan thrown over her shoulders. A string of pearls at her throat completed the outfit. She seemed to be staring at nothing in particular, but had a faraway look in her dark eyes and a gentle smile tugged at the corners of her mouth. Quinn felt Seth tense beside her.

"Mama," he called softly. "Good morning, Mama."

The woman turned to face them and a wide smile lit up her face. Seth breathed a sigh of relief that she recognized him.

"Seth," she called, her pleasure at seeing him obvious. "What a lovely surprise. You haven't been to see me in weeks."

"I was here last week, Mama," Seth reminded her gently.

"Were you really? I seem to have forgotten. Is that for me?" she asked, eyeing the box greedily.

"I brought you some chocolate-covered strawberries."

"I don't want strawberries. I want marzipan. You know it's my favorite," she said with a pout.

"I know, but you must watch your sugar intake. The strawberries in dark chocolate have much less than marzipan," Seth explained patiently.

"Oh, what difference does it make?" Mrs. Besson snapped. "I'd rather have marzipan than prolong this miserable existence you call life."

"Come now, Mama, you're hardly miserable."

"Oh? Would you like to come live here while I go home?"

Seth ignored the remark and turned to Quinn. "Mama, I brought someone to meet you."

"Have you finally gotten yourself a lady friend?" she asked, a wicked twinkle in her eye. "About time, I say."

"Mama, this is Quinn Allenby, and she's not my girlfriend." Seth looked like he was about to gag on his tongue, and Quinn stifled a smile. It was endearing to see a grown man so afraid of displeasing his mother. "She's my daughter," Seth choked out.

"What's that?" Mrs. Besson asked, staring at Quinn.

"Quinn is my daughter. She's just found me after all these years. I didn't know she existed," he added apologetically.

"Hello, Mrs. Besson," Quinn said, hoping the old woman wouldn't ask her to leave. It was still hard to believe this lady was actually her grandmother. "It's wonderful to meet you."

"Call me Rae, dear." Mrs. Besson patted the chair next to her. "Come sit down and let me look at you."

Quinn sat and allowed Rae a moment to study her closely.

"She doesn't look like you, Seth."

"No, but DNA doesn't lie."

Rae reached out and put her wrinkled hand over Quinn's, her eyes lighting up. "A granddaughter. Never thought I'd live to know such joy. And so beautiful. I'll have some words with your father in private later," she threw Seth a scathing look, "but I can't say I'm displeased. Never thought I'd have another grandchild, especially one that's grown." Rae continued to gaze at Quinn, a happy smile on her face. "Quinn, that's an odd name. One of them unisex names that are so popular now, is it?"

"Yes, it can be a man's name. I think my mother was hoping for a boy."

50

"And who is your mother, dear?"

"She's a girl I met in England, Mama," Seth cut in.

"You never told me you had a girlfriend in England."

"It didn't seem important at the time."

"Not important?" Rae huffed. "You made a child with her. I'd say that's important."

"My mother never told him about me," Quinn supplied. "We only just met this week."

"Shame Seth missed your childhood. But what a surprise to have a girl," she mused. "There hasn't been a Besson girl in centuries. Not a lucky family, the Bessons," Rae added.

"In what way?"

"In the way that matters. One boy in each generation. Just one. Why, I have dozens of cousins. I come from a big family. Three children was the minimum on my side. My sister had six. But the Bessons could barely squeeze out one baby."

Quinn bit her tongue before asking why Seth didn't have any siblings, but Rae anticipated her question. "Oh, we tried, girlie. We tried. I had three miscarriages before Seth and two after. Those babies just wouldn't take hold. Nowadays they'd have run tests and figured out the problem, but back then, they just told us to go home and hope for better luck next time. Don't know why this one lived," she pointed to Seth, "but he did. My one and only precious boy. I wanted a girl so badly. My sister has five daughters, God bless her, and one son. I always said to her, 'Let me have one, Jinny. Your husband won't notice. I'll take good care of her.'" Rae chuckled. "I would have, too. I would have taken one of hers in a heartbeat if she was willing. She was overwhelmed and tired all the time. A baby every year for six years. Imagine that. And then nothing."

"Did they stop having sex?" Seth asked, a twinkle in his eye.

"No, they didn't. They just weren't having it with each other," Rae replied. She patted Quinn's hand, her thumb caressing Quinn's engagement ring. "So, you're getting married. Where is your young man?"

"He's at home, in London."

"He let you come alone?"

"I didn't ask for his permission," Quinn replied with a smile.

"No, I don't suppose you would. Young women are different today. So, do you love him?"

"Yes, very much. Would you like to see a photo?"

"Oh, yes," Rae said, brightening up. "You got one of those smartphones?"

Quinn pulled out her mobile and found a photograph of Gabe.

"Handsome devil," Rae said, nodding in approval. "I always did like the dark ones, like Seth's daddy. I was blond myself, not that you can see that now," she said, patting her hair. "I was pretty as a picture."

"I'm sure you were," Quinn replied. She could see the young woman in Rae's face. She must have been quite striking in her day.

"And who's this little princess?" Rae asked, looking at a picture of Emma in her Disney regalia, posing next to Gabe.

"That's Emma. She's Gabe's daughter."

"So he's divorced, your man?"

52

"No, he's never been married."

Rae gave Quinn a look of pure disapproval. "Bit of a tomcat then?"

"No, he's not like that," Quinn replied, defensive on Gabe's behalf. "Gabe is very loyal, and very romantic."

"Yes, I can see that." Rae gave Quinn a knowing look and allowed her hand to gently brush against Quinn's stomach. "When's the wedding?"

"Next month."

"Better sooner rather than later." Rae nodded.

"Mama, what are you talking about?" Seth asked, as though oblivious to Rae's insinuation.

"Nothing, son. I just like weddings, that's all. I wish I could be there to see you get married. Never got to see my own girl as a bride. It would be nice to see my granddaughter walk down the aisle."

"Do you think you could travel to England?" Quinn asked.

Rae shook her head. "No, dear. I'm too old to travel across the street, much less to Europe. You'll have to send me a photograph. I want the old-fashioned kind, the kind I can put in a frame and show to my friends. None of this digital nonsense."

"Who will you show it to?" Seth asked, making Rae guffaw with laughter.

"I still have a few friends who aren't dead." Rae turned to Quinn. "Will you come back and see me before you go home? I want to say a proper goodbye."

"Of course I'll come. And it doesn't have to be goodbye."

"Darling, at my age it's important to say goodbye to those I love. Just in case. I might still be here when you return, but it

53

doesn't mean my mind will be. It's going, bit by bit. I just wish I'd forget the difficult parts instead of the happy memories, but we don't get to choose, do we? I hope I remember you, but if I don't, I want you to know I'm so glad to have met you. You've made an old woman happy today."

Quinn nodded in understanding. Rae reminded her a little of the grandmother she'd lost twenty years ago. They had the same wisdom and the same unflinching regard for the truth. Rae was too old for euphemisms, and looked reality in the face, frightened but ready to face the abyss.

"And you," Rae said, turning to Seth, "bring me marzipan next time. I have few pleasures left in life. Let me have my sweets."

"Mama, I'd like to give Quinn Amelia's fan," Seth said as they rose to leave. "I've taken it out of the safety deposit box."

Rae nodded. "As well you should. Not like you got anyone else to give it to. It's a lovely thing, Quinn. A piece of our past."

"I will treasure it, Rae."

"Give it to your own daughter someday. Tell her where her roots were planted."

"I will." Quinn kissed the old woman's papery cheek in farewell and smiled when Rae whispered into her ear, "This one is a boy, but maybe next time."

"Bye, Mama. I'll see you next week," Seth promised. He picked up the box of strawberries, but Rae snatched it out of his hand and pulled off the ribbon.

"I'll be waiting," she said as she took a bite of strawberry.

Quinn followed Seth out to the car. She couldn't wait to return to her hotel room and hold the fan. She was more than ready to learn its secrets.

Chapter 6

August 1858

New Orleans, Louisiana

Madeline sat perfectly still while Tess carefully removed the paper curlers and arranged Madeline's hair to her satisfaction. Fidgeting resulted in the dressing process taking longer, and Madeline barely had the patience for the three quarters of an hour it usually took to get her ready to face the day. She was hungry, and looked forward to going downstairs for breakfast. Breakfast was her favorite time of the day, since she always had it with Daddy, who rose from his bed in time to eat with her, regardless of when he'd come in the night before. It had become their ritual to eat together since Mama had died six years before when Madeline was just nine. She sometimes had bad dreams and cried out during the night, so Daddy always joined her for breakfast and tried to cajole her out of her melancholy, often taking her to walk by the river and pointing out the various boats sailing past or unloading goods.

Once it got closer to noon, Daddy would buy them molasses cakes from the Negro *marchandes* who walked along the banks of the Mississippi and sold their goods from flat boxes hanging around their necks by a rope. Daddy always brought a blanket so they could sit on the grass while they enjoyed their treat. The cakes were delicious and Madeline licked her fingers when no one was looking, to get the last bit of sweetness before dutifully wiping her hands with a handkerchief. Lately, her governess, Miss Cole, had begun to join them for walks by the river, but in the mornings, she took a tray in her room to allow father and daughter their time together.

Madeline descended the stairs, enjoying the sound of silk swishing against the damask-papered walls. Her new gown had hoops so wide they brushed the spindles of the banister and the wall along the stairs, making Madeline feel grown up. The silk was a sea-foam green, not one of the bland colors like pale yellow or rose pink that young ladies were expected to wear. The green was quite sophisticated, in Madeline's opinion, and since this was the first time she had worn the gown, it gave her a little thrill.

The table was already set for breakfast, so Madeline took her usual seat and spread a napkin in her lap.

"Coffee, Miss Madeline?" Mammy asked. While Tess helped Madeline dress, Mammy always prepared breakfast and waited in the dining room with a freshly brewed pot of coffee. Madeline hadn't liked the coffee at first, but her father drank cups of it every morning, so she'd learned to enjoy it and held up her cup for a refill whenever he did.

"Yes, please, Mammy. Has Daddy been down?" Madeline asked.

"Not yet."

"I'll wait for him, then."

"Yes, miss."

Madeline replaced her napkin on the table and got up to stand by the window. It was open to catch any movement of air, but already the day was oppressively hot and humid. Brilliant sunlight bathed everything in its merciless glare and the fragrance of flowers and sunbaked earth wafted into the dining room. Madeline didn't much like the brutal heat of August, but it beat the damp, foggy months of autumn and winter when life seemed to slow down and the world outside the door lay blanketed in mist so thick it was hard to even see the boats on the river.

The clock struck the hour and Madeline started. Daddy was usually down by this time, no matter how late he'd come in the night before. Her stomach growled. She had been feeling unwell last night due to her monthly visitor and hadn't eaten much at suppertime.

"Mammy, can I have a beignet while I wait?" she called toward the kitchen.

"Sho thing, Miss Madeline."

Madeline accepted a warm beignet and took a small bite. She felt guilty eating without her father, but she was starving. She'd just pretend she hadn't eaten by the time he finally made an appearance. She was almost finished with the beignet when there was a knock at the door. It was too early in the morning for anyone to call, and tradesmen usually used the back door when making deliveries, so Madeline remained where she was. She heard Tess's hurried footsteps as she went to answer the door and then muffled voices, one belonging to a man.

"Mr. Larson is here to see you, miss," Tess said as she peeked into the dining room.

"Did you tell him Daddy is not up yet?"

"It's you he wishes to see."

"Me?"

"Yes."

"All right. I'll see him in the parlor, unless he'd like some breakfast," Madeline replied. She knew Mr. Larson well. He was her father's close friend as well as his lawyer. He dined with them often, and had recently introduced them to his future wife, Lucille Heston. She was an attractive widow of middle years, and Madeline had felt instantly drawn to her. She reminded her of her own mother, who'd been kind and sweet-natured, although Corinne Besson had been dark of coloring, like Madeline, while Mrs. Heston was fair and blue-eyed.

"Good morning, Mr. Larson. I'm afraid Daddy is still abed. Would you care for some breakfast?" Madeline asked. She'd never had to play hostess before, but she liked it. She turned in a way that made the silk of her skirt swish, and smiled with satisfaction.

"No, thank you, Madeline. Would you be so kind as to ask Miss Cole to join us?"

Madeline looked at the lawyer in confusion. Why would he wish to see her governess? "Miss Cole is still in her room."

"I'm here," Miss Cole said from the doorway. She looked unusually solemn. Miss Cole had a sunny disposition, especially of late, and always counseled Madeline that charm and good manners were the most valuable currency. She looked at Mr. Larson with apprehension, then took a seat without a word of greeting to either of them.

"I must speak with you both," Mr. Larson began.

Madeline sat down and spread her skirts, showing off yards of green silk to its best advantage. She wished she had a fan, since she was perspiring, but it was up in her room and it would be rude to keep Mr. Larson waiting.

"What can we do for you, Mr. Larson?" Madeline asked, imitating the tone of a great lady.

"Madeline, I have some rather awful news. Your father attended a card game last night, where he suffered heavy losses."

"Is Daddy in debt?" she asked. She didn't fully understand what being in debt entailed, but she knew it was something to be avoided.

"I'll get to that," Mr. Larson replied softly. "He'd been drinking heavily and was quite inebriated by the time he left the game."

Madeline ignored the look of shock on Miss Cole's face. Daddy liked his drink, but he rarely went overboard. "Well, that explains why he's still sleeping. Doesn't it?"

"In his confused state, your father stepped in front of an oncoming carriage. He was badly hurt." Madeline opened her mouth to reply, but Mr. Larson cut her off. "Madeline, he died of his injuries an hour ago. I was with him till the last. I'm so sorry."

Madeline felt as if a horse had just kicked her in the stomach. All breath was driven from her body, leaving her gasping for air and shaking with shock. Her father was dead. He'd stepped in front of a carriage because he was drunk. Both her parents were now dead and she was completely alone in the world, with no one but Mr. Larson to turn to for advice.

Miss Cole's hand flew to her mouth and she let out a strangled moan. Her blue eyes filled with tears, and her face turned the color of curdled milk.

"Miss Cole, I asked you to be here because I know what you and Charles meant to each other," Mr. Larson said. "I thought it best you hear it from me."

Miss Cole nodded woodenly as tears spilled down her cheeks. She wrung her hands in her lap and sniffled, until Mr. Larson handed her his handkerchief, which she instantly used to wipe her streaming eyes.

"What do you mean?" Madeline asked, looking from Mr. Larson to Miss Cole. She had no idea what he was referring to, but that wasn't her immediate concern. "Wh-what will become of me?" she stammered. "Am I to come live with you, Mr. Larson?"

"No, my dear. Your father drew up a will after your mother passed. He left very specific instructions for your care should anything happen to him before you were of age or married."

"What kind of instructions?" Madeline felt as if she were floating on a thick mist, all sounds muffled by the moisture, and familiar objects seemed shrouded in shadow. She no longer saw the sunlight or felt the heat. Instead she felt cold and numb, and absolutely terrified. She might have expected some measure of support from Miss Cole, but she seemed lost in her own misery, rocking back and forth with her arms wrapped around her middle.

"Paula," Mr. Larson said, addressing Miss Cole, "I'm very sorry, but Charles made no provisions for you, since you weren't legally wed. You will be paid through the end of the month, and of course, you may take anything that Charles gave you as a gift."

Miss Cole stared at Mr. Larson, but her eyes looked blank, as if she didn't quite understand what the lawyer was saying to her. "I'm destitute," she whispered. "And unemployed."

"I will be happy to provide you with a reference, if that will help."

Miss Cole didn't reply. She sprang to her feet and fled the room, her sobs echoing through the house. Madeline looked after her, confused by this extreme reaction to her employer's death, but then understanding dawned. Her father and Miss Cole were fond of each other, and Miss Cole had nursed hopes of a marriage proposal. Knowing that her father was courting came as a shock, but at the moment, Madeline was too overcome with grief and uncertainty about her own future to give any thought to Paula Cole's predicament.

"Madeline, your father stipulated that you must go to live with your kin at Arabella Plantation should anything happen to him."

"I don't have any kin, Mr. Larson. It was just Mama, Daddy, and me. He always said so."

"Your father fell out with his family some years ago, but you do have relations—wealthy ones. You have a grandmother and a cousin. I sent a message this morning and received a prompt reply. They will be happy to have you."

"But I don't know them," Madeline cried. "Why can't I remain at this house until I'm of age? Mammy and Tess will look after me. We'll be just fine."

Mr. Larson shook his head. He suddenly looked older than his thirty-eight years and Madeline noticed that his hair was receding at the front. "Madeline, your father gambled frequently

60

and suffered heavy losses. His debts will need to be paid. I will have to sell everything of value, including Tess, to pay his creditors."

Madeline let out a cry of disbelief. Tess had been with them since before she was born. Both Tess and Mammy were family to her, the only family she had left. "And Mammy?" she breathed.

"You may keep Mammy since she's too old to fetch much at auction. She will come with you to Arabella Plantation. You have until Sunday to pack your most precious belongings. I have arranged for the funeral to be held on Monday. I will drive you out to the plantation after that. Again, I'm very sorry, Madeline. I know how bewildered you must feel."

"Thank you," she mumbled.

She drifted up the stairs, closed the door to her room and sank to the floor, completely indifferent to the damage it might do to her gown. Bewildered didn't begin to describe how she felt. Her beloved father was gone, her home was about to be sold from under her, and her trusted friend was about to be auctioned off to the highest bidder. Even Miss Cole, of whom she was very fond, would disappear from her life after the funeral, going to either another position or some dodgy boarding house until she could find new employment.

Madeline closed her eyes and rested her head against the cool wood of the door as hot tears slid down her cheeks. She had a grandmother and a cousin she knew nothing about. Why would her father tell her his entire family was dead? What could have happened to cause such a permanent and drastic rift between mother and son? They'd agreed to take her in. Had they known of her existence all along or had they just learned about her from Mr. Larson? It was all too much to take in.

"Madeline, are you all right, child?" Mammy called through the door. "Open up now."

"I just want to be alone, Mammy," Madeline croaked.

"Come now, open the door to your old Mammy. I will comfort you."

Madeline shifted away from the door, but she had no wish to see Mammy. No one could comfort her and no one could lessen the sense of mounting dread that threatened to engulf her. Only this morning her biggest concern had been ruining her new dress, but since then she'd lost everything she held dear. Well, everything except Mammy.

The older woman pushed her way into the room and pulled Madeline into a warm embrace. She smelled of fresh bread, coffee, and her own musky scent that was so familiar. Madeline buried her face in Mammy's ample bosom and wept. Mammy held her until the worst of her grief passed, then helped her to her feet and walked her to the bed. Madeline began to protest, but felt too exhausted to argue. She closed her eyes as Mammy drew the curtains to block out the harsh daylight.

"You'll be all right, child," Mammy said as she smoothed Madeline's hair from her brow. "The Lord is kind and forgiving and will not hold you accountable for the sins of your father."

"You mean the gambling and the drinking?" Madeline whispered, horrified that her father had sinned.

"That too," Mammy mumbled and left the room before Madeline could ask for an explanation.

Chapter 7

By the time Madeline came down, evening shadows had
chased away daylight, leaving the parlor nearly pitch dark, with
only the outlines of the furniture visible in the gloom. She walked
past the open door and headed to the dining room. Mammy and
Tess had retired to their rooms, having finished their chores for the
day, but Mammy had thoughtfully left a tray for Madeline,
knowing she'd get hungry eventually. She lifted the napkin and
examined the cold chicken, cornbread, and greens on the plate. She
sat down and ate slowly, savoring every bite as if it were her last.
Every task she undertook in this house would soon be her last. In
just a few days she would go into the unknown, and the
unexplained.

She tried to imagine what her father's family might be like
but drew a blank. Daddy had never spoken of his home or his kin.
He'd always said that both he and Corinne had been orphaned at a
young age and had no one but themselves to rely on. Madeline had
never had grandparents, aunts and uncles, or cousins. When her
mother had grown heavy with child, Madeline had nearly burst
with longing at the thought of the coming sibling. She wouldn't be
alone anymore. She would have an ally in life long after her
parents were gone. There were days when she'd prayed for a sister,
and other days when she'd thought it might be better to have a
brother. He wouldn't be able to protect her or look after her as an
older brother might, but it would still be nice to have a male
relative in a world where females weren't treated with respect
unless they were on the arm of a man.

Madeline pushed away her plate, no longer hungry. It had
been a boy, a brother to love and spoil, but he never drew breath.
He'd died before he was even born and took their mother with him.
Perhaps he'd needed her in Heaven. He'd been too little to be
alone, but Madeline had needed her mother too. She'd put on a
brave face for Daddy, who had seemed to lose the will to live after
losing his beloved Corinne and his long-awaited son. He'd stood
on the edge of an abyss, and Madeline had been the only one who

could coax him away and remind him that he still had a reason to go on. It had taken several years, and she'd thought Daddy was doing better. He'd smiled and laughed, and taken her on outings. They'd even had company on occasion, and now she'd learned that he had grown close to Miss Cole. Daddy had had everything to live for. Why would God take him now when he was finally on the road to recovery?

It weren't God that took him, child, it was the drink. Madeline could almost hear Mammy's voice in her head. Yes, it had been the drink. Daddy had been fond of drinking, and he'd grown reckless since Mama died. It had brought him comfort and helped him sleep, and now he would sleep forever next to his wife and son while Madeline was left on her own, stripped of all she held dear.

She heard a sniffle and turned to listen. She'd thought she was alone downstairs, but clearly someone was still here. She took the oil lamp and made her way down the corridor, shining the light into the empty rooms. She stopped when she saw Miss Cole huddled on a settee by the window, her head in her arms. Madeline walked softly into the room and set the lamp in a far corner, so as not to shine the light into Miss Cole's face.

The governess looked up. Her eyes were puffy from crying, her nose red, and her legs drawn up on the settee in a most unladylike way. Madeline took a seat across from her and held out her hand, but Miss Cole didn't take it. She seemed to draw even further into herself, her eyes fixed on some distant point beyond Madeline's shoulder.

"He said I'd never be on my own again," Miss Cole whispered. "He promised me a future, something I never dared to hope for."

"Did he say he loved you?" Madeline asked. She felt sorry for Miss Cole, but the idea of her father loving anyone other than her mother still hurt, even now that he was gone.

Miss Cole shook her head. "I know he didn't love me, not in the way he loved his wife, but he was fond of me and he would have come to love me in time. He was lonely. He needed someone."

"He had me."

"Men get lonely in a different way, Madeline. He loved your dearly, but he needed the love of a woman to let go of his grief. I could have made him happy," she added miserably.

"I'm sure you could have," Madeline agreed, but she didn't really believe it. Miss Cole was so different from her mother, so—what was the right word?—colorless. Corinne Besson had been beautiful and gay. She could tease her husband out of a sour mood in moments, and suddenly he would smile at her like a besotted boy and beg for a kiss, which she wouldn't give until she was good and ready, and sure that he was putty in her hands.

They had laughed a lot, her parents, and they had loved. Madeline had been young and ignorant of the ways of men and women, but she'd known happiness when she saw it. She'd known two people who couldn't be apart for long and gravitated toward each other whenever they were in the same room. Her father's hand had always reached for her mother, and she'd leaned into him when she thought no one was looking, her body fitting into the curve of his as if they'd been created as one and split into two halves, never truly whole unless together.

He'd never laughed with Miss Cole, and his hand had never reached out to her. They were two separate beings who could never become two parts of a whole. Madeline would have known if her father loved this woman; she would have sensed it. Perhaps Miss Cole had wanted to be part of a family so badly that she'd magnified what Charles Besson felt for her. Perhaps she had been the one truly in love and with plans for the future.

"What will you do now?" Madeline asked. She might have turned to Miss Cole for comfort before she knew of her feelings, but now Madeline felt resentful and annoyed. Miss Cole had been kind and caring toward her, but perhaps it was just a ruse to show Charles what a good stepmother she'd make and how loving she would be to a child.

Miss Cole shook her head. "I don't know. I have nowhere to go. Mr. Larson said I'll be paid till the end of the month, but that gives me very little time to find another position."

"Have you no savings?" Madeline knew the question was indelicate, but she was curious what a woman on her own could do in this situation. She might have found herself on her own if not for these mysterious relatives who were willing to take her in without having met her.

"I have some, but money goes very quickly when one has to pay for one's lodgings. If I don't find employment as a governess by the end of the month, I'll work as a seamstress. Mrs. Bonnard's shop always has openings, and she offers room and board."

"And a wage?" Madeline asked, curious. She sewed very well; her stitches were even and tiny, and her embroidery exquisite. Possible employment was something to keep in mind should things not work out with her relatives.

"Mrs. Bonnard pays a pittance," Miss Cole replied, her tone bitter. "The work is tedious and the hours are long, but it's a respectable place, and sometimes gentlemen come with their mothers and sisters."

"Why does that matter?"

Miss Cole looked up, a rueful smile tugging at her lips. "Madeline, my dear, you will discover very quickly that a respectable marriage is the only desirable option for a woman. Your only value lies in your youth, your beauty, and your innocence. Once those things are gone, you have nothing to bargain with. You will spend your days alone, in servitude to someone else, struggling to survive."

"You still have youth, beauty, and innocence, Miss Cole," Madeline replied, wondering if she misunderstood.

"I'm twenty-two." Miss Cole sighed. "And I'm neither beautiful nor innocent. Forgive me, Madeline. I shouldn't have said that."

Madeline didn't really understand what Miss Cole meant or why she needed to be forgiven, but decided not to pursue the topic. Perhaps she simply meant that she was more knowledgeable of the world than someone like Madeline. Mammy had said that men didn't like smart women because they made them realize what fools they really were, so perhaps Miss Cole was better off working as a seamstress after all.

"I'd better start packing," Miss Cole said as she slowly got to her feet.

"Will you come to the funeral?"

"Of course. I owe your father that much."

"Did he not leave you anything?" Madeline asked.

Miss Cole looked at Madeline, her eyes full of sorrow. "He left me something precious, but I must dispose of it if I am to survive."

"I don't understand," Madeline replied. Why did grownups always talk in riddles?

"No, you wouldn't. And for your sake, I hope you never have to. Go to your family, Madeline, and make the most of this opportunity."

Madeline watched Miss Cole walk from the room, her back straight and her head held high. She was damaged, but she wasn't broken. She'd find her way. Perhaps she wasn't as colorless as Madeline had once thought, or as uncomplicated.

Chapter 8

April 2014

New Orleans, Louisiana

It was past midnight, but the streets of the French Quarter were thronged with revelers out in full force, laughing and talking as they spilled from the numerous bars on Bourbon Street and dispersed in various directions, some stumbling toward the next watering hole while others tried in vain to catch a cab. The doors of the balcony and the hum of the air conditioner drowned out most of the noise, but Quinn still couldn't settle down. She tried reading and watching TV, but in the end she settled for a hot shower in the hope that it would relax her. She toweled her hair dry, pulled on one of Gabe's T-shirts, and climbed into bed. Tomorrow morning her hair would resemble a bird's nest, but she could always twist it into a bun to force it into submission. She sniffed at the T-shirt, wishing it smelled of Gabe, but of course, she'd taken a clean shirt instead of one he'd worn.

Quinn reached for the glass on the nightstand and took a sip of water, though she would have much preferred a glass of wine or even a shot of whisky to help her sleep, but water would have to do. She turned out the light and stared at the murky white ceiling. Why did she feel so unsettled? Why was every nerve ending in her body pulsating with anxiety? She'd spent the day alone, taking in the sights and sounds of New Orleans, or "Noo Awlins" as Seth pronounced it. Quinn would normally enjoy such a beautiful city with a rich history, but something about the place left her feeling like a little girl who feared the monsters under her bed.

It wasn't the history that put her off. New Orleans had seen its share of upheaval, but so had every other city in the world. Quinn never flinched when unearthing the bones of soldiers who'd been slaughtered in battle or examining the remains of plague victims tossed into shallow pits and doused in lime to keep the pestilence from spreading. She was a historian, an archeologist, so this was her bread and butter. But this place unnerved her. She was in a room by herself, safe and secure, but she felt something in the room with her, something dark and shapeless—something she couldn't name.

Was it fear? But what did she have to be frightened of? She'd finally found the father she'd been searching for, and given the circumstances of her conception, he wasn't nearly as off-putting as she might have expected. Seth was overjoyed to have found her, and although she'd known him for a grand total of four days, he seemed like a nice enough man. She now had another brother to get to know, and she had a physical portal into the past in the form of Amelia's fan. She might never find the answers about her psychic ability, because quite simply, Amelia Besson might not have been the one to have passed it on, but at least she would discover something of her family and its history.

Perhaps her ability had come out of nowhere as one of those strange things that showed up in families from time to time. Was there always a history of madness? Was there definitely a gene for creativity or an aptitude for mathematics? Did people like Nikola Tesla or Thomas Edison come from ancestors with a scientific background? She wasn't sure of the answer. Perhaps Quinn was the first in her family to have the gift of sight, and might be the last. What a relief it would be to know that her child would not be afflicted with the burden of seeing into the past. Human beings accumulated enough of their own baggage over the years, they didn't need to sift through someone else's dirty linen on top of that.

Quinn rarely saw anything happy or uplifting. Most of her visions inevitably led to misery, disappointment, and, more often than not, death. At times, it came peacefully at an age when dying wasn't unexpected, but it was usually a violent end that struck when the victim least expected it, and had decades of living stolen from them by hate, jealousy, or greed. It was a terrible burden to 'live' these memories, given the fact that Quinn could only watch, helpless to warn the victim or prevent whatever was about to happen. She experienced what the person felt, suffered their fears and shared their worries, but most of all she understood the hopelessness of their situation and tasted the terror of those final moments before life was extinguished and their story came to an end.

Quinn stretched out her arm and turned on the bedside lamp. She never needed a nightlight, but tonight she wanted to see every shadowy corner of the room to make sure she was quite alone and the threatening dark presence could not take her by surprise. She needed to feel safe, and she needed a distraction. Quinn reached for the fan.

Chapter 9

August 1858

River Road, Louisiana

Madeline trembled with apprehension as the carriage passed through tall wrought-iron gates and continued up the oak-lined drive toward the house. The slanting rays of the late afternoon sun shone through the leaves, the light diffusing when it filtered through the wings of moss that swayed from the ancient trees, giving the drive an almost magical appearance. Madeline imagined she had entered an enchanted kingdom where a fairy king and queen lived in the beautiful white mansion with a gabled roof supported by thick columns on all sides. A wraparound balcony with wrought-iron railings encircled the upper floor, and black wooden shutters flanked every window, the color adding contrast and character to the white walls and complementing the railing. According to Mr. Larson, Arabella Plantation was one of the grandest manor houses along the River Road, and that was saying a lot, since Madeline had never imagined the kind of splendor she'd witnessed as the carriage rolled passed one plantation after another.

Mr. Larson helped Madeline down from the carriage, but didn't extend his hand to Mammy, who sat on the bench next to the driver, her carpet bag on her knees. "The driver will take you round the back to the servants' entrance," he said. Neither Mammy nor Tess had ever used anything but the front door at their house in New Orleans, so this was the first difference Madeline had encountered, but she knew it wouldn't be the last.

"I'll see you soon," she said to Mammy, who nodded calmly, as though she'd expected this.

The carriage drove off and Mr. Larson escorted Madeline up the steps toward the front door, which was opened by a Negro butler dressed almost entirely in white. The brass buttons of his coat glowed in the sunlight, as did the chain of his pocket watch that stretched from one button to the pocket. The butler wore white gloves, and looked very fastidious and dignified.

"Mr. Larson, Miss Besson, the master will see you in the parlor," he said and led the way.

The parlor was bathed in the golden light of the late afternoon, its tall windows facing the front and side of the house open wide to catch any hint of a breeze. The room was beautifully decorated in shades of apple green and cream that gave an impression of freshness and coolth despite the August heat. Two women sat on settees facing each other, a low table with a pitcher of lemonade between them. The lemonade looked wonderfully refreshing, and Madeline nearly gasped in surprise when she noticed cubes of ice floating in the golden liquid. She'd heard that wealthy people imported ice from the North during the summer months, but had never actually met anyone who could afford such luxury.

"Mr. Larson, Madeline, do come in." A handsome young man with wavy light hair and luminous blue eyes peeled himself away from the mantel and came forward to greet them. He held out his hands, leaving Madeline no choice but to take them. He clasped her hands lightly and gazed into her face, smiling warmly. "Dear cousin, I have so looked forward to meeting you. I'm very sorry for your loss, and you're most welcome here."

He released Madeline's hands and turned to face the other two women. "Madeline, that great lady over there is your grandmother, Sybil Besson, and this fine lady," he added with a wink at the young woman, "is my lovely wife, Amelia." He never introduced himself, but it stood to reason that he was George Besson, the master of Arabella Plantation.

"Welcome, Madeline," Amelia said. Dark curls spilled from beneath her lace cap trimmed with blue ribbon. The most striking feature of her delicate, aristocratic face was her wide, dark eyes, which were fixed on Madeline in a frank gaze of appraisal.

Amelia remained seated, her pale hand resting on her rounded belly.

The older woman slowly rose to her feet and came to stand in front of Madeline, examining her as if she were a prize heifer. She didn't say anything, just nodded in acknowledgement of some private thought and left the room, her posture haughty and unyielding.

"Don't mind Grandmamma. She's still in shock," George said by way of explanation. "Mr. Larson, will you stay to supper?"

"Don't mind if I do, Mr. Besson."

"Amelia, dear, why don't you pour Mr. Larson and Madeline some lemonade? They must be parched after the long drive from town."

Madeline sat on the settee her grandmother had just vacated and gratefully accepted a glass of lemonade. It was cool to the touch and the drink was deliciously sweet-tart. She hoped that Mammy had been offered a cool drink and made to feel welcome.

"Supper is served," the butler they'd met earlier announced.

"Good. I'm famished," George said and offered Amelia his hand. She grasped it and lifted herself off the settee. Her pregnancy looked to be further along than Madeline had first thought, her belly like a watermelon beneath her cream-colored dress. George regarded his wife with undisguised pride and patted her hand when she slipped her arm through his.

Mr. Larson escorted Madeline into the dining room and held out a chair for her before taking a seat himself. The room was very grand, with butter-yellow walls and intricate white moldings. A huge gilded mirror hung over the sideboard, and a portrait of a handsome, if somewhat heavy-featured, middle-aged gentleman wearing a wig, an embroidered velvet coat in midnight blue, and white breeches adorned the space between two tall widows.

"That's Grandfather Jean," George explained as he took a seat beneath the portrait. "He died before I was born."

Madeline gazed up at the portrait. If Jean Besson was George's grandfather, then he was her grandfather as well, and must have been Sybil Besson's husband. Madeline studied the man's features. She saw something of her father, especially about the eyes, but Charles had never looked as arrogant or imposing as the man in the painting.

"And who is that?" Madeline asked, pointing to the painting directly across from Jean's. It was of a beautiful young woman, dressed in a frothy gown of dusky pink silk that accentuated her alabaster skin and luminous dark eyes. Her powdered hair was adorned with camellias and a long curl draped over one creamy shoulder.

"Oh, that's Grandmamma," George replied, as if it should be obvious. "She was the shining jewel of Crescent City society in her day."

Madeline turned to compliment her grandmother, but was surprised to note that Sybil Besson wasn't there. "Is Mrs. Besson not joining us for supper?" she asked.

"I'm afraid Grandmamma is rather tired. She'll have a tray in her room," George replied as the first course was brought out.

Madeline was relieved that the forbidding old lady wasn't there; she was nervous enough without her presence. George Besson and Mr. Larson chatted amiably about politics, escalating tensions with the North, and the price of cotton and sugar while Amelia tried to engage Madeline in small talk about the latest fashions. Amelia mentioned a few people she thought Madeline might know, but the names meant nothing to her, so Amelia moved on, searching for something they might have in common. Conversation flowed easily enough, but Madeline couldn't help noticing that no one made any mention of her father nor offered an explanation as to why they'd never met before. No one from Arabella Plantation had attended the funeral or sent a note of condolence. Madeline couldn't ask outright if George and Amelia had known of her existence before last week, but she was sure her father had never mentioned his mother, brother, or nephew within her hearing.

Madeline felt a moment of agitation when the meal finally came to an end and Mr. Larson thanked his hosts and prepared to return to New Orleans. It felt strange to know that she wouldn't be going back with the lawyer, but would remain here in this magnificent house, which was to be her new home.

"Don't hesitate to write to me if you need anything, but I think you're in good hands," Mr. Larson said and kissed Madeline's cheek in a gesture of farewell. He said nothing of inviting Madeline to his upcoming wedding, which made her feel even more displaced. Mr. Larson no longer saw her as a personal connection, but rather as a business obligation he'd seen to its conclusion.

"Don't worry, Mr. Larson. We'll take excellent care of Madeline. Won't we, Amelia?" George asked. He didn't seem to expect and answer and Amelia didn't bother to respond. Instead she wished Mr. Larson a good evening and turned to Madeline, who stood in the foyer, uncertain of what to do next.

"Cissy, show Madeline to her room," Amelia said once Mr. Larson took his leave. A young Negro woman stood at the foot of the stairs, curiosity about Madeline evident in her almond-shaped eyes. She smiled in welcome and Madeline smiled back, reminded of Tess.

"Your trunk has been brought up, and you should have everything you need. I gave you the Rose Room," Amelia added with a smile. "It's not the biggest, but it's beautifully decorated and has a view of the garden. You don't want to be looking at the slave quarters, do you?" she added, wrinkling her nose in distaste. "Summon Cissy if you require anything." She turned to her husband. "George, I'm tired. I think I shall go to bed."

"Sleep well, darling. I'll read for a while after I check on Grandmamma," George replied. "Goodnight, my love. Goodnight, Madeline."

Madeline and Cissy followed Amelia up the grand staircase with George trailing behind. They parted ways on the second-floor landing, each heading in a different direction. Cissy led Madeline to a bedroom at the end of the long corridor and threw open the door. Amelia had been right, it was a room of untold loveliness, the type of boudoir Madeline had never dreamed of having. Her own room at home had been pretty, but not nearly as opulent as her new bedroom. The walls were of cream-colored damask, and the bed hangings, drapes, and rug were all in shades of rose pink and gold. Madeline spotted her trunk at the foot of the bed. It appeared to have been unpacked and her belongings were already put away, her plain cotton nightdress laid out on the bed.

"Is there anything you be needing, Miss?" Cissy asked.

"Where is Mammy? Will she be coming up to see me?" Madeline's voice sounded small and frightened, and she saw sympathy in Cissy's dark gaze.

Cissy shook her head. "I'm sho I don't know. I ain't met your Mammy yet."

"Goodnight then, Cissy."

"Goodnight, miss."

Cissy let herself out, leaving Madeline alone. Worn out by the emotional turmoil of the past few days, she was more than ready for bed, but she belatedly realized she'd forgotten to ask Cissy where the water closet was located. At home in New Orleans, they'd still used an outhouse, but Arabella Plantation was very modern, with several water closets installed throughout the house, or so George had told Mr. Larson over supper. Unfortunately, Madeline had no idea where they were on this floor.

She let herself out of the room, leaving the door slightly ajar in case she forgot which one was hers, and wandered down the corridor. It would be terribly rude to just open every door, so she would have to find a servant and ask. She was just about to head downstairs when she heard voices from the room at the end of the long hallway.

"I don't want her here, George," Sybil Besson said, her voice gravelly and brusque.

"Come, Grandmamma, I've never known you to be uncharitable. You are always the first one to support a worthy cause. And she is your granddaughter, after all."

"She's no granddaughter of mine," Sybil snapped.

"Do you not mourn Uncle Charles in the least?" George asked, clearly shocked by his grandmother's attitude toward Madeline.

"I mourned for him years ago when he betrayed me and this family. Charles was dead to me long before last week."

"Grandmamma, what on earth did he do to hurt you so?" George's tone was indulgent and kind, the sort of tone one would use to tease a petulant child out of a bad mood.

"Don't ask me that, Georgie," Sybil replied, her voice softening. "I can't bear to speak of it."

"Even after all these years?"

"Some things can never be forgotten or forgiven. Please don't ask me to explain."

Sybil might have no room in her heart for her granddaughter, but it was obvious that George and his grandmother shared a warm and loving relationship, and he knew exactly how to talk to her.

"Surely it's important that I know, now that Madeline is here," he cajoled.

"What Charles did was unspeakable, and I will never forgive him, not even in death. And that girl is nothing more than a reminder of the son I lost. Find a school for her, George. There are plenty of establishments for girls who have no family. They live in year-round. Once she comes of age, she'll marry or find suitable employment, but she won't be our problem any longer."

"Grandmamma, I don't know what Uncle Charles did to hurt you so deeply, but Madeline is a sweet, charming girl who is in no way responsible for her father's actions. I am now the master of this house, and I say she stays. I don't ask you to care for her, but I would ask you to be civil."

"Hmm," Sybil scoffed. "You always were headstrong, just like your father. And equally misguided. He begged me to forgive Charles. They were close, those two, despite everything. I forbade Albert to have any contact with his brother and he obeyed, afraid that I would cut him out of my will and pass the plantation directly to you, but it seems I can't intimidate you as easily. I will honor your wishes, George. This is your house now, and you are master here. I'm nothing but an old woman whose opinion doesn't interest anyone. Go now. I am ready for my bed."

Madeline sprinted down the stairs when she heard George's footsteps approaching the door. She slipped around the corner once she reached the first floor and waited until George passed before continuing to the water closet she'd been shown earlier when she asked to wash her hands. Madeline found the room and shut the door. Just enough moonlight filtered through the window to keep it from being pitch dark. She splashed some water on her face and patted it dry with a towel.

Her heart was beating fast and there was a sinking feeling in her stomach. No one had ever shown such dislike for her before. She'd been protected, loved, and spoiled her whole life. She was deeply grateful to Cousin George for coming to her defense, but her grandmother's animosity shook her to the core. What had her father done that had caused his mother to banish him from her life? What would a beloved son have to do to cross the line so completely that he couldn't be forgiven, even in death?

Madeline slipped out of the water closet, wishing she could find Mammy, but the house was quiet and lost in shadow. The servants had finished for the day and gone to their own lodgings, and the only room still in use downstairs was the parlor, where George had retreated. Madeline saw a light beneath the door, but had no wish to confront George with her questions. She tiptoed back up the stairs and went to her room, where she lay awake for hours, too anxious and lonely to sleep.

Chapter 10

April 2014

New Orleans, Louisiana

Quinn set aside the fan and sighed with frustration. Her head hurt, and her brain felt as if it were wrapped in thick, fluffy cotton that prevented the firing of neurons and made her thoughts swirl in a lazy fog of sleeplessness. She'd finally fallen asleep in the wee hours of the morning only to wake up promptly at six. No amount of trying to get back to sleep had worked, so she'd made a cup of coffee in the coffeemaker provided by the hotel in an effort to get a jump start on her day. It hadn't worked.

Quinn laughed out loud when she caught sight of herself in the bathroom mirror. She looked like Medusa, her dark hair resembling writhing snakes that moved about her head in an uncoordinated dance of shiny coils. She cleaned her teeth, swallowed her antenatal vitamins, and decided to call for room service. She was too sluggish to go downstairs for breakfast, but her stomach rumbled with hunger. She was always hungry first thing in the morning, probably because eating at night gave her horrible heartburn and indigestion, so she avoided eating after six. Room service wouldn't get there for at least a half-hour and part of her longed to pick up the fan again, just for a few minutes, eager to learn more about Madeline.

Quinn's heart went out to the orphaned girl, but her mind, now a bit more active thanks to the belated boost from the coffee, teemed with questions. Who was Madeline, and why was she not listed on the family tree Seth had shown her? Seth had said that Charles Besson never married or had any children, but he'd been married to Corinne, and Madeline was clearly his daughter. Perhaps the stillbirth of Charles's son wouldn't have been recorded, but Madeline had been very much alive and known to her Besson relatives.

Seth had also mentioned that no girls had been born into the Besson family in more than two hundred years, but Madeline was a Besson, and most definitely a girl. And why did Seth believe the fan belonged to Amelia when, in fact, it had belonged to Madeline? Quinn wished she could simply put her questions to Seth, but how could she explain her sudden knowledge without telling him about her gift? He'd scoffed at the notion of psychic ability, and might ridicule her if she told him the truth. Would that bother her? Quinn wondered. Yes, it would, she realized with a start.

Quinn stared at her reflection in the bathroom mirror, no longer seeing her wild hair. Without make-up, she looked younger and more vulnerable, her hazel eyes clouded with confusion. Deep down she was still the little girl who longed to know who her birth parents were and hoped they wouldn't be disappointed in her if she ever met them. She and her biological father were as different as chalk and cheese, but she longed to establish a relationship with him now that she'd found him.

Quinn liked Seth well enough, but her mind still refused to cast him in a parental role. He was just a pleasant, friendly American man she'd met. She had to keep reminding herself that she carried his DNA, as did her unborn child. So far she hadn't discovered anything they shared, not even something as minor as a love of certain foods or a common interest. They were complete strangers on every level, so they had to tread carefully. Sharing her deepest secret with him was probably not a good idea.

Seth had invited Quinn out to dinner at his favorite restaurant tonight, and Brett would join them. Seth was excited about getting his son and daughter together in a formal setting, but Quinn thought it might have been best had they just met at Seth's house where Brett was on familiar ground. She couldn't imagine that he would be overly excited about her, not at this stage anyway. Logan had been curious about her and happy enough to meet her because he was older and settled into his own life. She was no threat to him. Jude, on the other hand, had seemed resentful and angry. Perhaps his moodiness had nothing to do with Quinn, but he was still young enough that he might not wish to share his mother with a daughter she was clearly excited about. Brett might feel the same about Seth. He was an only child who wasn't used to sharing the love of his parents with a sibling. She'd have to reassure him that she was in no way interested in taking his father away from him.

Quinn glanced at her watch. What was taking room service so long? She was famished. She checked her mobile while she waited, and discovered a message from her parents, a missed call from Sylvia, a text from Jill, and a voicemail from Rhys. Quinn took a deep breath and pressed 'play.'

"Please tell me I misheard your message and you didn't say you're in Louisiana." Rhys had every right to be annoyed. They still had to find a suitable subject for the season finale of *Echoes from the Past*, and his team was hard at work, since he'd pronounced that the last episode had to be mind-blowing. "What in the name of God are you doing in New Orleans?" There was a slight pause, just long enough for the penny to drop. "You're there to see Seth, aren't you? Well, I hope you find what you're looking for, Quinn. In the meantime, please allow me to remind you that you are under contract with the BBC, and we have to complete the series before October thirty-first. I have an idea I'd like to discuss with you. Ring me!"

Quinn was about to call Rhys when there was a knock on the door. She tossed aside her mobile and went to answer. She wasn't in the mood to deal with Rhys's peevishness, not before breakfast. She'd call him later, after spending the day in the way she found most productive, doing research. She'd hit the archives, the libraries, and the museums. The more she knew of the time period, the better she could understand the context of Madeline's story. And if she were really lucky, maybe she'd find some mention of her somewhere.

**

Quinn dressed for dinner with Seth and Brett, applied a little make-up, and ran her fingers through her newly styled hair, nodding with approval. She still had at least a half-hour till Seth came to collect her, so she might as well deal with Rhys. She selected his number on her mobile and smiled to herself when he answered, his voice gruff and unfriendly. This was vintage Rhys, but his bark was worse than his bite.

"And what time do you call this?" Rhys demanded. It was 6:00 p.m. in New Orleans, so midnight in London.

"You weren't in bed. In fact, if I know you, you're probably baking something sinfully delicious because you're stressing about the program."

"You're right, as it happens. I'm making a flourless torte, but it's not because I'm stressed," Rhys replied with a smile in his voice. "I've been invited to dinner tomorrow, and I said I'd bring the pudding."

"Must be someone special. You don't make homemade dessert for just anyone," Quinn joked. Rhys loved to bake, especially when he felt anxious or upset, but now that she knew him better, she also knew that he baked something special only for those he really cared about and wished to impress.

"Never you mind," Rhys retorted, but she could almost hear him blushing over the line. He was definitely baking for a woman.

"What did you want to discuss with me?" Quinn asked. "I'll be back in London next week. Can it wait till then?"

"We don't have anything lined up for the finale," Rhys said, terse again, automatically bouncing back to the persona of the demanding executive. "It has to be special and pack a ratings punch. Do you have anything in mind? Do you have any colleagues who have unearthed anything of interest lately?"

"Rhys, archeology is time consuming and painstaking. People don't just stumble onto royal burial chambers or the remains of dead monarchs buried beneath parking lots on a daily basis. Such finds are rare and special."

"I'm desperate here, Quinn. We need an outline for the final episode or we'll miss our deadline. The program has already been scheduled for a Sunday evening spot, just before *Downton Abbey*. That's a very desirable timeslot."

Quinn pinched the bridge of her nose, momentarily frozen with indecision. She had an idea, but she wasn't sure she was ready to share it with Rhys just yet. He would either hate it or latch onto it and there'd be no going back if she changed her mind or failed to find out anything exciting enough to fill an entire episode.

"I can hear you thinking," Rhys said, his tone impatient.

"And I can hear you chewing. You're more stressed about this than you're letting on. I don't know how you manage to stay so slim with all the baked goods you consume."

"Don't change the subject," Rhys replied, but the chewing stopped.

"Rhys, what if the final episode was about my own ancestors?" Quinn asked, hoping she wouldn't regret telling Rhys about Madeline.

"Go on," Rhys said, his tone lightening.

"Seth doesn't know much about his family history, but he does have a few documents and a family tree that his grandfather drew up based on extensive research."

"How does this make for good television?" Rhys asked, instantly critical. "My grandfather also dabbled in genealogy, but since I'm not descended from the kings of Gwynedd, my illustrious family is not exactly the stuff of legend."

"You really are an infuriating man." Quinn laughed. "Will you let me speak, or will you shoot down my idea before you even know what it is?"

"I'm sorry. I'm tired and grumpy."

"Really? I would never have guessed. I found something. I don't know exactly where this will lead, but there's definitely a mystery here, one worth pursuing."

"Tell me more," Rhys asked, his voice now silky and coaxing.

"I don't think I will," Quinn replied, a smile on her face.

"Tease."

"I need a few days, then we'll talk. In the meantime, get some rest and give my regards to Sylvia."

"How did you know I'd be seeing Sylvia?" Rhys asked.

"Because I know that you two have been spending time together and chocolate flourless torte is her favorite. Goodnight, boss," Quinn said with a chuckle and hung up before Rhys could confirm or deny her suspicions.

Chapter 11

August 1858

Arabella Plantation, Louisiana

"Shall I help you dress, miss?" Cissy asked as she pulled open the curtains. The blazing white light of the August morning flooded the room, making Madeline squint and cover her eyes with her arm. She'd finally fallen asleep in the early hours and woken groggy and muddled, and her eyes had a grainy feeling from lack of sleep. Had she been at home in New Orleans, she would have sent Mammy away and stayed in bed till noon, but this was her first day at the plantation and she couldn't be rude to her hosts.

Madeline stood like a dressmaker's dummy while Cissy did her best to stuff Madeline's unyielding limbs into the garments she'd prepared. The process took more than an hour, but Madeline couldn't help but admire the hairstyle Cissy had managed to wrangle from her unruly curls. Cissy had plaited several thinner braids into one thick coil and pinned it into a neat chignon at the back of Madeline's head. She had then used two side braids to crisscross at the back and snake around the chignon, and secured her creation with several pins decorated with tiny artificial flowers in palest pink. The effect was pleasing and made Madeline look ladylike and grown up.

"There now. How you like dem braids pinned like dat?" Cissy asked.

"It's beautiful. Where did you learn to do that?"

"I make up my own styles," Cissy answered with a shrug. "White folk's hair is easy to work with."

Madeline couldn't see Cissy's hair beneath her colorful turban, but she knew what the girl meant. Tess's hair never grew more than a few inches long, and looked like a spongy halo if left uncovered or unbraided. And she always began brushing it from the bottom rather than the top, and worked her way up. Mammy's hair wasn't as coarse as Tess's and grew longer, its natural color more brown than black. And it was very curly, the strands wound into tight spirals that sprang right back when Madeline had tried to pull on them as a child.

"You have a talent for coiffure," Madeline said.

Cissy shrugged again. "Don't know what *koifoor* means, but it don't take too much talent to twist braids into a bun."

Cissy turned her attention to making the bed and straightening the room while Madeline gingerly made her way downstairs. She wasn't sure where to go or what to do. She was hungry, but no one had said anything about breakfast the night before. Did the family breakfast together at a certain time, or was this the type of household where one helped oneself from a sideboard whenever one came down? Madeline wasn't sure which she'd prefer. It would be easier to eat by herself, but if she hoped to fit in she had to make an effort and begin building relationships with the Bessons. And she had to start from scratch, the most difficult part of all. They were complete strangers to each other in every way. How did one go from that to becoming a part of a family?

Madeline's vision blurred and she grabbed onto the banister for support as she recalled having breakfast with her father only last week. She'd taken her time with him for granted, assuming he'd be there to watch her grow into a woman and have a family of her own. The sheer power of her longing for him nearly undid her and she had to stand still for a few moments to regain control of her emotions. Her new relatives didn't grieve for Charles Besson, so she couldn't count on them to offer any comfort or sympathy in her bereavement.

Madeline was pleased to find Amelia alone in the dining room. She dreaded having to breakfast with her grandmother or even George. George seemed welcoming and kind, but having had

87

very little experience with young men, Madeline had no clue what to talk to him about or how to behave. And Sybil seemed to detest Madeline on sight, her obvious animosity not exactly a stepping stone toward a warm relationship.

Amelia smiled in welcome. She looked fresh as a daisy in a dress of blue and white gingham, unadorned except for a bit of lace at the sleeves and two strips of lace starting at the shoulders and meeting in a V at the waist. The style would have accentuated Amelia's waist, but instead the lace was like an arrow pointing to her protruding belly.

"I was hoping you'd come down soon. I hate eating alone. If you don't like bacon and eggs I can ask Cook to make you something different," Amelia offered as she poured herself a fresh cup of tea from a beautiful china teapot.

"Anything is fine," Madeline replied, not wishing to appear difficult. Mammy always baked fresh beignets and made hominy grits for breakfast, which she served with butter and a spoonful of molasses. Eggs and bacon were for Sunday mornings before church, but Madeline liked them just fine. She helped herself to some eggs from a covered dish and took two rashers of bacon.

"Have Cousin George and Mrs. Besson breakfasted already?" Madeline asked. She couldn't bring herself to refer to Sybil as her grandmother, especially after the heated conversation she'd overheard last night.

"George gets up early and goes out to ride his acres every morning before it gets too hot, then meets with the overseer and attends to plantation business," Amelia said. "It's cotton-picking time now, so he's gone for hours. And Grandmamma takes a breakfast tray in bed, so I eat alone every morning. I really am glad you are here. Perhaps it's selfish of me, but I did so long for a companion, and my prayers were answered through your misfortune."

"It's not as if you caused it to happen," Madeline replied in an effort to cheer Amelia up. She looked so forlorn.

"No, but it doesn't make it any less tragic, does it? I hope we can be of some comfort to each other over the coming months. You are in mourning for your father and I'm in my confinement, which is necessary but mind-numbingly dull." Amelia placed her hand on her belly. "I do miss society so, Madeline. George and I attended the most wonderful parties before... Well, never mind that. Perhaps after the baby is born," she added, her voice buoyant with hope. "It would be wonderful to have a Christmas ball to celebrate the holiday as well as the birth of our baby. My very own holy infant." She giggled happily. "Is that blasphemous?"

"When is the baby due?"

"Mid-November, so I still have a whole three months to go. I feel him kicking though. It's such an odd sensation. Like a fish on a hook thrashing to break free."

"Do you fish?" Madeline asked, surprised by the comparison.

"My father took me fishing once when I was little, but I didn't have the patience to sit there for hours quietly, so he never took me again. He said I disrupted his peace. I do remember what it was like to reel in a fish though. Father stood behind me and held the rod so I wouldn't drop it in my excitement."

"You said 'he,' referring to the baby," Madeline said.

"George wants a son, so I hope it's a boy for his sake. He needs someone to leave all this wealth to, or what is it all for? And Grandmamma will be pleased with me, if only for five whole minutes, if I deliver a boy."

"Do you displease her?" Madeline asked. Amelia seemed eager to talk, and any information Madeline could gather about George and Sybil could be helpful in her dealings with them. She felt completely out of her element, so perhaps Amelia could be her guide.

"She's very possessive of George. His mother died when he was three, so Grandmamma stepped in and raised him. He is more her son than her grandson, and even though I'm the lady of the house, she's the one who rules the roost. Did you see the ring of keys at her waist? She will not relinquish those until she's stone cold, and even then I'll probably have to pry them from her dead hand," Amelia said, but instantly backtracked, as though realizing she'd revealed too much. "She's been a tremendous help to me, of course. I knew nothing of running a household when I married George, so she kept doing things her way until I learned. I have yet to change a single thing."

Madeline nodded in sympathy. Her mother had never kept the keys at her waist, as though mistrustful of her servants and family, but for some ladies of great houses the keys were a symbol of power and a way to keep track of every ounce of food, every piece of silver, and every item of laundry touched by the hands of her slaves. Having the keys gave their owner the power to reward and the prerogative to punish. By keeping the keys, Sybil effectively usurped Amelia's place, treating her like a child instead of the mistress of the house, and judging by Amelia's baleful stare, she was fully aware of the insult.

"So, what would you like to do today?" Amelia asked.

"Can I see Mammy?"

Amelia pushed away her plate and busied herself with smoothing down the voluminous skirt of her dress. "I'm afraid that's not possible."

"Where is she?"

"She's in the fields."

"What? Why?" Madeline cried. "Surely she's too old to be picking cotton."

"That was one of Sybil's conditions for allowing you to come," Amelia said, her eyes sliding away from Madeline's gaze.

"Why does she hate me so?"

"I don't know, Madeline. I honestly don't. All I know is that she was more upset about having you here than about the death of her son."

"I'm going to speak to her." Madeline pushed her chair from the table with a scape that made Amelia cringe.

"Please don't," Amelia pleaded. "I don't want her to send you away. And she can, you know. She can talk George into just about anything. Don't worry about your Mammy. She'll be fine." Amelia gestured with her hands as if what she was saying should be obvious to anyone. "The slaves are used to that kind of work. Anyway, Cissy is young and knows about fashion. She'll take better care of you than some old, useless darkie."

Madeline gaped at Amelia. Mammy had loved Madeline since birth and cared for her every day of her life. She knew that some plantation owners saw their slaves as interchangeable and not possessed of human emotions, but Charles Besson had taught her to be respectful and kind to all people, no matter their background.

"I love Mammy," Madeline replied, her voice steely. "She's not a useless darkie, she's a person, and I won't have her mistreated."

"It's no longer your call to make," Amelia replied. "I'm sorry, Madeline, I really am, but Mammy belongs to the estate, and the estate belongs to Sybil. As long as she is alive, she will have a say in what goes on here, and George won't go against her, not on this. He defies her when he has no choice, but he loves her too much to upset her over something as trivial as an old slave woman."

Madeline blinked away tears of frustration. She was now at the mercy of these people, at least until she came of age. She had nothing of her own, nothing to fall back on, not even a good education that she might use to earn a living. No one would hire someone like her. Most people had slaves, and others hired poor white folk to work for a pittance. White laborers worked in awful conditions and died daily, but no one cared. Daddy had said that poor white folk were less valuable than slaves since a young male slave cost several hundred dollars and his death would be a financial setback to his owner, whereas a white man could be hired for as little as a quarter a day and if he died, the employer lost nothing at all. Plantation owners hired gangs of white men to cut cypress trees in the swamps, refusing to risk losing their slaves to swamp fever. Madeline had never understood the meaning of Daddy's words until today. Even old Mammy was worth more to an employer than Madeline. Mammy could pick cotton, work in the kitchens, or raise babies, but Madeline was suited to nothing and no one would pay her to do what someone else could do for less.

"Excuse me, Amelia. I need some air," Madeline said.

"It's hot as purgatory out there," Amelia replied.

"Nevertheless."

"Suit yourself. I'll have some cool lemonade waiting for you when you return."

"Thank you."

Madeline forced herself to smile as she walked out of the dining room. She had to control her temper and be respectful to her hosts. Once outside, she ran around the side of the house and headed for the slave quarters. She would find Mammy regardless of what Amelia had said.

Chapter 12

The slave quarters of Arabella Plantation were about half a mile from the main house—close enough to keep an eye on, but far enough to not be an eyesore to the family. About twenty cabins were clustered around an open space used for cooking, hanging out the washing, and doing various other chores that required elbow room. Given that the Bessons owned about two hundred slaves, about ten people slept in every one-room hut that boasted one small window and a narrow doorway.

Peering into the nearest hut, Madeline saw no furnishings except a couple of shelves on the walls and nails for hanging things. Rolled-up blankets lay neatly piled against one wall, waiting for their owners to spread them on the floor at bedtime. Madeline turned away, ashamed of her earlier bout of self-pity. She'd lost her father and her home, but she had no right to complain when other people lived in such barren conditions without hope of anything better. Mr. Larson had said the Bessons were good to their slaves. She'd hate to see what slave quarters on other plantations looked like, ones where the owners weren't as 'good.'

Madeline slowed her pace as she drew closer. Several women were hanging out the washing and cooking in large pots over open fires. Most of them had babies, either perched on their hips or in slings worn on their backs while they worked. Madeline noted with some surprise that the women looked too old to be the babies' mothers. The mothers were likely in the fields picking cotton, while the elderly stayed behind to look after the children and see to domestic chores. About a dozen pickaninnies ran around the yard, some completely naked, chasing each other and hooting with laughter. Some of the younger ones who could barely walk toddled behind the others, trying to get in on the fun. The women kept a watchful eye on the children as they went about their tasks.

Madeline stopped. The slave women would not welcome her presence and she had no wish to intrude. She found a shady spot and settled in to wait. It was close to noon, so the laborers would probably return soon for the midday meal, unless it was brought out to them in the fields. Madeline didn't yet understand the workings of the plantation, but she would learn soon enough if she remained watchful. Not that it mattered. Life on the plantation had a rhythm of its own, and she would have to adjust if she hoped to fit in and find some measure of contentment.

Her father had been gone for just six days, but already her life had taken on a surreal quality, flowing over her like a swift current that carried her along no matter how much she resisted. She had no say in anything that happened to her, not anymore. Her only choice was to be humble, grateful, and obedient.

Caught up in her somber thoughts, Madeline barely noticed the column of laborers making their way back toward the living quarters. They looked tired and dusty, but most of them appeared to be in good spirits, talking and joking amongst themselves and calling out to the women and children. Some of the children ran toward their fathers, who scooped them up and put them on their shoulders, the children's bare legs making a thick scarf around the men's necks. A few young women broke away from the crowd and reached for the babies, putting them to their breasts before they even had a chance to sit down or have a cup of water.

Madeline stepped forward and shielded her eyes with her hand, searching for Mammy. She spotted her eventually, way in the back, walking slowly, as if in pain. Madeline took off at a run and threw herself into Mammy's arms, blubbering like a baby. She had a speech prepared, but words deserted her, leaving her mind blank as she clung to the one person she still had left in the world.

"Come now, child," Mammy said, her voice as soothing as warm molasses. "Don't tear yourself up. It'll all be all right."

"Nothing will ever be all right, Mammy. How could they send you to the fields?" Madeline sobbed.

"Don't you worry about me. I've been in them fields before. It ain't so bad once you get used to it. Now, tell me how you been."

"Mrs. Besson hates me, but I don't know why. She keeps referring to something Daddy did that was unforgivable. She told George to send me away, but he refused."

Mammy nodded, as if Madeline had just confirmed her suspicions. "Now, you listen to your old Mammy. Your Daddy was a good man, and he loved you something fierce. Loved your momma too. That woman in that there house is your grandmother, no matter if she likes it or not. So you go back in there and you act like the granddaughter of the house. You hear? You make a place for yourself, and you hold on to it. You's got rights, baby girl. Don't forsake them."

Madeline stared at Mammy. Her plump face glistened with sweat and she looked worn out, but her eyes shone with determination and defiance. She wasn't broken, nor was she bitter. She'd accepted her fate and was urging Madeline to do the same.

"I will help you, Mammy. I promise. It might take me some time, but I'll see that you're treated right."

"You'll do nothing of the sort, child. You just look after yourself. There's good folk here, and I'm not treated unkindly. There's them that's much worse off than me, believe me. Why, you see all them little ones running around? That's all you need to know."

"Know what?" Madeline asked, confused. The children were sweet, but she hadn't given them another thought.

"There's some as have breeding farms and put the babies up for sale to make a profit. Tear them away from their mommas as soon as they's born. Here, families are kept together. No one takes the babies away, and no one suffers needless cruelty."

Madeline looked around. Workers sat around, enjoying their meal. The women served collard greens with large chunks of cornbread liberally smeared with fat and some kind of side meat. Some ate in silence, but most chatted and exchanged news and gossip with their friends. Madeline had never given much thought to the conditions the slaves lived and worked in before today. She only knew Mammy and Tess, and they had been part of the family. She looked at a young woman who rested her head on the shoulder of the man seated next to her, his arm going about her protectively. He held a small child in his lap, and tickled it with his free hand to make it giggle. The very idea that someone could simply take that baby away and sell it made Madeline's stomach churn with outrage.

"Now go back to the house. And don't go making things worse," Mammy instructed.

"I miss you," Madeline said, feeling sadder than she had before. There was a finality to Mammy's words. She was saying goodbye and telling Madeline to keep her distance for both their sakes.

"And I miss you, baby girl. I's loved you since you was born, and I will love you always. But your life is on a different path now, and you don't need me holding you back."

"You're not holding me back," Madeline protested.

"No, but I ain't helping you forward neither." Mammy reached out and pulled Madeline into an embrace. She smelled of sweat and dust, but Madeline didn't care. She buried her face in Mammy's shoulder, wishing she could stay that way forever.

"I love you, Madeline. I always will." Mammy gently took Madeline by the shoulders and held her away from her. "Go," she said softly. "Find happiness, my girl."

Chapter 13

Madeline muddled through the rest of the day, wishing only that she could retreat to her room and go to bed where she would no longer have to pretend to be a well brought-up young lady with not a care in the world. The brief moment of shame she'd experienced down at the slave quarters passed like a cloud over the sun and she felt more melancholy than before, her heart hollow in her chest, as if her loss had emptied it of blood and muscle and left a fragile shell in its place. She missed Daddy with an ache that was almost physical, and it reminded her of the desperate months after her mother had died, the loss leaving her so heartbroken that she'd cried and cried, forcing Daddy to put aside his own grief and do anything he could to soothe her.

Mammy, without being told, had cleared out all of Corinne's belongings, leaving nothing at all that could remind Madeline of the woman who'd loved her. Even her nightdress had disappeared, along with all her dresses and shoes. Madeline had buried her face in her mother's pillow, inhaling the smell of her hair, a smell that was achingly familiar. She'd fallen asleep clutching her mother's pillow and only woke when her father gently kissed her brow.

"Wake up, Maddy," he'd said. "It's time to go."

"Go where?"

"Go out. We've been cooped up in this house far too long, wallowing in our grief. Let's take a walk along the river and look at the boats. What do you say?"

He knew that Madeline wouldn't be able to resist. She loved watching the boats on the Mississippi. She especially liked the steamboats that dwarfed all the other vessels on the river, making them appear almost toy-like. And they were beautiful, too, like floating palaces with multiple decks adorned with lacy white railings, a huge paddle wheel on the side, and the boat's name painted in big black letters on the wood casing around the wheel.

Sometimes, music floated from the decks of a steamboat, a merry party taking place on the river. Madeline wished more than anything that she could attend such an event and stand on the top deck, her gloved hands on the railing, watching the water churching beneath the wheel and listening to sounds of gaiety coming from the salon within.

"Before we go, there's something I'd like to give you." Daddy had taken out a long, narrow box from his pocket and handed it to Madeline. "Open it."

Madeline ran her small fingers along the length of the box. It was made of polished wood, and felt smooth and cool to the touch. She carefully opened lid. Inside, nestled among folds of blue satin, lay a fan. It was made of ivory and lace, the ivory almost as delicate and transparent as the gauzy fabric.

"I bought this for your mama, but never got the chance to give it to her. She would have wanted you to have it, to remember her by," he said, chocking on the words.

"I will keep it always," Madeline said. She flipped open the fan, gazing at it in rapture. Her mother had loved beautiful things, and would have adored this fan.

"Someday, I will explain things to you, Maddy, but you are still too young and too naïve to understand. I want to keep you that way for as long as possible."

"What things?"

"Things that will change your view of the world, and of yourself."

Maddy shrugged. She had no interest in the world. She fanned herself, enjoying the delicate feel of the ivory in her hand. It was exquisite, and something of her mother's, which made it all the more special.

**

Madeline took out the fan and caressed the ivory with her fingers as silent tears slid down her cheeks. She wished she had something of her father's, but Mammy had disposed of all his possessions before the funeral. Madeline had begged for a memento, but Mammy had said that keeping Daddy's pocket watch or tie pin would only make Madeline sad. What made her sadder was the knowledge that Mr. Larson had taken everything of value to help pay Daddy's massive debts. The sale of the house and Tess had covered a large portion of the sum, but not all of it, and Mr. Larson had personally seen to the disposal of furniture, paintings, silverware, books, and jewelry. Everything had gone, even Daddy's clothes and shoes. Madeline briefly wondered if Mr. Larson had gotten his fee. In the past, she would have assumed that he would help as her daddy's friend, but now she wasn't so sure.

**

Madeline claimed a headache and asked to be excused from supper. She wasn't hungry, just very weary, and desperate to be alone. She allowed Cissy to undress her and climbed into bed. The lavender shadows of encroaching dusk filled the room. Faint stars twinkled in the sky, but grew bigger and brighter as a velvety Southern night cloaked the plantation. Through the open window Madeline could hear crickets and cicadas as they embarked on their nightly symphony, and a gentle breeze carried the strains of a haunting melody from the distant slave quarters.

Madeline was just drifting off to sleep when there was a light knock on the door. She thought it might be Cissy, but was surprised when George entered the room, casually dressed in a linen shirt and pants and carrying a single candle. He set the candle on the nightstand and parted the gauzy mosquito net before sitting on the side of the bed. The mattress sagged beneath his weight.

"Are you all right?" George asked. "You weren't at supper."

"I had a headache."

"I'm sorry. I heard you went to the slave quarters today."

"I wanted to see Mammy. Why was she sent to the fields, Cousin George? She's an old woman. Surely something could have been found for her indoors." Madeline hadn't meant to sound reproachful, but she was angry with George, and angry with the situation. She grew silent, hoping she hadn't made things worse for Mammy.

"You're right. I'll see to it that Mammy doesn't go back to the fields again. Perhaps the kitchen house. It's hot work during the summer months, but easier for a woman of her age."

"Why can't Mammy stay with me, George? I miss her."

"Grandmamma won't have it."

"But why?" Madeline exclaimed.

"There's history there, little one."

Madeline started, now wide awake. "History? They knew each other before?"

"Of course. Where do you think Mammy came from? Your father took her with him when he left. Your Mammy has family here—two sons and their wives and children. They haven't seen each other since Mammy left, but I'm sure they're happy to be reunited at last."

Madeline swallowed down nausea. Mammy had lied to her. She knew all about Daddy's family. She knew about the plantation and had lived here before. Mammy had children that Madeline knew nothing about, children she'd never thought to mention, not even today when Madeline had poured out her troubles to her. Madeline felt sick at heart. Did everyone always lie and deceive?

"And what about Tess?" she demanded. "Did she come from here as well?"

"No. Your father must have purchased her after he left."

"George, what did my father do?" Madeline asked, her need to know now driven by anger. "Why was he cut off by his family?"

George shook his head. "I don't know. I was very young when it all happened, and no one would have told me the truth anyway. I just know that he was cast out and told never to return. No one spoke of him again. I asked my father, but he told me I was better off not knowing. And Grandmamma will take the secret to her grave. She's a proud woman, and couldn't bring herself to forgive Uncle Charles, not even after my father died, leaving no one to run the plantation. She managed everything until I was old enough to take the reins. She put her heart and soul into this place, so I can't openly defy her."

"She holds me responsible for my father's actions," Madeline said, her tone bitter.

"She doesn't hold you responsible, but you are a reminder of something she'd rather forget. And perhaps, in some small measure, seeing you has made her question her judgement."

Madeline doubted it. Sybil Besson didn't seem like a woman who ever questioned her own judgment, only that of others.

"I know I'm young, but if I had a child, I can't begin to imagine what he'd have to do to have me cut him out of my heart this way," Madeline said.

"You are right, you are young. There are things you don't understand, little Maddy."

His use of her pet name startled Madeline. No one had ever called her Maddy except her parents. It was special, and private, but it would be rude to correct him.

"I'll let you get back to sleep." George leaned over and kissed Madeline on the forehead, the way her Daddy used to do. "Sleep well."

George pulled back the mosquito netting and adjusted it so there were no openings, then picked up his candle and left the room as quietly as he had come.

Chapter 14

April 2014

London, England

Gabe shut his laptop with the air of a man who'd just moved mountains. It hadn't been easy, but he'd rearranged several end-of-term meetings, locked in three guest lecturers to take his classes, and booked a flight to New Orleans. The Institute of Archeology directors would not be happy with him for taking two weeks off so close to the end of the school year, but Gabe had decided it was more important for him to be with Quinn. She'd sounded emotional on the telephone when she'd told him about meeting her father and brother, and now she was already immersed in the story of Madeline, thanks to an ivory fan Seth had given Quinn as a gift.

Whether Madeline had anything to do with Quinn remained to be seen, but the fact that the girl didn't seem to appear in any family records or old photographs was enough to arouse Quinn's curiosity, and in turn, Rhys Morgan's. Quinn had decided to extend her stay in Louisiana by a fortnight, and last Gabe heard, Rhys was waiting on approval from the powers-that-be for his request to send a camera crew to New Orleans to film Quinn's quest for her family history. And if anyone could smell a good story, it was Rhys Morgan, damn his overly sensitive nose.

Gabe's initial reaction didn't do him any credit. He was annoyed, and upset with Quinn's decision to extend her visit. This trip should have taken a few days, but she'd already been in Louisiana for nearly a fortnight, and would be staying for another fortnight to complete her research and the filming for the program. Gabe wanted her back. He was being selfish; he'd realized that after a night out with Pete and a conversation with his mother, who always put things in perspective, offering him a surprisingly unbiased point of view. She never took his side simply because he was her son. She just gave him her honest opinion, as did Pete, whose take on things had evolved over the course of his twenty year marriage to Brenda. So, perhaps, it was really Brenda's opinion that Gabe was hearing, but it didn't matter. All three of them were right.

"Don't you think you're being a bit unreasonable?" Pete McGann had asked him over a pint at their favorite pub. "This is important to her. After all these years, Quinn can finally put a name and a face to the people who brought her into this world. She's an archeologist, a historian; she needs to know her own story above all else."

"That's a very astute observation, Pete," Gabe had conceded, "and I completely understand Quinn's need to discover something of where she comes from, but I would just feel better if I were there with her."

"She's a big girl."

"She's a big girl who loves taking unnecessary risks." Gabe hadn't told Pete about Quinn's run-in with Robert Chatham at his Edinburgh hotel. Her lack of judgment on that particular occasion still rankled him, and frightened him as well. Quinn had managed to get away from Chatham, but things could have easily gone the other way. She could have been badly hurt, both emotionally and physically, and the repercussions would have been even more severe had Robert Chatham turned out to be her biological father. That scenario didn't bear thinking about, especially since Quinn's unplanned pregnancy was a direct result of that encounter and their subsequent row. Gabe still felt a pang of remorse when he recalled that night, and his own carelessness the following morning, but he couldn't feel regret about the baby. His heart fluttered with joy every time he thought of 'the little bean' and he couldn't wait to hold the child in his arms and finally see its sweet face.

Pete had looked at Gabe and burst out laughing. "I've known you since uni, mate, and I've never seen you like this. You are like the proverbial caveman who wants to drag his woman by the hair into his cave."

Gabe had set down his mug and stared at Pete. Did he really come off as some testosterone-driven Neanderthal? "I'm just feeling a bit overprotective. She's alone and pregnant, Pete, in a place where she knows no one."

"Except her biological father and brother. Sounds to me like they're getting on like a house on fire. Give her a chance to get to know her kin. Don't make this about yourself."

Am I making this about myself? Gabe had wondered as he headed home that night. Emma was already in bed, tucked in by Pete's wife Brenda, who'd volunteered to babysit so the boys could have a night out. Gabe missed his friend. He'd been busy with his growing family and Pete hadn't been around much of late due to his own family issues. Everything had finally resolved itself, but the tensions of the past few months lingered. Pete and Brenda's relationship with their son, who'd been accused of sexually assaulting a girl but had finally been cleared of all charges, was still strained. They'd questioned Michael and didn't immediately accept his version of events, and their lack of faith had cleaved an almost unbreachable chasm in their family. They had a long way to go until they could reclaim the easy and loving relationship they'd had with Michael, but hopefully, in time, he would see that his parents had had no choice but to question his story and try to get to the truth. Pete and Brenda would have still supported Michael, no matter what, but he was too young and vulnerable to see that.

"Pete's waiting in the car. Thank you for minding Emma."

"Oh, it was my pleasure. How I wish we'd had a girl. She's so lovely. Anyway, give my best to Quinn. When is she back?"

"Soon, I hope."

Gabe had seen Brenda out and settled on the sofa, remote control in hand, but couldn't focus on any program. He looked at his watch. His dad would probably be in bed by now, but Phoebe liked to stay up and read by the fireplace in the library with Buster at her feet until she felt tired enough to retire. Gabe didn't want to ring the house phone for fear of waking his father, but gave

Phoebe's mobile a try. She usually kept it in her handbag, but hopefully, she'd hear it.

Phoebe had answered on the second ring. "Hello, son."

"Hi, Mum. I didn't wake you, did I?"

Phoebe chuckled. "Of course not. Your father is snoring away, but I'm hooked on this new series of novels. It's rather titillating."

"Mum, I don't want to know," Gabe replied. The last time his mother had told him about a book she was reading, he'd actually felt himself blush, which had made his mother giggle like a school girl. His mum had a penchant for racy novels and had recently learned the meaning of S&M. Until then, she'd thought it was just someone referring to Marks & Spencer in the wrong order.

"What's on your mind, Gabe?"

"How do you know I didn't simply call to see how you are?"

"Because I am your mother and I know all the cadences of your voice. You sound in need of advice."

"Guilty as charged," Gabe had admitted, smiling. No one in this world knew him like his mum, not even Quinn.

"Out with it then."

"Mum, Pete has accused me of carrying on like some medieval overlord who wants to lock his lady in a tower to keep her from getting away from him. Am I out of line?"

Gabe could almost hear his mother settling more comfortably in her chair, ready for a meaningful talk.

"Darling, the woman you love, and who is carrying your child, is going through something very emotional and existentially defining. You are worried about her, and feel helpless because

106

you're not there to support her. Now, does that sound like the reasoning of a medieval overlord?"

"No, I suppose not."

"You are a sensitive man, and given all the emotional upheaval of the past few months, you're feeling protective of Quinn. That's nothing to feel ashamed of. Sometimes I wish your father would have been more protective and supportive of me. You know what he said when I went into labor with you?"

"Can't wait to find out."

"He said, 'Get on with it, old girl. I'll be at the pub.'"

"Did he really?" Gabe had asked, laughing. Knowing his dad, he wouldn't have expected him to say anything else, but it was still shocking to hear.

"He did, but things were different in my day. We all had our roles. Your generation is more in tune with each other's needs and feelings, and that's a wonderful thing. Quinn is an intelligent, independent woman, but that doesn't mean she wouldn't appreciate your support. Just because she doesn't need it doesn't mean she doesn't long for it."

"Are you saying I shouldn't have let her go on her own?"

"I'm saying she wouldn't be too upset if you showed up in New Orleans and shared this experience with her. Meet her father and brother, get to know them. I'm sure she's feeling a bit out of her element there. Bring her some digestive biscuits."

Gabe burst out laughing. "Thanks, Mum. I don't think Quinn is in need of biscuits, but you're right about her feeling out of her element. Would you be able to take Emma for a few days if I manage to clear my schedule at work?"

"Of course. We'd love to have her. In fact, there are some wedding plans she can assist me with. I need the perspective of a young person."

107

"Mum, she's four. What does she know about weddings?"

"She knows what she likes, that one. And she has a keen eye."

"If it were up to Emma, we'd all be dressed like the characters from Cinderella."

"Actually, you and Quinn probably resemble Aladdin and Princess Jasmine more, but I promise you, there'll be no magic carpets or mischievous monkeys. You just leave it to me and my granddaughter."

"Suddenly, I'm very worried," Gabe had joked.

"Worry about your bride; I'll take care of the rest."

"Thank you, Mum. I'll call you tomorrow and let you know for certain."

"Then I won't tell your father until then. I'd hate to tell him Emma is coming and then have to disappoint him."

"Goodnight, Mum."

"Goodnight, son."

Gabe had hung up, feeling infinitely better. He was going to New Orleans, and that was the end of it.

Chapter 15

Gabe bent down to retrieve his briefcase from beneath his desk and stood up to find Monica Fielding leaning against the door jamb of his office, studying him with her head to one side as if he were a particularly interesting specimen. She was holding a steaming cup of tea and seemed eager for a chat.

"I hear we are losing you," Monica said, advancing into the office without being invited.

"Only for a short while." Gabe patted his pockets in search of his mobile and keys. He hoped Monica would take the hint and leave, but she inched deeper into the room, heading for the chair facing Gabe's desk.

"You are right to go, of course," Monica continued as she perched on the edge of the chair and took a dainty sip of her tea. "Eight years is not something you can just erase, is it? I'd be worried too."

Monica rearranged her face into an expression of false sympathy as she waited for him to respond, but Gabe saw the eagerness in her eyes. . He felt as if he'd missed some integral part of the conversation.

"Sorry, I don't follow," he said, his keys momentarily forgotten.

"Didn't your bride run off to the States?" Monica asked, all innocence.

"Quinn went to New Orleans on some personal business. What are you getting at, Monica?" Gabe had never really had an issue with Monica before, but her treatment of Quinn had forced him to reconsider his attitude toward her. She really was a shrew, but he was stuck with her, since she was a long-standing member of his staff and he had no problems with her performance. It was her personality that could use some improvement.

"Oh, it's personal business all right." Monica took another sip of tea, her eyes fixed on Gabe over the rim of her mug.

Gabe placed his hands on the desk, leaning toward Monica in a way he hoped was intimidating. "Spit it out, Fielding," he said, his voice low and commanding. He was tired of this game, especially since Monica seemed to be enjoying it so thoroughly.

She exhaled dramatically, and leaned back. "I guess you haven't heard the gossip."

"I make it a point not to listen to gossip," Gabe countered, but in this instance he was willing to make an exception, since it clearly had something to do with his personal life.

"Luke and his lady love are no longer. Seems that American tartlet left him for a footballer or some such. I never thought they would last, and I told him so," Monica went on. "He is too mature for her, too intelligent. She was nothing more than a passing fancy. Young, beautiful, uninhibited. Who wouldn't want a piece of that?" She smiled guilelessly at Gabe. "She turned his head, but it was Quinn he always loved. He just seemed to forget it for a little while."

"Quinn's moved on," Gabe replied.

"But Luke hasn't. I spoke to him yesterday, and he was very interested to learn that Quinn is in the States. He realizes what a fool he's been, and I think he means to win her back." Monica couldn't keep the grin off her face. This was the kind of thing she lived for.

"Don't you need to get home?"

"Mark's away on a business trip, so I'm not in a rush."

"Really?" Gabe asked, matching her innocent tone. "I could have sworn I saw him by the Wesley Euston Hotel last night. With a woman. A colleague, no doubt."

Monica paled and sprang to her feet. "Mark's in Liverpool. He left two days ago."

"My mistake then," Gabe replied smoothly and reached for his coat. "Goodnight, Monica. Have a pleasant evening."

Monica walked out without replying, her back ramrod straight and her head held high. Gabe hadn't actually seen Mark, but rumors were rampant among the faculty. Archeologists liked digging up dirt on each other almost as much as they liked digging up the past. Perhaps even more. Monica's marriage wasn't as secure as she liked to believe. Mark might not have been at a London hotel last night, but he had been somewhere, and he probably hadn't been there alone.

Gabe shut the office door and walked out of the building. He wasn't proud of himself for stooping to Monica's level. He'd made that comment just to hurt her, but she'd hit a nerve and he'd reacted without thinking. Gabe had loved Quinn for years, but she had been devoted to Luke and planned to spend her life with him. Luke had walked out on her without a backward glance and accepted a teaching position in Massachusetts to be with his new American girlfriend, who'd been one of his students at the institute. Gabe needed to believe that Quinn hadn't come to him on the rebound and that she'd accepted his marriage proposal because her feelings for him were genuine and not just as a petty response to Luke's betrayal.

As he strode along the street, his anger mounting, Gabe wondered if it was possible she'd used him as an instrument of revenge. He shook his head to chase away the dark thoughts. He was sure of Quinn's love, but Monica had managed to stoke his insecurities, exactly as she'd hoped she would. Monica hated Quinn, and would like nothing better than to cause trouble for her in any way she could. She'd attempted to discredit Quinn as a historian, but failed, so now she was going after her personal life, using Gabe as her tool.

He stopped walking as he caught sight of himself in a storefront window. He looked angry and bitter. Monica's

111

insinuations had shaken him to the core because no other woman had ever made him feel as vulnerable as Quinn did, but no other woman had ever made him as happy. He would be lost and broken without her, and the magnitude of that realization left him reeling and helpless.

Snap out of it, you eejit, Gabe berated himself with disgust. *If you have no faith in Quinn then you deserve to be kicked to the curb.* He let out a slow breath and counted to ten, letting go of his anger and insecurity. He would be with Quinn tomorrow, and he couldn't wait.

Chapter 16

Gabe glanced at his watch and quickened his pace. He was running late. He normally collected Emma from the nursery school around five, but it was close to six, and she would be cross with him. She couldn't tell time yet, but knew exactly when to expect him based on the order the other children got picked up in. Most parents arrived at exactly the same time, so Emma knew when it was her turn and packed her belongings in anticipation.

Gabe cursed himself for an irresponsible fool when he saw Emma's nose pressed to the nursery school's window, her expression like a sad-face emoji. She always waved, but today she just stared at him through the glass, her gaze full of accusation.

"Darling, I'm sorry. I got held up at work," Gabe tried to explain as they left the building. Emma wore her Disney Princesses backpack that matched her pink coat. She threw him a look of pure disdain.

"I was the last one there," she said. "I thought you wouldn't come."

"Why would you think that?" Gabe had never given Emma any reason to doubt him. This was the first time he'd been late, and all thanks to the conversation with Monica, which he should have avoided like the Black Death.

"My mum was supposed to come, but she didn't," Emma replied, her voice turning tearful.

"Sweetheart, Mum was in a terrible accident. She would have come otherwise. You know that."

"You could be in an accident," Emma pointed out, making Gabe feel even worse. She was too young to think such morbid thoughts, but life had dealt her a terrible blow, and now she would always worry when someone failed to show up on time, fearing they might be dead.

"Emma, I got delayed at work," Gabe explained patiently. "But I'm here now. What would you like for tea?" he asked to change the subject.

"Can you make me chips and egg?"

"I can manage the egg, but we'll have to get take-away chips. I'm not that talented."

"Quinn makes good chips."

"I know. She'll be back soon."

"Let's go get her," Emma suggested. "Is New Orleans close to Disney World? We can collect Quinn and go to the park together. Quinn would like that," Emma said, giving Gabe her most winning smile.

"Only four years old, but already a ruthless negotiator," Gabe said, smiling.

"What's a negotiator?"

"Someone who gets what they want. Like you."

"Are we going, then?" Emma asked, her earlier pique forgotten.

"Someday, sweetheart, but not next week."

"You suck!"

"Pardon me?" Gabe gaped at her. She'd never said anything like that before and it came as a shock.

Emma instantly looked contrite. She was probably testing the waters to see how much she could get away with, and quickly realized that this kind of behavior wouldn't get her far.

"You will never speak to me like that again. Is that understood?" Gabe sounded sterner than he'd intended, but he wouldn't take this kind of guff from a four-year-old.

"Sorry, Daddy. I heard one of the teachers say it."

"To whom? To a pupil?"

"No, she was on her mobile. She was laughing, so I thought it was a funny thing to say."

"I'm going to have a word with your teacher," Gabe said. Who knew what else the children overheard during the course of the day? Gabe was sure the use of mobile phones was prohibited during class hours, but clearly, the teachers were bringing their personal lives into the classroom. It was a losing battle, really. Most of his students kept their mobiles on during lectures, despite being asked to turn them off, and often texted, looked things up, and even watched videos during class. As much as Gabe enjoyed modern technology, he found the lack of respect difficult to deal with, as an educator and as a parent. He snuck a sidelong glance at Emma. It was just a matter of time before she asked for a phone. He'd seen several of her classmates proudly displaying theirs, making the others green with envy. Well, he'd try to hold off on that conversation as long as possible.

"Don't," Emma said.

"Don't what?"

"Don't talk to Miss Aubrey tomorrow. She'll think I'm a snitch. No one will want to be my friend if they find out."

Gabe opened his mouth to reply, but closed it again, considering what Emma had said. She was right. No one liked a snitch. Perhaps he'd have to find some other way of voicing his concerns. Emma really liked Miss Aubrey and wished to remain in her good graces.

"All right. I won't say anything, I promise. In any case, you won't be going to school tomorrow," Gabe began, about to tell Emma that they would be going to see Phoebe and Graham when his mobile began to vibrate in his pocket. "Hold on," he said as he checked the display. "Hello, Mum."

"Gabe?" Phoebe's voice sounded strange, almost strangled. There was a shaky intake of breath on the other end of the line.

"What is it?"

"Gabe, you must come at once, but without Emma."

"Why? What's happened?" His heart began to beat faster, and his breath caught in his throat. His mother never summoned him home, so this had to be serious.

"Your father's had a heart attack. I'm at the hospital with him now."

"Mum, I'll be there as soon as I can. I just have to get a few things sorted." Gabe hung up and looked down at Emma. The expression on her face was way too serious for a child of four, and she slid her hand into his, needing reassurance that everything was all right.

"What's wrong with Grandad?" she asked, her voice small.

"Grandad is a little unwell, but there's nothing for you to worry about. Nothing at all," Gabe lied smoothly. Emma had been traumatized enough already; there was no need to frighten her. He'd tell her the truth once he knew what they were dealing with. But if he couldn't bring her to Berwick, what was he supposed to do with her? Gabe sorted through the options. He could ask Pete and Brenda to look after her, but Brenda often worked night shifts and Pete wasn't equipped to look after a little girl. Jill had her shop, which didn't close till seven, and Quinn's parents were in Spain.

Sylvia.

Gabe dialed her number and hoped she'd pick up.

"Gabe? Is Quinn all right?" Sylvia asked the moment she answered her mobile. The question surprised Gabe at first, but he quickly realized Sylvia would never expect a social call from him.

"Yes, Quinn is fine. Sylvia, I have a favor to ask. My father's been taken ill and I must leave for Berwick tonight. Would you mind terribly looking after Emma for a day or two?"

"I'd be delighted. Emma and I will have a wonderful time. She'll hardly notice you're gone."

"Brilliant. I'll drop her off in about an hour, if that's okay."

"Sure. Just remember to pack her pajamas, toothbrush, favorite film and toy, and several changes of clothes."

"Will do. Thanks again, Sylvia."

"Not a problem. Jude is actually at home until next Wednesday. Then he leaves for Dublin. He thought Emma was charming."

Gabe cringed inwardly. He would have preferred it if Sylvia could give Emma her full attention, but beggars couldn't be choosers. It was only for a few days.

"Em, guess what?" Gabe said, trying to sound like he was filled with excitement.

"What?"

"You are going to have a sleepover at Grandma Sylvia's."

"I am?" Emma sounded less than thrilled. "Why can't I come with you? I can look after Buster. He'll need someone to play with him."

"Don't worry about Buster. He's just fine," Gabe replied, avoiding the question. "Jude will be there."

"Really? I like Jude."

"Do you?"

"Yeah. He's fun."

Gabe hadn't noticed Jude being particularly fun or paying much attention to Emma, but if Emma saw Jude being at Sylvia's as a bonus, then so be it. "Come, let's go home and get your things."

"What about my tea?"

Gabe pulled out his phone again and texted Sylvia. "Grandma Sylvia is making you chips and egg, and your tea will be ready by the time we get to her house."

"I hope she has something for pudding," Emma mumbled, clearly disgruntled with the whole situation.

Chapter 17

September 1858

Arabella Plantation, Louisiana

The days flew by, as days tend to do, but even after several weeks Madeline still felt like an outcast. She'd lost her place in the world, and the people who'd been permanent fixtures in her life were all gone. Her new situation fit her about as well as someone else's shoes, something she was reminded of every single day. She saw Mammy coming and going from the kitchen house from time to time, but their relationship had changed. Madeline still missed Mammy and wished she could pour out her troubles to her and find some solace in Mammy's advice, but Madeline no longer trusted her old nurse, nor did Mammy try to seek her out. If anything, she tried to avoid Madeline, rushing away whenever she saw her coming.

Mammy had returned to her family, and she was happy in a way that Madeline could never hope to be. Mammy had a new vitality about her, despite doing harder work for longer hours. She reluctantly introduced Madeline to her sons, Zachary and Zane, who were strapping lads in their late twenties. Madeline thought they might be twins, but Mammy said they were born a year a part. Zack and Zane had five children between them and Madeline watched from a distance when she ventured to the slave quarters one evening, driven by loneliness, as Mammy joyfully played with her grandchildren. Madeline never went back. Mammy didn't need her any longer, and she had no wish to be a nuisance to her.

Sybil Besson was coolly polite, but treated Madeline much as she would a new chair or a potted plant. She looked through Madeline, but saw her well enough to avoid her whenever possible. She did, however, point out Madeline's poor posture, a wrinkle in her skirt, or the inappropriate nature of a book she saw her reading.

The criticism hurt Madeline, but it was Cissy who made her see her grandmother's comments in a slightly different light.

"Madame is not one to show affection," Cissy said as she went about dressing Madeline's hair for the day. "She likes to nitpick, but it only shows her interest in you, Miss Madeline. She grooming you to be a fine lady. She grooming you for marriage."

Madeline didn't reply, but took the comments to heart and spent several days mulling them over. Perhaps Cissy was right and her grandmother was beginning to warm to her, in her own way. If she wanted Madeline to look her best and be well versed in the ways of society, then she had plans for her, and that couldn't be a bad thing. Even if Sybil hoped to marry Madeline off at a young age to get rid of her, she was still thinking about her future and expecting her to make a good match, which was a start. Their relationship had begun on such a sour note that it could only get better, Madeline mused, grateful to Cissy for opening her eyes.

Madeline's only companion was Amelia, since George was rarely at home. It was the busiest time of the year for him, and he was out in the fields every day, too preoccupied with the harvest to pay much attention to anyone but his overseer and workers. The sheds were filling with cotton, and the cotton gin seemed to be going around the clock to prepare the cotton for shipping. Madeline had met the overseer, Mr. Diggory, several times when he came up to the house to speak to George. He was a man of late middle years, with a rounded belly that strained against his waistcoat and a balding pate that he always kept covered with a wide-brimmed straw hat when outdoors. His teeth were stained brown from chewing tobacco, a habit Madeline found disgusting.

Mr. Diggory had been very pleasant to Madeline when they first met and expressed condolences on her loss, something that George seemed to approve of. Madeline briefly wondered if Mr. Diggory might have known her father, but George later mentioned that the current overseer had been in his employ for only four years. She supposed it didn't really matter since she could hardly approach the man and question him about Besson family history. Even if he knew anything of the reason Charles Besson had been banished from the family home, he'd hardly tell her for fear of losing his position.

Amelia always joined Madeline in the dining room for breakfast and talked nineteen to a dozen while they ate, and for hours afterward while they worked on their embroidery or took walks in the grounds. Very little of what she said was of interest to Madeline, but at least it was some sort of companionship. Amelia wasn't unkind, just self-absorbed and totally vacuous. There was little substance behind her beauty, and at times, particularly at dinner, when Amelia and George were finally in the same room, Madeline noticed that Amelia's chatter irritated him.

She supposed it was normal for men and women to be interested in different things, but her own parents had enjoyed a much closer relationship, even after years of marriage. It was clear to Madeline that Amelia adored George, but she wasn't sure the feeling was mutual. He always treated his wife with the utmost curtesy and respect, but his eyes seemed to glaze over when she began to regale him with the latest fashion trends from Paris that she'd heard about from her dressmaker or bits of gossip she'd gleaned from letters from her friends, which came regularly. Amelia had been a fixture in New Orleans society before the pregnancy and couldn't wait to return.

Madeline's only salvation was the library, which was surprisingly well-stocked and always empty. She found a comfortable spot by the widow and spent hours reading, especially in the afternoons when Amelia rested and Madeline had time to herself. The library was a refuge, a place where she could hide from Sybil's critical stares and Amelia's constant prattling. There she could let her guard down and escape to a world of her choosing, finding friends among the characters in her favorite novels. Lonely and unsure of her place in the Besson household, she didn't think she'd ever feel like a real part of the family.

Even Cissy was distant. Whereas Mammy and Tess always talked and laughed with the family, Cissy never responded to Madeline's overtures of friendship. She said what she needed to say, which was usually surprisingly to the point, and then clammed up, turning her attention to the next task. Cissy made it very clear that Madeline was her mistress, not her friend. Madeline couldn't blame her. Cissy had lived all her life in an environment where the line between the masters and the servants was clearly defined, and she had no desire to cross it for fear of repercussions. Cissy never seemed frightened, but she was wary, so Madeline stopped making overtures.

Chapter 18

Madeline was surprised to find George seated at the breakfast table one morning, reading *The Times-Picayune*, which was delivered to the plantation several times a week. He read every edition cover to cover, even if it was several days out of date. George liked to keep abreast of what was happening in the world beyond his plantation, and there was much going on. He never spoke about politics in front of the ladies, but Madeline had glanced at the paper from time to time, when George carelessly left it lying around, and knew that tensions between North and South were escalating, as did the rhetoric, which was often incendiary and unpatriotic.

"Good morning, cousin," George said, putting aside the paper. "Did you sleep well?"

"Yes. Thank you. Where's Amelia this morning?"

"She's feeling unwell, I'm afraid. I told her to stay in bed today and rest. Grandmamma will look after her, which I'm sure will help Amelia make a miraculous recovery," George replied with a boyish grin. "She hates it when Grandmamma treats her like a child."

She treats everyone like a child, Madeline thought. *Even George.* "Can I go and see Amelia later?"

"You could, but you won't be able to."

"Why not?" Madeline asked, alarmed.

"Because I'm taking you on an outing. I'm in need of a companion, and you're in need of a change of scenery. You've been cooped up in this house for three weeks. Things would be different if Amelia wasn't near her time, but I'm afraid socializing is off the table right now, until after the child is born. Cissy, fetch Miss Madeline's bonnet and parasol," he said to Cissy, who had come in with a fresh pot of coffee and a plate of bacon.

"Sho thing, Mr. George."

"There's no need to rush. Miss Madeline hasn't had her breakfast yet, and I think I'll help myself to a bit more bacon." George held out his cup and Cissy refilled it before leaving the room. George popped a piece of bacon into his mouth and rolled his eyes in ecstasy, making Madeline laugh.

"Where are we going?" she asked as she helped herself to bacon and eggs.

"You'll see. I promise you'll like it."

Madeline felt a frisson of excitement. George was right; she had been cooped up. She didn't receive any social invitations of her own, and life at the plantation was quiet and uneventful. Madeline had nothing to compare it to since she didn't know what it had been like before Amelia's pregnancy, but she hoped there would be more diversions after the baby came. She rushed to finish her breakfast and accepted her bonnet from Cissy, who adjusted the angle and tied the ribbons just beneath Madeline's left ear before allowing her to leave.

"There now. That's better. You enjoy yourself, Miss Madeline," Cissy said as she handed her a parasol.

The butler, Jonas, held the door open for Madeline and gave her a respectful bow. "Have a good day, Miss," he said solemnly.

"Thank you. I am sure I will."

George was already outside, waiting for her by the carriage. The driver, whose name Madeline didn't know, was seated on the bench, and tipped his hat to her as if she were the daughter of the house. He would have ignored her at any other time, as almost everyone at the plantation did, but being with George elevated her status and suddenly made her visible.

For the first time in her life Madeline longed for something of her own. How splendid it would be to have her own home and

124

her own servants and not feel like a poor relation, treated like a charity case and constantly reminded of her good fortune to have been taken in and not consigned to the streets. It was a heady feeling to be treated with respect, especially by George, who made her feel like a lady as he held out his hand and helped her into the carriage, then took a seat opposite her, smiling broadly.

It was a glorious September morning and Madeline felt lighter than she had in weeks. Wherever George was taking her had to be better than spending the day hiding in the library, nursing her grief. The carriage rolled along the avenue and through the gates, then turned onto the River Road.

Madeline's mouth formed a little 'O' of disbelief when the carriage pulled up to a busy dock. The *Natchez V*, one of the most graceful and elegant steamboats she had ever seen, was in the process of being loaded with bales of cotton. About a dozen Negro men came and went, sweating profusely as they brought the cargo aboard while the crew waited for them to finish and urged them to hurry. Several passengers looked on from the upper deck, expressions of boredom and impatience on their faces. They'd seen this countless times, but for Madeline it was all new.

"That's our cotton," George said proudly. "It's going up the river to a mill in Ohio."

"Are we going to Ohio?" Madeline asked, shocked. She'd never been further than the Arabella Plantation, and the thought alarmed her. She didn't have anything with her except a small reticule in which she carried a handkerchief and a few coins.

"No, silly, we're only going as far as New Orleans. Amelia mentioned you have a fondness for steamboats, so I thought I'd bring you along. We can have lunch in town after I've completed my business and return by the River Road. I thought it'd make for a pleasant day."

"Oh, it will. Thank you, George," Madeline gushed. She'd never been on a steamboat despite begging Daddy to take her. He'd always promised to take her someday when she was older, but that day never came. Madeline wasn't sure how long the trip to New Orleans was, but just being aboard a boat would be an amazing treat all the same. "Can we go on the upper deck?" she asked, breathless with excitement.

"Of course. We can do anything you like."

Madeline beamed. George was so kind. He gave her his arm and they ascended the ramp. Had Madeline been younger, she'd have wanted to run around and explore the great vessel, but since she was fifteen she had to contain her curiosity and behave in a ladylike fashion.

"Let me give you a tour of the boat. It's not due to sail for another half-hour at the very least, so we can explore at our leisure."

"Yes, please."

George showed Madeline every inch of the boat. He even took her up to meet the captain, who knew him well and welcomed them inside like old friends. The captain was a short, round man of about fifty, with a neatly trimmed white beard and light-blue eyes in a face tanned to deep bronze by years spent on the water.

"Would you like to take the wheel?" the captain asked, grinning at Madeline. "No one is allowed to steer but myself and my first mate, but you can be honorary captain until we sail."

Madeline nodded. The wheel felt smooth and warm beneath her fingers. What would it be like to spend one's days on the river, just going from place to place, and never stopping anywhere long enough to put down roots? She gave the wheel an experimental nudge, wondering how far the Mississippi flowed. Did the steamboat sail as far as New York or Boston?

"How's your missus, captain?" George asked, dispelling Madeline's romantic notion of a rootless existence.

"Oh, she's peart. Thank you for asking, Mr. Besson. Blessed me with another boy this summer. I'm thankful they are both well, but a girl might have been nice. That's six boys I've got," the captain said, his chest swelling with pride. "Six fine boys."

"My congratulations to you both. I might have a boy of my own before long," George boasted, beaming at the captain.

"Well, it's about time, if you ask me," the captain replied, patting George on the back.

"It sure is."

"They've finished the loading, captain," a crewman informed him.

"We'll be off, then. You enjoy your river cruise, Miss Madeline," the captain said.

"Thank you, sir."

Madeline could hardly breathe as the great steamboat slid away from the dock, its smokestacks blowing black smoke and the paddle wheel slapping against the water. The boat glided smoothly away from the shore and toward the middle of the river where a pleasant breeze ruffled the curls surrounding her face and the lace trim of her parasol. She breathed deeply, inhaling the damp smell of the river.

"Like it?" George asked.

"It's wonderful. I wish we could stay here forever."

"Forever is a long time, Madeline," he said, grinning. "If you like it that much I'll take you along every time I go to New Orleans, although I usually go by land. It takes about the same amount of time, but I still have my carriage in town and can return any time I please."

"Do you go often?" Madeline asked.

"At least once a month."

George went on to talk about his business, but Madeline wasn't really listening. She drank in the scenery and inhaled the bracing air. She would have gladly continued all the way to Ohio, but all too soon the boat reached New Orleans and began to steer toward the wharf. There was a lot of activity as it docked and the ramp was lowered to allow the passengers off before unloading the cargo bound for New Orleans. George escorted Madeline down the ramp and away from the docks.

"This is an unsavory area," he said, referring to Rattletrap Square and the area around the docks. Madeline had passed the square before, with her father. She'd seen the poor white folk who lived like rats in tumbledown shacks and walked around barefoot all year round. Some of the children, who wandered around unsupervised at all hours of the day, were so filthy and thin that they looked half dead.

"There are some who say it's wrong for one human being to own another," George said as they passed the square, "but isn't it better to belong to a kind owner who offers his people three meals a day and a home in their dotage than to live like this?" He jutted his chin toward the smelly dwellings. "The mortality rate for poor white folk is much higher than it is for slaves."

"Not all owners are kind, though, are they?" Madeline asked, turning away from the poverty and desperation she saw.

"No, they're not. I treat my people well."

He sounded defensive, so Madeline let the subject drop.

"I have a meeting in Royal Street," George said. "It won't take long. You can wait for me in the reception area. I'm sure they can offer you a glass of lemonade."

"Can I stay here?"

"Alone?"

"I'll just walk by the river. You can come get me once you've finished. Please, George. I used to come here with my parents. I'll be safe on my own. I promise."

George considered this for a moment. "All right. But please, Madeline, don't stray from this spot. Had I known you'd want to walk around I'd have brought Cissy to accompany you."

"George, I'm fine without Cissy. I used to come here by myself all the time when Daddy was…"

"When Daddy was what?"

"Daddy started drinking after Mama died. And gambling. Mammy and Tess were too busy with household chores to come with me, so I often came on my own, just to take a walk. I like it here."

That wasn't quite the truth since Madeline had usually come with Miss Cole, but she had no desire to sit in some stuffy office, sipping lemonade and waiting for George, when she could be outside on this glorious morning, enjoying the sights and sounds of the river.

George took out a pencil and paper from his portemonnaie and scribbled an address. "This is where I'll be should you need me."

"Don't worry, George. I'll be fine."

He gave Madeline a quick peck on the cheek and walked away. She felt an odd sense of relief. This was the first time she had been truly alone since Mr. Larson took her to Arabella Plantation. It felt good not to have to explain herself to anybody or make excuses—not that her grandmother or Amelia cared much where she was. She began to walk, enjoying her solitude and freedom. Being back in New Orleans was bittersweet, and she had a brief urge to visit her old home, but quickly suppressed it. The house had been sold, and going back would do nothing but cause her pain. She wished she could see Tess. Mr. Larson had said she was still in New Orleans, but Madeline had no idea where she might be. She hoped Tess was happy and well treated.

Her thoughts turned to Mammy. Madeline had spent many a happy afternoon by the river with her mother and Mammy when she was little. Mama and Mammy had shared an easy relationship, and chatted and laughed like friends rather than mistress and servant. Madeline sighed. All the grownups she'd trusted had lied to her, or if not outwardly lied, withheld the truth. Only now had she begun to realize how little she really knew of her father, mother, and Mammy.

Mammy had never spoken of her past, never told Madeline where she'd come from or who her people were. She'd never mentioned she had children, and she must have had a husband at some point. Mammy had said that her sons' father was gone, but she must have loved him and missed him when she lived with Madeline's family in New Orleans. She hadn't even gone to his funeral or visited her sons in all the time she'd been away from the plantation. Had her parents known that Mammy had a family and refused to let her visit them, or was Mammy not welcome at Arabella Plantation? George had said there was history between her and Sybil Besson. Perhaps her father had taken Mammy with him for a reason.

And what did Madeline know of her mother's family? Or her father's? They'd never spoken of their parents or any siblings they might have had. Was it possible that Madeline had other kin she knew nothing about on her mother's side? Had her parents been protecting her or themselves when they kept her in total ignorance?

Madeline twirled her parasol as she walked. After a while the heady feeling of independence wore off and she began to feel lonesome. She saw several girls her age strolling along, chaperones in tow. The women were clearly the girls' mothers and they followed the girls at a discreet distance, chatting amiably. Madeline felt a stab of loneliness. She would never take a stroll along the river with her mother, or have her there to guide her through the pitfalls of adolescence or the wonders of marriage and motherhood. She'd have no one. Not even Mammy. There was so much she didn't know or understand, but she had no one to ask.

Lately, Madeline had begun to wonder about relations between men and women. She suspected there was more to getting married than simply going to live in your husband's house and sharing a room. She'd overheard Cissy chatting with one of the other household maids. They were giggling and talking in low voices, but Madeline had heard Cissy speak of kissing a man.

"Did you go with him?" Bette asked as she dusted the mantel.

"Not yet, but I will," Cissy replied. "And soon. When he lays his hands on me, I forget everything in the whole world, Bette."

"I felt like that with my man," Bette said, sighing. "And now, when he lays his hands on me I want to whack him over the head with a cast-iron skillet."

"Why does that happen, you think?" Cissy asked. "All that passion turns to hate."

"Because the man who whispered sweet nothings in your ear and took his time to please you becomes selfish and indifferent, and his eyes follow other women when he thinks you ain't looking. Not like they's so fine, dem other girls, but they's forbidden fruit, and you's nothing but a core left from an apple he's already eaten."

Cissy giggled. "You do have a way with words, Bette, I'll grant you that. You think I should wait?"

"I think you should be careful. If you get with child, you'll lose your place. They'll send you to the fields to pick cotton. Mrs. Besson won't have you in da house."

"Why's that?"

"Don't know. Don't like to see slaves breeding, I reckon, but that don't stop her from enjoying the benefits."

131

"At least they don't sell the babies on," Cissy said.

"For now," Bette replied. "If things get hard, they just might. Easy money to be had from selling babies, and no loss of labor."

"You got a point there," Cissy conceded. "I best mind myself. I don't want no baby."

"Then keep your legs crossed, my girl."

Madeline hadn't really understood what the women were talking about, but found their conversation intriguing. She had thought you had to be married to have a baby, but it seemed you could have a child without the benefit of wedlock. So how did the baby come about? If Cissy wasn't married and lived in the big house, sharing a room with Bette, how could she have a baby? Perhaps she could ask Amelia.

Madeline turned to see how far she'd come. Realizing she'd wandered a lot further than she'd planned, she decided to turn back. George would be finishing his business by now, and Madeline was getting hungry. She turned around and began to walk back at a brisk pace. She wasn't enjoying her stroll anymore.

Madeline was only a short distance from where she'd promised to wait for George when she saw a familiar face. Miss Cole hurried along, a paper-wrapped package beneath her arm. She might have hurried past, had Madeline not called out to her.

"Madeline, is that you?" Paula Cole seemed shocked to see her, and a bit dazed.

"I'm just here for the day," Madeline explained. "Cousin George brought me. He had some business in town."

"And he let you wander around on your own?"

"Only for a short while," Madeline replied, offended on behalf of George. She couldn't help but notice the pallor of Miss Cole's cheeks and her haggard appearance in the unforgiving bright morning light. She seemed to have aged years since the funeral. "Are you all right, Miss Cole? How are you getting on?"

Miss Cole tried to smile, but faltered. "I've been better, Madeline, but I have employment and a roof over my head. I work at Mrs. Bonnard's shop."

"You look so pale," Madeline said, hoping she didn't sound rude.

"I hardly see the light of day," Miss Cole replied. "All the seamstresses get up at dawn and sew for two hours, then have breakfast and go back to work until midday. We're allowed half an hour for our midday meal and then it's back to our stations till six. Then dinner. The doors are locked by eight. The only day we have off is Sunday, and even then we have to follow the rules. We must attend church, then see to our laundry and personal hygiene. No visitors are allowed."

"But you're out here now," Madeline said.

"The boy who delivers the packages took ill, so Mrs. Bonnard sent me to bring this to a client. I only work on collars, buttons, and hems, so she can spare me for an hour. I'm grateful for the respite, but since I get paid per the number of items I complete, I won't get paid for this time."

"But that's so unfair."

Miss Cole gave Madeline a strange look, like she was about to say something, but changed her mind. "It was good to see you, Madeline. I hope you appreciate your good fortune."

"I wish you well, Miss Cole," Madeline called as Miss Cole walked away, her back ramrod straight and her shoulders tense.

Madeline looked after her for a time. She'd spent the first fifteen years of her life being coddled, but now her eyes were beginning to open to reality. Miss Cole was stuck in the back room of the shop all day long, with no time to herself or any opportunity to meet new people. She had a job and a roof over her head, but not much more, and would likely remain trapped in this job until she either died or the shop closed its doors, in which case, she'd try to find a similar position. There were few opportunities for women, and as Miss Cole had no family to turn to, she had to do whatever it took to survive. Her life could have turned out very differently had Charles Besson lived. Had he remained at home that night, drank less at the card game, or left earlier, he might still be alive and all their lives would have gone on as before.

Madeline recalled the lesson on ancient mythology Miss Cole had taught about the Wheel of Fortune. At the time, Madeline had thought it was a silly fable, but now it seemed more real and sinister than she had been willing to admit. Fortuna had spun the wheel, and all their futures had changed in the blink of an eye.

"Enjoy your good fortune," Miss Cole had said. It was strange to think of losing her father and her home as good fortune, but Madeline had gained a comfortable future whereas Miss Cole had lost her only chance at happiness and comfort.

When I was a child, I spoke as a child, I understood as a child, I thought as a child;

but when I became a man, I put away childish things.

The Bible verse from Corinthians came to Madeline as she resumed her walk. She wasn't a man, but it was time to put away childish things. Life was no longer black and white, but countless shades of gray, and she had to adjust her thinking to this new reality. She had to stop mourning her old life and move forward.

Chapter 19

"There you are," George said and he strode toward Madeline. "I was getting worried. You weren't where I left you."

"I was just walking," Madeline replied, her mind still on Miss Cole's predicament. Their encounter had dampened her spirits, but she decided to put the governess from her mind for the time being. Her heart went out to Miss Cole, but she wasn't her responsibility.

"There's a lovely restaurant I want to take you to, but I thought we'd make a stop on the way. Do you mind?"

Though Madeline's stomach growled with hunger, she could hardly object to George's request after he'd been so kind to her. She'd been to a restaurant only once, on her fifteenth birthday, when Daddy had taken her to Antoine's. It had been a wonderful experience—or would have been had Daddy not overindulged in drink. Few other patrons had noticed, but it had upset Madeline. Perhaps the only reason he'd always had breakfast with her was because it was the only time he was truly sober.

Rather than hail a carriage for hire, George gave Madeline his arm and seemed all set to walk.

"Is it far?" she asked. The day had warmed up considerably since they'd disembarked the boat and she was beginning to perspire, even in the shade of her parasol.

"Not at all. It's just in Basin Street."

Madeline looked up at George in surprise. St. Louis Cemetery was in Basin Street. Her mother was interred there, but Daddy had never taken her to visit her mother's grave. He'd thought she was too young to go to the "City of the Dead," as he called it.

"Are we going to the cemetery?" Madeline asked as she tried to keep pace with George.

"I always visit my parents' vault when I'm in town, and I thought you might wish to visit yours," George replied. "My mother died when I was very little, but I knew my father well, and I miss him still. It eases me somehow to visit his final resting place." He gave Madeline a searching look. "We don't have to go if you feel uncomfortable. A cemetery is not a pleasant place."

"No, I want to go. I've never visited my mother's grave, and I'd like to see where Daddy is interred. I never really got the chance to say goodbye," Madeline added. Her father had been taken to a mortuary after his accident and funeral arrangements had been made quickly and without a fuss. There had been a service at St. Louis Cathedral, with only a handful of people in attendance, and then Mr. Larson had asked Tess to take Madeline home while he, his fiancée, Mammy, and Miss Cole went on to the cemetery to see her father interred.

Madeline drew closer to George as they entered the cemetery. Many paths branched off the central avenue, and they were narrow and bare of any greenery, the whole place like a sea of unyielding stone. Imposing tombs stood shoulder to shoulder, their windowless walls gray even in the autumn sunshine. Some had the family name engraved above the entrance, but others didn't, the identity of the occupants having been obliterated by time. Those who weren't interred in family tombs had been laid to rest in above-ground stone caskets that littered the surface of the cemetery as if the gravediggers had wandered off before completing their task.

"Where are your parents?" Madeline asked.

"The Besson family tomb is just over there," George said, "but your parents are not there."

I didn't think they would be, Madeline thought bitterly. Her parents had been outcasts, as she was just beginning to understand.

They walked until they had almost reached the wall surrounding the cemetery. Here, the caskets were plainer, more neglected, and even closer to each other, the dead laid to rest

136

practically one on top of another. George showed Madeline two stone coffins side by side. "Here they are. Your brother is with your mother."

Madeline stared at the inscriptions on the gravestones. The one on her father's looked fresh, but the lettering on her mother's grave was slightly weathered.

Corinne Besson

Died July 17, 1853

Aged 29

Charles Besson

Died August 4, 1858

Aged 37

Madeline traced the letters with her finger. Her brother wasn't even mentioned, having been stillborn. Had her parents given him a name or had he gone to his grave nameless?

"Would you like a moment alone?" George asked. "I'll just go pay my respects to my parents and come right back."

"Of course."

Madeline had no desire to remain by herself, but she could hardly deny George a few moments of privacy. She wanted to run from this place and never come back. How sad it was that all that remained of two vibrant, loving people were these gray stones with just their names and dates of death. If it wasn't for her, it'd be as if they'd never lived at all. Her father had done something to shame his family, and even in death he remained unforgiven and unmourned.

"Daddy, I don't know what you did to make your family despise you so, but I want you to know that I love you and miss you, and will continue to miss you for the rest of my days," Madeline said to her father's stone.

"And Mama, I feel the lack of you every single day. I've been really struggling since Daddy's death, but I'm doing my best to conduct myself in a way that would have made you proud." She kissed the tips of her fingers and pressed them first to her mother's stone and then to her father's. "Goodbye."

Madeline turned away walked in the direction George had taken. She didn't want to remain at the cemetery any longer. She saw George standing, head bent, in front of a grand mausoleum with the name *Besson* carved into the lintel above the door. He looked young and vulnerable and she felt a wave of affection for him. Her grandmother might be cold and unfeeling, but at least Cousin George cared for her, so perhaps that was enough.

George turned away from the tomb as Madeline approached. He smiled and his eyes lit up, the melancholy replaced by genuine warmth. "I'm starving. Have you ever been to Tujague's?"

"No."

"Then you are in for a treat. Their brisket with horseradish is not to be missed. I always have it when I'm in town. But today it will taste even better."

"Why's that?"

"Because I have such a lovely companion," George replied, offering Madeline his arm. "Let's go, Miss Besson."

Madeline accepted George's arm as they strolled out of the cemetery. She didn't mention it to George, but she felt her cloud of melancholy lift as they stepped back out into the street. She was grateful to George for taking her to visit her parents' resting place, but she had no desire to return. She'd carry them in her heart always, but the gray stone coffins were not how she wanted to remember her mother and father, or the little brother who would sleep with them for eternity.

138

Chapter 20

April 2014

New Orleans, Louisiana

Quinn left her hotel on St. Louis Street and walked toward the cemetery. It was another warm, sunny day, and her spirits were high despite the grim errand she was about to undertake. As an archeologist, she wasn't put off by cemeteries. At least the people buried there had a name, unlike so many whose identities had been forgotten by history—like Petra and Edwin, whose remains Quinn had unearthed only a few months ago, or Elise and James who'd been buried alive, their very existence obliterated by a vengeful husband and father. She'd given their identities back to them, but there were countless others who had simply vanished into the sands of time, forgotten before the earth could even claim them.

Quinn always felt pity for the nameless skeletons she came across in her profession. Those people hadn't been so different from modern-day people. They had loved, hated, worried about the future, and strove for whatever it was that was important to them. How fleeting all those feelings and needs were in the face of time. Human beings ended up being dead a lot longer than they enjoyed being alive, and she used the term 'enjoyed' loosely. Life, especially in centuries past, was all about survival, not enjoyment. Quinn was grateful to have been born in the twentieth century, and more grateful still that she got to pursue what she loved. Had she been born in a previous era, her life would have been very different, being a woman, and a bastard to boot. Her fate would have been sealed the day of her birth, her choices limited to only a few unpleasant options.

During the short walk to the cemetery, Quinn enjoyed the bohemian atmosphere of the French Quarter. A part of her wished she'd come in early March for Mardi Gras, which had been 'legendary,' according to Brett. He'd used a few other terms that

139

Quinn wouldn't have associated with a parade or a bar crawl, but she had some catching up to do on American slang and traditions. She smiled to herself when she thought of Brett. He hadn't seemed upset at all to find out he had a sister; in fact, he'd seemed pleased, and instantly turned the situation to his advantage.

"Good, now Dad can pin all his hopes and dreams on you and stop ruining my life," Brett said with a wink as Seth glowered at him. "How do you feel about inheriting a trucking business? It's so much more glamorous than it sounds," he added, oozing sarcasm. "Did I tell you how many different types of trucks there are, and which ones are used for which types of deliveries? Oh, and this is really exciting." He clapped theatrically, royally annoying his father. "We are about to invest in refrigerated trucks. Imagine the possibilities! Dad is already wooing several distributors of seafood and produce. When he told me, I nearly wet myself."

"You ungrateful little…" Seth hissed. "I should disinherit you and see how you like it."

"Dad, I'm just joking." Brett smiled and patted his father on the back. "I'm grateful for everything you do for me, and always will be, as long as you let me off the hook and allow me to pursue my own dreams. Quinn got to pursue hers. Did you always want to be an archeologist?" he asked, deftly changing the subject before his father could get any angrier.

Seth glared at Brett with annoyance, but didn't say anything, allowing him to prattle on. They'd clearly had this conversation before, and would again. Quinn chose not to comment, but she could sympathize with Brett's point of view. Few children chose to follow in their parents' footsteps these days, especially when those footsteps led to the less-than-posh offices of a trucking concern. Seth's business was clearly profitable, but the day-to-day operations held little interest for Brett, who had plans of his own.

"And your fiancé is an archeologist too. What fun you must have," Brett mused, putting on a comical face and a phony

British accent. "'How was your day, darling? Dig up anything good today?' 'Not really, sweetie, just some plague-ridden peasants of no historical account.'" Brett laughed at his own joke and blessed Quinn with a winsome smile. "Can I visit you at a dig one day? A cool dig, like if you find the missing Roman Ninth Legion. Man, what I wouldn't give to see that. Or maybe a royal burial chamber in the Valley of the Kings. Now that would be something."

"Are you interested in history, Brett?" Quinn asked, wondering if he was just taking the mickey. She couldn't quite tell with him.

Brett's expression grew serious and he nodded enthusiastically. "I am, but only in the really cool stuff. I'm not interested in pottery shards or ancient stone circles. I'll leave those to you. I like reading about famous battles."

"Any particular historical period?" she asked, hoping to find some common ground with her brother.

"Anything, really. Have you unearthed any ancient battlefields?" Brett asked, and previously stilted conversation began to flow, with Seth looking on happily as his children bonded.

**

As Quinn approached the cemetery, she reflected that she was actually glad of the time alone. Seth had something planned for her every evening, and although she was touched by his obvious desire to get to know her, she was a little tired and needed time to process what she had been seeing when she held the ivory fan. Daily texts and emails arrived from Rhys, demanding to know what she'd learned and whether Madeline's story would make for a dramatic episode of *Echoes from the Past*. It was too soon to tell, so Rhys was hedging his bets and searching frantically for another viable story should Madeline's prove not exciting enough. Quinn supposed that was what made Rhys so good at what he did, but it also bothered her that he didn't see the subjects of the program as actual people. To him they were nothing more than a path to ratings, and their stories didn't really touch him the way they touched her. But Rhys trusted her instinct and was more than willing to come to New Orleans in person should Quinn find it necessary.

She had mixed feelings about Rhys at the best of times, but having him in New Orleans would prove a welcome distraction from getting to know her father. Had Quinn ever been asked to describe her perfect dad, Seth Besson would be last in line. She found him to be generous with his time and money, and emotionally open to getting to know the daughter he'd never known he had, but he was also garrulous, a little overbearing, and as different from Quinn as it was possible to be. Every time she returned to her hotel after spending several hours with Seth, she tried to see if she could pinpoint anything they had in common, but even after a week of dinners, strolls around the city, visits to jazz clubs, and companionable lunches on Seth's patio, she still couldn't name a single thing that tied them to each other in that biological way of parents and children.

It wasn't easy with Brett either. Quinn had made an instant connection with Logan, but the younger boys were more difficult to reach. She wasn't giving up on Jude just yet, but her time with Brett was limited, so she had tried to get to know him in a way he wouldn't find intrusive. Too many questions came off like an interrogation, so Quinn allowed Brett to take the lead. He was more sarcastic and irreverent with Seth around, but more at ease on his own, and more willing to share. She had spent a pleasant morning with him the day before, when she finally visited the Arabella Plantation. She could have visited it sooner on her own, but decided to wait a few days and learn something more of life on the plantation before seeing it in person.

"Dad's busy at the office today, so he asked me to take you on a plantation tour," Brett said as he pulled up to the hotel in his sports car. He wore a baseball cap, and a faded T-shirt with some band's logo on it hung loosely on his thin frame. Mirrored aviator shades hid his eyes, so Quinn couldn't tell if he was pleased or annoyed at having to spend the morning with her. "He thought you'd like to see what your great-grandparents lived like. I'll save Arabella for last. It's not as grand as some of the others on the River Road, but still pretty impressive."

Quinn had seen the plantation in her visions and couldn't wait to see the real thing. Normally, she never got to see a place in person as it had actually looked in the past. It was like watching a film that took place at some point in history and then seeing the place for herself and finding it transformed into a bustling square or a busy street lined with shops and trendy restaurants. Many times, the original structure had been ground into dust, or all that remained of a building or a temple was a pile of rocks or broken columns. If the Arabella Plantation was frozen in time, she might actually get a glimpse of Madeline's world and see the room she'd slept in or the veranda where she'd often sat with Amelia, a glass of lemonade in hand. Quinn was also curious to examine the slave quarters. Having seen them through Madeline's eyes, she wanted to see them for herself and visit the place where Mammy had lived with her family.

"Do you mind if we skip the others and go directly to the Arabella Plantation? I'm feeling a little impatient," Quinn confessed.

"Sure, whatever you want," Brett replied, clearly relived to be spared a boring morning.

He turned off the air conditioning, opened the windows, and put down the top of the car. Quinn rested her arm on the car door as she took in the grandeur of the river that flowed lazily past and the lush landscape, so unique to Louisiana. A lovely breeze caressed her face and moved through her unbound hair. She closed her eyes and tried to imagine traveling down the River Road in a horse-drawn carriage. It had probably taken some time to get to the plantation houses, but it must have been a lovely drive. Today, the road wasn't as picturesque as it had been at the height of the antebellum period. They drove past industrial sites, strip malls, and several run-down farms where rusted machinery sat idle among a jumble of items Quinn couldn't quite identify. There were several

143

seedy bars with peeling signs, some of them boasting go-go dancers, and a few discount stores where one could buy anything from household goods to small appliances. The drive became a little more pleasant once they neared the historical stretch where dozens of plantations reigned in all their restored glory.

The Arabella Plantation manor house looked just as Quinn had envisioned it--a wedding cake whimsy of a house: white, elegant, and frilly in its decoration. The black wrought-iron balcony and shutters were just the same as she's seen in her visions, the paint fresh and glossy.

Brett parked the car and led Quinn into the foyer, where a small ticket counter stood unobtrusively in the corner. He purchased two tickets and helped himself to a map of the grounds.

"Is Ms. Aptekar Hill here?" Quinn asked the young woman manning the desk.

"Yes, she's doing a tour at the moment. She should be finished in a few minutes, if you'd like to wait."

"Yes, we would," Quinn replied. Seth had said that Ms. Aptekar Hill was the most knowledgeable guide, so Quinn wanted to take a tour with her instead of the bored-looking young man who'd been about to approach them.

A few minutes later, a small group of tourists left by the front door after thanking their guide for an informative tour. The woman turned to Quinn and Brett with a bright smile.

"Well, good morning. Are you ready for the tour? I'm Dina Aptekar Hill. Please call me Dina."

Quinn liked her on sight. She was one of those people who instantly made you feel at ease. She looked younger than Quinn had expected, with abundant blond hair pulled back into a ponytail and smiling blue eyes.

"The Arabella Plantation once belonged to the Besson family," Dina began.

144

"Yes, we know. We are the lucky descendants," Brett quipped.

"Are you really? What a treat. I've met Seth, of course, and his father and grandfather, but it's a pleasure to meet the younger generation. You must know something about the place then. Would you like me to do the tour, or would you like to just walk around and ask questions?"

"I'd prefer the tour," Quinn said. "This is all new to me."

Dina nodded. "You've come a long way to see it, haven't you?"

"Yes, I live in London," Quinn replied. "I've only recently discovered a connection to the Bessons. I never expected to find my roots in Louisiana."

"Very few people are familiar with their family history, beyond that of the most recent generations," Dina said. "I always thought my family emigrated from France, which they had, but it turned out that my maiden name is of Polish origin. Aptekar means pharmacist, or apothecary. One of my ancestors wound up in France at some point in the seventeenth century. Many immigrants changed their names in order to fit in, but that particular Aptekar decided not to, for which I'm very grateful. I wouldn't have been able to find him otherwise."

"Was it very difficult to track him down?" Quinn asked, intrigued. She'd found very little useful information about the Bessons, and wondered if Dina had encountered the same roadblocks when researching her own family.

"It's not difficult when you know where to look. I actually do this for a living," Dina added. "I fell in love with genealogy when I was in my twenties. At first, I did it as a hobby, helping friends uncover their buried past, but then I started my own business. I only do the tour-guiding part time."

"Do you have many clients?" Quinn asked.

"I do have some private clients, but my biggest clients are the estate attorneys who need to track down potential heirs. It's cheaper for them to hire a freelance genealogist than to spend their own precious time digging through archives and surfing databases."

"Do you get results every time?"

"Not every time, but most of the time. I make a lot of people very happy. Imagine suddenly getting a windfall you never expected."

"Must be nice," Brett chimed in.

"It is, especially when the estate in question is sizeable."

"Perhaps you can do some research on the Bessons," Quinn suggested. "I'd pay you, of course."

"Oh, no need, doll. I've already found anything there is to find out. How could I not, working here?" she asked with a grin. "I will gladly tell you all I know. The Bessons were a fascinating family, by all accounts."

"In what way?" Quinn asked, genuinely curious.

"Probably in the way that they were very unlucky. I'll start at the beginning, if you don't mind."

"Please."

"Maurice Besson built the original plantation house on this site at the end of the eighteenth century. He made a fortune trapping in Canada and brought his money to Louisiana, where prime land was going cheap. Maurice married Arabella Dupre, the only child of Andre Dupre, who owned the adjoining tract of land. It was probably a calculated move since Maurice consolidated his holdings as soon as the old man died. Maurice named the plantation after his wife."

"Did he love her?" Brett asked. The question surprised Quinn, but she remained quiet, allowing Dina to answer.

146

"I can only speculate, but I would say the answer to your question is yes. He did name the plantation after her, and he never remarried after she died in childbirth in her late twenties. Maurice was still a young man and could have had his pick of local beauties. Instead, he concentrated on growing his profit. He bought as many as one hundred slaves during his lifetime, and left a very profitable plantation to his only surviving son, Jean. We do know from letters that were found at the house that Maurice handpicked a bride for his son. Her name was Sybil Talbot, and like Arabella, she was the only child of a wealthy family. Sybil, and in turn her husband, inherited everything and invested it in the plantation. Another hundred slaves were purchased and put to work in the cotton and sugar cane fields."

"That doesn't sound very unlucky to me," Brett observed as he trailed after Dina from one opulent room to the next.

"What made the Bessons unlucky was the brevity of their lifespans. They had it all, but they never lived long enough to enjoy it. Maurice died in his forties, as did his son Jean, who caught swamp fever. Jean Besson's sons, Albert and Charles, both died at an early age, leaving only one child behind between them, Albert's son George. George was the one in residence at the plantation at the outbreak of the Civil War."

"Are you quite certain that Charles Besson didn't have any children?" Quinn asked.

"Charles never married, and was killed in New Orleans at the age of thirty-seven. He was run over by a carriage."

"Maybe it was suicide, à la *Anna Karenina*," Brett joked.

"Charles had a drinking problem, so it was ruled an accident. There are notes from the inquest in the library, if you'd like to see them," Dina replied.

"Might he have been married?" Quinn asked, wondering why Charles's marriage certificate had never surfaced among his papers.

147

"There's no record of a marriage anywhere in the state of Louisiana. Charles left the plantation when he was twenty-one and took a house in New Orleans. Nothing more is known about his private life since no letters or diaries were left behind after his death. The house and all the assets were sold to pay off his gambling debts. He lived modestly, and had one slave girl named Tess, who looked after him."

"And George. What happened to him?" Quinn asked. She knew she'd find out eventually from her visions, but she wanted to hear the official version of events.

"George joined the army as an officer at the beginning of the Civil War. As a plantation owner, he wasn't obligated to, since it was important to keep the plantations producing, but George was a true patriot and wanted to prove his mettle. It was the poor folk who were expected to do the fighting, since the loss of them did little to hurt the economy and they were largely seen by the wealthy as cannon fodder. They were fed a lot of hogwash about the North threatening their way of life and planning to kill them all in their beds. Few foot soldiers truly understood the reasons for the conflict, and even fewer realized that freeing the slaves would benefit them in the long run. They would have more jobs available to them and would be able to demand higher wages, since they would no longer be competing with slave labor," Dina explained.

"Did George survive?" Quinn asked, fearing the answer.

"I'm afraid not. He died of wounds sustained during the Battle of Gettysburg."

"And what became of the plantation?" Quinn's insides twisted with grief when she thought of young, beautiful George lying bloody and mangled on the battlefield, but she couldn't allow Dina or Brett to see her distress. As far as they were concerned, Quinn was hearing about George for the first time, so his untimely death would mean nothing more to her than an unfortunate slice of family history.

By this time, they had reached Madeline's bedroom and Quinn sucked in her breath in wonder as she gingerly touched the bed where Madeline had slept, and ran her fingers over the lovely rosewood dressing table. She'd seen Madeline sitting at this table, her hair spilling over her shoulders and her eyes aglow with excitement. Quinn stepped aside, not wishing to draw attention to her emotional reaction to a piece of furniture.

"What happened to the slaves owned by the Bessons?" she asked. "Were they freed after the war?"

"The Civil War and the Reconstruction that followed hit the Bessons hard. It hit most plantation owners hard, but some managed to rebuild and reinvent themselves. However, many of the plantations, like the Arabella, didn't survive. Once the system collapsed, the plantation owners no longer had the slaves to work the cotton and sugar cane fields, nor did they have the necessary funds to hire help. Some older slaves remained, fearful of a world they knew nothing about, but most of the younger people ran off as soon as they thought it safe. They had to find a way to support themselves and their families, which was unfamiliar territory for them. Some were actually worse off than they had been. The years after the war were chaotic and difficult for everyone, both black and white."

"And Mrs. Besson?"

"Amelia Besson stayed for as long as she could, but she couldn't manage and eventually left. She must have buried some silver and other valuables at the beginning of the war because as far as we know, she didn't arrive in New Orleans destitute. She lived comfortably until she remarried at the age of thirty-three."

"Did she have any more children?"

"No, just the one son she had with George. The boy became a doctor. A surgeon, actually. He was well known and respected in his day. He married in his late thirties and had one son. Neither father nor son lived to see fifty."

149

"What became of the plantation?" Quinn asked as they circled back to the foyer.

"Amelia held on to the plantation, knowing that if she sold it, it would have to be for a song. The plantation continued to molder, the vegetation all but swallowing the house after a century of neglect. It was Seth Besson's father who finally allowed the plantation to go out of the family. He dreamed of the house and grounds being restored to their former glory and put up a portion of the restoration costs himself. The house took years to restore and opened to the public in 1983, just over a hundred years after it was abandoned."

Dina brought Quinn and Brett back to where they'd begun the tour. Her next group, about twenty school children, milled around the foyer with expressions of indescribable boredom on their privileged young faces.

"You can tour the slave quarters on your own, if you like. There's also the cotton gin, the storehouses, and various other outbuildings. The kitchen house, which was quite modern by nineteenth-century standards, has been converted to a restaurant. It specializes in gourmet Creole cuisine and is open for lunch. I highly recommend the Cajun crawfish and shrimp etouffe. It's my favorite. There's also excellent jambalaya and chicken gumbo."

"Thank you, Dina. The tour has been very informative," Quinn said.

"Oh, it was my absolute pleasure. So few people are truly interested. They just rush through the rooms and head straight to the restaurant, which is what we are known for. I'm glad you enjoyed it, and hopefully, you have a clearer picture of your family history."

Quinn would have liked more time to linger in the main house, but they had to follow Dina's pace and had spent no more than a few minutes in each room. The house looked much as it had in Quinn's visions, but she felt nothing of Madeline in its echoing silence. It was beautifully restored and decorated almost exactly as it had been during its heyday, but it felt devoid of personality. The rooms had been vacant for far too long, lacking the human habitation that gave a house its character.

Quinn and Brett took their leave and walked toward the slave quarters.

"I'll have to look up the Battle of Gettysburg," Quinn said apologetically. "American history is not my strong suit, I'm afraid."

"I can tell you about it, if you'd like," Brett replied. He looked a little embarrassed by his enthusiasm, but Quinn could see he was eager to talk about it.

"Did you learn about it at school?"

"Yes, of course, but I also researched it on my own. I told you, I like reading about famous battles. Anyway, it was the bloodiest battle of the Civil War, with as many as fifty-one thousand casualties from both sides. It was the turning point, really. Huge victory for the North and crushing defeat for the Confederates. I didn't know that George Besson died there."

"Did your father never mention it?"

Brett shrugged. "Believe it or not, we've never really spoken about family history. It took your unexpected appearance to rake all this stuff up. I don't mind, though," he added. "It's actually pretty cool. I felt a connection when we walked through the house. That lady was knowledgeable, but honestly, I would have preferred to just wander around on our own for a while. You know, feel the place."

"You should have said so. We could have taken the tour later, after we'd had a chance to explore."

"We can still go back. The tickets are good for the whole day. Personally, I'd like to explore the restaurant after we check out the slave quarters. That etouffe sounds good. What do you say?" Brett asked.

151

"I say, I like the way you think," Quinn replied. "I've never tried etouffe, but it sounds lovely."

As they continued toward the slave quarters, Brett talked of the war and the Reconstruction in great detail. Quinn was interested, since she knew very little of that chapter of American history and was embarrassed by her ignorance, especially about the Reconstruction.

"It was the period after the war when the Union Army came to the South to regulate the transition," Brett explained. "It was difficult for everyone. The plantation owners were struggling to hold on to their land and way of life, but it was difficult for the freed slaves as well. People often assume that freeing the slaves was much like liberating prisoners from German concentration camps, but it wasn't really like that at all. Most of the slaves knew nothing but life in captivity. They were worked hard, and were often treated badly, but they didn't have to worry about earning a living. They were fed, clothed, and had a roof over their heads regardless of whether it was a good or a bad year, and they were not turned out once they got old. All that changed overnight."

Quinn found him knowledgeable and animated, something she hadn't expected from a teenage boy who made it a point to look bored and poke fun at those around him. She also noticed the hint of resentment when Brett mentioned the North, and the Northern do-gooders referred to as carpet-baggers who came to the South after the war as teachers, doctors, administrators, and clergy.

"They were nothing more than vultures picking over the bones of the Confederacy," Brett stated with great aplomb.

"You seem to know a lot about the period," Quinn said.

"The Civil War period is not a favorite of mine, but I've read a lot about it and seen tons of movies. It's always interesting to see what your ancestors went through."

"So, what's your favorite time period then?" Quinn asked, genuinely curious. "I know you mentioned an interest in the Roman Empire, and the lost legion."

"Yeah, I'll read and see anything about that period. Ever seen *Gladiator*? Awesome movie. I love stuff about the Vikings and Saxons. I've read all of Bernard Cornwell's books. Did you ever read those?"

"I have," Quinn replied, thrilled to have found something else they had in common. "I think they might be making the books into a television series."

"No shit? I hope we get that here. I love Uhtred." Brett made a sword-swinging motion and lunged forward. "My favorite character from the novels."

"I'm a fan of Uhtred myself," Quinn replied. "I read the *Warrior Chronicles* when I was a teenager."

"Neat. Have you ever excavated any Saxon burial mounds? I'd love to see the grave goods they buried with their dead."

"Sure. I have some photos of the artefacts we found, if you'd like to see them."

"Sweet. Show me over lunch."

The tour of the slave quarters didn't take long. There were several empty cabins clustered around an open space. Brett proclaimed that it wasn't much to look at and turned toward the Kitchen House Restaurant they'd passed on the way. Quinn peeked into every cabin, but found little of value—no furniture, tools, or anything of historical interest. Just bare boards. All traces of the people who'd inhabited the cabins had been obliterated. Quinn wondered what had happened to Mammy's descendants, but of course, there was no one to ask and she didn't know their surname, if they'd even had one at the time.

"Do you watch *Game of Thrones*?" Brett asked as he tucked into his etouffe.

"No."

"Too bad. Awesome show. Some of the storylines are off the hook."

"Whatever that means." Quinn laughed as she took a sip of water. The food really was delicious, if a bit spicy.

"It means like—you know—badass."

"Right."

"You are kind of badass," Brett said shyly.

"Me?"

"Well, yeah. You're an archeologist, and you get to go to all these exciting places. And you have your own show. God, I've never seen Dad so proud. He's telling everyone about you, as if he's had a hand in shaping the person you are. He might have lived his whole life and not known of your existence. And here you are."

"It must be very strange for you to have me here," Quinn said, sensing Brett's bitterness. He was Seth's only son. Surely Seth was proud of him.

"You could say that," Brett replied. "Anyway, it was fun to visit the plantation. I'm glad we came. Seeing all that splendor kind of made me wish the Confederacy had prevailed."

"Do you sympathize with the Confederate cause?" Quinn asked carefully. She knew there were many people in the South who still proudly displayed Confederate flags and memorabilia.

"I belong to a reenactment group," Brett replied, "but that's just for fun. It's kind of cool to put on uniforms, wheel out the cannons, and run around with antique guns. And the girls dig it," he added with a happy grin. "Got laid more than once while in my full Confederate get-up. The ladies look bitchin' in their hoop skirts and bonnets. Takes a lot of fumbling to get beneath all that jazz, but so worth it." Brett looked like he was about to reminisce some more, but then recalled the question. "I definitely don't support slavery or oppression of any kind. I enjoy learning about

that time in our history, but only from an academic point of view."
The statement sounded stiff and rehearsed, but he seemed to mean
it.

Quinn smiled. She might have nothing in common with
Seth, but Brett was a kindred spirit, even if he used history to shag.
He wouldn't be the first or the last person to enjoy a bit of role-
playing, and there was always plenty of tent-hopping at any dig.
After all, that was how she'd met Luke.

Chapter 21

Quinn stopped in front of the entrance to St. Louis Cemetery No. 1, the oldest cemetery in New Orleans, and it looked the part. The mausoleums and tombs looked weathered and neglected, the stone cracking and crumbling from centuries of inclement weather and the settling of the ground. Not a single headstone stood perfectly upright, and many of the more elaborate tombs looked like they might fold like a house of cards if a strong enough wind blew through the cemetery. But the cemetery had withstood Hurricane Katrina, so perhaps it wasn't as derelict as it first appeared, Quinn mused as she strolled down the central avenue. It certainly looked different than it had in Madeline's time, when most of the gravestones were still fairly recent. Several tourists milled around, but they remained mostly in the front part of the cemetery, taking photographs and reading the names on the tombs.

Quinn walked past the Besson vault, which had taken a beating over the years, and made her way toward the back wall, where Madeline's parents were interred. This part of the cemetery was completely deserted, the silence almost eerie. It took time to find the right tombs, since most of the lettering had been obliterated by time and weather, but, at last, Quinn found what she was looking for.

Charles Besson

Died August 4, 1858

Aged 37

Quinn looked from side to side, but couldn't see the headstone for Corinne Besson. She was sure Corinne's headstone had been to the left of Charles's, but there was nothing, save a crumbling stone coffin that had sunk into the earth and was barely visible. Quinn moved closer to see if the headstone might have

156

fallen backward, but it wasn't there at all. No headstone, no bits of broken masonry, and no indentation where the headstone might have once stood. Odd. Corinne had definitely been interred there. Quinn looked around to see if the stone might have been moved for some reason, but all the other tombs still had intact gravestones. Someone had removed Corinne's headstone. But why?

Quinn took a photo of the tombs with her mobile and hurried toward the exit. She'd visited countless cemeteries in her life, but this one set her teeth on edge. There was an atmosphere here, a presence almost, of something sinister and frightening that made her quicken her step. This was not a place of eternal rest, but a gateway to an eternity of torment and suffering. Quinn knew she was being fanciful and ridiculous, but she felt the hair at the nape of her neck stand on end, as if someone were walking just behind her, their footsteps crunching on the path as they drew closer.

She whipped around, her heart pounding with irrational fear, and drew up short, her eyes widening in surprise. She wasn't sure what she'd been expecting, but it certainly wasn't Luke, who appeared to have been following her down the narrow path leading back to the main avenue.

"Hello, Quinn."

"Care to explain?" Quinn asked. "You scared me half to death." With her heartrate slowly returning to normal, she was more annoyed now than frightened.

"I'm sorry. I didn't mean to startle you. I was walking toward your hotel when I saw you turning into the cemetery, so I followed. You seemed so intent on whatever you were doing that I thought it best to wait to speak to you after you had finished."

Quinn gazed at Luke in confusion. "Why were you walking to my hotel, and how do you even know which hotel I'm staying at? And what are you doing in New Orleans? Are you not living in Boston these days?" She resumed walking toward the exit with Luke close on her heels. She really had no desire to talk to him. She just wanted to get back to her room and call Gabe.

"Can I take you to lunch?" Luke asked instead of answering her questions.

"Actually, I already have plans," Quinn replied. She was due to meet Seth in half an hour in the lobby of her hotel. They had plans to visit the French Market and have lunch at Café de Monde. Seth had a light day at the office and wanted to spend a few hours with her.

"Quinn, please, wait," Luke pleaded. "I want to talk to you."

"Then you can talk while we walk."

"All right. Look, Monica told me you were in New Orleans, and I thought it was too good an opportunity to miss."

Quinn exhaled loudly in irritation. Damn Monica Fielding. Why was that woman always interfering in her business? And how did she know where Quinn was staying? Gabe would never have told her.

"She's friends with Gabe's PA," Luke said as if Quinn had asked the question out loud.

"Why are you here, Luke?" she asked, wary of his motives.

"Ashley and I split up."

"My condolences," Quinn replied sarcastically. Luke had hurt her, and she wasn't about to let him off the hook. She'd loved him for eight years, had trusted him, and had been loyal to him, and he'd betrayed her without a second thought.

"Quinn, walking out on you was the biggest mistake of my life. I grew too comfortable and too settled. I began to take you for granted. I suppose I stopped noticing you."

"But you noticed Ashley?" Quinn knew she sounded bitter, but it hurt to think she'd become invisible.

"I was dazzled by her. She seemed so confident, so uninhibited, so spontaneous. She didn't have any of that British reserve. She spoke her mind and did as she pleased, which was refreshing. But once I really got to know her, I realized her lack of inhibition was nothing more than an expression of selfishness. She said and did what she felt like because she didn't give a damn about the consequences or anyone else's feelings."

"She's thrown you over, hasn't she?" Quinn asked, giving Luke a smug grin. Now his unexpected appearance made sense. Free-spirited, uninhibited Ashley had grown tired of him. Perhaps it was his British reserve that had begun to grate on her American nerves.

"Quinn, I know I don't deserve a second chance, but I still love you. I didn't understand how much until I realized I'd lost you for good."

Quinn stopped walking and turned to face him. He was the same old Luke. His hair was tousled by the breeze and his blue eyes crinkled at the corners as he gazed at her with his best puppy-dog expression and a winning smile, but there was a wariness about him now, and telltale signs of middle age. Even golden boys grew old, their charm tarnished by years of playing the field and living a life of excess. Luke had never wanted the responsibility of a family. He'd kept putting things off, and making promises that he clearly had no intention of keeping, and Quinn realized she was glad, and grateful. Luke had spared her years of heartache by walking out, and with him gone, she had been able to finally see something that had been there all along, something solid and true, and more romantic than anything she'd ever experienced with Luke.

"Are you serious?" she asked. "Do you really think that coming here and telling me you're disappointed and full of regret will win me back? I've moved on, Luke, and I am happy. Gabe and I are getting married next month, but I'm sure you already know that."

"Yes, I heard," Luke replied, pulling a face. "Look, you didn't deserve to be treated unkindly, and I'm very sorry for breaking things off the way I did, but I didn't think you'd fall into Gabe's arms as soon as I was gone. Are you really that desperate?"

Quinn gaped at him. He'd never been spiteful, but this new side of him she was seeing was a revelation. She'd always tap-danced around Luke's feelings because he avoided confrontations like the plague, but now she meant to tell him the truth without mincing words. Standing in the middle of a cemetery reminded Quinn just how brief life was, and how important it was to be true to yourself and your dreams. All too soon, everything she stood for would be reduced to dust, and she'd be damned if she wasted another minute being unhappy or disappointed.

"No, Luke. I was desperate to stay with you for as long as I did. I was foolish, and blind, and way too trusting. Don't think for one moment that I don't know about your extracurricular activities. Ashley wasn't the first, and she won't be the last. But do you know what I realized once you were gone?" she asked, pausing to let him consider her question. "I realized that all the years I'd spend with you were a prelude to something better. You should have never been anything more than a summer fling, because a shag is about the only thing you've got to offer."

"Oh, is that a fact?" Luke sputtered, clearly cut to the quick by the insult.

"And do you know why our relationship was doomed?" Quinn continued. "Because whenever I needed a shoulder to cry on, or wanted sound advice, I never turned to you because I knew you were useless. It was always Gabe. You were always up for sex, but you were emotionally unavailable, and will probably be for the rest of your days."

"And now you will marry Saint Gabe and raise his spawn because he's so good at giving advice?" Luke snarled.

The gloves were off, and Quinn was glad. It was time they said what they meant and put their relationship to rest once and for all.

"And now I will marry Gabe and raise *our* daughter because I love him and want to spend the rest of my life with him. Now, please leave. There's nothing more to be said."

"There's plenty more to be said," Luke retorted, his anger heightening his color.

"Quinn, are you all right?" Seth's expression was as dark as a gathering thunderstorm as he strode down the avenue toward them. Quinn wasn't sure how much he'd heard, probably just the last bit, but he looked furious.

"Stay out of it, mate," Luke growled. "It's none of your business."

"It's very much my business," Seth replied, his voice dangerously low. "If you don't turn around and walk away from my daughter right now, I will knock you into the middle of next week, buddy. Am I making myself clear?"

"Your daughter?" Luke echoed, staring at Seth with new interest.

"Yes, my daughter. Now, get lost."

"This conversation is not over," Luke warned Quinn.

"This conversation is very much over," she replied and slid her arm through Seth's. "Ready to go?"

"I sure am." Seth gave her a brilliant smile and Quinn returned it. It was nice to have a tough dad. "They said at Reception that you asked for directions to the cemetery," he said as they walked toward the market. "Was there anything in particular you wished to see?"

161

"I just wanted to see the Besson family vault and the tomb of Charles Besson," Quinn replied. Seth didn't know anything about Corinne, and she wasn't about to bring her up.

"I'm a grown man, but that place gives me the creeps," he said with a chuckle. "We used to dare each other to go there on Halloween when we were kids. That place at night is not for the faint of heart."

"No, I would imagine not. It isn't very pleasant during the day either."

"Was that your old flame?" Seth asked conversationally as they entered the bustling market.

"Yes, that was Luke."

"Came back crawling with his tail between his legs, huh?" Seth asked. "Any regrets?"

"None. Seeing him was actually very therapeutic."

"Good, I'm glad. Now, let's get something to eat. I'm starving."

"Me too," Quinn replied, and realized she was.

Chapter 22

September 1858

Arabella Plantation, Louisiana

Rather than return from New Orleans by steamboat, George and Madeline traveled home by carriage, which had been sent from the plantation to meet them at the appointed time. It wasn't as magical as the steamboat journey, but still very pleasant. The open carriage rolled along the River Road, a gentle breeze caressing their faces as slanted rays of afternoon sun dappled the road and twinkled through the intertwined branches of the trees. Madeline felt languid and content, having tasted champagne for the first time with lunch. She barely recalled what she ate, so excited had she been to dine in a restaurant and sit across from George, who was so charming that all the ladies stole glances at him over the rims of their glasses. Not only had Madeline felt grown up, but surprisingly she'd forgotten her misery for hours on end and had experienced a glimmer of hope for the future.

"George, thank you for a wonderful day," Madeline said as the carriage left the city behind and entered a tranquil stretch of road. George sat across from her, with his back to the driver, who whistled under his breath as if they weren't even there.

"Are you happy?" George asked, smiling at her.

"Yes. And tired."

George came to sit next to Madeline, putting a protective arm about her shoulders. She rested her head on his shoulder, the way she used to when Daddy sat next to her on the settee at home. It felt companionable and natural.

"Enjoy the drive," George said softly. "We'll be home before dark. I'm glad you enjoyed yourself, Maddy. I was beginning to despair of ever seeing you smile."

Madeline looked up at and smiled just for him. She was still floating on a cloud of happiness when they arrived at the plantation. The sky was a deep shade of lavender, and the sickle of the new moon seemed to be suspended directly above the house, the delicate crescent surrounded by stars. The air was thick with the scent of flowers and freshly cut grass, and a chorus of insects filled the night with song. Madeline couldn't ask for a more perfect evening. Still full from lunch, she asked to be excused from supper and went up to her room, where she threw open the widows and snuggled into the widow seat, her arms wrapped around her legs.

For the first time since her father's death, Madeline saw a way forward for her. She would get used to life on the plantation, and in time, George would see to it that she was introduced to society and made a good match. Some girls married as young as fifteen, but there was no rush. Amelia had married George when she was eighteen and he twenty-one. That was the perfect age, Madeline decided as she finally left her perch by the window and prepared for bed. Cissy had helped her out of her hoops and corset when she first came in, so all she had to do was put on her nightdress and climb into bed. She stretched out on the cool white sheets, a small smile playing about her lips, and fell asleep as soon as her head hit the pillow.

Sometime in the middle of the night, she was jolted out of a deep sleep by anxious voices in the corridor and the sound of several pairs of feet treading up and down the stairs. Madeline got out of bed and went to the door, peering into the dim hallway. Sybil was standing at the top of the stairs, her expression stern, as Cissy and Bette—still in their nightclothes—brought up pitchers of steaming hot water and clean towels. A low moan came from Amelia and George's bedroom. The door was closed, but Madeline could hear a man's voice—not George's—speaking softly.

"What's happened?" Madeline asked Sybil. She rarely addressed her directly, but there was no one to ask except the servants and they looked harassed enough.

"Amelia's pains have started," Sybil replied brusquely.

"Is there anything I can do to help?"

"You can go back to your room and not get in the way."

Sybil's tone brooked no argument, so Madeline did as she was told and got back into bed, but sleep was impossible. After about an hour she retreated to the window seat where she wrapped a shawl around her shoulders and fitted herself deeper into the corner, making herself as small as possible as life went on just outside her room. Amelia's moans turned to screams, and Madeline heard George's voice several times, begging for news of his wife through the closed door of their bedroom.

"George, go downstairs and wait," Sybil replied, as if addressing an errant boy. "Dr. Holbrook will speak to you as soon as he is able."

Madeline heard George's footsteps as he trudged down the stairs. She considered joining him, but changed her mind, not wishing to intrude. Madeline found her dark corner comforting and remained in her hiding place, her ears attuned to whatever was happening down the hall.

The night dragged on. Amelia's screams grew more desperate and hoarse, and Sybil's commands to the servants more hostile. Madeline must have dozed off in the small hours because when she woke the house was silent. A faint strip of light rimmed the horizon as night finally gave way to morning, and a fresh wind moved through the trees, making the gauzy curtains billow like the sails of a ship. Madeline stretched her stiff muscles, fetched her dressing gown, and quietly stepped into the corridor. She couldn't hear any sounds coming from Amelia's room, so she made her way downstairs. Cissy or Bette might be up, although they would be exhausted after a night of boiling water and running up and down with kettles and towels.

The first floor was still dark, except for a faint light glowing beneath the parlor door. Perhaps George had fallen asleep and forgot to turn down the lamp. Madeline stopped on the stairs, unsure whether to return to her room or check on George, when she heard Sybil's voice coming from the parlor. She was speaking very low, but Madeline could still make out her words in the tomb-like silence of the house.

"Pull yourself together, George. The child didn't stand a chance. Surely you realized that as soon as Amelia went into labor. A few more weeks in the womb and it might have survived. I've known seven-month babies who suffered no ill effects, but this one came too early. Pity Amelia didn't die in childbirth," she added coldly.

"Grandmamma, what are you saying?" George sounded more bewildered than angry. His voice cracked with fatigue and bitterness, and Madeline was sure he'd been crying.

"I'm saying that Amelia has lost three babies. I really thought she'd carry this one to term, but it wasn't meant to be. You must get rid of her, George."

"She's my wife," George protested.

"A wife who can't give you a living child, and likely never will. Accuse her of adultery and start divorce proceedings against her."

"I will not!"

"So what do you propose? Staying married to a woman who's as good as barren? Don't be a fool, Georgie."

"Don't call me that. I'm not a child."

"You're carrying on like one. A man does what must be done."

"Grandmamma, Amelia just lost a child. Don't you think she's suffered enough? I will not be cruel to her. I love her."

166

Madeline heard Sybil's hiss of derision. "Love! What's that got to do with anything? Duty is what matters. You are the last living Besson male. It is your duty to run this plantation and make it profitable. It is your duty to produce an heir to leave the plantation to. And it is your duty to do what's right for future generations. Amelia is nothing but a cog in a wheel. When the cog breaks, you replace it with a new one."

"The way grandfather replaced you?" George asked, his tone mocking.

Madeline cringed when she heard the sound of a slap. "Shut up, you insolent pup! You will do as you are told."

"Or what?" George baited her. "What will you do?"

Sybil remained silent.

"That's what I thought. Perhaps you should consider taking a European holiday. It will do you good."

"The only way I will leave this plantation will be in a pine box," Sybil retorted.

"And that day will come sooner than you think if you continue to lord it over me, Grandmamma. You look tired. Perhaps you should get some rest."

Madeline crept up the stairs and returned to her room, reeling from the conversation she'd overheard. How could anyone be so cruel? How was it possible that Madeline's kind, loving father came from this heartless woman who didn't have a shred of sympathy for anyone? And what had George meant when he mentioned that Sybil's husband had replaced her? Replaced her with whom? But what troubled Madeline the most was the note in George's voice when he had threatened his grandmother. Sybil had pushed him too far, but could he really be capable of doing her harm?

Madeline waited until the usual time, then returned downstairs. The dining room was set up for breakfast, but neither

Cissy nor Bette was there. Madeline was surprised to see Mammy coming into the room with a platter of eggs and bacon.

"Good morning, Madeline," Mammy said. "And how are you today?"

"Sad."

"Losing a child is a sad business," Mammy agreed as she set the dishes on the sideboard.

"Mammy, did you know my grandmother when you were young?"

Mammy pursed her lips and looked away from Madeline. She pretended to busy herself with rearranging china on the table.

"Mammy?"

"Yes, I knew her. And she knew me. And it made neither of us very happy."

"What do you mean?"

"I mean that history is best left in the past, child. Now, eat your breakfast. You's growing too thin."

Madeline opened her mouth to ask more questions, but Mammy walked out of the dining room and closed the door behind her, signaling that the conversation was over. Madeline helped herself to some eggs and a strip of bacon, but she didn't have much of an appetite. Only two days ago she had sat here with Amelia, discussing layettes and baby names. Amelia had planned to call the baby George, but if it happened to be a girl, she favored Rosalie or Josephine. She'd said that George didn't like either name and thought it might be nice to name the baby Arabella, after the original mistress of the plantation.

Madeline turned around at the sound of the door opening. She thought Mammy had returned, but it was George. He looked gray and tired, his eyes red-rimmed from exhaustion and grief. He was still wearing the clothes he'd worn yesterday and dark-blond stubble covered his lean cheeks.

"George, I'm so sorry," Madeline said. She wished she could hug him, but it didn't seem appropriate, so she remained where she was.

"So am I." George collapsed into a chair and poured himself a cup of strong black coffee.

"Are you hungry?" Madeline asked.

"Strangely, yes."

Madeline filled a plate for George and set it in front of him. He picked up his fork and began to eat, but his motions were jerky and unnatural.

After a few forkfuls, George pushed the plate away in disgust. "These eggs are too salty."

"Should I ask Mammy to make you some fresh ones?"

He shook his head. "There's no need. I only came in here to see you. I just couldn't bear to be alone."

Madeline wasn't sure what to say to that, so she just remained silent and allowed George to talk.

He lowered his head and pinched the bridge of his nose, as if he had a terrible headache. He likely did. "Amelia is asleep. Dr. Holbrook gave her something to sedate her. She was devastated, poor thing. She thinks it's her fault."

"How can it be her fault?"

"It isn't, but she lost two babies before this one. The other miscarriages were early on in the pregnancy, so she thought this time she'd carry to term. Dr. Holbrook advised bed rest for the last six months of the pregnancy, but Amelia refused. She said she couldn't bear the thought of lying down for six months, especially when she was feeling so well. Now she blames herself." George sighed and shook his head in disbelief. "The child will have to be interred. And named."

George covered his face with his hands as a sob tore from his chest. His shoulders shook and Madeline went to him and wrapped her arms around him. He didn't push her away. Instead, he turned around and buried his face in her middle, his arms going around her waist.

"He's so perfect, Madeline," he muttered. "So beautiful. It's like he's sleeping. Oh, how I wish he was. And now I have to put him in a box and shut him away in the Besson tomb, next to my parents. It's so unfair," George sobbed.

"I know. I'm sorry. I wish there was something I could do."

"Just be there for Amelia. She'll need understanding and support."

And she won't get it from Sybil, Madeline added silently.

George pulled away and used the back of his hand to dry his eyes. "I better clean up and change. I have a plantation to run." He walked from the room without a second glance.

Chapter 23

Madeline was coming out of the library when she saw the undertaker's carriage through the open door. He had several tiny coffins in the back, ready to show his wares to the grieving parents. George came out to greet him, pointed to a highly polished dark-brown box, and walked away, his shoulders slumped in misery. The undertaker took the coffin George had selected and headed into the house, walking past Madeline toward the door to the cellar. Madeline hadn't thought about it until that moment, but she supposed they had taken the baby's corpse to the coolest place in the house to keep it fresh until the funeral, and to keep Amelia from coming across it should she get it into her head to get up and wander around the house in search of her baby.

Sybil swept past Madeline and followed the undertaker down into the cellar. In her hands was a tiny embroidered gown, the one Amelia had been working on when Madeline had first arrived at the plantation. Sybil glared at Madeline before shutting the door.

"Amelia is awake. Go to her."

"Yes, ma'am." Madeline climbed the stairs with a heavy heart. What could she say to a young woman who'd just lost her baby?

Amelia was sitting up in bed, propped up by several pillows. She looked wan and listless and her eyes were red-rimmed from crying, but her hair had been brushed and plaited and she wore a clean nightdress. The room showed no trace of last night's tragedy. The sheets looked clean, and someone had taken away the soiled towels and linens. Madeline hovered in the doorway, unsure whether to enter, but Amelia held out her hand.

"Come in, Madeline," she said. Her voice was almost a whisper, hoarse from hours of screaming.

"I'm so sorry, Amelia," Madeline said as she sat in a chair someone had left by the bed.

Amelia nodded in acknowledgement.

"Are you in pain?"

Amelia began to cry quietly, as if her grief were something to be ashamed of. She covered her face and hunched over, rocking back and forth in her despair.

"Is there anything I can get you?" Madeline asked. She hated feeling so helpless in the face of Amelia's suffering.

Amelia shook her head. She removed her hands from her puffy, tear-stained face and turned to face Madeline, her eyes full of anguish and fear. "The physical pain will go away, but not the pain in my heart. This is the third baby I've lost, Madeline. And now I've lost George as well."

"You haven't lost George. He loves you."

"A man rarely loves a woman who can't give him what he wants, and what he wants is a child."

"You'll have another baby, a living baby," Madeline insisted.

Amelia shook her head as tears slowly slid down her pale cheeks once again. "Madeline, you are too young to understand, and I probably shouldn't be using my pain as an excuse to disillusion you, but girls like you and I are only good for one thing. We are bred for only one purpose. We are a bridge to the next generation. None of this is worth anything," Amelia made a sweeping gesture, "if there's no one to leave it to. George is the last Besson descendant. If he dies without an heir, everything dies with him."

"Amelia, you're still young," Madeline protested.

"Do you know what Dr. Holbrook said to me?" she asked, the look of desolation in her eyes replaced by burning anger. "He said I should pray for forgiveness and acceptance. Forgiveness because I'm clearly to blame, and acceptance because he doesn't believe I can carry a child to term. He said as much to Sybil. Sybil is obsessed with this place, and she's very possessive of George. She will not allow her family's legacy to crumble into ruins."

Madeline was about to disagree, but having overheard Sybil's advice to George, she couldn't bring herself to lie. She had thought Amelia was oblivious to the undercurrents around her, but now Madeline realized Amelia had been a lot more aware than she'd given her credit for.

"You need to rest," Madeline said as she got to her feet. Amelia did look exhausted, but that wasn't the reason Madeline needed to leave. She'd rather be anywhere than in this room. Amelia was drowning in her desperation and Madeline felt as if Amelia would drag her down to the bottom with her. At fifteen, Madeline wasn't equipped to deal with the depth of Amelia's grief or her fears for the future. She could barely handle her own.

"Yes, you're right. Thank you for coming to see me." Amelia's voice sounded flat again, and all the emotion left her eyes. She leaned back deeper into the pillows and closed her eyes, giving Madeline an excuse to leave.

Chapter 24

May 2014

Berwick-Upon-Tweed, England

A churchlike hush settled over the hospital once visiting hours came to an end and the patients were settled in for the night. Only a few visitors remained, those whose loved ones might not make it through the night. A low light burned over the nurses' station where two efficient-looking representatives of the caring profession held down the fort, mugs of tea in hand. Gabe could just see them through the partially open door of his father's room.

Graham Russell looked like a stone effigy—white, still, and lifeless—but his breathing was even and he appeared to be asleep rather than unconscious. Gabe reached over and took his mother's hand. She never looked away from her husband, but the gesture seemed to bring her back to life.

"You were born here, you know," Phoebe said as she shifted in the uncomfortable plastic chair.

"I know."

"Never did like this place. Looks like a dungeon," Phoebe added. "I haven't been here in years. Not since your grandmother passed. It hasn't changed much."

The Berwick Infirmary did have the appearance of a stronghold, or a Victorian lunatic asylum. Built of gray stone, it had a tower that must have at some point housed a bell. There was a strict no mobile phones policy on the ward, for which Gabe was grateful since it gave him an excuse not to call Quinn, who'd rung twice since he left London. He longed to talk to her and share his worry and fear, but didn't want to upset her. It wasn't as if she could do anything to help. He'd ring her in the morning, once he had something definite to say.

"Mum, what exactly did the doctor say?" Gabe asked. He'd arrived in Berwick-upon-Tweed only an hour ago and spent most of it arguing with the night porter, who had tried to turn him away and advised him to come back in the morning when visiting hours began.

"He said your father had a cardiac event," Phoebe replied. She didn't elaborate, and Gabe didn't press her. He could see for himself that things were dire, and making his mother reiterate the details would only upset her further.

"Can I get you a cup of tea, Mum?" Gabe felt an overwhelming need to get up and walk, having spent the past eight hours in the car. He'd dropped off Emma, then spent over an hour in rush-hour traffic, followed by the additional six hours it took to get to Berwick. Now that he was finally here, he felt like a caged animal who, despite its limitations, couldn't sit still and paced its cage for hours on end.

"Yes, tea would be lovely. Have you called Quinn?"

"Not yet. I didn't want to worry her."

Phoebe nodded, but didn't reply. Gabe left the room and went in search of tea. He found a vending machine at the end of the corridor, but the tea would be weak and lukewarm at best, so he returned to the nurses' station.

"Any chance of a cup of tea for my mother?" he asked the nurses, hoping they'd take pity on him. The older nurse looked annoyed and was about to direct him back to the vending machine, but the younger one smiled and nodded. She was in her early twenties and seemed to have a sunny disposition.

"We have a kettle set up in the breakroom. I'll make you a fresh brew. Back in a tic."

"Thank you, miss," Gabe said. His father would have said something like "Thanks, luv," but having been a college administrator for years, Gabe had learned the art of political correctness. Some women wouldn't mind being called *luv*, but others might find the endearment condescending or even sexist. Monica bloody Fielding had even filed a sexual harassment complaint against one of the older professors who called everyone *luv*, *pet*, or *dear*. Gabe had had to call the man in, read him the riot act, and extract the promise of an apology to Monica, who had gloated as if she'd won a million-dollar harassment suit.

The young nurse returned with two plastic cups of strong tea and extracted a half-eaten package of biscuits from her pocket, which she held out to Gabe.

"Your mum's been here for hours. She must be starving."

"That's very kind," Gabe replied and took the biscuits. He was hungry himself, not having had time to grab anything before leaving London. He'd bought a cup of coffee at a petrol station, but hadn't thought to grab a sandwich, which would have come in handy by dinnertime.

Gabe returned to his father's room and handed the cup of tea to Phoebe, who accepted it gratefully.

"Would you like a chocolate biscuit?" He held the package out to her.

Phoebe took one and bit into it, chasing it with a sip of tea. "I hadn't realized I was hungry," she said, as if surprised that such a thing were even possible in the face of the day's events.

"Mum, let me take you home. They'll ring us if anything changes. You look exhausted," Gabe suggested, though knew what she'd say.

Phoebe shook her head. "No, I can't leave. You go on if you want. I'll wait for the doctor."

"I don't think anyone will come till morning."

176

Phoebe didn't reply. She drank her tea and set the cup on a low plastic table. Her gaze never shifted from Graham's face, and her grim expression remained in place. She stayed that way for hours, until the patch of sky outside the window lightened to a deep gray and the stars began to fade in preparation for sunrise.

Gabe's eyelids felt heavy from lack of sleep and his stomach reminded him that he hadn't eaten anything since lunchtime yesterday. He glanced at his watch and wondered if Emma was already up and running rings around Sylvia. He hoped Sylvia would make her a good breakfast. Emma didn't like breakfast cereals or plain toast. Quinn always made her a hot breakfast before school, and Gabe had been trying to do the same, despite his very limited cooking abilities. He could manage a boiled egg and toast soldiers though, and instant porridge, which Emma liked with raisins and a spoonful of honey. Thinking about breakfast made Gabe even hungrier. He'd have to step out and get something soon.

He forgot all about food when Phoebe shifted, her head swiveling toward the door as if on cue. A young doctor entered the room, followed by a male nurse.

"Good morning. I'm Dr. Abigail Spencer," the doctor said. "I'll be Mr. Russell's attending physician today."

"What happened to Dr. Lorde?" Phoebe asked, clearly annoyed by the switch.

"Dr. Lorde is not on call today, I'm afraid, so you'll have to do with me."

Gabe glanced at his mother. She was probably thinking that Dr. Spencer looked too young to be anyone's attending physician, but Phoebe wore the look of stoic acceptance she'd perfected over the years. The nurse checked the IV drip and emptied the bag attached to the catheter, while Dr. Spencer looked at the chart and checked Graham Russell's vital signs.

"I've consulted with Mr. Russell's cardiologist, Dr. Nixon. He would have spoken to you himself, but he's been called away

177

and he's still not back. We've run a battery of tests, including an electrocardiogram, an echocardiogram, and a CT, as well as a full blood workup. Mrs. Russell, when was the last time your husband saw his GP?"

"About two months ago, I'd say."

Dr. Spencer shook her head in amazement. "The tests show that Mr. Russell has suffered several minor cardiac events over the past year, usually a warning sign that a more severe attack is likely, which is what's happened. Had Mr. Russell been experiencing any chest pains prior to this?"

Phoebe shook her head. "He's been more tired of late, and complained of a pain in his neck a few days ago, but no chest pains."

"Sometimes pain in the neck, back, or chest is indicative of a heart attack. Has he had any dizziness?"

"Not that he told me. How bad is it, Dr. Spencer?"

"Mrs. Russell, I don't wish to frighten you, but yesterday's event, coupled with previous undiagnosed attacks, inflicted considerable damage to the heart muscle. The next heart attack could be fatal."

"So, what do we do?" Phoebe looked ashen, and Gabe put a hand on her shoulder to steady her.

"Mr. Russell will remain under observation for the next few days. Once we feel it's safe to release him, he will need to be on bed rest for at least a week, and then start to gradually resume his daily activities. Of course, modifications will need to be made to his medication and his diet, and physical activity will need to be restricted to short walks. If he has to climb stairs to get to the bedroom, perhaps it would be wise to set up a cot downstairs. Stress is to be avoided as much as possible. Do you have any questions?"

"Will you tell him?" Phoebe asked, jutting out her chin toward her husband. "He won't listen to me."

"Dr. Nixon will explain everything to Mr. Russell when he gets in this morning."

"Will Graham be alert when he wakes up?"

"Mr. Russell might be a bit woozy and irritable as a side-effect of the medication, but that will pass. I will be back to check on him when he wakes."

"Thank you, Doctor," Gabe said and watched Dr. Spencer walk away. "Mum, are you all right?"

"I'm frightened, Gabe," Phoebe replied. "Your father has always been so strong, so indestructible. Seeing him like this…"

"I know. It's very difficult."

Phoebe suddenly looked up at Gabe, her eyes pleading for understanding. "Oh Gabe, the wedding."

"Don't worry, Mum. The wedding can be postponed. Quinn will understand. I'll tell her today."

"Gabe, go to New Orleans. I'll look after your father."

"And who will look after you?"

"I don't need looking after," Phebe retorted.

"Of course you don't, but I'd like to all the same. I'll stay here with you until Dad wakes and then I'll take you home, where you will rest. While you're sleeping, I'll take apart the bed in the guest room and set up a bedroom for Dad downstairs, so he won't have to climb stairs when he comes home."

"But Gabe," Phoebe protested.

"No buts, Mum. I'm staying."

Chapter 25

Staying in his old bedroom always made Gabe feel like an adolescent, but his problems had come a long way from worrying about exams and not making a fool of himself in front of some girl. He was grateful that his father had survived the heart attack and would be coming home in a few days, but he felt a deep sense of unease at not being able to get to Quinn. He was being ridiculous, he knew that, but something about this whole situation continued to trouble him. He was desperate to speak to her, but it was still very early in New Orleans, so he'd have to wait several hours until he was sure she was up.

Gabe sighed and folded his arms behind his head, staring at the cracked ceiling. The house needed major repairs, but his parents were in no condition to deal with contractors and workmen, and Gabe hadn't been around enough to help as much as he should have. Just another thing for him to feel guilty about as his father remained in Urgent Care, hooked up to machines. He had been disoriented and woozy when he finally woke up, but Dr. Spencer had assured them that Graham was doing as well as could be expected.

It had taken Gabe nearly an hour to persuade his mother to return home for some food and rest. She was currently napping in the library, huddled beneath her husband's favorite blanket. Gabe had come up to his room for a kip, but despite the sleepless night, couldn't fall asleep. He'd promised his mother that he'd wake her no later than one in the afternoon and take her back to the hospital. It was now half twelve, so Gabe decided to go downstairs and make some sandwiches for when Phoebe woke up. She'd be in a rush to get back to his father, and she needed to eat, since she'd fallen asleep before he could even offer to make her breakfast.

Gabe found some bread, ham, cheese, and tomatoes. That would do. He popped a piece of ham in his mouth and reached for his mobile. It'd be after seven in New Orleans, so hopefully he wouldn't wake Quinn. The call went straight to voicemail, so Gabe left a neutral message and returned to the task at hand.

Phoebe appeared in the doorway precisely at one o'clock. She looked tired and her hair stood up on end, but the look in her eyes was one of pure determination. "It's time to go back."

"You're not going anywhere until you eat," Gabe replied. "I made some sandwiches, and you will have two. Understood? I'll make you a cup of tea. Or would you prefer coffee?"

Phoebe made a face at him and shrugged, but obediently took a seat at the old kitchen table and reached for a sandwich. "You're starting to sound like a parent," she observed as she accepted a mug of tea. "I like it."

"Well, all children eventually start to parent their parents."

"Is that so? I'm not senile yet, son. You don't need to parent me. Just drive me to the hospital."

"Sorry, Mum. I wasn't implying that you're senile," Gabe replied with a guilty smile. His mother was as sharp as ever, and that included her tongue.

Phoebe bit into her sandwich. "Not too bad. I should teach you how to make some simple dishes, so you can help Quinn once the baby comes. I hear you can now boil an egg," she added with an impish smile. Once she finished her meal, she ran a hand through her hair to tame it. "I'll just pop into the loo and meet you outside. I hope your father has eaten," she added, checking the time. "Do you think we should bring him something? I can't imagine he'll be very pleased with the lunch choices at the hospital."

"I don't think Dr. Spencer would approve. You can make him all his favorite dishes, minus fat, salt, and taste, once he's back at home."

Phoebe nodded. "You're probably right. He'll have to suffer hospital food if he hopes to get better, but he won't be happy about it."

"No, he won't be."

Gabe held the door for his mother and followed her down the corridor toward his father's room. The hospital was much busier now, with patients being wheeled or escorted down corridors, harassed nurses dashing from place to place, and a lunch cart making its rounds. The corridor smelled of mashed potatoes and some sort of meat. Phoebe hurried along, narrowly avoiding a collision with a nurse who came out of one of the rooms. She stopped dead when she reached Graham's room.

"He's not here," she said, turning to Gabe.

"They probably took him for some test." Gabe walked over to the nurses' station. The nurses from last night had been replaced by a young blond woman and an older black nurse, the latter on the phone. "Excuse me. We're here to see Graham Russell," Gabe said.

"Are you next of kin?" the blond nurse asked. She looked uncomfortable and wouldn't meet Gabe's gaze.

"Yes."

"I'll just page Dr. Spencer for you," the other nurse promised, having finished the call. "She's just down the hall, I believe. Why don't you have a seat?"

Gabe led Phoebe to a row of plastic chairs and took a seat next to her. His mother's head swung from left to right like a pendulum as her gaze searched for either her husband or the doctor, but she spotted neither. It took a good ten minutes for Dr. Spencer to finally appear. She walked briskly down the corridor, her face unreadable.

"Mrs. Russell, Dr. Russell," she said by way of greeting. She suddenly looked very young and vulnerable.

"Where's my husband?" Phoebe demanded.

"Mrs. Russell, I'm terribly sorry," the doctor began.

"Sorry about what?"

"Mr. Russell became very agitated when Dr. Nixon informed him that he'd have to remain in hospital for several days. He said he wanted to go home and tried to get out of bed. He became quite irate."

"So you moved him?" Phoebe asked, her expression hopeful.

Dr. Spencer stared at her shoes, her face pale against her white coat. "Mrs. Russell, we tried to calm him down, but he became so upset that he suffered another cardiac event. We did everything we could."

"Are you saying he's dead?" Phoebe whispered.

"We tried to resuscitate him, but I'm afraid his heart was too badly damaged. He died almost immediately."

"Why didn't you call me?" Phoebe cried.

"We did, but you must have already left for the hospital. We thought it best to tell you in person and not break the news to you while you were driving," Dr. Spencer explained. "I'm terribly sorry."

Phoebe sank into the chair she'd vacated only a moment ago. She was white as a sheet, her eyes glazed with disbelief. . "He's gone," she muttered. "Just like that. Can I see him?" she asked, her head snapping up to confront Dr. Spencer.

"Yes. He's been moved to the mortuary."

"The mortuary," Phoebe whispered in disbelief. "He won't like it there. It's cold."

Dr. Spencer glanced at Gabe, as though hoping he'd step in.

"Mum, why don't I take you home?" Gabe suggested. He was gutted by his father's death, but his first priority was his mother, who was clearly in shock.

"I have to see your father. I'm not leaving until I do."

"All right. We'll go see Dad." Gabe nodded to Dr. Spencer. "If you would…"

"Of course. Come with me, please."

Gabe linked his arm through his mother's to steady her. She looked as if she could barely walk, but she shuffled after Dr. Spencer. She looked confused and terrified, and Gabe wished he could spare her this.

"Mum, how about I go see Dad and you just wait outside?" he suggested, but Phoebe shook her head.

"No, son. I need to see him and say goodbye privately. We were married for over forty years. I can barely remember my life before Graham," she said, her voice wistful. "He was difficult at times, stubborn and opinionated, but he was honest, hardworking, and loyal to a fault. He loved me, and I loved him. Thank you." She suddenly looked up at Gabe.

"For what?"

"For Emma. She made him so happy. I'm so glad he got to meet her before…" She didn't finish the sentence, but Gabe knew what she meant. "I'd like to go in alone," Phoebe announced.

"Are you sure?"

"I'm sure. You wait outside, you hear?"

Gabe nodded and watched his mother disappear with Dr. Spencer through the mortuary door, then turned away. Though he wanted to support his mother, he was grateful not to have to see his father laid out on a metal slab. He'd see him at the funeral where Graham would be dressed in his best suit, with his hair brushed and his moustache trimmed. His father would appreciate that final

184

bit of vanity. Graham Russell would hate for anyone to see him in his hospital gown with gray stubble covering his cheeks and his thinning hair in disarray.

Gabe sank into a chair and covered his face with his hands as silent tears slid down his unshaved cheeks. His father was gone. His mother was a widow. Emma had just lost another person she loved. And he would have to tell her.

Chapter 26

The clock struck midnight, but Gabe's mind was too restless to go to sleep, despite the fact that he hadn't slept at all the night before. His mind kept replaying the events of the day. Gabe couldn't help wondering if giving in to his mother and remaining at the hospital instead of taking her home to rest would have made any difference. Was he responsible for his father's death? Had she stayed, would Phoebe have been able to calm her husband down and prevent another heart attack? Dr. Spencer didn't seem to think so, but it was possible, and for the rest of his days Gabe would have to live with the guilt.

Phoebe regained her self-control when she came out of the mortuary, but the ride from the hospital was a sad one, the silence broken only by Phoebe's sighs. Gabe wanted to comfort her, but there wasn't much he could offer besides the usual platitudes, and he knew his mother wouldn't welcome those. Halfway home, Phoebe asked Gabe to turn around. He pulled over and looked at her. Her helplessness and frustration had been replaced by a look of determination.

"Take me to a funeral home. You know, the one that did your uncle's funeral. Charles Mace and Son."

"Are you sure you want to do this now?" Gabe asked.

"Yes. I want to have the funeral this week. Tomorrow, if possible."

"Why, Mum? What's the rush?"

Phoebe turned to face him, the glint of resolve in her eyes positively frightening. "Your father didn't want any fuss. We talked about this, and that was what we decided. He asked to be cremated."

"Did you know he'd had previous heart attacks?"

"No, but no one lives forever, and once you get to a certain age, you must look reality in the face," she said bravely. "I'll ring everyone tonight. Whoever wants to pay their respects will be there, and whoever doesn't will make an excuse whether we hold the funeral tomorrow or next week."

"I'll stay with you, Mum," Gabe said. "For as long as you want me to."

"You'll do no such thing. You will attend your father's funeral and then you will go to New Orleans. And you will get married next month." Phoebe pinned Gabe with a look that dared him to argue with her at his own peril.

"Mum," he protested.

"Don't 'Mum' me. Gabe, your father was an old-fashioned man. He was born in the 1930s, lest you forget. He was thrilled that you and Quinn finally got together, but he wanted to see his grandchild born to parents who are legally wed. He recalled the stigma of being born a bastard all too well, and he didn't want that for your baby."

"But Dad wasn't a bastard," Gabe replied, confused.

"No, but his older brother was. Your grandfather got a girl pregnant before he went off to fight the Huns in 1914. He was barely sixteen. Lied about his age to enlist. He would have married her had he known, but she didn't find out about the baby until after he'd gone. She died of influenza shortly after the child was born. The boy was raised by her parents, but your father knew him."

"Were they close?"

"No. Lance hated your father, and blamed him for being the legal heir to the Russell estate. It was quite sizeable in those days. Your grandfather provided for Lance, but he wanted the lot. He was very resentful."

"What happened to him? Dad never mentioned him."

187

"He was killed in the Second World War. His widow moved to Canada. She had family there." Phoebe reached out and took Gabe's hand. "Promise me you will get married."

"I promise," Gabe said, hoping Quinn wouldn't think it callous of him to want to get married a month after his father's death.

By the time all the arrangements had been made and Phoebe rang everyone, it was dinnertime, but neither one of them was hungry. Phoebe took a sleeping tablet and went to bed, while Gabe reluctantly called Sylvia. The thought of telling Emma about her grandfather's death made his heart feel as if it were wrapped in barbed wire. She was too young to know this much loss. The only saving grace was that she wouldn't see the coffin glide toward the flames of the crematorium as the doors closed on Graham Russell for the last time.

"I'm very sorry for your loss, Gabe," Sylvia said once he told her. "I hoped you'd have better news."

"So did I."

"Well, don't worry about Emma. She's just fine. You take all the time you need."

"May I speak to her?"

"Of course. Emma, Dad's on the phone," Sylvia called.

"Hello, Daddy," Emma said. She sounded breathless, as if she'd come running.

"Hello, darling. How are you getting on?"

"I'm okay," Emma replied. "When are you coming back?"

"Not just yet." Gabe opened his mouth to tell her about Graham's passing, but the words just wouldn't come. He couldn't bring himself to break her little heart, so he decided to wait. What was it his mother always said? *Good news will keep, and bad news won't leave.* "What did you do today?"

"I went to the zoo with Logan and Jude. Logan had the day off," Emma explained.

"Oh? How was that?"

"I like the one in Edinburgh better because Mum used to take me there," Emma added, her tone wistful. "Anyway, Logan and Jude had a big row, and then Jude left."

"What did they argue about?" Gabe asked, curious what caused the bust-up between brothers.

"Well, Logan said that Jude needs to go to a method one program because he's addicted to being heroic. Jude is nothing like a super-hero," Emma added. "But maybe that's just his disguise."

"Maybe." Gabe took a deep breath and exhaled to keep his voice even. "And then what happened?"

"Jude told Logan to mind his own business. He used a lot of bad words, and then he called Logan a pouf. What does that mean?"

"I'm not really sure," Gabe lied. He wasn't about to explain to a four-year-old what sexual orientation meant or that 'pouf' was a derogatory term for homosexual. "Did you tell Grandma Sylvia about the row?"

"No. Logan told me not to."

"I see. But you had a good time otherwise?"

"Yes, it was good," Emma replied. "Logan bought me ice cream and a stuffed giraffe. I am going to call him Cecil."

"Well, that sounds like a fine name for a giraffe. But remind me not to ask for your input on a name for the baby," Gabe said.

"What's wrong with Cecil?" Emma whined.

"Nothing, darling. I was only joking."

"Anyway, I want to call the baby Aidan."

"Why's that?" Gabe asked. He hadn't expected Emma to have a say in naming the baby, but she'd clearly given it some thought.

Emma giggled. "Because there's a boy named Aidan at school," she replied shyly.

"And you like him?"

"I think he's nice. Don't tell Miss Aubrey," Emma warned, her tone suddenly serious.

"I won't. Your secret is safe with me."

"I have to go. Grandma Sylvia is calling me to take a bath now. Come home soon, Daddy."

"I'll come for you as soon as I'm able. I love you."

But Emma had already hung up. Gabe tossed his mobile onto the bedside table and went to pour himself a large whisky. He needed to calm his nerves before calling Logan. He'd suspected, of course, that Jude was using, but if Jude was a heroin addict, Gabe didn't want Emma anywhere near him. He wondered if Sylvia knew, but believed she didn't realize the extent of Jude's addiction, which was why Logan had asked Emma not to say anything.

Under normal circumstances, Gabe would have gotten in his car and fetched Emma home right away, but he could hardly leave, especially with the funeral looming tomorrow afternoon. For the moment, he had to put everything aside: Jude's drug habit, Luke's imminent return, and Quinn's newfound family. Tomorrow he would see his father on his final journey. Then, life would resume.

Chapter 27

Quinn stowed her mobile back in her purse and meandered along the river. On this sunny, crisp morning, the Mississippi sparkled and shone like an endless ribbon of light. It was vast, wider than any river Quinn had ever seen, and there were many different boats, both commercial and private. She saw several steamboats docked at various points, their crews preparing for cruises down the river. Quinn briefly considered taking a cruise, but changed her mind. She wasn't in the right mood to appreciate it. In fact, she was in a terrible mood. She'd tried to reach Gabe all day yesterday, but her calls had gone directly to voicemail. She'd texted him and received a terse reply telling her that he would ring her as soon as he could. He had rung early in the morning, but she'd been in the shower and by the time she called back, he didn't pick up.

That wasn't like Gabe at all. Quinn woke up every day to a loving text wishing her a good morning and telling her that he was waiting for her call. Speaking to Gabe before starting her day made her feel cherished and safe. A day without him felt all wrong, especially after her unexpected encounter with Luke. Quinn was grateful he hadn't come round again, but he'd never been one to give up on an idea easily, not when he really wanted something. Did he want her, or was he just testing the waters to see if she was gullible enough to take him back? She wasn't. Their conversation had left her feeling soiled and angry. She didn't want to rehash their relationship or explain why she was with Gabe. Her private life was no longer any of Luke's business, and she wished he'd leave well enough alone.

But Luke had spoken to Monica Fielding, and Monica, being an evil witch, would probably run straight to Gabe and try to plant seeds of doubt in his heart. Gabe Russell was a smart, sophisticated, confident man, until it came to his feelings for Quinn. He'd waited a long time for her, and although he never mentioned Luke, she knew some small part of him feared she might harbor regrets and consider taking Luke back if he ever came groveling. Now that she was carrying Gabe's child, his fear would be even greater because he stood to lose not only Quinn, but his baby. Since they weren't yet married, and given what had happened with Jenna McAllister, he had every right to worry.

Quinn leaned against the metal railing and stared sullenly over the water. She felt very much alone and homesick, and wanted nothing more than to book the next flight to London and leave New Orleans. She needed to see Gabe in person, and tell him he had nothing to worry about—ever. Luke was in the past, and she would never, even if things didn't work out between them, try to keep Gabe away from his child.

Quinn sighed with frustration. She would have booked a return flight today if it weren't for the call she's had from Rhys last night. He had set things in motion, and there was no turning back. He'd sounded brusque and businesslike on the phone, his mind already on the project.

"Quinn, sending a camera crew to the States will put a serious dent in our production costs, so I came up with the next best thing. I reached out to a freelance cameraman we've worked with in the past, and he just happens to be between assignments. He'll be arriving in New Orleans sometime tomorrow. He's based in Charleston, South Carolina, but he said traveling to Louisiana for a job is not a problem for him. He'll call you when he gets there. His name is Jason Womack."

"What do you want him to shoot?"

"Get footage of whatever you think is important, particularly the interior of the plantation house, the slave quarters, and the French Quarter. That's where Madeline lived before her father died, correct? We'll use the footage to build sets and shoot the episode on a sound stage. And get shots of the bayou."

"I haven't had any visions of Madeline in a bayou," Quinn replied.

"That doesn't matter. The bayou is mysterious and picturesque, and always associated with Louisiana. We'll find a way to use it."

"All right, Rhys. How's the weather in London?"

"Pissing as always. And it's cold. By the way, I'm meeting Sylvia for lunch tomorrow. She's bringing Emma. Any suggestions? I don't often do lunch with four-year-olds."

"Sylvia is bringing Emma?" Quinn asked, confused. Emma wouldn't be at school on a Saturday, but why would she be with Sylvia?

"Emma is staying with Sylvia for a few days. Didn't Gabe tell you?"

"Yes, of course," Quinn lied. She had no desire to explain to Rhys that she hadn't been able to get in touch with Gabe and had no idea he'd dropped Emma off at Sylvia's, a decision Quinn couldn't easily explain. Gabe barely knew Sylvia and wouldn't leave Emma with her unless he was in dire straits. What the heck was going on? "I forgot. Just go anyplace that has a children's menu."

"Right. Good idea. I'll call you on Monday."

Quinn pushed away from the railing and began walking again. She needed the exercise after all the rich food Seth had been plying her with on a daily basis.

Quinn still had mixed feelings about the man, but she'd learned to accept that he would never be the father she'd envisioned. She had come to like him, though, and would maintain a relationship with him once she returned home. Maybe he could even visit her one day.

She would miss Brett, who was undemanding company and seemed to enjoy spending time with her. Their shared interest in history and certain types of literature gave them something to talk about that wasn't too personal or awkward. Brett came round most days after finishing his classes, and often took her to places of historical interest that he thought she might enjoy.

"Guess who used to live here?" Brett asked gleefully as they walked past an imposing house with wrought-iron balconies and black shutters. The house was lovely, in a Gothic sort of way, but its aura smacked of something dark and forbidden.

"I have no idea. Who?"

"Anne Rice," Brett announced after a dramatic pause, obviously expecting a reaction of some sort.

Quinn searched her memory, but drew a blank. "Who's Anne Rice?"

"Oh, come on. Are you serious?"

Quinn smiled and shrugged. "Sorry, the name doesn't ring any bells."

"*Interview with the Vampire. Lestat. Queen of the Damned.* Have you never read the Vampire Chronicles? They're awesome."

"I'm not big on vampire lore."

"It's not lore, it's fiction, and it's brilliant. You have got to read it."

"All right, I'll look up the first book when I get home. Maybe I'll have time to read it while I'm on maternity leave from the program."

"Maternity leave?" Brett's eyes widened. "Does Dad know?"

Quinn blushed furiously. She hadn't told Seth she was expecting. It just seemed odd to blurt that out, and she wasn't ready for his reaction. Early on she'd explained that she didn't drink, putting an end to Seth offering her glasses of wine and shots of Bourbon. This would be Seth's first grandchild, and he might want to be involved in its life. Quinn would not prevent him from forging a relationship with her child, but she simply wasn't ready to figure out how it would all work. This baby was everyone's first grandchild, and would have more grandparents than any child alive. There would be rivalry, and there would be much awkwardness if Sylvia and Seth found themselves in the same room, or if Quinn's parents had to share their grandbaby with Quinn's biological parents.

"No, I haven't told him yet. Haven't found the right moment, I guess. Please don't say anything, Brett. I'll tell him in my own good time."

Brett shrugged. His cheerful mood vanished, and he suddenly seemed ill at ease. "Look, do you mind if we go back to the hotel now? There's something I need to do. You know, for school."

"Sure. I'll see you tomorrow?" Quinn asked, wondering why Brett seemed so out of sorts.

"Yeah, sure. Tomorrow."

Brett walked Quinn back to the hotel and gave her a peck on the cheek. "Congratulations, Quinn. Dad will be thrilled when he finds out. See ya." He gave her a lopsided smile and walked away, his mind already on other things.

She hadn't seen Brett since she told him about the baby two days ago, but he'd texted her several times to find out if she'd made any plans for the weekend. She'd replied that she was free, but that might change now that Jason Womack was due to arrive. She needed to make a list of places to visit with Jason and figure out the best time to drive out to Arabella Plantation.

Tired of walking, Quinn found a bench. She reached into her bag and pulled out her mobile to call Dina Aptekar and ask about shooting some footage at the plantation. One glance at the screen told her there'd been no calls from Gabe. Not even a text. But there was a text from Jill, asking her to call.

Quinn decided to get business out of the way first, and called the Arabella Plantation. Dina came on the phone after a brief hold.

"This is a bit unorthodox, but since you're a Besson and this is your family's history, I suppose we can make an exception and let you have a private tour," Dina said. "However, I don't think you can use the footage for anything but private viewing. Give me a call tomorrow and I'll figure something out. Maybe you can come a half-hour before we open to avoid random tourists wandering into the shot. Would that be enough time to get what you need?"

"I think so," Quinn replied, although she wasn't sure. She'd have to talk to Jason and see what he thought. Quinn wished that Rhys had given her Jason's contact information so she could find out exactly when he was planning to arrive and what hours he preferred to work. She supposed morning light would be best for filming the plantation, but Jason might want to get some twilight shots or even some footage of the mansion and the slave quarters by night.

Quinn put Rhys and Jason out of her mind and rang Gabe's number. Again, the call went directly to voicemail. Quinn felt a pang of worry. Why wasn't he answering? She fired off a text to him and then selected Jill's number. She needed to hear a friendly voice, and Jill would be at her shop at this time.

"Hey, Jilly, how are things?" Quinn asked, relieved when her cousin answered on the first ring.

"Not too bad," Jill said. "How's sunny New Orleans? I reckon you don't even need an umbrella. This weather is getting me down. What happened to bloody spring?"

"It's England, Jill," Quinn pointed out.

"Don't I know it? Lord, I'd trade my firstborn for a week in the Maldives."

"You don't have a firstborn."

"Hypothetically, love. Speaking of firstborns, how are you feeling?"

"I'm all right. Just a little more tired than usual. And I've had trouble adjusting to the time difference. I miss home."

"When are you back?"

"I was planning to fly back at the weekend, but Rhys thinks there's a story here, so he is sending a cameraman my way."

"What story?" Jill didn't know anything about Quinn's ability to see into the past, so Quinn instantly backtracked. She had been making too many slips of the tongue of late.

"Rhys just thought it might be a nice change of pace to have an episode set in mysterious old antebellum South. Something to shock British audiences out of their complacency. You know what they expect—castles and medieval maidens. This will be something very different."

"It sure will. Can't wait to see it."

"Jill, have you heard from Gabe?" Quinn asked carefully.

"No. Why?"

"He's not answering his mobile, and Rhys mentioned that Emma is staying with Sylvia for a few days."

"And how does Rhys know that Emma is staying with Sylvia?" Jill asked, instantly latching on to that bit of information.

"I gather they've been spending time together."

"As what?"

"I'm not quite sure, and I don't think it's my place to ask. But I am concerned about Gabe."

"Sounds like he might have left town. Have you called his parents?"

"I don't want to alarm them, or make Gabe feel as if I'm checking up on him," Quinn replied.

"Look, Quinn, Gabe probably has a perfectly logical explanation, being the perfectly logical bloke that he is. Have faith. He loves you."

"Oh, I don't think…" Quinn allowed the sentence to trail off. What exactly did she think? "Jill, I don't think Gabe is with another woman. I think something's wrong."

"Quinn, whatever happened, Gabe will deal with it. He probably just doesn't want to worry you, especially since you can't do much from where you are. Don't worry, coz."

"Thanks, Jill."

"So how are things with your new American family?" Jill asked, deftly changing the subject.

"Things are going well. Seth makes me feel a bit smothered, but he's just excited about finding a daughter. I like his son—my brother," Quinn amended. "He's an interesting bloke. Perhaps he'll come to England one day. It'd be fun to show him around. He's a history buff, like me."

"And what about Seth? Do you two have anything in common?"

"Not a blessed thing." Quinn laughed.

"I think you do," Jill replied.

"And what might that be?"

"Your drive. You must get it from him. He sounds like someone who sets his sights on something and goes for it. Like you."

"I haven't thought of that, but I suppose you're right."

"Isn't genealogy fun?" Jill asked, dripping sarcasm. "Now you can try to figure out what *wonderful* traits you got from your birth parents."

"I don't think I really want to go there, Jill. Sylvia is as wily as a fox, and Seth is the proverbial bull in a china shop."

"It's a wonder you turned out halfway normal, given the zoo you come from." Jill giggled.

"Did I?"

"I was being kind. Ooh, a customer. Gotta dash."

"Talk to you later."

Quinn disconnected the call. She felt much better after talking to Jill, and more focused. She'd stay for another week, get footage for Rhys, spend a few more days with Seth and Brett, and then she'd go home.

Chapter 28

September 1858

Arabella Plantation, Louisiana

"You sit still now, Miss Madeline, so I don't burn you," Cissy said as she expertly applied hot tongs, turning Madeline's naturally wavy hair into artful ringlets atop her head. Cissy suggested clipping Madeline's hair at the front so she could curl the shorter pieces and arrange them into a fashionable hairstyle. The rest of the hair was pinned high at the back of her head with long ringlets cascading over her shoulders. Madeline normally wore her hair parted in the middle and twisted into a simple knot, so this was quite a departure for her. Cissy said that the most fashionable hairstyle was called "à la giraffe," but Madeline flat-out refused to allow Cissy to try it out.

The effect of the shorter curls around her face was rather pleasing, but Madeline's mind wasn't on her hair. George had invited her to accompany him to a dinner party tonight given by his friend Preston Montlake in honor of his guests, Mr. and Mrs. Monroe of Kingston, New York. Madeline had never been to any type of formal gathering, so her nerves were stretched to the breaking point. She felt an overwhelming desire to yank up the bodice of her gown, which was off-the-shoulder and had a rather daring décolletage, accentuated with wide flounces made of lace. She wore layers of petticoats beneath the bell-shaped skirt, and her corset was laced so tight she could barely breathe. Silk opera-length gloves and a small jeweled reticule would complete the ensemble. And, of course, she would take her mother's fan.

"George, I really don't know," Madeline said when George brought up the party several days ago. "I wouldn't know how to behave in such company. I'll be the youngest person there, won't I?"

"Come, Maddy. Please, do me this favor. It's darn awkward to attend a gathering like this by yourself, and Amelia is refusing to leave her bed. I would gladly decline, but Mr. Monroe owns one of the largest textile mills in the North, and he's looking to increase his supply of cotton. Preston is already under contract with him, and he means to give some of us an introduction. I'd be a fool to miss out on such an opportunity."

"I haven't anything appropriate to wear," Madeline said. She had no idea what a lady would wear to a dinner party, since her mother was long gone and Amelia hadn't gone out anywhere since Madeline arrived at the plantation.

"Cissy will find just the right thing. She always attended on Amelia when we went out or entertained at home. Is that a yes?"

Madeline nodded. She couldn't let George down, not after he'd been so good to her, and perhaps this would be an opportunity to learn something of this world she'd been thrust into. Sooner or later, Amelia would recover and there would be gaiety at Arabella Plantation once more. Amelia had told Madeline of the parties they'd hosted and described the food and her gowns in exquisite detail. She obviously enjoyed socializing, so it couldn't be all that unpleasant.

"There you are," Cissy said, admiring her handiwork. "You sho look pretty, Miss Madeline."

Madeline's hand went to her hair, but Cissy deftly caught her wrist. "Don't touch it. You'll ruin it."

"Sorry," Madeline muttered.

"Here, let me put your bonnet on, and be careful when you take it off. Do it just so." Cissy made a lifting motion with her hands. "Straight up, without touching the sides."

"All right."

"And take a shawl. It'll be getting chilly by the time you'll be returning tonight."

If Madeline felt uneasy wearing Amelia's finery, it was nothing compared to her discomfort when she came downstairs and saw the look on Sybil's face. Sybil didn't say anything, but her eyes narrowed and her head tipped to the side, as if she were appraising a side of beef. Madeline expected to be sent straight back upstairs to bed, but Sybil nodded in approval.

"She'll do," Sybil said to George, who came out of the parlor. He wore a navy-blue tail-coat with fawn-colored trousers and a silk cravat tied in a bow, and held his top hat under his arm. He looked handsome and youthful, and the smile that lit up his face erased the lines of his recent bereavement.

"Maddy, you look like a proper Southern belle. Doesn't she, Grandmamma? Just look at her."

"You do look lovely," Sybil admitted in a rare moment of generosity. "Your father would have been proud."

Tears welled in Madeline's eyes. This was the first kind thing Sybil had ever said to her, so perhaps she was finally warming up to her.

"We should get going. It's a half-hour drive to Preston's plantation," George said.

"Are you taking a fan?" Sybil asked Madeline.

"Yes. I have my mother's fan."

Sybil paled at the mention of Corinne, and turned to Cissy. "Fetch one of Miss Amelia's fans," she barked.

"I will take my own," Madeline said.

"Another fan will go better with your gown," Sybil insisted, but Madeline wouldn't back down. The fan was the only item that was truly hers, and she meant to bring it.

"I'm partial to this one."

"As you wish." Sybil swept past her. "Have a good evening, George," she called over her shoulder, completely ignoring Madeline as she mounted the stairs.

"We shall. Come, Maddy."

George escorted Madeline to the waiting carriage and they set off into the purpling twilight of the September evening. Madeline was glad she'd brought the shawl, especially when the carriage entered the wide avenue leading away from the house. It was cooler beneath the trees, and very dark. The wings of moss swayed like loose ends of ghostly shrouds, contributing to the eerie atmosphere.

Madeline stole a peek at George, who looked completely at ease as he leaned back against the seat. He was still grieving, but no one would ever guess that his fondest hopes had just been cruelly dashed. George was skilled at masking his feelings, and that was a lesson Madeline needed to learn. It wouldn't do to wear her heart on her sleeve. She had to be charming, courteous, and gracious, and never draw attention to herself for the wrong reasons. She hoped she wouldn't embarrass George by doing or saying something inappropriate.

It will be all right, she thought as she peered at him from beneath her lashes. *George will guide me.*

Chapter 29

Madeline had worried about encountering all kinds of pitfalls during her first dinner party, but one thing she hadn't anticipated was mind-numbing boredom. She wondered why George had even bothered to bring her as she added little value to the gathering, but she had noticed Mrs. Montlake sizing her up when she thought Madeline wasn't looking. The Montlakes had a son of eighteen who had cast her shy looks all evening and tried to engage her in conversation while the guests were served pre-dinner cocktails in the parlor. Madeline enjoyed her mint julep a lot more than her talk with Gilbert Montlake, who was as tall, thin, and intense as his father. She was grateful when George joined them, rescuing her from Gilbert's awkward attempts at flirtation. George seemed amused and treated Gilbert with great consideration, asking his permission to steal away Madeline for a few moments.

"What do you make of young Gilbert?" he asked with an amused smile.

"He's nice," Madeline replied. In truth, she didn't think anything at all, but George seemed to expect an answer.

"He's a fine chap, and an only son," George added, his meaning clear. "And he seems very taken with you."

"Is that why you brought me here?" Madeline watched George's face carefully. She knew she'd be paraded in front of potential suitors eventually, but she hadn't expected it this soon.

George leaned in and kissed Madeline's cheek. "My darling cousin, I brought you here as my dinner companion. As a matter of fact, I wasn't even aware Gilbert would be joining us. I'm devastated that you'd think I had ulterior motives for inviting you tonight."

"I'm sorry, George," she muttered, chastised. "I just thought…"

"Not to worry. Would you like another mint julep?"

Madeline nodded happily and George motioned for the maid to bring another drink. He raised his glass and clinked it with Madeline's playfully. "To the most beautiful girl in the room," he said and smiled.

She lowered her eyes as a tell-tale heat bloomed in her cheeks. No man had ever paid her a compliment before —well, no man besides Daddy—and she was overcome. George had called her beautiful. She caught Gilbert watching them from across the room, but pretended not to notice his wistful stare. He was nice, truth be told, but George was much nicer, and Madeline felt giddy with pride when he escorted her into dinner.

Talk around the dinner table centered mostly on politics, and the conversation became heated when the subject of abolition came up, as it inevitably did whenever men got together. Mr. Monroe, although amiable and charming, had some harsh views on slavery and believed that paying a man a fair wage for a day's work was the way of the future. His wife, a pretty young woman with wide dark eyes and ebony curls, didn't say much, but Madeline noted the look of panic in her eyes. No doubt this very conversation took place everywhere they went, and she knew exactly what to expect, and dreaded it.

"Ladies, why don't we adjourn to the parlor for some coffee and allow the men to continue their fascinating discussion," Mrs. Montlake suggested and led the ladies from the dining room.

Madeline breathed a sigh of relief. The end of the dinner party was in sight. She couldn't wait to go home and climb into bed where she could stop smiling and nodding like an idiot in false support of issues she knew next to nothing about. She strongly suspected the rest of the female guests felt the same. They had contributed little to the conversation and seemed to be on hand only to grace the arms of their husbands, who paid them scant attention as they discussed business and politics.

Madeline followed the ladies into the parlor and accepted a cup of coffee from the same maid who'd served cocktails earlier. She wanted to thank the girl, but the servant never made eye contact with any of the guests, and retreated to the corner until someone required a refill, cream, or a clean serviette.

Mrs. Montlake settled on a settee in front of the low coffee table where several offerings of dessert were displayed. There was molasses cake, pineapple upside-down cake, and baked rice pudding, which Madeline would have liked to sample had her corset not been laced so tightly. She would probably be ill if she tried to eat anything more. Even a few sips of coffee made her feel as if she couldn't breathe.

The ladies applied themselves to the dessert, but the tension from the earlier conversation lingered, particularly with Mrs. Monroe, the only Northerner in the room.

"Pardon me for saying," Mrs. Clinton began as she pushed her plate away, "but I just don't see any sense in the abolitionist point of view. Why, freeing the slaves would be an act of unspeakable cruelty. They are as helpless as children. What would they do with themselves if they didn't have us to care for them? How would they feed themselves? We give them a home, plentiful food, clothes, and even days off from work. We're generosity itself when it comes to those the good Lord made inferior."

The rest of the ladies nodded in agreement, but Mrs. Monroe glanced toward a portrait hanging on the opposite wall, and remained resolutely silent.

"What do you think, Mrs. Monroe?" Mrs. Clinton asked, smiling at the poor woman like a cat who had a mouse by the tail.

"I wouldn't know, Mrs. Clinton. I've never owned slaves."

"But surely you must have an opinion on the subject," Mrs. Clinton persisted.

"The Negroes I know are perfectly capable of taking care of themselves and are in no way mentally inferior," Mrs. Monroe replied. "In fact, they're a lot more intelligent than some white folk I know." She clearly meant to slight Mrs. Clinton, but the woman

206

didn't even notice the insult, too scandalized by what Mrs. Monroe had just implied.

"You socialize with Negroes?" she squeaked.

"Yes, I do. Some of them are my friends."

There was a collective gasp from the ladies in the room, but they instantly recovered from shock and tried to smooth things over.

"You are very generous of spirit, Mrs. Monroe," Mrs. Montlake exclaimed. "That's most Christian of you. We are all God's children after all. Are we not?" She cast a warning look at Mrs. Clinton, who ignored her completely.

"This whole thing will be old news by Christmas," Mrs. Clinton said, referring to talk of secession. "It's absurd, is what it is. Imagine, breaking up the Union. I quite enjoy my summers in Saratoga. I wouldn't care to give them up. Harold and I have many friends in the North, and they are perfectly agreeable people."

"How do they feel about you owning slaves?" Mrs. Monroe asked. She gave Jane Clinton a sharp look, but Mrs. Clinton was only too happy to reply, as though thrilled to have finally goaded Mrs. Monroe into a confrontation.

"Oh, they don't give a picayune, my dear. They enjoy our company and we enjoy theirs. We don't spoil things with talk of slavery. Harold and I do not keep company with those holier-than-thou types; they do tend to go on and on about their views."

"Perhaps their opinions are worth listening to," Mrs. Monroe replied.

"Why? What do they know of our life?" Jane Clinton asked, looking around the room for support from her fellow Southerners. "They will not be affected by the abolition of slavery because they own none, but our whole way of life will fall apart if it comes to pass. Our God-given way of life, I should add. I hope it doesn't come to that, but Harold and I would fully support seceding from the Union if abolition became inevitable."

"What will happen to us if we leave the Union?" Mrs. Roberts asked. She was about eighteen, and newly married.

"Not much, I expect," Jane Clinton retorted. "We don't need them. It's they who need us. Their tea will be very bitter without our sugar, and their gowns awfully threadbare without our cotton. They best learn to mind their own business and see to their own problems, of which they have many."

"You seem very well informed, Mrs. Clinton," Mrs. Roberts said, clearly impressed with the older woman's vehemence.

"My Harold likes to discuss things with me," Mrs. Clinton said proudly, as though to imply most women were kept ignorant of current events. "Does your husband discuss matters with you, Mrs. Monroe?" she asked sweetly, but Madeline could see she was gunning for the Northern woman once again.

"Yes, Clayton discusses things with me, and I discuss things with him, such as my involvement with the abolitionist movement. Clayton supports me in my beliefs, and has made a sizeable donation to a fund for runaway slaves."

"That's theft," Jane Clinton fumed. "You are harboring someone's property."

"No human being should be anyone's property, but I know you disagree, so perhaps we ought to talk of something you find easier to comprehend, such as fashion, or the weather, which is lovely, by the way. There's autumn in the air in Upstate New York, but here, summer just goes on and on," Mrs. Monroe replied airily, a small smile playing about her lips. She'd retaliated skillfully with the insult to Mrs. Clinton's intelligence, and seemed quite pleased with herself.

Madeline sank deeper into her wingchair, grateful that Mrs. Clinton hadn't tried to draw her into the conversation. Were grownup gatherings always like this, all barbed comments and sly looks dressed in layers of floral silk and adorned with pearls? She had much to learn of adult society.

"Ladies, I bought the most darling bonnet the other day," Mrs. Montlake chimed in desperately. Offending Mrs. Monroe could threaten her husband's business arrangement with Clayton Monroe, and it was Mrs. Montlake's duty as hostess to keep the peace, even if she wholeheartedly agreed with Jane Clinton. "It's decorated with flowers that are so lifelike, a bee actually tried to pollinate one." She smiled around the room, silently calling for a truce.

"Yes, I saw you wearing it, Constance. It's absolutely charming," Mrs. Roberts said, clearly relieved by the change of subject.

"That's a lovely fan, Madeline," Jane Clinton said as she held out her coffee cup for a refill.

"It was my mother's," Madeline replied, belatedly realizing that Jane Clinton was stirring up controversy once again. She must have overheard Madeline mentioning the fan to Daisy Roberts when she complimented her on it earlier.

"Really? Isn't it strange how we never met your mother, or your father for that matter. What caused the great family rift? Do tell us, my dear."

All eyes turned to Madeline, who wished the floor would open up and swallow her whole. She opened her mouth to reply, closed it again when the door opened. The gentlemen came into the parlor, smiling at their wives as if they hadn't seen them in days. They seemed in good spirits, having likely downed a considerable amount of brandy, and their clothes gave off the repellent smell of cigars.

"George, please, can we go?" Madeline whispered, close to tears, as he came to stand behind her chair.

"Of course. Preston, Constance, we thank you for your hospitality. And Mr. and Mrs. Monroe, it was my pleasure to meet you. I hope we shall speak again soon, Clayton. Goodnight, all." George bowed from the neck, and slipped his arm through Madeline's. "Come, Maddy."

"Goodnight," Madeline said.

"We hope to see you again soon, Madeline. She's charming. Isn't she charming?" Jane Clinton exclaimed, loud enough for Madeline to hear, making her feel like a poodle that everyone wanted to pet.

"Pay her no mind," George said as they waited for their carriage to be brought around. "Jane Clinton has a sharp tongue, and a dull mind."

"She's vicious," Madeline said.

"She's angry."

"At what?"

"Her husband has a beautiful young mistress. The girl's hardly more than eighteen. And everyone knows about the affair, which is the greatest insult of all."

Madeline considered this information. Jane Clinton appeared to be in her late twenties. Despite her unpleasant personality, she was quite beautiful, with golden curls and wide blue eyes fringed with unnaturally dark lashes. Her husband had to be at least forty. He had a florid complexion that spoke of a fondness for drink, and was quite portly. His thinning dark hair made his forehead appear unusually large. What beautiful young girl would wish to be his mistress?

"She's an actress," George explained. "Harold has installed her in a fine house in New Orleans, and visits her often, sometimes for several days at a time. Jane is livid."

The carriage drew up and George helped Madeline in. She drew her shawl closer as she settled in, glad they had taken the closed carriage since the outside air had become chilly and the carriage was cozy and warm. George got in across from her, and the conveyance pulled away from the house. As the carriage rolled down the avenue toward the front gates, the lanterns affixed to its sides illuminated the great oaks but did little to dispel the darkness inside.

"Thank you for coming with me tonight, Maddy. I know it wasn't much fun for you," George said. He took off his top hat and set it on the seat next to him, then leaned back, finally allowing himself to relax after an evening of having to put on a performance.

"I was happy to help," Madeline replied, and meant it.

George sat up and looked at her across the dim confines of the carriage. "I'm sorry your father died, Maddy, but I'm not sorry that his death led you to me. I hadn't realized how lonely I've been until you came along."

"How can you be lonely? You have your grandmother and Amelia. They love you."

George gazed out the window for a moment, his eyes following the dark outline of the trees. "Grandmamma's expectations are non-negotiable. She's the most unyielding person I've ever met, but I suppose that's what has kept her going all these years, through the loss of her husband and both sons. I think there were other children who died in infancy, but she never speaks of them." George sighed. Child mortality was normal and expected, but speaking of it was difficult in view of his recent loss.

"She came to Arabella Plantation when she married my grandfather. She was fifteen. The plantation has been her life for fifty years, Maddy, and it's the only thing that truly matters to her. It's her legacy, and the only constant in her life. The thought of losing it is enough to drive her mad. She might have loved me once, but now she only sees me as a tool for keeping her dream alive."

"And Amelia?" Madeline asked.

"Amelia and I were happy when we were first married. We had such dreams. But grief and loss take a toll on a marriage, and love often turns to resentment."

"Do you resent her?" she asked, shocked by George's candor.

"She resents me, Maddy. She thinks that I see her as a failure, and a disappointment."

"Do you?"

"I see a young woman who's suffered. I don't blame her for the loss of the children. How can it be her fault? I just wish she'd recover something of her spirit, but that isn't easy with Grandmamma lording it over her and reminding her every blessed day that I'm the last of the line."

"George, what will happen to the plantation if you die without leaving an heir?" Madeline asked. It was an indelicate question, but since he'd brought up the subject, she wanted to know.

"I suppose it'll go to you."

"Me?"

"You are the next in line. The family name will die out, but not the family. So, there's hope."

"There's time, George. You and Amelia are still young."

He shook his head. "There'll be no more babies, Maddy. Dr. Holbrook said that Amelia is not strong enough to suffer another loss. Three miscarriages in four years have taken their toll. I won't put her through that again."

George went silent and stared out the window into the darkness beyond. They remained quiet for the remainder of the journey, each lost in their own thoughts.

Chapter 30

May 2014

New Orleans, Louisiana

When her ringtone interrupted Quinn's vision of the past, she reluctantly set aside the fan and reached for her mobile, her mind still on Madeline and George. The bitter atmosphere in the carriage permeated Quinn's own mood, making her less than eager to speak to Seth, who had no doubt found another great place to take her to for dinner or a jazz performance that couldn't be missed. She appreciated his zeal, but would be happy with a sandwich and an early night. And a phone call from Gabe.

"Hello, darling. How's my girl today?" Seth asked. He was always pumped in the mornings. He said it was because he was a morning person, but Quinn strongly suspected it had something to do with the triple espressos Dolores brewed for him as soon as he got up.

"I'm well. And you?"

"Super. Listen, I hope you won't be too upset with me, but I've planned a party for this Saturday. In your honor. I don't have much family besides a few cousins, but I want to introduce you to my friends and business associates. I hope you don't mind. It would mean a lot to me."

"No one's ever thrown a party in my honor before," Quinn replied. In truth, a party was the last thing she wanted, but she couldn't bear to disappoint Seth. He seemed so excited, and so eager to make her happy.

"I've even invited Kathy. She's eager to meet you, and I think we can put our differences aside for one night. She's glad that Brett has a sibling. What say you? Will you attend and allow me to show you off?"

"Of course. But Seth, I must return home soon. I'm going to book a flight for next week."

"Aww. Must you go? We're just getting to know each other."

"This time with you has been very…eh, special, but I have commitments at home. I'm getting married in a few weeks, and my fiancé seems to be missing in action."

"Don't worry, sweetheart. I'm sure he's fine. Probably planning his bachelor party," Seth joked.

"Probably," Quinn agreed, impatient to get off the phone.

"Want to meet for lunch?"

"Actually, I already have plans for today. I'll see you later, if that's okay."

"Of course. Have fun, whatever you're doing. I'll check in with you before I leave the office."

Quinn rang off and called Gabe again. The automated voice informed her that his mailbox was full. "Damn you, Gabe. Where are you?"

She swung her legs off the bed and headed for the bathroom, hoping a cool shower would refresh her. She'd had a lingering headache for the past two days, and her normally trim ankles looked swollen. She'd missed her prenatal appointment at the clinic in London and would have to reschedule as soon as she returned home. And now she'd have to find a dress for the party. She hadn't thought to bring anything smart to wear, assuming that her meeting with Seth Besson would be casual and brief, but since she'd stayed longer than expected she'd had to buy several new outfits to accommodate her busy social schedule as well as her expanding waistline.

"Are you all right in there?" Quinn asked the baby as she stood naked in front of the bathroom mirror. She turned sideways to examine her belly. It had noticeably rounded over the past week, the little bump firm and the skin sensitive to the touch. Her breasts were fuller and crisscrossed with bluish veins, like rivers on a map, while her nipples had grown darker and larger. Quinn laid a hand over her stomach and waited. Some expectant mothers said they felt movement as early as sixteen weeks, but she was close to twenty and hadn't felt anything yet. She longed for confirmation that her baby was well. There was no reason to think otherwise, but she hadn't been feeling well the past few days. Perhaps it was the food, or the humid New Orleans weather that she couldn't get used to. Her face looked flushed, even in an air-conditioned bathroom.

Quinn stepped into the shower and allowed the water to cascade over her shoulders. They felt stiff with tension. She pressed her forehead to the cool tiles to try to alleviate the headache that had been building instead of improving. She wished she could just take a day to rest, but Jason Womack would be meeting her in the hotel lobby at ten, so she had to get ready. He'd gotten in later than expected, but sent a text to schedule their meeting. It'd be a long day.

When she got out of the shower, Quinn checked her mobile again and found a voicemail from Gabe. Finally.

"Hello, love. Sorry I haven't been around. Hope you're having a grand time with your dad. Talk to you soon. Love you."

Quinn tried calling Gabe back, but the call went to voicemail again. This wasn't like him. Even his message sounded odd. He had a deep, melodious voice, but he sounded almost breathless, as if he were nervous. What was going on? Quinn was about to call Phoebe when the room phone trilled.

"Ms. Allenby, there's a Jason Womack here for you."

"Thank you. Please tell him I'll be right down."

Quinn pulled on her clothes, twisted her still-damp hair into a bun, and threw her mobile into her bag. She'd have to call

216

Phoebe tomorrow, since it would be too late to call by the time she returned to the hotel. Perhaps she was just being paranoid and homesick.

Quinn came downstairs to find a burly, curly-haired man in a baseball cap waiting for her.

He smiled and came toward her, hand outstretched. "Dr. Allenby. A pleasure. I'm all yours until the end of next week, so if you'll just give me an outline of what you'd like to cover, we can get started."

Quinn shook Jason's hand. He looked to be in his mid-thirties and had a disheveled look, but the warmth in his eyes and the lift at the corner of his mouth when he smiled put Quinn at ease. She had no worries about going off with him, especially since Rhys had recommended him so highly.

"I'd like to start with filming the River Road and the plantation itself," she said, "and then move on to the slave quarters and fields. I can add a voiceover later. Let's just get as much footage as we can, so Rhys can pick and choose what he'd like to use."

"May I suggest taking a boat into the bayou?" Jason said as he picked up his bag. "Perhaps we can do that tomorrow."

"I have no reason to believe that anything pertaining to this episode happened in the bayou," Quinn replied, although it was a good idea. She still didn't know exactly what had happened to Madeline, and the bayou was synonymous with Louisiana. It couldn't hurt to have the footage should a need for it arise. "Yes, let's do that."

"May I make another suggestion?" Jason asked as they stepped into the balmy morning and walked toward his SUV.

"Of course."

"Let's not ask the museum staff for permission to film."

"Why ever not? I've already mentioned it to one of the guides."

Quinn glanced at her watch. She'd left a message for Dina Aptekar Hill last night to make an appointment, but never heard back from her. The plantation had already opened to visitors this morning, so if Jason wanted to shoot when the place was empty, they'd have to do it on a different day. She explained this to Jason, who shook his head.

"They will most likely refuse, since this footage will be used for commercial purposes. We will need a permit, and that could take weeks to obtain. Are you familiar with the expression 'slow as molasses'?" he asked, chuckling at the disbelief on Quinn's face. "File the paperwork and have them send the permit directly to Rhys Morgan, with the understanding that you will return to film the plantation. Rhys will have it on file should any issues arise once production starts. And in the meantime, we simply act as tourists. I have a small hand-held video camera. I can shoot discreetly inside the house without anyone thinking it's anything more than a vacation video of a historically minded couple on their honeymoon."

"Honeymoon?" Quinn asked in surprise.

"People love honeymooners. Everyone needs that assurance that love and romance are alive and well. They'll be less likely to harass us. Besides, you are engaged, are you not?" he asked, cutting his gaze to Quinn's ring. "Who's to say I'm not the lucky man?"

"You've really put some thought into this, haven't you?"

Jason smiled and put on an exaggerated Southern accent. "My granny always said you should be prepared for any eventuality if you hope to succeed in life."

"What else did your granny say?"

"She said it's easier to apologize after the fact than to ask for permission, get denied, and then do it anyway and get caught red-handed."

"You make it sound like we're going to rob a bank."

"Some people take their history very seriously and believe it belongs only to them. Hey, Rhys said this is the story of your family. Is that so?"

"Yes. I've just recently discovered that my roots come from Louisiana."

"And you with that posh British accent." He chuckled. "Well, that's even better. Who can deny a lovely young lady a tour of her family's ancestral home?"

Quinn followed Jason and got into his truck. She wondered if he'd ever moonlighted as a paparazzo. He seemed like the kind of man who'd hide in the bushes or use a zoom lens to get a prize shot, indifferent to the rights of the people he was photographing and intent only on getting what he needed. Perhaps that was necessary in his line of work, but she didn't feel overly comfortable with his methods. She'd mention it to Rhys later. In the meantime, she hoped Dina wouldn't be at the plantation this morning to foil Jason's plan.

Chapter 31

September 1858
Arabella Plantation, Louisiana

Madeline slept late the morning after the dinner party. She'd thought the mint juleps and the soothing rocking of the carriage would make it easier to fall asleep once she undressed and climbed into bed, but her mind had refused to settle, picking over the details of the gathering and trying to make sense of the undercurrents that had shaped the conversation. She might have slept longer, but Cissy roused her when she came in and threw open the curtains with an air of defiance. Cissy had chores to attend to and didn't take kindly to her schedule being disrupted. She helped Madeline dress and arranged her hair into a simple style, which took hardly any time since Cissy clearly had no patience for anything more elaborate.

Madeline went downstairs, hoping to find Amelia seated at the breakfast table. Amelia hadn't left her room since the night she lost her baby, but she had to come out sometime. Instead, Madeline found a trunk by the front door.

"Bette, is Mr. George going on a trip?" she asked the maid as she rushed by with a basket of laundry.

"I wouldn't know nothing 'bout that, Miss Madeline," Bette replied.

"It's Amelia who's leaving," Sybil said as she stepped out of the parlor.

"Where is she going?" Madeline asked, surprised to see her grandmother up so early, since she rarely made an appearance before ten. But Sybil was up, dressed, and in something resembling good spirits.

"Amelia is going to visit with her family in Boutte. I think it will do her a world of good to spend some time with her mother and sisters. Won't it, Amelia?"

Amelia was descending the stairs, parasol in hand. She'd lost weight and her skin was as white as bleached cotton, but at least she was out of bed, which had to be a sign of progress.

"I expect so," Amelia replied. The dead-eyed stare of the past two weeks had been replaced by something resembling an interest in the world around her.

"Enjoy your visit, Amelia," Madeline said, glad to see Amelia up and about but sad to see her go. The house would be very quiet with just Sybil for company. George was too busy to pay her much attention, and the servants kept their distance, all too aware of Sybil's displeasure if they got too friendly.

"Thank you, Madeline. I'll be back before you know it."

"Ready, Miss Amelia?" Jonas asked, having come back inside after making sure Amelia's trunk was securely stowed in the back of the carriage.

"Yes."

Madeline stepped outside with Amelia. The morning was cool and fresh, and full of promise. Perhaps she'd take a walk after she waved Amelia off.

Amelia's head snapped up when she noticed a rider approaching from the direction of the fields. George galloped up to the house and leapt off his horse before it fully stopped. Madeline would have expected Amelia to be pleased that he had made it in time to see her off, but she frowned as if she'd been hoping to get away without seeing her husband.

"Were you going to leave without saying goodbye?" George demanded. He looked wounded and Madeline felt a pang of sympathy for him.

"George, I…" Amelia looked flustered. "I thought it best."

"It's never best for a wife to leave her husband without a word of farewell." George took Amelia by the shoulders and gazed into her eyes. "I will miss you, Millie, but I want you to stay as long as you need. I want to see you smile again."

Amelia's eyelashes shimmered with unshed tears. "Thank you, George. I appreciate your kindness."

George leaned in and kissed Amelia on the forehead in a fatherly fashion. "Be well, Millie."

He helped Amelia into the carriage, shut the door, and gave the driver the go-ahead. The carriage began to move and was halfway down the avenue within moments, growing smaller as it rolled toward the gates. George stood still, staring after the conveyance long after it had disappeared from view.

"I think we need to cheer ourselves up, Maddy. What do you say?" George asked as he came back in the house and joined Madeline in the dining room. He held his cup out for coffee and reached for a beignet.

"Aren't you going back to the fields?"

"Not today. What do you say to a picnic lunch by the lake?"

"Really?"

"Absolutely. But wear something plain. You can't sit on the ground in those silly hoop skirts. It would be like trying to sit while wearing a church bell. Quite a sight, to be sure, but not very comfortable."

Madeline giggled. "All right. I will wear something simple."

"Excellent. Meet me in the foyer at noon."

"Shall I ask Mammy to pack us a basket?" Madeline asked, her spirits rising by the moment.

"Leave all the planning to me. You are my guest." George winked at her and gulped the last of his coffee before springing to his feet and presumably heading for the kitchen house to place his request. Madeline hastily finished her breakfast and stepped outside. She had over two hours until she had to meet George, and she felt too restless to remain indoors. She walked for about an hour, going all the way to the River Road and back down the main avenue, then headed inside to change. Cissy *tsked* with disapproval, but removed Madeline's hoop skirt and helped her into a dress of simple sprigged muslin. Madeline wore a ruffled petticoat beneath, and a pair of sturdy shoes, suitable for walking on the grass.

"Don't forget your bonnet, Miss Madeline. You must keep the sun off your face to protect your complexion."

"I know, Cissy," Madeline replied. Everyone always seemed concerned with her complexion. She couldn't help it if her skin turned a golden brown the moment it was kissed by the sun.

"Ready?" George asked as she came downstairs. He was holding a wicker hamper and had a colorful blanket slung over his arm. "Cook packed us freshly baked corn bread, cold chicken, cole slaw, and plums for dessert. A feast fit for royalty, I'd say," he joked. George normally dressed like a fashionable town swell, even when at the plantation, but this afternoon he was wearing light-colored trousers, a linen shirt, open at the collar, and comfortable shoes. The simple attire made him look younger, and more vulnerable somehow, not at all like the wealthy scion of an aristocratic family.

Madeline walked with George to the lake. She'd seen it from her window, but never actually walked there because it was too far to go alone. The water shimmered in the afternoon sun, and a gentle breeze caressed her face. Madeline wished she could take off her bonnet and remove the pins from her hair. It would be so lovely to turn her face up to the sun and not worry about getting too tanned or behaving improperly.

"I think this is a good spot," George said as he spread the blanket under an old leafy oak. "Come and sit down, Maddy."

Madeline carefully lowered herself to the ground and spread out her skirts around her, making sure to cover her ankles. The tips of her shoes peeked out from beneath the fabric, and she sat stiffly, her legs directly in front of her and her hands folded in her lap.

"Seriously, Madeline. Have you never been on a picnic? Take off your bonnet, kick off your shoes. You can even roll down your stockings and wet your feet in the lake. I won't tell anyone. It's just you and me here, and no one to judge us."

George demonstrated what he meant by taking off his shoes and socks and rolling up his trousers. He walked to the edge of the lake and dipped his toes in. "The water is gorgeous," he said. "Want to go for a swim?"

"No."

"Are you sure?"

"I've never gone swimming."

"There's a first time for everything. Come on. I won't let you drown, I promise. It's so refreshing."

Madeline glanced at George from beneath her lashes. The water did look awfully tempting, but she felt shy about removing her clothes.

George experienced no such qualms. He removed his trousers, pulled his shirt over his head, and waded into the lake wearing only his cotton drawers. Madeline sucked in her breath as she watched him. She'd never seen an unclothed male, not even her father. Charles Besson had always been meticulously dressed, complete with a waistcoat and a necktie. George's skin glowed in

224

the sunlight and his muscles rippled as he swam out to the center of the lake.

"Come on, you ninny," he called as he waved to her. "Look, no hands," he cried out and lifted his arms above his head, promptly sinking beneath the glittering surface and then reappearing moments later. He shook the water from his eyes and smiled broadly.

Madeline could resist no longer. She removed her dress and rolled down her stockings, remaining only in her camisole and pantaloons. She walked to the edge of the lake, gasping when the water swirled around her ankles. It was cool and inviting, but the bottom of the lake felt slimy and treacherous. Madeline inched forward, afraid of slipping on the cool mud.

George swam back toward the shore to meet her. He shook his head and sprayed Madeline with water, making her giggle and turn away from the flying drops, and the sight of him. His near-nudity embarrassed her, but George seemed oblivious to her maidenly sensibilities.

"Give me your hand," he said. "The bottom is slippery."

Madeline gave George her hand and allowed him to lead her waist-deep into the water.

"Lie back and allow yourself to float. I'll hold you. There's nothing like floating on a calm lake and looking at the clouds," he said as he slipped his hand beneath her calves and lifted her legs up while easing her back into a reclining position.

Madeline complied and leaned back on George's arm. Her arms and legs floated on the surface of the lake, her limbs relaxing of their own accord. She felt weightless as she gazed up at the sky. It was peacock blue, with wispy white clouds lazily sailing overhead and passing in front of the shimmering sun. All sound faded as Madeline's ears dipped beneath the water. The moment felt oddly peaceful, and timeless. She could be content to float this way forever.

George removed the arm from beneath Madeline's legs and stretched out next to her, but his right arm still supported her from beneath, making her feel safe. They floated side by side, staring up at the endless sky for what felt like hours.

"This is the happiest I've been in a long time," George said after they finally emerged from the water and reclined on the blanket to dry off.

Madeline glanced in embarrassment at her see-through undergarments, but he didn't seem to care. His drawers were soaking wet, and she could see the bulge of his manhood as he folded his arms behind his head and closed his eyes, sighing with pleasure. He remained like that for some time, but then his eyes flew open, as if he'd just remembered something important.

"I'm hungry," he said. He sat up and rummaged in the basket, taking out the food the cook had packed for them, as though searching for something. "I asked Cook for lemonade, but she only packed a bottle of wine."

"I don't usually drink wine," Madeline replied. She didn't mind the bubbly taste of champagne or the minty flavor of the julep, but the sourness of wine didn't appeal to her. Lemonade would have been perfect, but it was too far to walk back to get some.

"Just a small glass." George poured her a glass of wine. The liquid looked blood-red as it caught the rays of the sun.

Madeline accepted a plate of food and took small sips of the wine. The food was simple, and the wine warm from sitting in the sun, but it was the most delicious meal she'd ever had. She felt so happy just sitting there with George, enjoying their al fresco lunch and drying off in the warm sunshine. The wine gave her a pleasant feeling of peace, and she didn't protest when he refilled her glass. Her limbs felt languid, and her mind slowed, thinking only uncomplicated thoughts.

George set aside his plate, leaned forward, and kissed Madeline lightly on the lips.

"What are you doing?" she asked. She wasn't shocked, just curious.

"I'm showing my love for you. Being with you makes me happy."

"I like being with you too, George."

He kissed her again. This time the kiss was longer and more demanding. His tongue slid into her mouth, exploring it leisurely and inviting her tongue to do the same. The sensation was odd, but strangely pleasurable. Her breasts pressed against his chest as he gathered her to him and held her close. She'd never kissed anyone before, but once she kissed him back, it came naturally and she melted into him, eager for more.

Madeline barely noticed when George pushed her down on the blanket and covered her body with his own. Some inner voice told her what he was doing was wrong, but it felt good and she didn't want him to stop. Her loneliness and need for affection refused to let her push him away. He was giving her the love she craved so desperately. How could she reject him?

George pushed down her damp camisole and cupped her breast, massaging her nipple with his thumb until she shuddered with pleasure. She'd touched her breasts many times while bathing, but it had never felt like this. She roused to his touch, and her reaction spurred him on. George lowered his head and caught her nipple between his lips, sucking gently until Madeline let out a low moan. How could something so simple feel so wonderful?

"George, you shouldn't," she murmured.

"Give me one good reason to stop," he whispered, capturing her lips once again.

Madeline tried to think of a reason, but her brain seemed to have turned to jelly. She couldn't think, she could only feel, so when George's hand slid between her legs, she arched her back, eager to discover what other delights he had in store for her.

227

"You are so beautiful, Maddy. So ripe for the picking."

"I'm not fruit." Madeline giggled, surprised by the comparison.

"Oh, but you are. You are ripe, and delicious, and bursting with juice."

Her cheeks heated. He must be referring to the strange wetness between her legs. She tried to clamp them together, but he shook his head and parted them with his knee.

"Don't ever be ashamed of your desire," George murmured. He slid down and pulled off her pantaloons, making Madeline gasp with embarrassment. She opened her mouth to protest, but changed her mind since George was leaving a trail of kisses down her belly as his fingers explored the part of her that no one had touched since she was a small child, leaving her breathless with pleasure.

Madeline cried out when his tongue found her center. He lapped at her like a lazy kitten, not hungry enough to eat quickly, but not full enough to walk away from its bowl. His tongue was slow and persistent as it probed and stroked her. Madeline shuddered with the sensation, too aroused to ask him to stop. She was vibrating like a tuning fork, her whole being focused on the spot George was working on.

"You like that?" he asked with a low chuckle.

"Yes."

"Now we'll do something I like."

George moved back up and pinned Madeline's wrists with his hands, kissing her urgently. She tried to wiggle away from him as she felt the tip of his manhood push inside her. This had gone too far. Her virginity was for her future husband and had to be preserved—or so Miss Cole had said when she'd counseled Madeline in lieu of her mother. She had no idea what would happen if George actually penetrated her or how her husband

228

would know that someone had been there before him, but it felt wrong and had to stop.

"George, no, don't," she pleaded, but he ignored her. He pushed harder, overcoming her body's resistance to this unexpected intrusion. Madeline cried out as pain tore through her and then George's hard shaft filled her, her tender flesh stretching to accommodate it. Despite the pain, the sensation was strangely fulfilling. He began to move within her and Madeline forgot about the discomfort as waves of pleasure radiated through her lower belly.

"Open up to me, Maddy," George whispered into her ear.

Madeline did as she was told and spread her legs, arching her back as George drove deeper into her. They moved together in rhythm until he let out a strangled moan and collapsed on her. Afraid to move, she lay beneath him, still quivering. The unfamiliar throbbing between her legs felt so good, she wished he would take her again.

Without saying a word, George flipped onto his back and stared at the sky, folding his arms behind his head.

"Did I please you?" Madeline asked, worried he wasn't happy with her.

George turned onto his side and cupped her cheek. "More than words can say. I love you so much, Maddy, but we must keep this between us. Some people wouldn't understand."

Madeline nodded. No, they wouldn't understand. She wasn't sure she understood either, but she wasn't about to question George. He was the only person who'd shown her any real kindness since her father died, and losing his love was the worst thing she could imagine. She glanced down and was shocked to see blood covering his softening penis.

"George, what…?"

"Don't worry. It's normal to bleed the first time."

"Is it? How do you know?"

George laughed and kissed the tip of her nose. "You are so wonderfully naïve, Maddy, and so innocent. I'm proud to have been your first."

"Shouldn't my husband have been my first?" she asked.

"Don't worry. He'll never know the difference if you cry out in pain and squirm a little on your wedding night. Men believe what they want to believe. You'll only have to pretend the first time."

"Do people do this often?"

"They do it all the time. And it gets better and better. You'll see."

Madeline felt a warm glow in her belly. George was pleased with her and they would do this again, and as long as it didn't cause problems with her future husband, she was more than happy to oblige. Nothing had ever felt as wonderful as having George inside her and knowing he loved her and she'd made him happy.

"Go in the water and wash off the blood," he instructed. "You don't want Cissy seeing blood on your bloomers."

Madeline did as she was told and then allowed George to help her dress.

He kissed her again, very tenderly. "Say you'll always love me, Maddy."

"Always, George."

"That's my girl."

Chapter 32

The next few months were the happiest Madeline had ever known. With Amelia away, she took on the role of the lady of the house. George treated her as if she were his wife, and even Sybil's attitude toward her had thawed, finally allowing Madeline to forge a fragile friendship with her grandmother. They spent hours sewing or reading in the parlor and even entertained guests, who came more frequently since Amelia's departure. Mr. and Mrs. Clinton called several times, as well as Mr. and Mrs. Roberts, and Mrs. Montlake came for tea with Gilbert every other week. Gilbert had lost some of his reserve and spoke to Madeline of horses, which he loved, and the family business. He was being groomed to take over for his father when the time came, and found he enjoyed the challenges and rewards of running a plantation.

Preston Montlake had recently taken Gilbert along on a trip to New York to visit the Monroe Mills, and Gilbert was full of stories about life in the North. What seemed to have impressed him most was the cold, and the glorious foliage of Upstate New York as autumn swept over the mountains and valleys, painting the landscape in crimson, gold, and burnished orange. Gilbert was wise enough, or maybe too cowardly, not to engage Madeline in political discussions, and their conversations remained easy and light. He was a pleasant enough young man who seemed to genuinely enjoy her company. Madeline thought George might resent the time she spent with Gilbert, but he didn't seem to mind in the least.

"It's only natural that young men will be interested in you, Maddy," he said. "Gilbert is a family friend and you should be kind to him. Take him for a walk in the garden, or play a card game. You need friends who are closer to your own age."

"But I want to be with you," Madeline replied as George nibbled her earlobe.

"You *are* with me, but we can't make our feelings for each other public. Not yet."

"George, what will happen when Amelia returns?" she asked with trepidation. The question had permeated her every waking moment since that day by the lake, making her sick with worry. She had tried to hide her insecurity from George, but she was sure he was aware of her fears and probably harbored some of his own.

He gazed down at Madeline, his head resting on his hand. He looked very serious, which didn't happen often, so she braced herself for whatever he was about to tell her.

"Maddy, my relationship with Amelia is fractured beyond repair. We haven't shared a bed in nearly a year, not since she found out she was pregnant again. As you saw yourself, she tried to leave without even saying goodbye. But she recently lost a child, and I won't be cruel to her. She is my wife, and the woman who carried three of my children. In due course, I will obtain a divorce, but for now, you must be patient and keep your feelings for me to yourself."

"What if Amelia doesn't want a divorce?"

"Amelia has been gone for months. If I wished to file for divorce, I could cite abandonment as grounds for my petition, but there's no rush. It will all work out. I promise. Now, come here," George said and pulled Madeline toward him, his hand sliding between her legs. She opened up to him, but her thoughts lingered on their conversation. He meant to obtain a divorce. Did that mean he would marry her? Would this really be her life? And was it possible to retain this kind of happiness for long?

George came to Madeline's room nearly every night and often stayed till morning, making love to her into the wee hours and sleeping next to her as if they were husband and wife. He encouraged her to tell him exactly what pleased her and what didn't, and after a time she let go of her inhibitions and began to explore his body freely and learn what brought him pleasure. He wasn't shy about showing her what he enjoyed, but never insisted she do anything she didn't want to.

232

"George, was it like this with you and Amelia?" she asked, jealous of her rival. Amelia was never far from her thoughts, and Madeline alternated between feeling possessive of George and eating herself up with guilt. Amelia was her friend, and didn't deserve this, not even if she thought her marriage was at an end.

"It was in the beginning. We sailed to France for our wedding trip. We hardly left the cabin that first week," George said with a wistful smile. "We were so happy."

"Did Amelia know how to please you?"

"Not at first. I had to teach her, just as I'm teaching you."

"And how did you know? Who taught you?" Madeline knew very little about this aspect of human nature since no one had ever mentioned this kind of intimacy in her presence. Now that she knew what took place behind closed doors, she regarded the people she knew through different eyes, wondering if they did the things she did with George, and whether they enjoyed it. Had her father shared his bed with Miss Cole? Did Mr. and Mrs. Clinton, who seemed so uptight, spend hours in bed taking turns pleasuring each other? It seemed highly unlikely, but Madeline realized appearances could be deceiving.

"There are places in New Orleans where men go, Maddy, where there are women who are paid for their favors. They like nothing more than an innocent young man to educate."

"Do you mean a brothel?" Madeline asked, scandalized that George would admit such a thing to her. She'd only recently learned what a brothel was, and was still shocked that such places existed openly and that many married men went there regularly.

"Yes, a brothel. After my father died, Preston Montlake took me under his wing. He took me to an exclusive establishment that he frequents and paid for my education."

"Did you not wish to remain pure for your wife?" Madeline could hardly fathom the idea of prim and respectable Mr. Montlake frequenting a brothel, and she couldn't help wondering if Mrs.

Montlake knew of her husband's activities and turned a blind eye. Was that normal in a marriage?

George laughed softly and kissed the tip of her nose. "Believe me, Maddy, no woman wants a bumbling idiot in her bed, which is what I was my first time. A woman's first experience defines the rest of her life, and I wanted to make it special and wonderful for my wife."

"Like you did for me?"

"Was it special and wonderful?" George whispered, and then ran his tongue along Madeline's lower lip.

"You know it was."

"Then I served you well. And I will do so again."

Madeline tried to put Amelia from her mind, but her conscience gnawed at her, reminding her every day that she was usurping Amelia's rightful place. The letters from Amelia didn't help. She'd written several times, inquiring after the family and regaling them with news of her hometown. Amelia seemed in better spirits, and begged George's forgiveness for not rushing home. She was regaining her health and vitality, and praised his generosity of spirit in putting her needs before his own. Sybil ranted and raged at Amelia's selfishness and her shortcomings as a wife, but Madeline wished that Amelia would never return. Amelia was happy with her family, and Madeline was happy with George. It could all be so simple if everyone just did what they wanted.

Madeline sometimes caught Mammy's worried gaze on her, but she'd barely seen the old woman in the past few months. Madeline had no reason to visit the kitchen house, and Mammy had no call to come into the main house. Their paths rarely crossed, and the ache caused by the betrayal of her old nanny began to heal. Madeline still grieved for her father, but the pain lessened every day as she blossomed from an innocent child into a sensual young woman. She was young, she was in love, and she was happy for the first time since her mother had died.

George spoiled her, and often took her for carriage rides and on his monthly visits to New Orleans. They didn't go on a steamboat again, but Madeline cherished the memory, and instead enjoyed riding in a fine carriage with her handsome George by her side. She was almost sixteen, but she felt like a woman of the world when she accompanied him to restaurants or joined him for an evening at the theater. George always introduced Madeline as his beloved cousin, and treated her like a charming ingénue in front of his acquaintances. She didn't mind. She understood his obligations to Amelia and gladly acted the part, playing the innocent and gazing at George with adoring eyes, the easiest part of all, as he squired her about town.

As October gave way to November and then December, the plantation grew quieter and grayer. The cotton-picking season had ended, and after weeks of ginning the cotton, finished bales were sent down the river to their various destinations. George sent nearly five hundred bales of cotton to Mr. Monroe's textile mill in Kingston, New York, a transaction he was very pleased with.

A quantity of cotton was held back, to be carded and then spun by the slaves. The finished cotton would be used on the plantation for new bedding and clothing. Sybil supervised the carding and weaving process, and then allocated the finished cloth to various purposes. Madeline was given lengths of cotton to make new undergarments and night dresses for herself under the supervision of Sybil, who was practical to a fault.

"Why should we pay a seamstress when we can easily do this ourselves?" Sybil demanded. "Idle hands are the devil's workshop," she added, giving Madeline a meaningful stare.

Madeline cringed under her grandmother's gaze. What if she knew about her intimate relationship with George? What would she do? She'd been eager to send Madeline away to a school for girls, and perhaps she would insist on it before Amelia returned. But Sybil said nothing more and Madeline began to relax.

She didn't mind sewing since the weather wasn't suited to walking and George spent much of his time at the neighboring plantation. The sugar cane at the Arabella Plantation was still processed by hand, a long and laborious process that required several steps and all able-bodied slaves. Mr. Campbell of Oak Ridge Plantation had recently invested in a steam-powered mill and George was smitten. He spent hours at Oak Ridge, discussing the charms of the steam engine with Mr. Campbell, who was only too happy to show off his new 'baby.'

But eventually, all the cotton was shipped, and all the sugar had been ground, and the plantation entered a period of quiet contemplation as the end of the year approached. This was a time of rest for the slaves, and a time of idleness for the owners. The new sugar crop would not go in until January, so George had nothing to occupy him till then. He became listless, since he no longer rode his acres every morning. The fields were bare and brown, the endless acres often shrouded in a soupy fog in early morning. George still consulted with his overseer every day, discussing the rotation of the fields to ensure the soil didn't grow depleted, and making plans for the spring planting.

The days grew cooler, the fecund humidity of summer replaced by drier, brighter weather. George often left in the morning and didn't return for a day or two, joining his friends in various entertainments, since everyone now had more free time. Madeline missed him when he was gone, but didn't utter a word of reproach, waiting patiently for George to return. Even Gilbert's visits became less frequent as his family attended various parties and prepared for their own Christmas ball, to which the Bessons were invited.

Sybil took Madeline to New Orleans to order a new gown for the social event of the season. Madeline hoped to see Miss Cole at Mrs. Bonnard's establishment, but there was no sign of her in either the front parlor, where the gentlemen waited for their ladies to finish the fittings, or the back rooms, where numerous seamstresses crouched with a mouthful of pins, tucking and adjusting until the gowns fit just right and the hems were perfect.

Madeline hoped that Paula Cole had been able to escape the hardship of her new life and found employment as a governess. It lifted her spirits to think that Miss Cole had moved on to something better.

Madeline had her last fitting on her sixteenth birthday. She hadn't told anyone it was her birthday, fearing they would feel obligated to celebrate and get her presents, but she intended to enjoy her outing to New Orleans, particularly since George had promised to take them to lunch after they finished their business at the dressmaker's. Madeline was taken to the back room by herself, since Sybil's gown was finished and ready to take home. Her grandmother elected to have a cup of tea in the parlor, especially since the proprietress, Mrs. Bonnard, asked if she might join her. The two women had known each other for years, and as much as Sybil pretended not to care, she enjoyed a good gossip now and then.

The fitting room was nearly empty, with only one customer being fitted for a silk ball gown in a startling shade of green. The bright color made the woman look sallow, but she seemed quite pleased with the dress, turning this way and that and admiring herself in the long mirror. The lady appeared to be hard of hearing and yelled at the poor seamstress as she crouched on the floor pinning the hem.

Madeline's gown was the color of liquid gold. It wasn't a shade she would have picked for herself, but Mrs. Bonnard had suggested it, and she had been right. The color brought out Madeline's dark hair and hazel eyes, and made her look youthful without appearing too prim in a gown of white or cream. Her father used to say that her eyes were the color of the bayou on a sunny day. How proud he would have been to see her looking so lovely, and so mature. She was no longer the girl he'd loved, but a woman, ready to shape her own destiny.

"How does that feel, miss?" the seamstress asked as she stood back, surveying Madeline with a critical eye. "I had to let it out a bit at the waist, and I took up the hem another inch. It was still too long."

237

"It feels fine," Madeline replied. Cissy hadn't laced her corset as tightly as she usually did, which accounted for the loosening of the waist, but Madeline didn't mind. She hated the feeling of not being able to take a deep breath, especially when dancing. Her waist was small enough that she could get away with this tiny indulgence.

"Would you have a forwarding address for Miss Cole?" Madeline asked as the seamstress began to unbutton the gown, her fingers deft on the cloth-covered buttons.

"Miss Charlotte," Madeline called to her when she failed to respond. "It is Charlotte, isn't it? Miss Cole used to be my governess, and I would like to write to her and find out how she's faring in her new position. You wouldn't be betraying her confidence if you told me where she's gone."

"She's gone to the cemetery, Miss Besson," Charlotte replied quietly, so the other seamstress wouldn't overhear.

"What do you mean?" Madeline whispered. "I saw her only recently, and she seemed well enough."

The seamstress came closer to Madeline and began to adjust her sleeve, so her face was close to Madeline's ear. "If you tell anyone, I'll deny you ever heard it from me, but Paula Cole died of severe hemorrhage."

"Did she cut herself?" Madeline gasped.

Charlotte looked exasperated, but then must have remembered Madeline's tender age and rearranged her face. "She was in the family way, Miss Besson, not that I should be telling you that," she whispered. "But as you knew her, maybe you'll mourn for her. She had no family, and Mrs. Bonnard didn't see fit to pay for a fancy funeral. She just used whatever was owed to Miss Cole to pay for a pine box and a burial service. Not even a stone to mark her life."

Madeline shook her head. "I don't understand. What brought on the hemorrhage?"

Miss Charlotte looked distinctly sorry that she had ever opened her mouth, but it was too late to back out now. She had to explain. She helped Madeline out of the gown and assisted her in dressing in her own clothes while she waited for the other seamstress to leave the room.

"You see, whoever the father was, he had no wish to marry her, and Mrs. Bonnard would have cast her out without a reference, and possibly without paying her wages once it became known she was with child. Paula tried to get rid of the child before her condition became apparent."

Madeline thought she was going to be sick. She sucked in a deep breath to calm her heaving stomach, but it didn't help much. She'd been too young and naïve to comprehend what Miss Cole had been referring to, but now she understood very clearly.

"Well, we're all done now. Good day to you, Miss Besson," Charlotte said, raising her voice slightly as a new customer was brought back for a fitting. She wanted Madeline to leave, which was understandable. Telling her about Miss Cole was a breach of etiquette, which would have been treated with the utmost severity if Mrs. Bonnard ever got wind of it. Charlotte had taken a great risk in telling Madeline.

"Thank you, Miss Charlotte," Madeline said. "You've been very helpful. I look forward to wearing my new gown." She laid a hand on Charlotte's arm, her eyes telling the young woman that she would never betray what she'd done. "I'm grateful."

Charlotte gave a slight nod and hurried away, taking the gown with her to be folded and stored in a box with tissue paper so Madeline could take it home.

Madeline stood stock-still for a moment. She needed to get her feelings under control before going to find Sybil in the parlor, and her reflection in the mirror stared back at her with wide, startled eyes as if she'd just seen a ghost. Perhaps she had. Paula Cole had already been a ghost the last time Madeline saw her. No wonder she'd sounded so bitter. She'd been carrying the child of a man who could no longer make a respectable woman of her. Charles Besson would have married Paula Cole in a heartbeat had he known. But Madeline's father was gone, as was his mistress and their baby—Madeline's brother or sister.

She forced a smile onto her face as she stepped out of the fitting room. Sybil would be waiting for her, and George was supposed to join them directly after the fitting. After lunch, they planned to visit several more shops to purchase new gloves and silk stockings, and order a bonnet to be ready in time for Christmas. Madeline had looked forward to this outing for weeks, but now she only wanted to return to the plantation and hide in her room where she could grieve for Paula Cole and her baby in private. The food tasted like ashes in her mouth, and she could barely recall which bonnet she'd agreed to in the end. Madeline was relieved when it was finally time to return home, and sat quietly all the way back to the plantation, lost in her own thoughts despite George's valiant efforts to draw her out.

"Let her be, George," Sybil said irritably in response to George's chatter. "Madeline's tired, and she's had too much champagne."

George cast a worried look toward Madeline, but didn't argue. He remained silent for the rest of the ride, his gaze averted from her.

Madeline went directly to her room, glad to finally be on her own. She undressed with Cissy's help, got into her dressing gown and lay on the bed, book in hand, but she couldn't focus on reading, not after what she'd learned. She closed her eyes instead and allowed the tears to fall, crying not only for Miss Cole and her child, but for herself as well.

She barely noticed when the door opened and Mammy slipped into the room. She held a small paper-wrapped package and approached Madeline hesitantly.

"Miss Madeline, I wanted to give you a small token to mark the day."

Madeline nodded, unwrapped the package and took out a cotton handkerchief, beautifully embroidered with vines and pink flowers.

"I asked Cissy for some colored thread," Mammy said. "I hope you likes it."

"Thank you, Mammy. It's very pretty," Madeline replied. A year ago she would have been delighted with the gift, but no amount of kindness could rekindle the affection Madeline had once felt for her nurse. "It was kind of you to remember my birthday."

"Like I could ever forget," Mammy replied. "I was there the day you was born. I helped bring you into this world, and I was the first person to hold you."

Madeline felt a pang of sadness at Mammy's words. They had loved each other once. Why had she lied? Why had she withheld so much?

"Well, I won't keep you. You enjoy your evening, Maddy."

Mammy rushed off, leaving Madeline feeling even more forlorn. How different life had been only a year ago. Her father had been gone for four months, but she felt as if she'd aged a decade since his death.

Chapter 33

May 2014

New Orleans, Louisiana

Quinn fled the main salon and stepped out on deck, eager for a breath of fresh air. The dusky sky twinkled with countless stars and the moon hung unusually low, its glowing belly grazing the dark outline of the treetops in the distance. The banks of the Mississippi slid by as the *Natchez* cruised past the well-developed shores of the river. There were other boats nearby, but the massive steamboat dwarfed them and made them look like children's toys bobbing along on the waves it created.

Jazz music floated from the main salon and several other guests stepped out on deck for a breath of air or a stealthy cigarette. Snatches of conversation and laughter erupted every time the door opened, and everyone who came out of the salon made a passing comment to Quinn, since the guest of honor couldn't be ignored. Quinn didn't know any of them, but she smiled in greeting when her grandmother came out on deck with her nurse. Seth had made sure his mother could attend the party, and hired a nurse to look after her for the evening.

"Good evening, dear." Rae returned Quinn's smile. "It's nice to see you again."

"I'm so glad you're here," Quinn said, taking the older woman's hand. She didn't know anyone else at the party besides Seth, Brett, and Dolores. And Brett had introduced her to his mum.

"Oh, me too. I can't remember the last time I've been to a party. And Seth knows how to throw a party," Rae added. "I am looking forward to dinner. They serve slop not fit for pigs at that nursing home. Were you the one who made the arrangements?"

"No, Seth took care of everything."

Rae looked confused. "But aren't you his secretary? He always speaks so highly of you. I told him he shouldn't hire such pretty young girls, especially not while his wife is pregnant. It makes her feel insecure. She's having a boy," she confided. "Kathy wants to name him Brett, but Seth is trying to talk her into naming the baby Seth Junior. I prefer Brett myself. Everyone should have their own name. Don't you think?"

"Yes," Quinn muttered. She wasn't surprised her grandmother didn't remember her, given her diagnosis, but it made Quinn feel sad. She might never see the old woman again, and it would have been nice to share this moment with her.

"Well, you enjoy the party." Rae turned to her nurse. "Seth is so good to his staff," she said as they walked away. "Probably a lot more generous than he should be. That young woman should be working, not behaving as if she were a guest."

Quinn looked around, desperate for a more private spot where she wouldn't be quite so noticeable or feel so vulnerable. She needed a moment to compose herself before going back inside. She didn't want to ruin the evening for Seth. He'd pulled out all the stops with the party. The food was superb, the music quickened the pulse like a shot of caffeine, and the dozens of guests he had invited were all friends, business associates, and relations of the proud father.

Quinn had had every intention of blending into the background, but Seth had made that impossible. Once the *Natchez* had pulled away from the dock and everyone got comfortable and made at least one trip to the open bar, Seth had called for silence and beckoned for Quinn to join him on the small stage set up for the band. He smiled at her warmly and took her hand, as if she were a little girl.

"Good evening, everyone," Seth had said, beaming like a lighthouse at the assembled guests. "I'm not going to bore you all with long speeches or flowery toasts. I just want to raise a glass to

243

by beautiful girl, Quinn. I thought I had a pretty good life until this amazing woman walked into it and showed me exactly what I was missing. I thank God that she found me, and I couldn't be prouder of the daughter I didn't even know I had. And not only is she beautiful, brilliant, and successful, she's going to make me a grandfather. I love you, kiddo."

Seth leaned in and planted a kiss on Quinn's flaming cheek. She hadn't told Seth about the pregnancy, but Brett must have spilled the beans after she unwittingly told him her news. It was silly to feel so upset about her personal business being made public when anyone who looked at her closely could probably see the gentle swell of her belly beneath the flowing skirt of her dress, but Quinn felt as if she were standing under a huge spotlight, stark naked in front of all the guests.

Seth downed his champagne and motioned for the waiter to refill his glass. "And a mineral water for the mommy-to-be," he'd added, noting that Quinn's glass was empty.

"I just need some air," Quinn said as she slipped her hand out of Seth's grasp. Seth looked like he might follow, but became distracted by some friends who came approached congratulate him.

"Quinn, are you all right?" a voice broke into Quinn's reverie.

Kathy, Seth's ex-wife, leaned on the rail next to her, her eyes full of concern. "You looked very flushed in there."

"Just a little embarrassed, that's all," Quinn replied. "I'm not used to parties thrown in my honor."

"Who is?" Kathy laughed. Her long blond hair moved in the breeze and she wrapped a shawl closer about her shoulders, but her dark eyes never left Quinn's face. "You were flushed before Seth made the toast. Do you mind?" she asked as she reached for Quinn's wrist. She stood perfectly still, her head cocked to the side as she took Quinn's pulse. "Your pulse is very rapid. Has anything been bothering you?"

"I've had a headache for the past few days, and my ankles are a bit swollen, but I think that's just from the humidity. I'm also rather tired," Quinn admitted.

She'd been on her feet for the past several days with Jason, traipsing all over the plantation and its outbuildings, including the sugar mill, which was within walking distance, but still a trek from the main house, and covering nearly every inch of the French Quarter. They had also spent a day sailing down the bayou in a hired canoe. The boat trip hadn't been strenuous, but Quinn had felt a growing sense of unease as they drifted deeper into the swamp. When she'd begun to feel oddly claustrophobic, she asked Jason if they could turn around and return to New Orleans.

"How far along are you?" Kathy asked.

"Nearly twenty weeks."

Kathy nodded. "Are you sleeping?"

"Not well. I've had difficulty adjusting to the time change for some reason."

"Have you felt movement yet?"

"No," Quinn confessed. She hadn't meant to crumple in front of Kathy, but sudden tears slid down her cheeks. "I think there might be something wrong," she wailed. "I can't feel the baby."

Kathy wrapped Quinn in a warm hug and patted her back as though she were a colicky baby. "Have you had any spotting or full-on bleeding?"

Quinn shook her head.

"Quinn, I have a friend who's an obstetrician. Do you mind if I give her a call? There's no cause for panic, but I'd like her to have a look at you, just as a precaution."

"All right," Quinn replied, still sniffling. "I want Gabe," she said, sounding like a child desperate for the comforting presence of a parent.

"Have you spoken to him?"

"I've had a text, but I can't seem to reach him in person."

"Nothing to worry about, I'm sure. Just the time difference and all that. Here, let me call Annette." Kathy made a brief call and turned to Quinn with a reassuring smile. "Annette is on call tonight at the Tulane Medical Center. She'll meet us there after the party."

"Maybe we should see her tomorrow," Quinn suggested.

"I'd rather not wait. Now, let's go back inside. When did you last eat?"

"I had a few canapes when we first boarded."

"Let's get you something to eat, and another mineral water. You must stay hydrated, but don't drink anything alcoholic. And try to enjoy the party, Quinn," Kathy said with a smile. "I promise you, if there was any urgency, I'd have Seth turning this boat around and an ambulance standing by. Everything will be all right. Okay?"

"Okay," Quinn said, feeling marginally better. She was hungry, and needed to sit down.

Kathy took Quinn's arm and led her back inside and over to a table where Seth was sitting with Brett. The dinner was buffet-style, since Seth didn't want his guests to be limited to just one delicacy, and Seth and Brett already had full plates.

"Seth, get Quinn something to eat. Nothing too spicy," Kathy said, her tone brooking no argument. "And Brett, ask one of the waiters for a bottle of mineral water and a glass of ice."

"Is everything all right?" Seth demanded, his protective paternal instincts kicking in.

"Everything is just fine. Quinn's feeling a little lightheaded. It's not uncommon in pregnant women." Kathy took a seat next to Quinn and patted her hand. "You'll feel much better once you've eaten. In fact, you'll feel well enough to dance with Seth. I know he's been looking forward to having a dance with you since he won't get to have a father/daughter dance at your wedding."

"I wish I could invite him, but…"

"It's complicated. I know. My mom remarried when I was two. Both my dads were at my wedding and both wanted to walk me down the aisle and have the father/daughter dance with me," Kathy said, smiling at the memory.

"So, what did you do?"

"I had both of them walk me down, and then my stepdad cut in halfway through the dance. It made them happy and kept the peace."

"I think it might be more complicated than that, given my birth parents' history."

"Yes, Seth told me. Don't worry about him. He's a big boy. It's your big day and you should do whatever you're comfortable with," Kathy advised. "To be honest, if I had to do it all over again, I would talk Seth into running off to the Caribbean and getting married on some beautiful beach. Big weddings are overrated."

"So you would still have married Seth?" Quinn asked, smiling at Kathy.

Kathy laughed, as though realizing what she'd said. "You know, I would. But I would have done things differently, and I'm sure so would he. We were happy for a long time, until we weren't. I wouldn't have been so selfish about having more kids. Seth begged me to have another baby, but I refused. My career came first, and I paid the price with my marriage. But hindsight is twenty-twenty, as they say."

"So I hear," Quinn agreed, making a mental note never to start taking Gabe for granted or ignoring his needs. If he wanted to have more children, she'd never deny him, unless he planned to have enough kids to start his own football team.

**

"I'm coming with you," Seth announced once they disembarked the *Natchez* and Kathy informed him she was taking Quinn to see her friend.

"There's really no need, Seth. We'll be just fine, and I'll see Quinn back to her hotel," Kathy said.

"But I'm worried," Seth persisted.

"And I will text you as soon as I know anything," Kathy replied firmly. "Now, take Brett home. He doesn't have a ride. I'll talk to you later."

Seth looked like a dejected puppy, but didn't argue. He kissed Quinn's cheek and went in search of Brett, who was chatting up some girls who'd been on the cruise with their parents. Kathy got her car and drove Quinn the short distance to the medical center.

"Page Dr. Glahn, please," Kathy told the woman at reception.

A few minutes later, a slight woman with a pixie cut and fashionable specs came down to reception. She smiled at Quinn and held out her hand. "Annette Glahn. It's a pleasure to meet you. How was the party?" she asked conversationally as they got into the elevator.

"Oh, you know, typical Seth," Kathy replied with a chuckle. "Always throwing money around and showing up his friends. He did seem genuinely happy though. I haven't seen him like that in a long time. Quinn has brought out his emotional side, something Brett was never able to do."

"The father/daughter dynamic is always different," Dr. Glahn replied. "Men want sons, but dote on daughters. My dad was hard on my brothers, but I could do no wrong in his eyes," she added with an impish grin. "I'm in my forties, but I'm still his baby girl. How is it for you, Quinn, meeting your father at this stage of your life?" the doctor asked as she led them to a vacant examining room.

"It's a bit strange, but I'm glad to have the chance to get to know my father after all these years."

Dr. Glahn patted the examination table, inviting Quinn to sit. She chatted amiably while she took Quinn's blood pressure, listened to her heart and lungs, and palpated her stomach.

"Fill this for me please," she said, handing Quinn a plastic cup. "I need to check for protein in your urine."

Quinn did as she was told and returned to the room. She hadn't noticed any signs of alarm in the doctor, and began to relax. Maybe she was just being a worrywart.

"Have you had a sonogram recently?" the doctor asked.

"I had a scan about a month ago," Quinn replied. "Everything was fine then," she added, her apprehension returning.

"Everything looks fine now as well, but we can do a sonogram just to put your mind at rest. Lift up your dress for me."

The doctor squirted some clear gel onto Quinn's stomach and sat next to her, probe in hand. She turned the screen toward Quinn and began to move the probe around gently on her stomach. Quinn exhaled in relief when she heard the whoosh of the baby's heartbeat.

"Aha, there we are!" Dr. Glahn exclaimed when the fetus appeared on the screen.

Quinn could clearly see the baby. Its legs were bent at the knees and one foot was slightly raised. The baby appeared to be

249

sucking its thumb. "What is it doing?" she asked as she stared at the screen, unable to look away.

"Just chilling," the doctor replied with a smile. "Would you like to know the sex?"

"Yes," Quinn said, then quickly backtracked. "No. Not without Gabe."

"Okay, I'll keep mum then. The baby looks healthy and is developing normally, so relax, Mommy."

Quinn wiped off the gel and pulled down her dress before swinging her legs off the table.

"Just one thing before you go," Dr. Glahn said as she turned off the sonogram machine. "Headaches, swollen ankles, and elevated blood pressure can be just that, but they can also be a sign of preeclampsia. The onset is usually later on in the pregnancy, but I think you should mention these symptoms to your doctor at your next checkup. If the headaches persist and the swelling gets worse, don't wait; see someone immediately."

"How high is my blood pressure?" Quinn asked.

"It's slightly elevated, but not enough to be of concern. Yet. Stay off the caffeine, lower your sodium intake, and drink more water. It will help with the swelling as well. And it's all right to take over-the-counter medicine for the headache. You don't need to suffer."

"I'm not familiar with American medicine," Quinn confessed.

"Tylenol should be fine. Here, I have some one-dose packets. Keep them in your purse."

"Thank you, Dr. Glahn."

"Oh, it was my pleasure. I know how anxious first-time moms can be. And it's especially worrying when you're in a foreign country and don't have a doctor you feel comfortable with. When are you returning home?"

"By the end of next week," Quinn replied as she slipped on her shoes and reached for her bag. "I'm a bit homesick."

"That's understandable. I hope you'll visit us again."

Quinn nodded. She hadn't thought of returning to Louisiana, but now that she had family here, it was a definite possibility.

Dr. Glahn walked Quinn and Kathy to the elevator and bid them goodnight. "I'd love to stay and chat, but I have a patient in labor," she said. "She's getting close."

"Feel better?" Kathy asked as the elevator doors closed on Dr. Glahn.

"Yes. Thank you so much, Kathy. Where do I pay?"

"You don't need to pay. Annette saw you as a favor to me. I'm just glad all is well with the little one. Where to?" Kathy asked as they got into the car.

"To the hotel, please. I'm tired."

"Get some rest. You look like you need it. And track down that man of yours and tell him his baby is fine."

Chapter 34

December 1858

Arabella Plantation, Louisiana

The Christmas ball was wonderful, filled with music, dancing, and the type of male admiration Madeline had never experienced in her young life. George had warned her ahead of time that he would only partner her once, leaving her free to dance with all the other young men at the party. She waltzed with Gilbert at least three times, and two other young men begged for dance after dance, but had to be rejected after two turns about the floor in favor of other partners. Madeline didn't enjoy dancing with the older gentlemen, like Mr. Montlake, who claimed her for a polka, but it would have been churlish to refuse, so she put on a smiling face and did her duty to the host. He reeked of brandy and tobacco. Normally, Mr. Montlake chewed his tobacco, but having been forbidden by his wife to indulge in the disgusting habit at the ball, he smoked cigar after cigar as the night wore on.

George danced with all the ladies, young and old, and paid Madeline exactly the amount of attention appropriate to bestow on a young female cousin. She didn't mind. He had given her a beautiful cameo locket for Christmas, saying it was also for her birthday, which he'd unwittingly missed.

He'd chastised her for not telling him and pretended to be angry with her until Madeline kissed away his scowl and got him to smile at her once again. George fastened the locket around her neck and she spent several joyful moments admiring herself in the mirror. The cameo was suspended on a thin gold chain and depicted the profile of a young woman on a shell-pink background.

"When I saw it, it reminded me of you," George said, kissing Madeline's neck and pulling her away from the mirror. "But she doesn't do you justice. You are much more beautiful."

"Why?" she asked. The woman in the cameo had perfect features and flowing hair. How could Madeline be more beautiful than her?

"Because you are real," George replied with a casual shrug, as if the answer should have been obvious.

"I will wear it always," Madeline promised, kissing his cheek. "May I have a photograph of you to put inside?"

"Are you sure you should carry a photograph of your cousin so close to your heart?" George joked. "Poor Gilbert might get jealous."

"I don't care about Gilbert." Madeline pouted. "Why do you keep mentioning him?"

"Because maybe I'm the one who is jealous."

"What reason would you have to be jealous?"

"I'm jealous because he's free to marry you, and I'm not," George replied, his expression growing serious. "You might tire of waiting for me."

"Don't be silly, George. You're such a fuddy-duddy sometimes," Madeline said, laughing. "I love you. I will wait for you forever, if that's what it takes."

"Forever is a long time, Maddy, especially when you're sixteen."

When Cissy arrived to help Madeline dress for the ball, she ejected George from the room.

"You must leave now, Mr. George," Cissy said sternly, brandishing the hair tongs. "I've much to do. Joe has polished your

253

shoes and brushed down your coat. I'll come by and tie your cravat for you after I'm finished with Miss Madeline."

George gave Cissy a thoughtful look. "Perhaps I should have my hair curled. What say you, Madeline?" he asked, flipping his hair and batting his eyelashes.

Madeline and Cissy both giggled. "Go on with you," Cissy said, "or I'll make you look like that fellow in the alcove."

The bust in the alcove was of some Roman god whose hair was so curly it looked as if he were wearing his brain outside his skull. George gave the two women a look of mock horror and departed for his dressing room, where he would likely read the paper and smoke a cigar until it was time for him to don his suit. He didn't require two hours of preparation.

A joyful smile stretched across Madeline's face as she slowly woke the next morning. She stretched luxuriously. The sun was already riding high in the sky, but she'd gone to bed just as the first rays of the morning sun lit up the wintery sky, so it was all right to sleep in.

She thought back to her conversation with George as she reverently touched the locket. Warm from her body, it felt like a living thing rather than a piece of jewelry. She found it endearing that George worried about losing her. She'd wait as long as it took for him to extricate himself from his marriage. He had assured Madeline that Amelia wouldn't object, so there was nothing to worry about.

"Planning on getting up today, Miss Madeline?" Cissy asked as she swept into the room. "'Tis past noon, and Mrs. Besson would like a word."

Madeline reluctantly got out of bed and walked over to the dressing table. She laughed out loud when she caught sight of herself. She looked like a wild woman with her hair as unruly as a lion's mane and her face flushed and slightly puffy from all the punch she'd enjoyed the night before.

Cissy shook her head in dismay as she picked up the brush and motioned for Madeline to sit down. "This will take some doing," Cissy said as she ran the bristles through the first tangled section of hair.

"Ow, that hurts," Madeline complained.

"Should have brushed and plaited it before going to bed," Cissy replied, unfazed. "Now sit still."

Madeline complied and tried not to yelp every time Cissy combed out a particularly nasty tangle. The only thing that made Cissy's ministrations bearable was that Bette brought Madeline a cup of coffee and a buttered roll fresh from the oven.

"I thought you might be hungry," Bette said. She exchanged loaded looks with Cissy and left.

Madeline took a sip of coffee and sighed gratefully. It was strong and hot and made her feel less muddle-headed.

Half an hour later, Madeline was finally ready to face the world—and her grandmother. Sybil had seemed pleased with her last night, watching her as she danced with Gilbert and smiling at Mrs. Montlake as she commented on the waltzing pair. She'd even discussed the ball with Madeline in the carriage on the way back, while George stared out the window, half asleep after all the cognac and brandy he'd consumed.

Madeline knocked on the door and entered Sybil's private parlor. She'd never been in there, and the feminine loveliness of the room surprised her. Sybil was all sharp angles and harsh words, but the room was nothing like its occupant. It was charming, with rosewood furniture upholstered in pale yellow silk and matching drapes. Several competent landscapes hung on the walls and a daguerreotype of George and Amelia on their wedding day held pride of place in a heavy silver frame. Sybil sat in an armchair by the hearth, a pot of coffee on a low table at her side. There were two cups, which Madeline found encouraging.

"Good morning, Grandmother. I hope you slept well," she said, hoping to recapture the unexpected camaraderie of last night.

Sybil took a sip of coffee and set the cup down before acknowledging Madeline's greeting with a nod. Madeline expected her grandmother to invite her to sit down and have a cup of coffee with her, but Sybil didn't offer the seat or the coffee. She looked Madeline up and down instead, displeasure curling her lip into a snarl. Madeline took an involuntary step back, wondering if she'd done something to offend Sybil without realizing it.

"Cissy informs me that you haven't bled in three months."

Madeline's cheeks heated. Menstruation was not something she ever discussed with anyone. It had been Mammy who had explained things to her when she got the curse at the age of twelve, and Mammy who showed her how to care for herself and protect her clothes. Cissy left the necessary supplies in a bedside table, and replenished them when they ran low, but never asked Madeline about her courses or made any mention of the fact that she hadn't used up the cotton napkins Cissy left for her.

"Do you understand what that means?" Sybil demanded.

"Am I ill?" Madeline croaked, suddenly frightened. She hadn't given it much thought, glad not to have to deal with nearly a week of bleeding and cramping every month. It was a relief, especially since George could come to her any time.

"You're not ill; you're pregnant," Sybil announced, her eyes boring into Madeline.

"But I can't be. I'm-I'm not married," she stammered.

"Has no one ever explained these matters to you, you foolish child?"

"No," Madeline muttered.

256

Something like pity moved behind Sybil's eyes, but she gave Madeline no quarter and continued her interrogation. "Have you not been indulging in sin with my grandson for months? Oh, did you think I don't know?" she asked, correctly reading Madeline's expression of shock.

Madeline hung her head, too ashamed to look at her grandmother.

"You took advantage of his bereaved state and lured him into your bed as soon as Amelia left. He was heartbroken, and you preyed on his vulnerability," Sybil accused.

"It wasn't like that," Madeline interjected, stunned. "It was George…"

"Be silent!" Sybil roared. "How dare you argue with me when you've disgraced this family, you little trollop. I suppose I never should have expected anything better from you, given your parentage. Measures will have to be taken to protect your reputation, and ours."

"What measures?" Trembling with fear and shame, Madeline was shocked to the core to learn what had happened to her without her knowledge or understanding. Surely George must have known about the possible consequences of his actions. He was a married man, and many years her senior. Madeline covered her face with her hands and hunched over, as if in pain. Tears slid between her fingers and ran down her hands. She didn't even have a handkerchief in her pocket, a small oversight that only added to her misery.

Sybil handed her one and pushed her into a chair. "Clean yourself up," she said, not without sympathy.

Madeline tried to get hold of herself, but the tears wouldn't stop falling. She was so woefully uninformed about the whole process that the magnitude of what had happened to her was too much to bear. Only an hour ago, she had been basking in the afterglow of her first ball, and now she was here, her future uncertain and her grandmother, whose approval she'd tried so hard to win, ashamed and disgusted by her.

"I'm sorry," Madeline wailed. "I didn't know this could happen."

"No, I don't suppose you did," Sybil replied. "Stop sniveling, Madeline. You're not the first or the last foolish girl to fall pregnant before marriage. Of course, the fact that George is already married does complicate matters. Had this child been Gilbert's, we'd have had you married before the end of the year. There'd be gossip, of course, but eventually, everyone would tire of your disgrace and move on to something else."

"What's going to happen?" Madeline asked, her pleading eyes on her grandmother. Sybil was so strong, so capable. She'd have the answers.

She had opened her mouth to reply when Cissy ushered Mammy into the room. Mammy looked ashen, her eyes wide with apprehension.

"Take Madeline to my bedroom and examine her," Sybil ordered Mammy. "I need to know how far gone she is."

Mammy looked as if someone had just upended a bucket of ice water over her head. Her gaze flew to Madeline's face, but Madeline couldn't bear to meet her shocked gaze and stared at her hands folded demurely in her lap, clutching the soiled handkerchief.

"Did you hear me?" Sybil demanded. "You delivered half the children on this plantation in your time, so I must rely on your knowledge. I can hardly call Dr. Holbrook, given the circumstances."

"Yes, madam," Mammy replied. "Right away."

Mammy took Madeline by the arm and led her into Sybil's bedroom. Madeline didn't notice anything except the sea-green bed hangings, which made her feel like she was drowning. She felt sick to her stomach, and terrified of what this examination would yield.

"Lie back, child," Mammy said softly.

Madeline obediently lay on the bed and allowed Mammy to push up her skirts and pull down her pantaloons. She was embarrassed, but Mammy seemed very matter-of-fact and talked to her softly, telling her to relax. Madeline cried out as Mammy slid her fingers inside her and felt around before removing her hand and palpating Madeline's stomach. Mammy's eyes were moist with tears and her hand shook as she wiped it on a towel after completing the examination and they both walked back into the parlor.

"Well?" Sybil demanded.

"'Bout three months gone," Mammy said.

Sybil nodded and turned to look at Madeline. "You will begin to show soon, and I won't have scandal tainting this family. Not again. You two will go to a cabin in the bayou and remain there until the child is born. Everyone will be told that you went to visit with your mother's relations in Charleston."

"My mother had relations?" Madeline asked, brightening.

"No, you dimwit, that's just an explanation for your absence. Your Mammy will deliver the child. She's good at that," Sybil added bitterly.

"What will become of it?" Madeline asked, realizing for the first time that an actual living child would be the result of this catastrophe.

"It will be taken from you and given to George and Amelia to raise as their own. And you will not breathe a word of it to anyone."

"I need to speak to George," Madeline cried.

"George is gone."

"Gone where?" She felt desperate now, cornered by this cold woman who couldn't spare Madeline an ounce of compassion in her hour of need.

"George has gone to fetch his wife home, and beg for her forgiveness. He will be back after the New Year, by which time you'll be long gone, off to South Carolina to visit with your loving kin," Sybil added, her tone dripping with sarcasm and chilling Madeline's blood.

"And what will happen to me after the baby is born? Will I be allowed to come back?" Madeline asked. Would she be expected to remain in this house with George and Amelia, and her baby? If she had felt lonely and unwelcome before, this would be so much worse. George would denounce her, Amelia would despise her, and Sybil would never truly forgive her for her fall from grace. The thought of living that way brought fresh tears to Madeline's eyes.

"Gilbert Montlake is smitten with you. A month after you give birth, your engagement will be announced and you will marry shortly thereafter. You will leave this house and never return. Do you understand? You will never be alone with George again, and you will never see your child, except perhaps on social occasions. Thankfully, Gilbert is too innocent to suspect what you've been up to, and if you're convincing on your wedding night, this episode need never come up again."

"But I don't want to marry Gilbert," Madeline protested. "I don't love him."

Sybil looked like she was about to chastise Madeline for her stubbornness, but seemed to reconsider. She leaned back against the chair with a sigh and allowed her shoulders to relax, as if she were tired.

"We'll discuss the marriage at a later date. Gilbert might lose interest in you while you're gone and meet someone he likes better. Life can be unpredictable that way. Don't distress yourself. It's not good for the child, and the baby should be your first priority right now. You will be quite comfortable at the cabin, and Joe will bring you supplies every week. It will all be all right, Madeline." Sybil sounded almost maternal. Her voice had softened and her face relaxed into something resembling concern. "You just look after yourself. This baby is precious to us all. He's the next generation."

"It might be a girl," Madeline retorted, just to be defiant.

"It might, but she'll still be a Besson, which is what matters. Now, go back to your room and get some rest. You look ill." Having dismissed Madeline, Sybil turned her attention to Mammy. "You will go to the cabin today," she said, her voice edged with steel again. "It must be prepared for habitation, since it hasn't been used for some time."

The look that passed between the two women could have frozen Lake Pontchartrain over, but Madeline hardly noticed. She felt too shaken and dejected to care.

"Take what you need and tell no one," Sybil continued. "Just say you're accompanying Madeline to South Carolina. Joe will bring her by the end of the week. Now, get out. Both of you."

"Mammy," Madeline began once they were alone in the hallway, but Mammy shook her head in dismay and walked away, leaving Madeline completely alone.

Chapter 35

May 2014

London, England

Gabe experienced a flutter of nervousness when he finally heard Quinn's voice. He felt guilty as hell for avoiding her calls these past few days, but every time he picked up the phone to call her, he wound up putting it down again, unable to tell her what had been going on for fear of bursting into tears like a child. After the initial shock, the death of his father had hit him like a steam train, and he'd needed a few days to lick his wounds. He was still at the start of the grieving process, but at least now he could be honest with Quinn without upsetting her more than necessary and making her worry about him. There were other things he needed to discuss with her, and he wished he could put off that conversation forever. He'd turned her life upside down when he discovered the existence of a daughter he never knew he had, and now, with his father gone, he had to ask Quinn to deal with yet another life-altering situation.

"Where in blazes have you been?" Quinn demanded. She was understandably angry, but Gabe also heard relief in her voice. "Are you all right, Gabe? I was so worried."

"I'm sorry," Gabe replied. "I tried to call. Several times, in fact, but I just couldn't seem to find the strength to tell you the news." He tried to sound calm, but the tremor in his voice was unmistakable.

"Gabe, for God's sake, just tell me what's wrong. You're scaring me. Is Emma all right?"

Gabe cursed himself for a fool. He hadn't wanted to upset her and now she was close to tears. "Yes, Emma is fine. Quinn, my father suffered a fatal heart attack. We buried him on Friday."

Gabe had been expecting words of sympathy, but what he got instead was a stunned silence. He could hear a sharp intake of breath as Quinn processed the news.

"Quinn?"

"You buried him on Friday?" she finally asked.

"Yes."

"And you didn't think to call me? You didn't think I would get on the next flight home to be there to pay my respects to your father, whom I'd known for years and cared about? You didn't think I should be by your side to support you and your mother in your loss?" Quinn demanded, her voice trembling with hurt and disbelief.

She sounded so wounded that for a moment Gabe actually forgot all about his own grief and focused on Quinn's instead. All his reasons for not calling her seemed ridiculous and he now realized how callous he'd been to leave her out. He'd wanted to protect her, but instead had made her feel like an outsider, whose presence was optional rather than as necessary to him as the air he breathed.

"Quinn, I'm so sorry," Gabe pleaded. "I wasn't thinking. It all happened so quickly. One minute the doctor said he was on the mend, and the next he was gone. We came to the hospital to find his bed empty. He was already at the mortuary, lying on a slab, like a piece of meat. They referred to him as 'the body.'" Gabe nearly choked when he uttered the words. He hadn't realized how profoundly the term had affected him. "We weren't there when he passed. He was all alone."

Gabe angrily wiped away the tears that snaked down his cheeks. He'd promised himself that he'd remain in control, but here he was, blubbering like an idiot.

"Oh, Gabe," Quinn breathed, her own anger forgotten. "I'm so sorry. I wish I'd been there for you. I can't begin to imagine how devastated you must have been."

"I was always closer to my mother," Gabe confessed. "I kept my father at arm's length. He was so old-fashioned and set in his ways. I didn't think he could ever truly understand me or see my point of view, but now that he's gone, I realize how unfair I was. It would destroy me if Emma felt that way about me. I wronged him, Quinn, and now it's too late to make amends."

"Gabe, your father loved you, and he knew that you loved him. He wasn't an easy man to talk to, and yes, he was set in his ways, but he was raised during a different time, when people weren't as open about their feelings and needs. He didn't parent you the way you parent Emma, but then again, most people of his generation didn't."

Gabe used the back of his hand to rub at his eyes. "No, I don't suppose he did. He never hugged me or kissed me when I was a child. He thought it inappropriate. Instead, he'd pat me on the head, or clap me on the shoulder and call me a 'good lad.' He was proud of me, though. He told my mother."

"Of course he was proud of you. You are the perfect son."

"Hardly. I had a child out of wedlock with a woman I barely knew. In my father's eyes, that was shameful," Gabe said softly.

"Gabe, your father lit up like a Christmas tree whenever Emma walked into the room. He doted on her, and she made his final months so much more rewarding. She might not have come about in the way your father expected, but she was a gift, and he treated her as such."

"He was worried about our baby being born a bastard," Gabe confessed, cringing at the word.

"Was he really?" Quinn asked. She sounded incredulous. "We will get married eventually, but now it won't be next month. We'll have to wait until after the baby is born, maybe even until next year."

"Quinn, he would have wanted us to marry. That was part of the reason my mother wanted to have the funeral as quickly as possible. She wants the wedding to go on as planned."

"You can't be serious," Quinn replied. "You father died a few days ago, and your mother is in mourning. How can we possibly go on as if nothing has happened?"

"We can't, but maybe we can just go to a registry office. We can have a party later, after the baby is born."

Gabe heard Quinn's sigh of resignation. "If that's what you want, then that's what we will do."

"Would you be all right with that?" he asked.

"Yes," she said, sounding as if she'd just agreed to march to the guillotine.

"There's something else, love," Gabe said, bracing himself.

"Oh?"

Gabe sighed. There was no turning back now. "We might have to move to Berwick."

"What? Why?"

"My mum can't handle the house on her own, and she will go mad living there alone."

"Do you think she might agree to sell the place and move to some nice, modern flat in the heart of Berwick?" Quinn asked carefully.

"Not a chance." Gabe had suggested that exact same thing, but Phoebe was adamant about staying in her husband's ancestral home. "The de Rosels settled on that bit of land right after the Norman invasion and have remained there since. My mother would see it as the ultimate act of betrayal to sell the lot and move to some flat. She says it's my birthright, and she wants our son to be the next lord of the manor."

265

"Right." Quinn said. "But what about your job? And mine? What about our homes?"

"I can find another job. And we can keep my London flat, so you can stay there when you need to be in London. It's too small for a family anyway. We're bursting at the seams already, and once the baby comes…"

"Yes, I've thought of that," she conceded. They would have to move sooner rather than later.

"There are ten bedrooms at the manor house. Just think of how many children we can have," Gabe said, smiling at the possibility.

"Is that your invading ancestor speaking through you? You want to keep me barefoot and pregnant for the next decade?" Quinn joked.

"Hmm, the thought is strangely appealing," he replied, making her laugh.

"What about my house?" Quinn asked.

Gabe knew she loved her little converted chapel. It was her home, her sanctuary, the one place where she felt completely at peace, even when she was alone. "That's up to you, but you won't have much use for it once we move. The four of us can hardly fit into one room."

"In the Middle Ages, there'd be a dozen of us, and we'd have all our domestic animals living indoors with us," Quinn replied. Only a fellow historian would see the humor in that, and Gabe chuckled at the image that sprang to mind.

"We can try it out, but I don't think the reality would be nearly as 'glamorous' as the fantasy. So, you would consider moving?" he asked carefully. "Mum would love to help us with the children. It would give her something to do to keep her mind off Dad."

"Gabe, if we have to move to Berwick-upon-Tweed, then we will move. I wouldn't dream of forcing you to sell your 'ancestral stronghold.' Hey, do you think they buried any treasure or the bodies of their enemies on the property?"

"Anything is possible. They were a bloodthirsty lot. We can start digging anytime you like," Gabe promised, enjoying the banter. He felt lighter than he had in days, and it made him hope that in time, he would learn to live with his loss.

"That's what I like to hear. Imagine if I were marrying an accountant," Quinn quipped. "My life would be so dull."

"Good thing you're marrying a college administrator then. Imagine the adventures we shall have," Gabe replied, making her laugh. "If you prove yourself worthy, I might even trust you to file some budget reports."

"You're all heart, Dr. Russell."

"I am, and it belongs only to you," Gabe said simply. "Are you feeling well?"

"I've actually felt a bit off, so Kathy—that's Seth's ex-wife—took me to see a friend who is an obstetrician. She said all is well," Quinn assured him. "She did a scan and I saw our baby. It's so perfect, Gabe. I think it was waving at me. She asked if I wanted to know the sex."

"Did you find out?" Gabe asked, trying to keep the pang of hurt out of his voice.

"No, of course not. I wouldn't want to find out without you there."

"Thank you. I appreciate that. Can you forward me a picture of the scan?" he asked, desperate to feel a part of what Quinn was experiencing.

"Of course. It's a bit blurry, but you can see still it," she replied. "And you can't guess at the sex because it has its legs crossed, the little devil."

"I don't want to know the sex."

"Neither do I. Everyone says it's a boy anyway."

"Who's everyone?" Gabe asked. Only his mother had tried to guess the sex of the baby, as far as he knew.

"My grandmother," Quinn replied, her tone becoming heavier. "She has Alzheimer's. She was lucid the first time I met her, but couldn't remember me when she saw me again on Saturday."

"I'm sorry."

"It's all right. At least I got to speak to her once. It felt surreal, knowing I'm directly linked to this little old woman of whom I knew nothing my whole life. Even being with Seth is still strange."

"Quinn, when are you coming home?" Gabe hated the desperation in his voice, but he missed her the way an amputee missed a limb.

"I'd get on a flight tomorrow if it wasn't for Rhys," Quinn complained. "Jason forwarded the footage we shot, but Rhys has a few requests and wants us to get more coverage of the bayou and the slave quarters."

"How do you feel about the episode focusing on your family's past?"

Quinn was silent for a moment. "I'm not sure. On the one hand, I want to resurrect Madeline. I still don't know what became of her, but I'm pretty sure she didn't live happily ever after. On the other hand, it feels awfully personal. Even though I've just found out about this branch of the family and have no real connection to the South, I feel strangely responsible. It shames me that my American ancestors owned slaves."

"Quinn, during that time many Brits owned slaves as well. It was a different world, so you can't take their transgressions upon yourself. It's history, and it's up to you to tell it. That's what we do as historians."

"Easy for you to say. Your whole ancestral line is nauseatingly heroic," Quinn replied, only half-joking.

"Hardly. I have no doubt that my ancestors raped and pillaged with the best of them. That's what conquering armies did, after all."

"Yes, I suppose you're right. Look, I've got to go. Jason is picking me up in a few minutes and we're off to the swamp again. That place scares me. It's like entering some cursed kingdom that's been slumbering for hundreds of years, but it's not really asleep, just pretending, and waiting to pounce when you least expect it."

"I've never heard you speak this way about any other place."

"It's otherworldly, especially at twilight."

"Don't get all fanciful on me, Dr. Allenby. Just finish the assignment and come back to us. We miss you."

"I love you, and miss you. Give my love to Emma. I can't wait to see her."

"I will. I love you, Quinn."

Gabe disconnected the Bluetooth and fixed his eyes on the road. All in all, the conversation hadn't gone as badly as he'd feared. Quinn was well, if a little spooked and homesick, and not completely averse to moving up north. And the baby... Gabe couldn't wait to meet his child. Quinn had been hardly showing when she left, but he hadn't felt the baby move, so on some level, it still didn't feel quite real. He wished he'd been there for the scan and seen the little one with his own eyes.

A few more months. Be patient, Russell.

He pressed his foot on the gas pedal and the Jaguar roared into life. It was time to get his girl back.

Chapter 36

Quinn grabbed her handbag and sunglasses, remembering to slip a bottle of water into her bag before heading for the elevator. She'd been making a conscious effort to drink more fluids. She did feel better, and the headaches were not as severe, but a dull ache still hovered behind her eyes, ready to escalate if she allowed herself to get stressed or overly tired.

She rode the elevator to the ground floor of the hotel, hoping to have a cup of decaffeinated tea at the restaurant before leaving for the day. Perhaps Jason would join her when he arrived. She'd had breakfast in her room already, so she ordered a pot of tea and settled in to wait for Jason. He'd know to look for her here.

Her conversation with Gabe was still fresh in her mind, and truth be told, she was more than a little upset despite the brave face she'd put on for him. The fact that Gabe hadn't called her when Graham passed away rankled, even though she'd accepted his apology and understood his reasons, and the sudden prospect of moving to Northumberland didn't thrill her either. She understood Gabe's dilemma, and wanted to be there for Phoebe, but she liked being in London, and was just beginning to forge a relationship with Sylvia and Logan. She'd miss Jill too. Quinn popped into Jill's shop whenever she was near, but now she wouldn't see her cousin for months on end, possibly longer.

Quinn stirred sugar into her tea and took a sip. The tea was hot and strong, and just what she needed. As she lifted her head, her eyes fell on a familiar figure walking toward her table. She carefully set the cup down. Her hand was shaking and she felt a now-familiar flush spreading from her neck up toward her cheeks.

"May I join you?"

"What do you want?" Quinn asked warily. "I thought we'd finished our conversation."

271

"Quinn, I'm sorry. I didn't mean to upset you," Luke said as he sat down opposite her and signaled to the waiter. "I only wanted to talk to you, but things got out of hand. And then that man showed up."

"That man is my father."

"Yes, I gathered that. How on earth did you find him?"

"I found my biological mother first," Quinn replied. "Or, more accurately, she found me."

"Will you tell me about it?" Luke asked after ordering a cup of coffee. He leaned in closer and gazed into Quinn's eyes. "I know how much this means to you. You must be thrilled to finally have the answers you've been seeking."

She knew exactly what he was doing. She'd seen him do it countless times. He was trying to disarm her, to win her over with his interest and undivided attention. Did he really think that was all it would take to get her back?

"Luke, I'm meeting someone in a few minutes," Quinn said, implying he should leave, but he ignored the hint and added cream to his coffee, his movements relaxed and unhurried, as though there were nowhere else he'd rather be.

"Quinn, please give me a chance. Have dinner with me. We'll have a nice meal, talk, and maybe you'll forgive me just a little bit."

"I am not sure how I can say this in a way you'll understand. We're done. There'll be no dinners, no conversations, and no apologies. I bear you no grudge, and I wish you well. And I hope you can do the same for me."

"It's not as if you've never made mistakes," Luke replied. The casual posture was gone, replaced by a tensing of his shoulders and the tightening of his jaw.

Quinn instinctively leaned away from him, not wishing to engage.

"You drove me away," he hissed. "You always put your career first. You never had time for me."

"Then you should be glad to be rid of me," Quinn replied, gathering her things. "You are now free to find a woman who will make you the center of her universe. Goodbye, Luke. Please don't come here again."

Quinn was about to walk past Luke when he grabbed her arm. "Quinn, come on. You see what you do to me? You make me lose control because I care so much. Please sit down."

"Everything all right?" Jason asked as he approached the table. Normally, he looked like a big teddy bear, but at the moment, there was nothing cuddly about him.

"Let me guess. Your newfound brother?" Luke asked sarcastically. "Will he threaten to rough me up as well?"

"If the situation calls for it," Jason replied calmly.

"I'm ready, Jason. Let's go," Quinn said and turned away from Luke.

"Quinn!" he called after her, but she didn't turn around.

"Are you all right?" Jason asked as he held the truck door open for her and then climbed into the driver's seat.

"Perfectly. But thank you for coming to my rescue," she said with a smile.

"Damsels in distress are my particular specialty. Look, all jokes aside, if you're uncomfortable with that guy, just say the word."

"Thank you," Quinn said and put her hand on Jason's arm. "I think he got the message loud and clear."

Jason nodded and started the engine. "Off we go then. I hear the swamp calling."

Chapter 37

January 1859

Arabella Plantation, Louisiana

Madeline floated through the house like a ghost in the days following the Christmas ball. She was alive, but she no longer felt a part of the physical world. She was a shell, a husk of her former self, a gift box discarded after the present had been removed and enjoyed. George had forsaken her, and now she would be sent away, tucked away from prying eyes until her shame could be erased. George and Amelia would get a new beginning, while Madeline would be disposed of as soon as was decently possible. She supposed many girls would thank their lucky stars for a chance at a respectable marriage and a husband who cared for them, but the thought of marrying Gilbert left Madeline feeling even more desolate than the promise of exile.

Having experienced love with George, she couldn't begin to imagine having that type of intimacy with Gilbert. The thought of sharing his bed made her feel sick, and the idea of carrying his children brought the bitter taste of revulsion to her mouth. She wouldn't be the first woman to marry someone she didn't love, but perhaps it was easier if you had never loved, and had never known the kind of rapture she'd known with George. She supposed that deep down she had always known their liaison would end in disaster, but she was young and naïve, and most of all trusting. Had George truly cared for her, as he'd professed, or had he simply used her to fill a void left by the death of his child and the desertion of his wife? Perhaps he had wanted to get back at Amelia for leaving when he needed her more than ever. Madeline supposed that in time she'd know the answer. She would see George again sooner or later, and his behavior toward her would answer all her questions. But for now, she had to bide her time.

She had to endure a visit from the Montlakes the day before she was set to leave for the cabin, and having to pretend that everything was well took more out of her than she could have imagined. Sybil had informed Mrs. Montlake and Gilbert that Madeline would be leaving to visit her mother's family in Charleston, and Madeline had to deliver her carefully prepared story to divert suspicion from her sudden departure.

"May I write to you?" Gilbert asked as she walked him to the door.

"You may send your letters here," Sybil responded in Madeline's stead. "We will include them with our own."

"That's very kind of you," Mrs. Montlake said.

"I hope you'll not forget me and write back," Gilbert said. He looked like a dejected puppy, a state that Madeline had come to associate with him.

"Of course she'll write back," Sybil replied with a tinkling laugh. "What girl wouldn't wish to correspond with her young man?"

Gilbert's eyes lit up, his expression hopeful. "There are things I'd like to talk to you about when you return," he said softly. "But I will wait. Mother says there's a time for everything, and today isn't that time."

"No, today is not the time," Madeline agreed. It would never be the right time, but she could hardly say so in Sybil's hearing. All she wanted was to go back to her room and ask Cissy to loosen her corset. She could hardly breathe. Already her body had begun to change, and the tiny belly that protruded when she stood in front of the mirror in her camisole needed to be contained to avoid any suspicion.

Gilbert leaned in and planted a chaste kiss on Madeline's cheek. "I'll miss you, Madeline. Come back soon."

"Oh, she'll be back before you know it. Won't you, Madeline? By March, at the latest," Sybil promised. Of course, Madeline wouldn't be back by March, or even by April or May, but Sybil could hardly tell the Montlakes that Madeline wouldn't be returning until after she delivered her bastard. Some excuse would be made, and lies would be told.

Madeline smiled brightly as she said goodbye to the Montlakes and accepted their good wishes. She breathed a sigh of relief when they'd finally climbed into their carriage and could no longer see her face.

Sybil turned on her heel, ready to walk away. She'd hardly spoken to Madeline since the morning after the ball, addressing her only when the story needed to be worked out for the sake of the neighbors.

"I suppose you'll expect me to write to Gilbert," Madeline said to Sybil's back.

"You suppose correctly. Joe will pass on his letters, and you will respond. Your letters to him will be light and airy, full of trivial details and girlish observations. You must keep him on the hook, Madeline."

"Or what?"

"Or your future will be a lot dimmer than even you can imagine," Sybil replied and walked away, leaving Madeline standing alone in the foyer.

Madeline recalled the gaunt and pale face of Miss Cole when she last saw her a few months back. She'd become a shadow of her former self, a drudge who lived from payday to payday, dependent entirely on the whims and moods of her employer. Madeline sighed and trudged up the stairs to her bedroom. Some practical part of her brain told her it was never too late to become a seamstress or a governess, because once set on that path, there'd be no coming back, so despite her misgivings, she had to go along with Sybil's plan—for the time being.

277

Madeline glanced at the clock. It was nearly noon, and Joe would be taking her to the cabin in about an hour. He'd returned from the bayou yesterday evening, having delivered the last of the supplies, and informed her grandmother that all was in readiness. Mammy was awaiting Madeline's arrival. Madeline supposed she was ready to go.

She paced the length and breadth of her bedroom, and then wandered to the hallway, restless and filled with dread. Madeline wasn't sure what had made her go there, but she found herself in the nursery. It had been cleaned and prepared for the baby that never came, the crib polished to a shine, and soft cotton bedding embroidered with pink and blue flowers covered the tiny mattress. Bette had scrubbed the floor and cleaned the old toys that lined the wooden shelves. She'd dusted every nook and cranny, but now a fresh layer of dust covered all the surfaces, the nursery abandoned once more, patiently waiting for a child to fill it at last.

Would Madeline's baby occupy this nursery? Would Sybil summon one of the nursing mothers from the slave quarters and oust Madeline from her baby's life as soon as it was born, fearful of the love that would bind the child to its mother? Of course she would. This would be Amelia's baby, and it would crave Amelia's love.

Loneliness and desolation sweep over Madeline. How had she come to this impasse in her life? Only a few months ago she had been in New Orleans, happy with a father who loved her, and spoiled and indulged by Mammy and Tess. She'd still been a child, an innocent. She still felt innocent, despite the sin she'd committed and the unlawful love she'd made with another woman's husband. Deep down she'd known she was doing wrong, but had given in to her loneliness and desire to be loved. Mammy had often said that there's a price to pay for every moment of happiness, and now Madeline finally understood what she'd meant. She would be paying for her recklessness for years to come, maybe even for the rest of her life.

278

Madeline sank down onto a window seat. A polished wooden horse's head on a stick, the kind boys liked to play with and pretend they were riding a fearsome stallion, gleamed in the sunlight streaming through the window, its painted eyes staring straight at Madeline. She reached out and touched its brown mane made of yarn. It was shaggy and soft.

Madeline yanked her hand away in fright. She thought she saw two boys in front of her, fighting over the horse.

"Let me play. It's my turn," one of the boys whined.

"It's mine. I got it for my birthday."

"Why can't you share, Charles?" the younger boy cried.

The imagine faded, leaving Madeline wondering if she'd imagined the whole thing. She reached out and carefully touched the horse again, her fingers pressed to the sun-warmed wood. The boys reappeared. They were about six and eight, both dark-blond with light eyes and fair skin. Their matching outfits made them look even more alike.

"Leave me alone, Albert. I only just got it yesterday. You can play with it tomorrow. I promise," Charles replied, and held the horse out of his brother's reach. He straddled it and began to prance around the nursery, smiling slyly at his brother's disappointment.

Madeline yanked her hand away and slumped against the back of the seat, panting with shock. Was she imagining things or had she really just seen her father and his brother playing in their nursery? How was that possible?

She looked around. The room was silent, and dust motes floated peacefully in the shaft of light from the window. No one had occupied this room since George was a child, so why couldn't she see him? Madeline touched the horse again.

This time the boys appeared to be a little older, possibly eight and ten. The horse stood forgotten in the corner as they sat side-by-side at the table, an open book in front of them. A bearded and bespectacled middle-aged man stood before them, slate in hand, droning on in a voice reminiscent of boring church sermons that seemed to go on forever. He appeared to be teaching them arithmetic. Madeline couldn't help smiling when she noticed Albert elbowing Charles when the tutor wasn't looking and making him spill ink on his work. Charles kicked him back under the table, and a scuffle broke out.

"If you're not back in your seats in two seconds, I will tell your mother, and then you know exactly what will happen," the tutor said.

The boys froze in the act of pummeling each other and immediately slid back into their seats, eyes on their teacher.

"That's better. I would hate to see you two punished again. If I recall correctly, you couldn't sit for several days."

The boys nodded in unison, their eyes pleading with the tutor not to tell.

"Whoever solves this problem first, and correctly, will have an extra ten minutes to play after lunch."

The boys bent their heads to their notebooks, all playfulness forgotten as they applied themselves to the problem.

Madeline let go of the horse and got to her feet. If she could see the past by touching the horse, might there be other objects that could show her something? She went around the room, laying her palm on various toys and books. Nearly half the objects in the nursery seemed to be imprinted with memories of their owners, but the newer ones showed Madeline nothing. Perhaps they'd belonged to George and were purchased long after Charles and Albert had outgrown playtime.

Madeline replaced the last toy on its shelf and moved toward the door. It had been comforting to see her father as a boy, but a little unnerving too. Why was she seeing these strange things? Perhaps it was just her mind playing tricks on her because she was so distraught.

She returned to her bedroom and curled up on her bed. Silent tears slid down her cheeks, but no one came to comfort her. She was a pariah.

Chapter 38

May 2014

London, England

It was dinnertime by the time Gabe pulled up to Sylvia's house in Ealing. He'd picked up a sandwich and a cup of tea just after noon when he'd stopped at a petrol station, but now he was hungry and tired after driving for most of the day and sitting in rush-hour traffic for nearly an hour once he entered London proper. He hoped Sylvia had given Emma her tea so he could just give her a bath, read her a story, and put her to bed as soon as they got home. He needed a quiet evening, and a large glass of something very alcoholic to dull the anxiety he'd been feeling over the past few days. Tomorrow morning, he'd call the airline and see if there were any seats left on his upcoming flight. Emma would be coming to New Orleans with him.

Gabe just barely squeezed into a spot and thanked the gods of parking that he'd been able to find a spot so quickly. The lights in Sylvia's front room were on, so thankfully she was at home and he wouldn't have to wait. He rang the bell and allowed himself a happy smile. He couldn't wait to scoop Emma up and give her a great big hug. He'd been gone for less than a week, but he felt as if they'd been apart for a month.

Sylvia yanked open the door and stared at Gabe with a look of pure trepidation. She paled visibly, and stepped back to allow him to come inside.

"Is something wrong?" Gabe asked, taken aback by Sylvia's obvious distress. "Where's Emma?"

"I don't know," Sylvia admitted. "I thought you were Logan."

"Sylvia, what's happened?" Gabe demanded, his voice rising by several octaves. "Where's my daughter?"

Sylvia sank down onto the sofa, as if her legs could no longer hold her up. She wrung her hands and her unfocused gaze slid around the room to avoid meeting Gabe's intent stare. The house was ominously quiet, only the ticking of the clock audible over the hush. It felt to Gabe as if all the air had just been sucked out, leaving him and Sylvia suspended in a vacuum, their movements reminiscent of some strange pantomime.

"Sylvia," Gabe barked, forcing her to look at him.

"Emma was taking a nap, so I asked Jude to mind her while I ran out to the shops. I wanted to pick up some chops for our tea. There was a line at the till, and I took longer than expected. When I came back they were gone."

"Have you rung Jude?"

"Of course. I've been trying for hours. He's not answering and his mailbox is full."

"Where's Logan?" Gabe demanded.

"Logan and Colin went out to look for Jude and Emma. Logan knows Jude's favorite hangouts. He thought it was worth a try."

Gabe sank onto the sofa and covered his face with his hands. His stomach felt hollow and his chest tight, as if a cinder block rested on his ribcage. He was a horrible parent, the kind of parent who allowed something awful to happen to their child through thoughtlessness and negligence. He should have never left Emma with Sylvia. He hardly knew her, and what he knew of Jude made his blood run cold. Emma would have been devastated by the death of her grandfather, but at least she would have been safe. Now she was out there somewhere, alone with a drug addict who'd taken her out hours ago without telling anyone where he was going.

"We've got to call the police," Gabe said, springing to his feet.

"Gabe, no, please," Sylvia wailed. "Not yet."

Gabe stared at her, confused, and then the penny dropped, and his fear escalated to new heights. "Jude's got a record, doesn't he?"

"Yes. He was arrested for heroin possession and dealing a few years ago. He spent six months at a juvenile hall since he was still a minor."

"So you left my child alone with a druggie and a felon, and merrily went off to the shops?" Gabe roared, fighting to control an overwhelming desire to grab Sylvia and shake her until her teeth rattled. The impulse shamed him, so he drew in a few deep breaths to calm his temper.

"He's my son, Gabriel. I don't think of him in those terms," Sylvia replied with a defiant lift of her head.

"Well, Emma is my daughter, and you have no bloody idea where she is. She's four, Sylvia. She's vulnerable and trusting. I'm calling the police."

"Gabe, I beg you. Wait. It's only been three hours."

"That's three hours too long."

Gabe was about to call the police when the doorbell rang. Sylvia ran to answer it, but the light of hope went out of her eyes when Logan and Colin came in, looking tired and worried.

"We didn't find them," Logan said. "None of his mates have seen him today."

"Oh, God," Sylvia moaned. She tried to stay Gabe's hand as he called 999, but he wouldn't be deterred. Night was coming, and Emma would be out there alone with a strung-out heroin addict. It didn't bear thinking about. Gabe calmly gave all the pertinent information and disconnected the call. The police were on their way.

"I'll make some tea," Colin offered. "I'd prefer something stronger, but it won't do for the police to think that anyone in the house might be under the influence."

Sylvia resumed her seat on the sofa, Logan next to her. Gabe couldn't sit still, so he paced the room like a caged tiger, ready to pounce on anyone who dared to cross his path.

Everyone jumped to attention when a key turned in the lock and Emma exploded into the room. She was wearing shimmering fairy wings and had a fuchsia streak in her black hair. She twirled around to show everyone her beautiful wings and then jumped into Gabe's arms, thrilled to see him back.

"Daddy, I have pink hair!" she cried, clearly delighted with her new do.

Jude walked in after her. Emma's Disney Princesses backpack was slung over his shoulder and he carried her jumper in his hand, since she couldn't wear it over her wings. Jude had shaved the sides of his head, and the hair on top stood in sculpted spikes, the tips colored electric blue. Around his neck he wore a leather collar studded with metal grommets.

"Where the hell have you been?" Gabe snarled, barely controlling his temper so as not to frighten Emma. He wanted to take a swing at Jude and watch him go down in a heap, but under the circumstances that wasn't an option. Some part of Gabe's brain reflected that becoming a parent had turned him into an unhinged lunatic who would probably need to enroll in an anger-management program before long.

Jude looked around, his expression confused. "What's everyone freaking out about?" he asked, finally noticing Logan and Colin's anxious faces and Sylvia's deathly pallor.

Gabe was about to respond when the doorbell rang. A pair of plain-clothed detectives were at the door. They identified themselves before stepping into the entryway.

"We've had a report of a missing child."

"I'm sorry to have troubled you," Gabe said, his voice low. "There seems to have been a misunderstanding. She's home and she's all right."

The officers looked around the room, taking in the subdued adults and the child, who was happily twirling around, her wings shimmering in the light as she hummed to herself. Emma was oblivious to the drama playing out around her, caught up in some childish fantasy.

"That's the best outcome we could have hoped for. Goodnight, sir." The policemen turned to leave, but not before bestowing a look of irritation on Gabe. He'd wasted police time, which under certain circumstances, was a crime.

Gabe closed the door and returned to the front room, where Emma had stopped twirling and was hopping from foot to foot.

"I have to go to the toilet," she announced.

"Come, darling, I'll take you," Sylvia said, ushering Emma out before emotions had a chance to boil over, and closing the door behind her.

Jude stared at Gabe in utter disbelief. "You called the cops? What did you think I'd done with her?" he yelled. "Did you think I sold her on the dark web to pay for drugs, you arsehole?"

"Where were you?" Gabe asked, ignoring the insult.

"We went to a hair salon. I wanted to change up my look a bit before our next gig, and my friend Bridget had an opening."

Gabe felt a momentary pang of regret when he saw tears of hurt in Jude's eyes, but he was still furious. "You didn't answer your mobile. What were we supposed to think?"

"You weren't supposed to think anything. My battery died and Bridget didn't have a charger. What's the problem, mate? We've only been gone for a few hours, and Emma had fun," Jude cried, obviously devastated by the implication that he would have done anything to hurt Emma. "We are back in time for tea."

"She has colored hair," Gabe said, but the anger had gone out of him, leaving him tired and overwrought.

"She asked for a pink streak, so Bridget did it for her. It's no big deal, man. It's just one strand. It'll grow out in a few months. She loves it. Did you really think I'd hurt her?" The hurt had turned to anger as Jude advanced toward Gabe, fists clenched.

Logan instantly came between them and put a restraining hand on Jude's arm.

"I didn't know what to think, given your history," Gabe replied. He had no intention of backing down. Emma was his child, and he had every right to be worried. And if Jude's feelings were hurt, well that wasn't his problem. "You should have told someone where you were going."

"Fuck you, man. And the same goes for the rest of you," Jude said just as Sylvia and Emma returned to the room. "Not you," Jude amended, looking at Emma. "You are a cool kid."

Jude stormed out of the house and slammed the door behind him. Sylvia sank into a chair, her shoulders heaving with silent sobs while Emma hid behind the sofa, frightened by the exchange.

"Mum, he'll be back," Logan promised. "He just needs a little time to cool down."

"No, he won't. And I wouldn't blame him. We should have had more faith in him. How's he ever supposed to get better if no one trusts him?"

"What's going on?" Emma demanded from behind the sofa. "Grandma Sylvia, why are you crying?"

"I'm just glad you're back," Sylvia replied, avoiding a lengthy explanation.

"Of course I'm back. It was fun. Why did Jude leave? He said we could watch a film tonight."

"Jude is a little upset, Em," Gabe said. "He needs time to think things through. He took you without telling anyone and we were worried."

"Well, that's silly. He's my uncle."

"I know, sweetheart, but he still should have told someone where he was going."

Emma nodded, already bored by the heavy conversation. "I'm hungry."

"Why don't we all go out for a pizza?" Logan suggested. He glanced at his mother, whose mouth was compressed into a thin line as she gave Gabe a hard stare.

Gabe ignored her. He wasn't sure if Sylvia knew that Jude was using again, but he did, and he'd had every right to demand an explanation, especially given the fact that Jude kept pulling down his sleeves while they spoke. The leather collar on Jude's neck did explain the marks Gabe had seen before, so he was glad that at least Jude wasn't risking his life for an orgasm. Or maybe he was, and used the leather collar to cover up the bruises. It wasn't any of his business, but he wouldn't be leaving Emma with Sylvia again in a hurry.

"I'll stay here and wait for your brother," Sylvia said to Logan.

"Mum, he won't be back tonight. Give him some space. He's angry, but he'll come round. He'll understand that we were simply worried."

"Gabe called the police on him," Sylvia cried.

"And I would do it again," Gabe replied calmly. "Now, can we put this behind us?"

"Not just yet," Sylvia replied. She was still angry, but the fight had gone out of her. "You go on. I'll talk to you tomorrow."

"Come on then," Colin said, eager to lighten the atmosphere. "Emma, what kind of pizza do you like?"

"Just plain. Can I wear my wings?"

"Only if we walk to the restaurant. They'll break in the car."

"I'm tired of walking. Jude made me walk. Here." Emma turned to Gabe, allowing him to remove the wings. "Keep them safe."

"I will. You can wear them tomorrow."

Emma smiled hugely. "And I'll have my pink hair for months," she said, pleased with herself. "Bridget has purple hair. Jude said it looks fierce. What does that mean, Daddy?"

"Means it looks great."

"Do I look fierce?" Emma demanded.

"You are the fiercest of them all," Logan interjected. "You make me want to get pink hair."

"Logan, pink is for girls."

Logan and Colin exchanged looks and burst out laughing.

"Come, I'm starving," Logan said and they trooped out of the house, leaving Sylvia to stew.

Chapter 39

May 2014

New Orleans, Louisiana

Quinn set aside the fan and exhaled the breath she hadn't realized she'd been holding. She finally had her answer, the answer she'd been searching for since she was a little girl. Madeline was the one with the psychic gift, and she must have passed it on to her child, who appeared on the family tree as the son of Amelia and George. But how had Madeline come by her ability, and what had become of her? Why was there no record of her existence? Had she died during the Civil War, which began shortly after her baby was born, and been forgotten by history, or was there something more sinister behind the obvious omission?

Quinn buried her face in her hands. She didn't want to know. She really didn't, but she couldn't stop now. If her hypothesis was true, then Madeline was her ancestor, her only link to those who came before her. And if Madeline had come to a violent end, Quinn needed to know. Madeline's story had to be told, and her voice needed to be heard one last time.

The fan lay on the bed, an inanimate object from a bygone era, a lacework in ivory, and a ghostly reminder of a girl who had lived long ago. Quinn had searched every source, both digital and physical, and every archive in New Orleans. She'd even gained access to cemetery records in the hope that she would find a reference to Madeline Besson, but she'd come up empty-handed. Madeline had vanished like a puff of smoke.

"What happened to you, Maddy?" Quinn asked the silent room. "Where did you go?"

Quinn leaned her head against the padded headboard and considered that question. Perhaps nothing had happened to

Madeline, other than an ordinary life. There could be another scenario that fit, one that was ridiculously simple. She might have handed over her baby to Sybil and left the plantation. She wasn't wanted there, and her father's banishment was the reason her birth and death were never recorded in the family records. She'd never wished to marry Gilbert Montlake, so it stood to reason that she'd married someone else at a later date. Madeline could have gone on to have a long life, and was probably safely buried somewhere, her death listed under her married name. There had been countless Madelines in the archives, countless women whose lives had not taken a violent turn and whose legacy lived on in their descendants, just as Madeline Besson's lived on in Quinn.

There was only one way to find out, so Quinn gingerly reached for the fan and closed her eyes, ready to witness the next chapter.

Chapter 40

January 1859

Louisiana Bayou

Madeline sat on the hard wooden chair, her eyes fixed on the stagnant water of the bayou. The water sparkled in the bright sunshine that managed to penetrate the gloom of the towering trees and shine a light onto this forgotten corner of Louisiana. She shuddered with revulsion when the scaly head of an alligator broke the surface, dangerously close to shore. The cabin could only be accessed by steep wooden steps, so they were safe, but the hideous creatures sent shivers of fear down Madeline's spine every time they came near. Mammy didn't seem bothered. She said that alligators tasted just fine, when barbequed over an open flame and basted regularly to prevent the meat from getting tough.

Madeline tore her gaze away from the gator and looked off into the distance, hoping to glimpse a canoe nosing its way toward the cabin. Joe came every Monday, bringing supplies and news of the outside world. But it wasn't Joe Madeline was waiting for—it was George. The New Year had come and gone, and January was almost at an end, so George had to be back at the plantation, even if he'd decided to visit Amelia's family for a few weeks. He had to be back, and he had to know about the child and Madeline's banishment.

"He'll come for me, Mammy. You'll see," Madeline said over and over again, trying to convince herself as much as Mammy.

Mammy nodded, her expression glum. She was always glum these days, going about her daily chores with a permanent scowl on her face. She was kind to Madeline, but Madeline could see anger bubbling just beneath the surface. Perhaps Mammy was upset about being separated from her family again, Madeline reasoned, as she spent her days moping aimlessly, desperate for something to occupy her time besides waiting for George.

"If you says so, child," Mammy would reply. "If you says so."

There was little to do at the cabin, so Madeline spent hours sitting on the tiny porch and reliving the happy moments she'd shared with George, her mind conjuring bittersweet images of that golden time. In her mind's eye, she saw George laughing and spraying water on her when he shook his hair after swimming in the lake. George in her bed, tender and passionate, whispering that he loved her while he moved deep inside her. George promising to take care of her always, no matter what happened. He wouldn't just discard her as if she meant nothing to him and go back on everything he'd said. It might take him some time to smooth things over with Amelia and extricate himself long enough to come to Madeline, but he would come; she was sure of it. Even if he no longer cared for her—a thought that left Madeline feeling hollow and hopeless—he'd never forsake his child, and as long as the child lived within her, they were one and the same.

Madeline placed a hand on her belly. It had changed over the past month, growing firmer and rounder, as had her breasts. Her skin felt unusually sensitive, even the smooth fabric of the linen shift she wore as irritating as the rough surface of the pumice stone Mammy used to remove callouses from her feet. The barely noticeable movement deep inside her womb reminded Madeline of the rippling in the water after an alligator slithered by. Mammy said it was the baby moving. Madeline's baby. Hers and George's.

The child hadn't seemed real before, but now it was as real as the loneliness that gnawed at her insides day and night, and the fear that gripped her heart as she lay in bed, sleepless, wondering what would become of her if she refused to comply with Sybil's wishes. She dutifully wrote to Gilbert every week, not because she cared what he thought or wanted to keep him interested, but because it was a way to stave off the loneliness for a short time. She made up amusing stories about her pretend family, and described events that never took place, unwittingly replaying her outings with George. The restaurant her aunt and uncle took her to was just like the restaurant where George had taken her for lunch, and the carriage ride along the river was as picturesque and dreamy as the one she had shared with George the night of the dinner party.

Gilbert wasn't much of a correspondent. All his letters were similar. He missed her. He looked forward to her return. He went to New Orleans with his father, or paid a social call with his mother. He was learning about the running of the plantation and taking on more responsibility. At times, Gilbert mentioned the growing unrest between the North and the South, but the sentiments he expressed were taken directly from his father's mouth, the views harsh and unyielding. Gilbert wasn't man enough to think for himself, or even man enough to choose his own bride. His mother and Sybil Besson had decided to pair them up, and Gilbert simply went along with their wishes. He wasn't passionate enough to care either way. He'd marry Madeline, but if she turned him down, he'd probably wed someone else just as happily, given enough time. He would be a good husband and a caring father, but he would never know true desire or feel life-shattering loss. He didn't have it in him to feel such extremes of emotion.

Madeline gave up on watching for the canoe and headed back inside the cabin. She needed to use the chamber pot again, and she was thirsty. Mammy was out back, hanging out the washing, so Madeline drank a cup of water, then squatted over the pot, sighing with relief. She was just about finished when she noticed something shiny beneath Mammy's cot. Curious, she used the handle of the broom to reach for the object. It was nothing but an old button, but it looked to be from a fine garment, not from something worn by a slave. Madeline picked up the button and held it up to examine it more closely. A strange feeling came over her as she was transported to another time, the experience just like the one she'd had in the nursery several weeks ago.

Madeline saw a handsome white man lying on the cot, his arms folded behind his head and a lazy smile tugging at his sensual lips. He was ten to fifteen years older than George, and a little

294

darker in his coloring, but the family resemblance was unmistakable. The man's well-toned body glistened with sweat, and a damp forelock fell into his eyes as he gazed upon a woman pouring a cup of beer from an earthenware jug. She stood with her back to him, her mocha skin glowing in the light from the open door. She wasn't thin, but she was shapely, with long legs, rounded buttocks and full breasts that strained against the thin linen of her shift.

"You're so beautiful, Clara. Take off that silly shift. I want to look at you."

"You ain't so bad yourself," the woman replied, and turned to smile at him.

Madeline sucked in her breath. The woman was Mammy, she was sure of it. She looked to be only a few years older than Madeline was now, but she couldn't mistake the features, or the familiar timber of her voice.

"Come back to bed," the man drawled. "I'm not finished with you yet."

Mammy handed him the cup and watched him drink. "You's the lustiest man I've even known."

"And have you known many men?" he asked, his tone playful rather than angry.

"Enough to know you's a fine one, and I'm lucky to have you."

"You don't have me, my African queen. My wife has me, by the balls most of the time, but you have my love, which is something she'll never get."

Mammy raised her brow in a way that made the man laugh. "I can't buy my freedom with your love." She said the words with a smile, but there was steel in her voice.

"I will grant you your freedom, but only once I've tired of you. You'll leave me before the ink is dry on your papers, and I will perish without you."

"You'll find another 'African queen' to warm your bed," Mammy replied, not without bitterness.

"Don't say such things. I only want you."

"And you has me," Mammy replied with a sigh. "You has me, and you owns me."

"I like your spirit. Now come here. I'm ready for you." The man threw aside the sheet that covered his middle to expose a stiff cock that rose proudly from a thicket of dark curls. "In your mouth this time," he said, closing his eyes in anticipation.

Mammy climbed onto the bed and crouched between the man's legs, taking him obediently into her mouth. It was obvious from the revulsion in her eyes that she didn't want to perform this unsavory task, but she did it just the same, as much a slave in bed as out of it. The man moaned with pleasure, oblivious to Mammy's distaste.

Madeline dropped the button, appalled by what she'd seen. Who was the man, and why had Mammy allowed him to treat her that way? He'd seemed playful and relaxed, but would he have forced her or had her whipped if she refused?

"What you doing?" Mammy asked as she came back in the cabin, an empty basket on her hip.

"Clara. Your name is Clara," Madeline said. "I never knew that."

"You never asked." Mammy tilted her head and gazed at Madeline, a look of profound sadness transforming her face. "You saw me, didn't you?"

Madeline nodded. "Mammy, am I going mad? I keep seeing things. Things from the past. What's happening to me?"

296

"It's nothing to be afraid of," Mammy replied as she set her basket down and poured herself a drink.

"But I don't understand," Madeline cried. "Why will no one tell me the truth about anything? A few months ago I was still a child, living with a father who loved me, and believing myself safe from harm. Since then I've been orphaned, disgraced, lied to, and banished. And none of it was my doing. There isn't a person in this world who genuinely loves me," Madeline cried.

"I love you, child," Mammy said and sat down next to Madeline. She put her arm around Madeline's heaving shoulders and kissed her temple. "I love you more than you'll ever know."

"Then tell me the truth. I'm a grown woman now, and I have a right to know."

Mammy sighed. "I tried to protect you, Madeline. I thinks it best that you don't know. But you's right. It's time you knew the truth. Come, let's sit outside. It's too hot in here, and too crowded with memories."

Madeline followed Mammy outside and took her customary seat, while Mammy took the chair on the other side of the open doorway. Her gaze seemed to glaze over as she stared out over the silent bayou. The water shimmered in the hazy winter sunshine, and the gnarled branches of the trees pointed to the sky like wasted limbs. The sinister beauty of the bayou was timeless and eerie, and made Madeline feel as if she couldn't breathe. She wanted to leave this place and never come back, but not before she was armed with the truth that had been withheld from her for so long.

Mammy didn't look at Madeline as she began to speak, her voice low and husky. "My mama was born in Trinidad. She was a healer, a wise woman. White men called her a witch doctor or shaman, but she be no witch, just a woman who knew things. She learned from her own mother, who learned from hers. The knowledge was passed down generation to generation, but only to the women. A marriage had been arranged for her with the son of an important man who was also a Dougla."

"What's a Dougla?" Madeline asked.

"A person of African and East Indian blood. My mama was to marry him when she turned sixteen."

"Did she?"

Mammy shook her head. "She was taken by a Dutch slaver when she was out collecting plants and roots for her medicines. He took her away."

There was no anger in Mammy's voice. She spoke as though in a trance, detached from what she was feeling, but Madeline didn't believe her demeanor for a moment. Mammy was like the deceptively calm surface of the Mississippi, hiding powerful currents beneath the surface. She wasn't one to feel nothing. In fact, she probably felt too much, and had no wish to relive this part of her family's history, which she'd buried deep inside and never shared with anyone.

"What happened to her?" Madeline asked, ashamed of how little she knew about the person she'd claimed to love. Mammy had been there for her, a loving, caring presence for as long as she could remember, but Madeline had taken what she had to give without giving anything back, without ever truly seeing Mammy as a person in her own right.

"He brought her here, to Louisiana, to sell. It was a long sea voyage. They made many stops and loaded more slaves. The Dutchman wanted a woman to warm his bed on lonely nights at sea, so he took my mama. By the time she came off that ship she was pregnant. She begged him to keep her, to protect their baby, but he was deaf to her pleas. He sold her at auction, and demanded a higher price 'cause the new owner was getting two for the price of one."

"That's barbaric," Madeline exclaimed, outraged by the man's indifference.

298

"That's life, child."

Madeline grew silent, thinking on what Mammy had said. How could a man sell his woman and child? How could a man take someone who was free and sell them for his own profit without a twinge of conscience? How could such a man live with himself? Without any remorse, Madeline assumed. There were many others like him, men who didn't see the people they enslaved as human beings, and didn't recognize the children they'd created as their offspring.

"What happened to her?" Madeline finally asked.

"She was bought by a cruel man. He didn't beat her, or work her too hard, but he took her baby away. He sold me on when I was six, old enough to remember my mama, but not old enough to fend for myself. He sold me to George's great-grandfather, Maurice. Maurice Besson was a frugal man. He didn't want to waste money on strong men, so he bought children and worked them like adults."

"Did you ever see your mother again?"

Mammy shook her head. "No. But I remembered the things she tried to teach me. She tell me to take every chance, and never trust anyone with my heart."

"Who was that man I saw you with in my vision, Mammy?"

"That be Jean, Maurice's son and George's grandfather. He took a shine to me, so I came to him willingly, hoping I might benefit if I please him."

"Was he kind to you?" Madeline asked, wondering if the man's playfulness was just a prelude to cruelty.

"He was kind enough, but his wife would have skinned me alive, given half a chance."

"Sybil?" Madeline said, finally understanding the animosity between the two women.

"Jean brought me here many times. He liked his pleasure uninterrupted."

"Did Sybil know?"

"Not at first," Mammy replied. "She was mad in love with him, that girl. He was handsome and charming and liked to give pleasure as much as he liked to receive it. Sybil was too innocent to think he might be laying with other women, especially slaves, who, in her mind, were lower than cockroaches. But there came a time when things couldn't be kept hidden any longer."

"How did she find out?" Madeline asked, although she thought she already knew.

Mammy smiled ruefully at Madeline, her gaze glazed with memories of that time. "Jean got me with child, and when my baby came out nearly as white as Sybil's own children, she knew. My baby had three white grandparents," Mammy said by way of explanation. "She was beautiful. She had green eyes like my father. My mama always spoke of his eyes. Clear green, with dark blond lashes. The Dutchman was a handsome man, if a heartless one."

"What happened to your baby, Mammy?" Madeline hadn't seen any white slaves at Arabella Plantation. Perhaps Jean Besson had sold the child to hide his infidelity.

"My girl was allowed to remain with me until she was eight, but then she was taken into the big house to serve the family. Sybil thought it was the best way to remind her of her place, and to punish me and her wayward husband. She served her own father and his children, and suffered daily humiliation from his wife."

"Where is she?" Madeline asked softly. "What happened to your girl?"

300

"She was too pretty to remain invisible. The son of the house fell in love with her. He wasn't like his father, who lied and promised me my freedom to keep me sweet. He freed my girl by marrying her." Mammy turned to face Madeline. "My daughter was your mother, Maddy. She was my beautiful Corinne."

Madeline stared at her, mouth open in shock. "You're my grandmother."

"Yes, child. I'm your grandmother, and I've passed on my mama's gift to you. You can see the dead when you touch their things. Corinne could too. She hated it. It frightened her, so when your daddy married her and took her away to New Orleans, he buy everything new for her. When your mama died, I took away all her things right away. I didn't want you to see."

"But you left her fan," Madeline protested.

"She never got to use the fan. It was safe to leave you something of her. She loved you, Madeline. So much."

"Did my father know, Mammy? Did he know my mother was his sister?"

Mammy shook her head. "Sybil was too proud to tell him. She cast him out for marrying a woman with Negro blood, but she didn't tell him the whole truth, and Jean was gone by then, carried off by yellow fever. Charles never knew. When they married, I went with them. Sybil was angry, but she did nothing to get me back. She couldn't bear to look at me. In her eyes, I'd ruined her life. She was still too proud to blame her own man."

"It must have been awful for you to have to return here."

"It was, but I got to see my boys. I found me a man after Jean tired of me, and we had a family. He loved my Corinne like she be his own, but I hadn't seen him or my boys in fifteen years. My man died two years ago," Mammy choked out.

"I'm sorry, Mammy," Madeline whispered. "I never knew what a hard life you've had."

301

"Oh, it wasn't a bad life, Maddy. I had my girl, and I had you. I was happy to see her free, and respectable. Your daddy, he loved her something fierce. Loving her is what killed him in the end."

"And George? Does he know?"

Mammy shook her head. "Sybil is too ashamed to tell her grandson that his uncle married a slave girl who was his half-sister. Too dirty, too shameful. But George, he no different from his grandfather. Handsome, charming, and ruthless."

"Oh, Mammy, you don't think he ever loved me, do you?" Madeline cried.

"Oh, he loved you, child. He loved you lying beneath him and taking what he had to give. He only cared for his own selfish needs. And now there's a baby in your belly, and it's an added benefit, unless it comes out black. Wouldn't that be a hoot?" Mammy asked, her tone bitter.

"Can that happen?"

Mammy shrugged. "I wouldn't know, but it's possible I s'pose. 'Tis in the blood, ain't it?"

"Mammy, what do I do?" Madeline wailed, more confused than ever. She had believed that George cared for her and would make things right once he found out about the baby, but if Mammy was to be believed, he had simply used her, much as the Dutchman had used Mammy's mother and like Jean Besson had used Mammy and then discarded her when he got bored. Were all men so callous?

No, Madeline thought defiantly. Her father had married her mother, despite the cost to himself. He could have inherited the Arabella Plantation. He could have enjoyed a life of wealth and privilege, but he'd chosen the woman he loved over money and reputation. There were good, honorable men out there. There had to be.

"You give that baby to George. Let it take its rightful place in the family," Mammy said, giving Madeline a hard, calculating look.

"It'd be the ultimate revenge, wouldn't it, to have your great-grandchild inherit it all?" Madeline asked, smiling for the first time.

"I ain't looking for revenge; I'm looking for justice. Let that baby be blessed and happy. It deserves it. You—you go away from here. Ask George for money and go away. Make a life for yourself away from this place. Build a future, a family of your own."

"Will you come with me?"

"They own me, my girl. I can't just leave unless George frees me. They'd hunt me down. Sybil would like nothing better than to whip me senseless, even after all these years. Her hurt runs deep. And I have my boys here and their children. No, you must go on your own. You'll find your way. You'll survive. You's got it in you."

"I'm afraid, Mammy. I've never been on my own."

"No one's ever been on their own till they is. You'll be fine, child, as long as you has George's money. You set yourself up nice, and find a good man to look after you. A kind man. It ain't hard for a pretty girl to find a suitor. And when you finds him, you tell him nothing, you hear? You tell him you're as pure as spring water."

"Won't he know I've had a baby?" Madeline asked, intrigued by the idea of a clean slate.

"He'll know nothing, unless you tells him. Give him his own baby, and he'll love you for it."

"My head hurts," Madeline said. "I need to lie down."

"You go. I'll wait for Joe."

Madeline went inside and stared at the cot with fresh eyes. Her mother had likely been conceived in that bed. It was an odd thing, knowing that. Madeline lay down and closed her eyes, but sleep wouldn't come. She understood now why no one had told her the truth and why Sybil could barely look at her. Would Sybil be capable of loving Madeline's baby, a child born of a mother conceived in incest and a father who was the mother's first cousin?

Madeline laid her hand on her stomach and felt a flutter of movement. What a heavy burden for a child to carry. Perhaps Mammy was right and she should just leave and allow her baby to grow up in security and comfort. It would never learn the truth, and the sordid details would die with Mammy and Sybil. She owed her child that much. She owed it freedom from shame.

Chapter 41

May 2014

New Orleans, Louisiana

Quinn stepped out onto the wrought-iron balcony. The French Quarter pulsed with life, as crowded with locals and tourists as the City of Westminster on an average day. The day's balminess had dissipated, replaced by a comfortable coolness. Quinn leaned against the railing and inhaled the fragrant air of the Southern night. She heard distant music and bursts of laughter as a group of people walked by, the women teetering tipsily on high heels and responding playfully to their men, who were teasing them. One of the men grabbed a woman around the waist and pulled her close, planting a passionate kiss on her lips as she melted into him, clearly eager for more. Quinn looked away, surprised by the twinge of envy in her gut.

She'd traveled for work many times, had been away from her parents, partner, and friends, but this was the first time she'd felt such desolation. It wasn't just being away from Gabe; it was being here, in this place. Something about it disturbed her, challenged her, and left her reeling. She wasn't alone, but she felt emotionally adrift and completely out of her element. For years, she'd wanted to know the truth about her lineage, her family, but now that she knew where she'd come from, she felt nothing but anger and sadness.

Did every family have buried secrets? Did every family try to hide that which they thought shameful or unpleasant? She supposed they did, but it angered her that her father and brother had no idea they were descended from a slave woman captured in Trinidad. Madeline, their link to the past, had been erased, forgotten, discarded after her child had been taken from her. Quinn knew what had happened to the child, but she still had no clue what had happened to Madeline, who'd been only sixteen when the

305

child was born. She'd had her whole life ahead of her. What had she done with it?

"I hope you found happiness, Maddy," Quinn whispered into the night. But no one answered. No whisper on the wind told her what she longed to know and was afraid to find out.

Quinn glanced at her watch. She desperately needed to hear Gabe's voice, to share what she'd learned with him, but she couldn't possibly call him now. It was just past two in the morning in London, and her call would wake Emma, a light sleeper at the best of times.

Quinn imagined Emma curled up in her bed, Mr. Rabbit clutched in her arms. She still had frequent dreams about her mother and grandmother and often woke up crying. She loved Gabe, but when she missed her mother she turned to Quinn, the closest thing she had to a mother. It surprised Quinn to realize she missed Emma as much as she missed Gabe. A few months ago, she'd still secretly thought of Emma as Gabe's daughter, but now she thought of Emma as her own child, and wanted to be her mother. Quinn knew that Gabe worried about how Emma would react to the new baby. She might be thrilled to have a brother or a sister, or she might feel resentful and displaced in the affections of her parents. That was normal, even with children who hadn't lost a parent.

I'll do something special with Emma when I get back, Quinn thought as she stepped back inside the room and locked the door to the balcony. *We'll have some mother/daughter time and do fun, girly things.*

Imagining all the things they could do together made Quinn less lonely, but she still needed to talk to someone. What she'd learned in her last vision was too big and shocking to keep to herself even a moment longer. She couldn't possibly share her discovery with Seth or Brett, and the only other person she could think of was Rhys. He might still be awake, but even if he wasn't, he wouldn't mind being woken for a good story. Rhys's passion in life was to tell the best story he could, in the most eloquent way, and he would welcome the middle-of-the-night call, even if he pretended to be grumpy at first.

Funny, but being away from home made Quinn feel closer to Rhys. She'd blamed him for what had happened to Sylvia and held him to account, but somehow she couldn't muster the same amount of resentment for the man who had fathered her. Perhaps it was time to let Rhys off the hook; Sylvia had, and Quinn had no desire to hold on to her anger.

Even after speaking to all three culprits who had been there the night she was conceived, Quinn was still no closer to the truth. Sylvia stood by her story. Rhys appeared to be contrite and was working hard to make amends. Robert Chatham was defiant, but there was a hint of truth to his account, despite his aggressive, bullying manner. And then there was Seth, who claimed to have no recollection of that night at all. Perhaps it was easier for him to pretend it had never happened, but Quinn knew him well enough now to believe he was telling the truth. So she still didn't know with any certainty whether she'd been conceived during an act of violence or if she was simply the result of an alcohol-soaked orgy in which her mother had been a somewhat willing participant. Whichever it was, it was time to move forward and forgive the guilty parties, one of which was her boss.

"This better be good, Quinn," Rhys growled when he answered his mobile.

"It is. I'm sorry to disturb you, but this simply couldn't wait."

"I wasn't sleeping," Rhys replied. "I just came back from Sylvia's. She was upset."

"Why? What's happened?" Quinn demanded. Rhys sounded more annoyed than worried, so it couldn't have been anything catastrophic.

"Jude buggered off. He had a run-in with Gabe and took off. Sylvia thinks he's using again. Personally, I don't think he ever stopped. Logan's been trying to get him into rehab for months."

"How do you know all this?" Quinn asked. She had no idea Rhys had grown so close to Sylvia's family.

"Quinn, there's something I have to tell you, and I hope you won't take issue with it. Sylvia and I are seeing each other. I know it's the last thing you might have expected, given our history, but there's something there—a connection, if you will, and we both want to explore it further."

"Rhys, the only thing I find shocking about your revelation is that you're actually interested in a woman your own age," Quinn joked.

Rhys laughed. "I know. I'm still recovering from the shock myself. I like her, Quinn. She understands me, and I can talk to her as an equal. It's refreshing."

"I'm happy for you both. Truly." Quinn smiled as she pictured the two of them together, but her smile faded as Rhys's words sank in. "Why did Jude have a run-in with Gabe? What could they possibly have to argue about?" She had a sinking feeling in her gut. Gabe didn't get worked up often, but when he did, it was usually for a good reason, and the only thing connecting Gabe to Jude was Emma, since she'd stayed at Sylvia's while Gabe was in Northumberland.

"It was nothing, Quinn. Just a misunderstanding."

"It had to be more than that if Jude took off," Quinn mused. "Did he leave because of Gabe?"

"Not really."

"He either did or he didn't."

"Look, Quinn, young men his age often harbor a lot of anger and self-loathing. Jude is an artist. He's very emotional and overly sensitive. Gabe was well within his rights in everything he

308

said, but Jude is too angry to see reason. He'll come round in his own good time."

"Or he'll go off the deep end," Quinn replied. She didn't know Jude well at all, but he was her brother and she worried about him.

"You can't keep that from happening. He has to take responsibility for his own life. No one will be able to talk sense into him until he's ready to listen."

Quinn sighed. Rhys was right, of course, but it was easier said than done. Now that Quinn had Emma and another child on the way, she could understand Sylvia's angst. Jude was a grown man, but to Sylvia he was still her son who needed saving, in this case, from himself.

"Now, what did you want to tell me?" Rhys asked, no longer interested in Jude's problems.

Suddenly Quinn wasn't sure she wanted to share her news with Rhys, but he'd find out soon enough anyway. Rhys was all about the program, and he wanted the series finale to be unforgettable. What Quinn learned would make it memorable, but it would also expose her family's history to the world, and although she wanted to tell Madeline's story, it all felt awfully personal.

"Rhys, I know where my ability comes from," Quinn said, nervous and reluctant to speak the words out loud. Once she told Rhys there'd be no going back. He might use her story to get ratings.

"Tell me," he said, his voice soft but commanding. "Tell me, Quinn."

And she did.

"Oh, Quinn, what a story. I couldn't have asked for more compelling drama," Rhys exclaimed. "No matter what ultimately happened to Madeline, this makes for excellent television." Quinn could almost hear him gloating at future ratings. "But how do *you* feel about it?" he asked, transforming from producer to human being and friend.

"I feel too many conflicting emotions to actually put them into words," Quinn replied truthfully. "I suppose it's nice to finally know the truth, but it's also painful and confusing, and utterly shocking. I worry about my baby. It'll be years before I know if the child can see things, and even then, I won't be able to do anything to stop the visions."

"No, you won't, but you'll be able to understand what the kid is going through and explain what's happening. Your parents had no idea you were seeing things and you had to deal with it all on your own. At least your child will have someone to talk to and ask questions."

"Yes, that's true. But I just really wish I could keep this gift from being passed on. I don't want to burden my baby."

"It can be wonderful," Rhys argued. "I wouldn't say no to possessing your gift."

"You say that now, but you'd feel differently if you had to actually 'live' these people's lives. It's never pretty, Rhys. I've never come across anyone who's had a normal, peaceful life. Some stories are dramatic, but some bring me to my knees."

"Like Elise and James's?" Rhys asked softly.

"Yes, and Petra and Edwin's. I still have nightmares about that child being stoned to death."

"I know, Quinn, and I'm sorry to have to put you through this. We don't have to use Madeline's story if you don't want to. As your boss, I would give my right arm to bring this to the screen, but as your friend, I will respect whatever you decide. We can find another skeleton, another murder, and another cover-up. God knows there's no shortage of drama buried beneath our feet, just waiting to be dug up. If this is too traumatic, I will understand and forget everything you shared with me."

Quinn found herself shaking her head, even though Rhys couldn't see her. "Thank you, but no. I want this story told. It's very personal, and I know that once the truth about my ability comes out people will never view me through the same lens, but I need to give Madeline her voice back. I need to tell her story, and the story of Corinne and Clara. These women were discarded by history, but they live on in me, and in the gift they've passed on through their blood."

"Good girl," Rhys replied gleefully. "I'll assign someone to research Trinidad and the slave trade in the eighteenth century. And of course, voodoo. That ought to shake things up."

"All right," Quinn replied, with more resolve than she actually felt. "You have my permission."

"Quinn, finish up and come back. Gabe looks like a lost puppy without you, and Sylvia needs her daughter to talk to. I have a feeling things are not about to calm down with *Jude the Obscure.*"

"Don't call him that," Quinn protested. She'd read the book in school and never forgot the dread and hopelessness the story had induced in her.

"That boy will get a lot worse before he gets better," Rhys replied. "Sylvia will need your support."

"And yours."

"I'll be there this time. I promise," Rhys vowed.

"Goodnight, Rhys. And thanks."

"For what?"

"For offering me an out. I appreciate it," Quinn said.

"I owe you, Quinn."

"Not anymore."

311

Chapter 42

May 1859

Louisiana Bayou

Madeline picked at her bowl of gumbo, unable to eat. She'd been feeling unwell the past few days and the heavy food seemed to lie in her stomach like a stone. She'd have been happy with a glass of milk and buttered bread, but milk products didn't keep in the heat, not even if submerged in a tightly covered crock deep in the cool water of the bayou to keep fresh. Everything they ate had to be well cooked or they would get sick. It had happened once already, so Mammy was extra careful what she prepared, refusing to allow Madeline to eat anything questionable in her delicate state.

Madeline's ankles were swollen, and she felt so overheated most of the time that she thought she might burst into flames. She had fond memories of lemonade with bits of ice clinking in a tall glass and ice cream occasionally served for dessert at the plantation. Her large, round belly protruded from her thin frame, making her look deformed. Her back ached and her breasts felt tender to the touch, engorged in preparation for a nursing infant.

Madeline pushed her plate away and fled outside, where the air was a bit cooler, but the oppressive humidity made her skin glisten with sweat. She'd given up on wearing gowns and hoop skirts long ago and spent her days in her camisole and petticoat or just a linen shift, refusing to don extra layers of fabric when there was no one to see her anyway. A long braid snaked down her back, the hair no longer dressed and curled to satisfy fashion. Mammy wore a faded cotton skirt and a camisole, her hair covered with her ever-present turban. Joe was the only person who ever came to see them, so it seemed pointless to put on airs and create extra laundry.

"We're living like savages," Mammy remarked as she joined Madeline outside. She seemed to have lost her appetite as well.

"We are savages," Madeline retorted.

Mammy didn't reply. She'd been careful around Madeline's feelings the past few months, trying to offer her comfort without lecturing her on how to feel, most likely because she was at a loss for words. Madeline's emotions had gone from hope to simmering anger and disappointment. With every week that passed, she'd grown more resentful and frustrated, finally realizing that George wasn't going to come. She might have accepted his decision not to help her, but the fact that he didn't even have the courage to talk to her in person left Madeline eviscerated by his betrayal. She refused to answer Gilbert's letters and wouldn't talk about the future.

"I have no future," she replied when Mammy tried to cajole her into making plans.

"I won't listen to that kind of talk," Mammy replied, hands on hips, her eyes glowing with anger. "You have been lied to and betrayed, but George is not the only one to blame."

"Isn't he?" Madeline snapped, annoyed at being challenged.

"No, he ain't. You might have been a child, but still a child old enough to know right from wrong. You knew he was married, and you didn't say no to his advances."

"Are you saying this is my fault?" Madeline cried, glaring at her belly.

"As much your fault as it is his."

"Why are you being so cruel to me?" Madeline whined. She was moody at the best of times, and close to tears more often than not. And Mammy seemed to be baiting her on purpose.

"Because I won't see you waste your life on one foolish mistake. When life knocks you down, you get up and keep going. A woman has to fight for her happiness in this world."

"I am too tired to fight," Madeline replied, but the anger had gone out of her.

"No, you ain't. You have a way out, a chance. You not going to be alone, bringing up a bastard on whatever pittance you can earn taking in laundry or scrubbing floors. You can marry Gilbert what's-'is-name or you can go your own way. George Besson will pay—handsomely, if you makes him feel guilty enough."

"Oh, Mammy. You make it all sound so simple."

"Nothing is ever simple, girl, but you have to grab the opportunities life hands you."

"Like you did?" Madeline asked, a trifle nastily.

"Yes, like I did. Now, stop sniveling and eat your dinner. You'll need strength to bring that baby into the world."

A tremor of fear went through Madeline. She tried not to think about the birth, but it was getting closer, and the day would come when this huge thing inside her would be ready to come out. Madeline hated being pregnant, but she feared the birth even more. The physical pain would end, if she survived the birthing, but her inner turmoil would not. What if the child came out black? Would George and Amelia still want it? What if they claimed it was a child of one of the slaves and denied it its freedom?

And what if she never saw her baby again? How could she get on with her life knowing she'd left a piece of herself behind? How could she think of marrying and having other children when in her heart she was married to George and already had a child? How did one set such feelings and fears aside and simply moved on? The answer was that it wasn't simple, nor would anything she did be straightforward. Heck, her very existence wasn't straightforward.

314

Madeline had spent the past few months mulling over Mammy's revelations, but she was no closer to making peace with what she'd learned. She no longer had a sense of herself or her place in the world. As someone with Negro blood she would be treated no better than a slave should anyone find out, and as a child of incest, she would be an abomination anywhere she went. No one had to know, of course, but she now knew, and that changed everything. No matter where she wound up, her secrets would remain with her, and eventually the truth would come out. It always did in the end. What kind of future could she hope for? What kind of man would want to marry her if he learned the truth?

"Where do I go, Mammy?" Madeline asked for the hundredth time. "Who'll have me?"

Mammy's answer had always been the same: "Any place is better than here." But today her reply was different. "Go North, Madeline. You'll be safer there. Freer."

"Why do you think that?" Madeline asked, surprised by this new viewpoint.

"I seen some of them Northern ladies when they comes to visit. They's different, Maddy. They's learned, admired. They not like Southern ladies, dressed up to look like upside-down flowers and expected to do nothing but look pretty for their menfolk. They have choices up North."

"Choices to do what?"

"To be more."

Madeline pondered this new idea. To be more. The thought appealed to her. She'd never longed to be more, but perhaps she'd never realized such a thing was possible. The extent of her ambitions had been to marry well and have children. She would still like to marry someday, but maybe she could continue her education, or get involved with a cause. She'd heard of the abolitionist movement, of course, but in the South it was as good as saying you'd decided to worship the Devil. Madeline had agreed with that in the past, but she knew better now. She was no longer who she'd thought she was, and the world looked somewhat less back and white. They said a war was coming between the North and the South, and she didn't want to be on the South side when it began. She had no wish to see men dying by the thousands, fighting for the right to oppress others and play God with their lives. She wanted to be on the side of justice, on the side of good.

Madeline looked at Mammy. "I will. I will go North. Thank you, Mammy, for putting up with me these past few months. I know it hasn't been easy." It was the closest Madeline would come to offering an apology, but Mammy seemed satisfied with the effort.

"I failed you, Maddy."

"You didn't," Madeline protested.

"I did. I should'a been honest with you. I should'a warned you. I knew what Besson men were like, and I kept silent, thinking George wouldn't come after you. Don't think there's no Besson bastards in them huts. My Corinne wasn't the only one, but she be the only one that came out white."

"I was horrible to you," Madeline said. "There's no excuse for that."

"Think no more on it, child. You's my flesh and blood, and listening to your ramblings is the least I can do. You've a right to be angry, and you've a right to be hurt. Just don't let your anger rule your heart. Let it go, Maddy. Be free."

"That might take some time," Madeline replied.

"You's got time. You's young."

"I don't feel young," Madeline said sadly.

Mammy just nodded. She understood.

Chapter 43

June 1859

Louisiana Bayou

The oil lamp glowed brightly, casting a pool of golden light that didn't extend to the corners. The night outside was dark and filled with sounds of the bayou. Madeline usually found them sinister as she lay in her bed at night, trying to get to sleep, but tonight the chorus of cicadas or the loud splash of a gator sliding into the water didn't trouble her. She was filling the bayou with a new kind of sound, the hoarse screams of a woman in prolonged labor. Her shift was soaked through with sweat and her damp hair felt hot on her neck. Mammy's round face glistened with perspiration and she'd undressed down to her undergarments, unable to bear the suffocating humidity of the bayou in the summer.

"I'm scared, Mammy," Madeline wailed as another contraction tore through her exhausted body. She'd been in labor for two solid days, but was no closer to bringing the child into the world. "I don't want to do this anymore."

"I know, child," Mammy said in her best soothing voice. "No woman wants to do it, but there ain't no going back now."

Tears rolled down Madeline's cheeks. She'd never been so scared in her life. Her body seemed to have turned on her, the pain of the contractions so visceral that it obliterated every thought from her mind, but how could she make it stop? Mammy had said the baby hadn't descended into the birth canal yet, but it felt like a huge boulder had lodged between her hip bones and was pushing them apart with merciless persistence.

"My bones will break," Madeline cried. "I can feel them cracking."

"I've seen many a woman give birth, and no one suffered broken bones," Mammy replied.

"I'll be the first."

"You remember this pain before you lie with a man again."

"I want to die!" Madeline screamed as a new contraction rolled over her. "Just let me die."

"Ain't no one's going to die," Mammy said firmly. "Not today. Now stop carrying on like a little girl. You're a woman now, like it or not, and you's got to get this baby out before it dies in your womb. Time to push."

"Push what?"

"Gather all your strength and bear down."

"I don't want to," Madeline cried. "It'll hurt more."

"You want this child out or not?" Mammy demanded as she positioned herself above Madeline's stomach. "You push and I'll press on your belly to help it along."

Madeline did as she was told. She felt like her eyes would pop out of her head from the internal pressure this created, but she did it again and again, desperate to expel the infant from her body.

"Once more now," Mammy said, her voice calm and authoritative. "The head's out."

"I can't. I just can't."

"You can and you will. Do it."

Madeline gathered what was left of her strength and pushed. The baby slid into Mammy's waiting hands and Madeline slumped back on the pillows, grateful the ordeal was finally over. She could barely feel her nether regions and she was sure she'd soiled herself while pushing. Mammy didn't seem concerned. She used her cooking knife to slice through the slimy cord that

318

connected the baby to its mother and set the knife aside. She held up the child for Madeline to see before taking him over to the table where towels, a blanket, and a basin full of warm water awaited his arrival. He began to cry. It wasn't the thin wail Madeline had expected of a newborn, but a loud, lusty cry that jerked Madeline out of her stupor.

"He's a big one. A fine, healthy boy," Mammy said as she cleaned the child, wrapped him in a thin blanket and handed him to Madeline.

Madeline held her son carefully and gazed into his face. He was red and wrinkly, his eyes shut tight against the morning light that had begun to creep into the shadowy corners of the cabin, dispelling the darkness. Dark blond fuzz covered his head, and a small hand pushed its way out of the wrapping, the fingers curled into a tight fist.

"He looks like George," Madeline whispered, amazed that they'd made this little person together.

"That he does," Mammy agreed, frowning with disapproval. "He'll be a proud daddy, that's for sho."

Madeline hadn't been sure how she'd feel once she saw the baby, but now that he was here, and he was a boy, pride overwhelmed her. She'd given George what Amelia couldn't, a healthy son. And she wanted to be there to see him grow, to take his first steps and say his first words. She wanted to see the joy on George's face when he beheld his son for the first time, and bask in the warmth of his approval. Maybe once George saw their baby, he'd love Madeline again. He'd set Amelia aside for the mother of his child. Amelia would be all right; George would see to that. He would provide for her and make sure she wanted for nothing. Why should Madeline be the one set aside when she'd been able to do the one thing Amelia couldn't?

"Mammy, what if I...?"

"No!" Don't even think such things. This baby is for them, the next one for you."

Madeline slumped over the baby, hot tears falling on his tiny face. "I don't want to give him up. He's a part of me."

"Do you love him?" Mammy asked. She stood over Madeline, hands on hips. For a moment, Madeline had forgotten that this child was Mammy's great-grandchild, but then she saw a momentary softening of Mammy's gaze. She loved him too, in her own way.

"Yes," Madeline sobbed. "I love him more than I thought I ever could."

"Then do what's best for him."

Madeline nodded, tears still falling. "I want to name him."

"You can't."

"Why?"

"Because naming him is laying a claim to him, and you ain't got no claim. They will name him."

"Mammy, how can you be so cruel?"

"I'm not cruel. It's life that's cruel, and nature. It's always the women that suffer." Mammy sat on the bed next to Madeline and pulled the sobbing girl to her bosom. "This will make you stronger, Madeline. This will make you wiser. This will make you more cunning. This a hard lesson to learn, my girl, but you can't trust no one in this world. Everybody wants something, and if you let them, they'll trample you beneath their feet to get it."

"Oh, Mammy, do you really think that's what George did?"

"Maybe it wasn't his intention to hurt you, Maddy, but that's what he done. It weren't Jean's intention to hurt me neither, but he near ruined my life. Had Sybil had her way, she'd have sold my girl to punish me. She'd have had me whipped till strips of skin was hanging off my back, and still she wouldn't have been satisfied. Jean forbade her to hurt me, but I could never feel safe. I cried for days when he passed, terrified of what she'd do to me and my children."

"But she didn't do anything," Madeline replied.

"No, your father wouldn't have let her. But he ain't here now." Mammy held out her hands and took the child from Madeline. "You sleep now. You need your rest. I will look after the boy."

Madeline lay back. Exhaustion dragged her along and swept her under like a powerful current and she fell into a deep, dreamless sleep.

Chapter 44

For the next few days, Mammy allowed Madeline as little contact with the child as possible. She kept him in her own cot and took him away as soon as Madeline fed him. Mammy referred to the baby only as 'the Boy' and refused to engage in any conversations about a future in which Madeline got to be his mother.

Madeline still felt exhausted and bruised, and her body did things she hadn't expected it to. She'd thought that giving birth would be the end of her ordeal, but she'd been wrong. Her breasts were engorged with milk and painful to the touch. She'd even had a touch of fever when the milk started to come in, and sweat so profusely that Mammy had to keep washing out her shifts and handing her clean ones before they even had a chance to dry out. She was still bleeding, and her belly felt like a sagging sail after the wind had died, leaving the fabric to hang limply off the mast. Mammy said her body would return to normal, but it needed time, and the help of a tight corset.

"No, Mammy, not yet," Madeline pleaded. "I can't bear it. And it's too hot."

Mammy shook her head. "You want to get your figure back or not?"

"Yes, but I'm still so uncomfortable."

"No one said birthing children was a comfortable business," Mammy countered. "The sooner you back to normal, the sooner you can go."

But Madeline didn't want to go. She wanted to stay. The thought of never seeing her son again filled her with such unbearable pain that she pushed it away, again and again, refusing to even picture a future in which he wasn't with her.

"Mammy, let me hold him," Madeline pleaded, but Mammy refused.

"It'll only be harder to let him go."

"Mammy, please."

"He ain't yours to hold," Mammy reminded her cruelly.

Madeline turned her face to the wall and wept. She knew Mammy was only trying to protect her, but her heart longed for the child, and her arms stretched out to him whenever Mammy brought him for a feeding. Madeline studied him as he suckled at her breast, his cheeks puffing out in a way that would have been funny if it didn't break her heart to know that once Sybil learned of the birth, she'd never hold her baby again.

Madeline secretly named him George. She hated George for abandoning her, but she still stubbornly believed he had loved her. He was just too weak to stand up to his grandmother, who'd dominated him all his life. Madeline would see George once she went back to the plantation, and then all would be resolved between them. They would not be lovers again, but perhaps they could still be friends, and maybe he would allow her to be a part of their son's life. He had the power to do that, surely.

Sybil came three days after the birth, alerted by Joe, who had visited every other day over the past two weeks to check on Madeline. Mammy had sent him away with strict instructions not to say anything to Sybil until after the baby came. She hadn't wanted Sybil anywhere near Madeline during the birth. She couldn't do much to help her granddaughter, but she could help her in this. Birthing was a harrowing enough business without someone hovering nearby, ready to snatch up the child as soon as it came into the world, and Madeline needed a few days to recover, and to come to terms with what was about to happen—not that she ever would.

Seeing the baby and holding him in her arms had undone all the careful work Mammy put in, talking to Madeline and trying to get her excited about the future she could build for herself away from Arabella. But Madeline was like any other woman, besotted with her newborn child, and utterly ruled by her emotions. Had she not cared for George, it might have been easier for her to turn her back on her infant, but Madeline loved George with all the innocent passion her still-childish heart could muster, and believed that somehow he would make things right despite evidence to the contrary.

Mammy and Madeline were sitting outside, the baby asleep in Mammy's arms, when Sybil arrived. He was completely unaware of anything but his own needs, which at that moment were all happily fulfilled. Sybil's expression softened for a brief moment as she beheld her great-grandchild. Perhaps he reminded her of George when he was an infant, or perhaps she was relieved to finally have the heir she'd prayed for. The future of the plantation was secure, so she could rest easy and enjoy the fruits of her labors.

"Well done, Madeline," Sybil said. "He's a fine boy."

"What now, Madame Besson?" Mammy asked, staring Sybil squarely in the face.

Sybil looked from Mammy to Madeline, as though gaging the level of hostility before replying. "You two will remain here until Madeline is fully recovered. You will bind Madeline's breasts immediately to stop the milk. Once she is ready, she will return to the plantation and accept a proposal of marriage from Gilbert Montlake, who's been eagerly awaiting her return. A house in New Orleans has been rented, and Madeline will reside there, with myself as a chaperone, for the duration of the engagement, which will be mercifully short. If anyone questions this arrangement, we will simply tell them it's more convenient to plan a wedding in New Orleans. After the wedding, which will be lavish, Madeline will move in with her husband's family, as is proper. During her sojourn at Arabella, she will have no dealings with either George or the child. George has already agreed to these terms, as has Amelia. Madeline, I'll need your word that you will honor these conditions."

"And if I don't?" Madeline asked. She felt Mammy tense beside her, but she couldn't help her defiance. Her whole life had been laid out for her, all the players given their lines, and the stage set for the final performance—her wedding to Gilbert, who had about as much sense as a lamb being led to slaughter.

"If you don't, you will be cast out without a penny to your name. Do you find that alternative preferable to a life of luxury and comfort with a man who adores you?"

"He hardly knows me—the real me," Madeline retorted.

"All a man needs to know when getting married is that he's anxious to bed his bride, and believe me, Gilbert can't wait to get you in his bed. His father made sure he's well prepared for the occasion," Sybil added with a knowing smirk.

"You mean he's been taking him to brothels, and partaking himself," Madeline stated. "I wonder how Mrs. Montlake feels about that."

Sybil's eyes widened in surprise. "There's nothing wrong with a man satisfying his needs, Madeline. You will learn to turn a blind eye, as all wives do."

"You mean as you did," Madeline taunted. Some inner voice told her to be quiet, to apologize, but she couldn't stop. She was shaking with helpless rage. If she didn't say something now, her baby would be lost to her forever. This was her only chance, her only hope. She knew she had no right to insult Sybil. Sybil wasn't the one who had lain with a married man and borne his child. She was only trying to protect the family and offer Madeline's child a brighter future, but Madeline was so overwhelmed by her emotions that she couldn't and wouldn't think straight.

Sybil stared at Madeline, her mouth opening in shock as her gaze turned to Mammy. Sybil looked murderous, but didn't say a word. Instead, she held out her arms.

Mammy handed over the baby with some reluctance. "He'll be hungry soon," she said.

"I've already found a nursemaid for him. She'll be honored to suckle Miss Amelia's son," Sybil replied. Madeline's anger was all bluster, as far as Sybil was concerned, and she chose not to engage in an argument that she'd felt she already won.

"Everyone will know he's mine," Madeline cried.

"No, they won't. The only people who know the truth are Bette, Cissy, and Joe, and if they breathe a word of it to anyone they know there'll be hell to pay. Amelia is in her bedroom even as we speak, ready to exchange the pillow beneath her petticoat for a live baby. We will then announce the joyous news to the world," Sybil said with a smile that didn't reach her eyes.

Sybil carefully handed the baby to Joe. "Get him settled in the boat," she barked.

Joe put the sleeping child into a Moses basket that was lined with clean linen and padded with a soft blanket, and positioned it in the center of the canoe where it couldn't tip over.

"Joe will come for you next week, Madeline, by which time I hope you will have seen sense," Sybil said. She was about to leave when Madeline grabbed her by the arm, forestalling her.

"That child is mine, and I won't let you take him away from me. I have no intention of marrying Gilbert Montlake, nor will I stand by and allow Amelia to claim my baby. My heart goes out to her. Only now that I've had my own baby can I even begin to comprehend her pain, but it's not for me to save her from it. You will tell George to obtain a divorce. And if you don't, I will tell everyone what I know."

"And what might that be?" Sybil asked, yanking her arm out of Madeline's grasp.

"I'll tell them your son married his own sister, who was the daughter of a slave. You will be disgraced, and all doors will slam in your face."

Sybil turned to Mammy, her face white to the roots of her hair. Her eyes narrowed to mere slits, and her breath came in shuddering gasps.

"I hated you," Sybil spat out. "I lay in bed every night thinking up new ways to hurt you. I would have had you flogged until your skin hung off your back in ribbons of bloody flesh. I would have sold your children. I would have plunged a knife in your heart and watched the lifeblood drain out of your body," Sybil sputtered. "But I didn't. Do you know why? Because deep down, I knew you had no choice. My husband wanted you, and he had you. You were as much a victim as I was."

"Madam…" Mammy began, but Sybil held up a finger to silence her.

"I brought Corinne into the house to shame him, to torment him with guilt, but he didn't care. She was nothing to him; just another slave girl to pour him coffee and shine his boots. I didn't punish Jean; I punished myself. I lost my son," Sybil cried. "I lost the person I loved most in the world."

"I'm sorry," Mammy mumbled.

"Are you?" Sybil screeched. "I let you go. I let you be with your daughter, and I was good to your sons and their families. I never took my anger out on them. It wasn't their fault, or yours. But this is," she hissed, pointing a finger at Mammy. Her breathing had calmed and her voice now had a granite edge to it. "You told her, and now everything I hold dear is threatened once again. Well, this time I won't be so forgiving."

"What do you mean?" Madeline cried. She'd only said what she had to gain some leverage over Sybil. She'd never meant for Mammy to get the blame, but Sybil's wrath was directed at her grandmother, who was now entirely at Sybil's mercy. "I begged Mammy to tell me the truth," Madeline tried to explain. "I wanted to know why my father was banished."

"Well, now you know the truth. And are you better for it?" Sybil cried. "You're an abomination, a stain on the family name. A demon sent by God to torment me for all my days. And it's all her fault," Sybil roared.

Sybil looked deranged, the years of keeping the sordid secret finally giving way to madness. She yanked a handgun from the pocket of her gown and pointed it at Mammy, who stood stock-still, her eyes wide with shock. The gun was ridiculously small, almost toy-sized. The ivory handle was intricately carved and fit perfectly into Sybil's hand, and the silver barrel glowed as it reflected the morning sunlight. It was difficult to imagine that something so small and pretty could actually kill, but if the weapon were as deadly as the look in Sybil's eyes, Madeline would not escape unscathed.

"No!" Madeline screamed and lunged at Sybil. The noise that erupted from the handgun was no louder than the popping of a champagne cork, but the bullet wasn't as harmless. Madeline felt a searing pain in her chest as a bloody flower bloomed on the front of her camisole. She tried to breathe, but gurgled instead, unable to draw air into her lungs.

Sybil looked momentarily horrified by what she'd done, but the gun went off a second time, and Mammy crumpled into a heap next to Madeline.

Madeline stared up at the sky. It was so blue, so clear. Only a crane, startled by the shot, marred its perfection as it took flight. The baby began to cry, but quieted quickly. Paralyzed with pain and shock, Madeline used the last of her strength to reach for Mammy. She inched her arm closer to her grandmother, finally closing her fingers around Mammy's hand. It was still warm, but Madeline knew in her heart that Mammy was gone. The bullet had found its mark, and Mammy had met a quick end, unlike Madeline, who gasped for breath and wheezed as the air leaked through her damaged lungs.

"Missus!" Madeline heard Joe gasp in horror. "What have you done?"

"Joe, toss Clara into the bayou," Sybil ordered. "Let the crocodiles have her."

"No," Madeline rasped. "Please…"

"Shall I go for the doctor?" Joe cried. "Miss Madeline is still alive."

"Are you mad?" Sybil had regained control and was now all business. "I will be accused of murder and sent to the gallows. Unless, of course, I tell the sheriff that you murdered Clara and Madeline, in which case you will be sent to the gallows," she said calmly. "One word of this to anyone and you will swing. Understood?"

Joe nodded miserably.

"Well, go on then," Sybil prompted.

Madeline tried to hold on to Mammy with all her strength, but Joe yanked Mammy's hand out of her grasp. He tried not to look at her, but Madeline could see the tears in his eyes. He was a good man, but he didn't have much choice. Sybil wouldn't hesitate to shoot him as well or turn him over to the law, if that's what it took to cover up her crime. A dragging noise was followed by a loud splash as Mammy's body hit the water and began to sink.

Madeline saw colored spots in front of her eyes. Her chest heaved as she tried to breathe, but her body was running out of oxygen. She knew she didn't have long. Her mind began to wander, going over every moment she'd spent with her son. She saw her mother's face. Corinne was smiling, and beckoning to her.

"Don't be afraid, Maddy," she whispered.

I'm an abomination, Mama, Madeline thought, *an affront to God.*

"Nothing that comes out of love can ever be an affront to God, my love," Corrine replied, still smiling.

It's my fault Mammy is dead, Madeline tried to explain.

Her mother shook her head, but didn't reply. The image faded. Madeline could still see Corrine's hand, beckoning to her, but she wasn't ready to go, not as long as she heard her son crying for her. She didn't see Sybil leave the porch, but she heard her voice as she boarded the canoe.

"Joe, take me back to the plantation," Sybil barked.

"What about Miss Madeline?"

"You will come back for her later."

"Shall I summon the doctor then?" Joe asked, his voice hopeful.

"She'll be dead by the time you come back, you fool," Sybil said. "Wait until dark, then wrap her body and take her to New Orleans. Lay her in my family tomb. I'm the last of the Talbots, so no one will go in there ever again. Her remains will never be found. And clean this place. No one must ever know what happened here."

"Yes, missus."

"Oh, and bring me her fan. It's the only thing that can give me away."

"As you wish. What do I tell Mr. George if he ask for Miss Madeline?" Joe asked.

"You tell him that Madeline refused to marry Mr. Montlake and decided to leave with her Mammy instead. I gave her a sum of money and wished her well," Sybil replied calmly. "She mentioned her desire to visit Europe."

"Yes, missus."

Madeline heard the splash of paddles as the canoe glided away from the bank. A lusty wail pierced the air, baby George announcing that he was ready for a feeding. Sybil's voice carried over the water as she cooed to the baby, sounding for all the world like a happy grandma.

Madeline's fingers clawed at the rough boards of the porch as she gasped for air, her mouth opening and closing like a landed fish. Her chest heaved and her legs convulsed like those of a hanged man. Terror overcame her, but after a few moments the pain receded, leaving a feeling of peace and calm. She was no longer suffering, but floating on a gossamer cloud, free as a bird. A choking sound escaped her chest as blood gurgled from her mouth.

Madeline's hand went to the hole in her chest, but never quite made it. It fell to her side as the light went out, replaced by eternal darkness. She didn't hear the hungry cry of her baby or the screech of a bird as it exploded from a nearby tree and shot into the sky, its wings flapping wildly. She was gone.

Chapter 45

May 2014

New Orleans, Louisiana

Quinn hurled the fan against the wall. The fragile accessory shattered with a satisfying crack as ivory met plaster. This time she didn't weep. She was furious. Sybil Besson had gotten away with a double murder since it was obvious no one had ever wondered what became of Madeline and Clara or bothered to investigate their disappearance. They weren't mentioned anywhere, least of all in the history of the plantation presented with such flair by the museum staff. George and Amelia got their baby, and Sybil had gone to her grave knowing that she had assured the continuation of the line. Very commendable!

"Well, that's about to change," Quinn told the empty room. There wasn't much she could do about Clara, since she rested at the bottom of the swamp, but she would find Madeline's remains and bring the crime to light. Madeline would get a proper burial, with her name etched into a gravestone that would be erected next to Charles Besson's. Corinne's gravestone would need to be restored as well, since whoever had destroyed it, likely Joe acting on Sybil's orders, had done a thorough job. Quinn wondered if Corinne's stone had been removed during Sybil's lifetime or at some point after. She couldn't see why someone would desecrate her grave after Sybil's death, but anything was possible. Perhaps George had learned the truth of Madeline's parentage from his grandmother and wished to erase all traces of the family's shameful past.

It might be possible to trace Clara's descendants, Quinn mused as she walked into the bathroom and splashed cold water on her flushed face. She didn't know Clara's surname; she probably hadn't had one, but there was bound to be some sort of list of slaves at the plantation, and since Quinn knew the names of Clara's sons, she could follow the thread into the present.

As she plopped into a chair, she wondered if Clara's descendants would appreciate learning the truth or resent the interference. What good would it do them to discover that Clara's death had gone uninvestigated and unpunished? It would be yet another crime committed against their family, a crime they could do nothing about at this stage. It wasn't as if they could hold Seth Besson accountable. Nor should they, since it wasn't his fault his ancestors were slave owners and murderers. Seth would suffer needlessly, and so would Brett by association.

Or maybe Clara's family already knows, Quinn thought as she sprang out of the chair and began to pace the room, too restless to sit. Zachary and Zane must have searched for their mother when she failed to return from the bayou. It was even possible they had learned the truth of what happened from Joe. He must have told someone what he'd witnessed that day, despite being threatened by Sybil. Or had he chosen to remain silent to shield himself from Sybil's wrath and to save Zach and Zane from helpless fury?

She'd never know unless she spoke to the family, which she would have to do before the show aired in Britain. It wouldn't be shown here in New Orleans, but information had a way of spreading, especially through the internet, and Clara's descendants might get wind of the program. Besides, the BBC would probably need their consent to tell that part of the story, unless they changed Clara's name in order to avoid getting mired in legal proceedings. Was there a precedent for this kind of situation? She'd need to run this by Rhys so he could clear the finished script with the Legal Department.

In the meantime, Quinn would focus on Madeline. She glanced at the alarm clock on the bedside table. It was just past two in the afternoon. She had no plans with Seth tonight, since he had a meeting after work, but perhaps Brett was free. For some reason, she felt reluctant to do this alone.

Quinn called Brett and was happy when he answered in person. "Hey, sis."

"Hey, yourself. Listen, I need a favor. It's a bit gruesome actually, so I'll understand if you say no."

"Do tell. I'm all ears." Brett sounded like an excited child.

"I need to break into a tomb."

"You're joking. Have you stumbled upon some archeological mystery in our boring old NOLA?"

"NOLA?"

"New Orleans, Louisiana. It's an abbreviation," Brett explained patiently. "Anyway, what have you discovered?"

"I'll fill you in later. Will you help me?"

"Hell, yeah! Whose tomb?"

"It's the tomb of Sybil Besson's family. I believe she was the last of that line, so the tomb wouldn't have been opened since her parents were interred."

"Why would you want to break in there?" Brett asked. He sounded distinctly less enthusiastic than before, his voice now tinged with doubt and suspicion.

"I believe I will find evidence of a crime that has gone unpunished for over one hundred and fifty years."

"And how would you know about a crime that took place that long ago?"

"I can't really explain, but it's sort of an extrasensory ability."

"Like a sixth sense?" Brett sounded wary, but Quinn was too emotionally overwrought to explain. Now that she knew what she had to do, she didn't want to waste another minute.

"Yes, something like that."

"You are wonderfully weird, you know that?"

"Yes, so I've been told. Oh, and bring a shovel."

"That's the first time anyone has asked me to bring a shovel, but hopefully not the last." Brett chuckled. "Have you told Dad about this little unlawful expedition?"

"No, I haven't told anyone. I want to see if I'm right first. If I'm not, then we'll just clear off and pretend it never happened."

"Sounds like a great plan. I'll pick you up in twenty minutes."

"I'll be waiting."

Chapter 46

Quinn dressed in a pair of leggings, a T-shirt, and trainers. This could be dirty work, and she had no desire to soil her good clothes. Hopefully, no Good Samaritan would report two people breaking into a tomb in the middle of the day. Disturbing someone's final resting place was a crime, even if they did nothing to desecrate the actual remains.

Quinn smiled. It was nice to have a brother willing to come on short notice bearing a shovel. That was what she'd been missing all her life—an accomplice. Of course, Gabe would have been there with bells on had this been England, but he was safely in London, doing the school run and marking end-of-term papers. Quinn fired off a quick text to tell him she missed him and hoped to see him in a few days. Once she found Madeline's remains there would be no reason to stay in New Orleans any longer. She would have everything she needed for the program, and had spent sufficient time with her new family to have established a lasting bond. It was time to go home. Quinn grabbed her bag, phone, and key-card and headed out.

Brett was waiting for her in the lobby. His face lit up with anticipation when she came toward him. "So, why are we doing this?" he asked as he kissed her cheek and followed her outside. "Come on. Tell me the whole story. Since I'm about to commit a crime at your behest, I'd at least like to know why I'm doing it and if it's worth risking my unblemished reputation and enviable future for. I considered robbing a bank when Dad cut off my allowance in seventh grade, but I never expected to resort to grave robbery. Even I have standards."

Quinn smiled at him. He seemed very pleased with his own wit and his exuberance was contagious. She really wished she could simply tell him the truth, but she wasn't ready to share her secret with him. He was too young to understand and would probably label her a freak and a fraud, as many people would once they found out.

"I will tell you everything if I find what I'm looking for. How about that?" she replied.

"Will this assignment be on a need-to-know basis, like in the army?" Brett joked.

"Exactly. This way you wouldn't be able to reveal too much if tortured for information."

"The only person likely to torture me is Dad. He'll be furious if we get arrested."

"And if we don't?" Quinn asked, amused by Brett's choice of words.

"Then he'll want to know all the details and complain about not being invited along."

"He'll complain about a lot more if I'm correct," Quinn muttered.

"What is it you're hoping to find, Quinn?" He was serious now, his eyes anxious as he searched her face for answers.

"Proof of murder."

Saying the words out loud doused Quinn's high spirits. This was no laughing matter, and some part of her wished she could leave this alone and forget what she'd seen. Apprehension tugged at her heart as she climbed into Brett's car. She wanted to find Madeline, but coming face to face with her remains would not be pleasant. Quinn had seen many skeletons in her profession and had always kept a sense of detachment, but this was personal. Madeline was personal, and for the first time, Quinn was directly linked to the victim.

Brett parked the car close to the cemetery and they walked toward the gates in silence. Brett's hold-all gave a metallic clang as he slung it over his shoulder.

"What did you bring?" Quinn asked. A shovel was noticeably absent.

"A screwdriver, a crowbar, and metal clippers. Not like the door is unlocked," Brett pointed out. "Besides, no one is buried underground. They are all nicely laid out on shelves. No need for a shovel, unless what you're looking for is buried inside the mausoleum. I have a shovel in the trunk, but thought it might be too conspicuous to be prancing about with it in the middle of the afternoon."

Quinn nodded. He was right, of course. Brett was a better accomplice than she'd anticipated. Some part of her was glad of this bonding experience with her brother, but her mind was on Madeline. She could recall Madeline's face as the gun went off and the bullet ripped into her chest, the impact knocking her backward. She looked so young, so innocent. She'd been only sixteen, a girl whose life had barely begun. In this day and age, Madeline would have had someone advocating for her rights, protecting her. There were laws, and George would have been held accountable for what he'd done. But in the nineteenth century there had been no one to turn to. Clara had been the only person who truly cared for Madeline, but she'd been powerless to do anything except try to advise Madeline to move on and rebuild her life, which she'd desperately tried to do.

Quinn wiped away an angry tear. This was no time to get emotional. First things first.

Brett extracted a pass from his pocket and showed it to the attendant at the ticket booth. His forethought impressed Quinn. Visitors to the cemetery had to pay a hefty admission fee, but locals who had family buried in St. Louis Cemetery could obtain a pass to enter the cemetery for free. The attendant waved them through without bothering to examine the pass. He had his mobile out and was too preoccupied with whatever he saw on the screen to care.

It took a while to find the right tomb since it was located in the most neglected and dilapidated part of the cemetery. The massive stone monument leaned a bit to the side, and chunks of stonework were missing, gouged out by storms and time. The stone lintel was so weathered that the name 'Talbot' was almost

338

completely obliterated. A wrought-iron fence surrounded the tomb, and although the gate was unlocked, it screeched with disuse when Brett pulled it open. Sybil had chosen wisely. No one had opened the Talbot vault since the nineteenth century. She'd committed the perfect crime.

"You should have seen this place after Hurricane Katrina," Brett said as he lowered his hold-all to the ground. "It's a wonder any of these old tombs are still standing."

"They were built to last."

"Yeah, that's what I love about those times," Brett replied. "When people did something, they did it like they meant it. They were strong and determined, not like the people of today who are paralyzed by ridiculous social constraints. They simply got on with it."

"Well, that's one way of looking at it, but social constraints were very much present in nineteenth-century society," Quinn replied, barely paying attention to him. She stared at the crumbling stone edifice, her hands shaking. It wasn't too late to walk away and leave this particular Pandora's Box closed. She knew what had happened to Madeline. Perhaps that was enough. She could simply tell Rhys that she'd changed her mind and this story was too personal to air. They could find another grave, another skeleton, another story.

"What other way is there? People today are so soft," Brett went on. "I mean, if something needs to be done, just do it and deal with the consequences later."

"Let's do it then," Quinn said. Brett was right. This needed to be done. The truth had to come out, and consequences be damned. Madeline deserved to be acknowledged, and it was time Quinn made peace with her gift. If people ridiculed her, so be it. She was done hiding.

"You sure?" Brett watched her closely, his eyes full of anxiety.

"Yes, I am."

The double doors of the tomb, which at some point must have been painted dark green but were now faded and peeling, were kept locked with an old iron padlock. The chain that slithered through the handles was flaking with rust, but when Quinn gave the lock an experimental tug, it held fast. She brushed the orange rust off her hands and peered closely at the door.

"Maybe we can unscrew the door handles with your screwdriver," she suggested.

"It's easier to just clip the chain," Brett replied. "There's no one here. No one will notice."

He extracted a pair of large pliers from his bag and applied them to the rusty chain. It took a few tries, but he was finally able to cut through one of the links. The chain rattled to the ground, and the lock fell at Quinn's feet. Brett picked up the lock and chain and tossed them behind the tomb. He stowed the pliers in his bag and opened the doors. The hinges whined with years of disuse, but the doors opened, revealing the inside of the vault. The tomb exhaled a breath of damp earth and decay.

"After you, Madame Tomb Raider," Brett said with a wicked grin.

Quinn peered inside. The tomb was filled with gloom, even on this sunny day. Four shelves held the remains of the last Talbots to have been interred in the vault, thankfully still in their coffins. The wood had warped and rotted over the years, especially after the flooding caused by the hurricane, but it was still intact, holding its grisly contents in check. A dozen bags lined up against the far wall had what appeared to be tags attached to them, but the tags were yellowed with age and the ink faded and illegible. The bottoms of the bags showed evidence of water staining, which meant that water had gotten into the vault and had eventually drained away.

"What are those?" Quinn asked as she peered at the bags.

"These family vaults can only hold so many coffins, so after someone has been dead for two years, they move their bones to a bag and burn the coffin, making room for new arrivals," Brett explained.

"Not a very pleasant way to spend eternity."

"What does it matter? They're dead," Brett replied with a shrug. "And these customers have been dead for centuries."

Quinn turned on the flashlight on her mobile and shone a light into the tomb, illuminating its darkest corners. She wasn't interested in the coffins or the labeled bags. No one would have bothered to label Madeline's remains. She was looking for something that seemed out of place. It wasn't hard to find. Beneath the lowest ledge was a burlap sack, or what remained of it. Most of the cloth had rotted away, revealing the white gleam of bone. Even without disturbing the remains, Quinn could clearly see the hand and the narrow, delicate wrist. They were small, like those of a child or a young woman. She exhaled loudly.

"I think that's her."

Quinn turned away from the sack to look at Brett. She expected him to ask questions, to demand to know who she'd been searching for, but he stood motionless just inside the vault. Even in the dim light, Quinn noted his pallor. He looked like he was about to cry.

"Brett, are you all right?" Quinn asked. "I'm sorry if you find this disturbing."

Brett continued to stare, his gaze fixed on the sack and its contents. "What do you plan to do, Quinn?"

"First, I must label and pack the bones. Then, I will take them to a forensic archeologist, who will examine the skeleton and tell me everything there is to know about her, from what she ate for breakfast to how she died."

"Leave her be," Brett said. His voice shook with emotion as his gaze traveled from Madeline to Quinn and back again.

"I must tell her story, Brett. She was murdered when she was sixteen."

"I know," Brett said as he moved a little closer to Quinn.

"You know?" she asked, but then recalled that she'd mentioned she was looking for proof that a murder had been committed as they were leaving the hotel.

"Yes, I know. Leave her be, Quinn. Please, just walk away. No one needs to know about this."

"Of course they do. Madeline's story will be the subject of the *Echoes from the Past* finale," Quinn replied as she crouched to snap photos of the remains. Since Jason wasn't there to film the process, she'd have to supplement her narration with photos of the remains in situ. She then stood and faced Brett.

"Quinn, I know about her. I know who she is and why she's here," he exclaimed, shaking with rage. "I saw her. I held her fan many times, before Dad locked it in the safe."

Quinn stood frozen, staring at Brett as realization dawned. He had the same gift. He could see into the past. "You saw her?" she whispered. The gift wasn't passed only down the female line after all. Seth had denied all knowledge of it, but maybe it had bypassed him, or he simply had no wish to acknowledge it.

"Yes, I saw her, just as you obviously did. I hoped I was wrong. I thought I was the only one. Neither of my parents are psychic, and I had no idea this ability came down the Besson line, but once you started talking about breaking into the tomb, I began to suspect. I kept probing to see if you actually knew about Madeline or if you were on the scent of something else. I agreed to come with you for a reason. I needed to see for myself."

"And now you have." Quinn was still bemused, but excitement was building within her. They shared the gift. They

342

were connected on a deeper level. They were two halves of a whole.

"Quinn, I need you to delete those pictures and walk away," Brett said. His tone turned threatening, his face all harsh lines and shadows.

"Why would I walk away now, when I just found her?" Quinn asked. "Are you afraid your ability will be revealed if Madeline is discovered? No one has to know."

"I'm afraid that my heritage will be revealed," Brett said, bearing down on her. "This is the South, in case you haven't noticed. Prejudice is alive and well, and I have no desire for the world to know that I'm descended from a black slave. You might not care, but I do. I will not have the world know there's a stain on the family name."

"A stain? Did you really just say that?"

"Yeah, I did. I have no intention of living with this shame. Nor do I want to pass it on to my children. It's bad enough that we lost the war and all those slaves were set free to desecrate the South and its traditions. Families like ours lost everything, and had to bow and scrape just to survive. I won't have it be known that I'm the spawn of some ignorant witch from Trinidad."

Quinn stared at Brett in shock and disbelief. How could she have misjudged him so spectacularly? *We lost the war*, he'd said, as if the war had happened in his lifetime and he'd been personally vested in its outcome. He participated in reenactments, but Quinn thought it was just something he liked to do for fun, not because he truly believed in the lost cause of the South.

She backed away from him, appalled and disgusted by this young man she'd been proud to call her brother only a few moments ago.

"You're mad," she said, noting the maniacal gleam in Brett's eyes.

"I'm the sanest person you'll ever meet," Brett replied. "I'm also the last person you'll ever meet."

Quinn cried out as he pushed her with all his strength. She crashed to the stone floor of the tomb, landing against the bags of bones lining the back wall. Something jabbed in her back and her knee turned at a weird angle, making her gasp with pain. Her head shot up as she heard the doors slam.

"Brett?" she cried. "Open the door."

No answer.

Quinn sprang to her feet and rushed toward the door, pushing on it as hard as she could. The door wouldn't budge. "Brett, please," she cried. "Open the door. Let's talk."

Quinn's heart hammered wildly when she heard a metallic sound from outside. "Brett, open this door right now!" she screamed. And then she heard the click of a lock. This wasn't the old lock Brett had thrown aside. He'd come equipped with a new one, ready for every possible outcome. He'd planned to lock her in all along if she proved to know the truth and failed to agree to his terms. "What are you doing?" she screeched as she pounded on the door with her fists.

Brett's voice was muffled, but she heard him clearly enough. "Did you really think you could show up out of nowhere and ruin everything? Not only are you about to reveal a secret that will destroy my family, but you're about to take half of what's mine. I've had to put up with my father's bullying my whole life. I've had to live with his incredibly high expectations and criticism, thinking that I only had to make it until I was twenty-one and could access my trust fund, and then you appeared. Beautiful. Perfect. And pregnant. You are everything he's dreamed of in a kid. And you're going to give him a grandchild. He's obsessed with you. So obsessed that he's changing his will—in your favor, no doubt. He will leave you everything: the house, the business, the investments, and I will be left with nothing. Well, not going to happen, Miss Britain 2014. I'll tell him you left, and when he doesn't hear from you or get an invitation to the wedding or get to see your kid, he'll start to hate you and turn to me, as he did when Mom finally left him after all his affairs. He'll need me again, and he'll appreciate me being there for him."

Brett's words came out in a torrent, as fears he'd been harboring for years came to a head.

"Brett, I don't want your father's money. I only wanted to know where I came from. Look, I won't tell anyone about Madeline. I'll erase the photos and we'll forget this ever happened. I'll call my boss and tell him he can't use the story."

"It's too late, Quinn. I gave you an out. I was willing to forgo half my inheritance to save your life, but you made your choice. You chose some half-breed over me, and now you'll spend what's left of your life with her. Goodbye, Quinn. I hope it doesn't take you too long to die."

"Brett!" Quinn shrieked, but no reply came. He was gone.

Chapter 47

"Brett!" Quinn cried again as she put a shoulder to the door. The wood was old, but the doors were thick, and as Brett had pointed out, built to last. She tried several more times before giving up. Her shoulder throbbed, her breath came in ragged gasps, and her heartbeat grew more erratic as her panic escalated.

"Calm down and think rationally," Quinn told herself as she leaned against the door for support. She took several deep breaths and waited for her heart rate to slow down before formulating a plan.

She would find her phone and call for help. She'd have some explaining to do, but she'd much rather get into trouble with the law for breaking into a tomb than wait for Brett to come to his senses and return for her. He would come back; she was sure of that. He might be angry and misguided, but he wasn't a murderer. He'd meant to teach her a lesson, and he had. She should have taken his feelings more seriously, even if she didn't agree with his way of thinking, and she would tell him that as soon as she got the opportunity. If he felt this strongly about Quinn sharing Madeline's story then she would give him her word that the episode would never air. Rhys wouldn't be happy, but he'd respect her wishes. After all, he had offered her the option to back out only a few days ago.

Quinn crouched down and searched for her mobile. She'd dropped it when Brett locked the door, but it had to be nearby. She just had to make sure not to step on it. She breathed a sigh of relief when her hand closed around the cool metal case of her iPhone. She was one step closer to getting out. She pressed the button and stared at the screen. The phone was almost fully charged, which was a blessing. Quinn decided to try Seth first. He'd be angry, but he'd probably want to avoid involving the police. She selected his number and waited for the call to connect.

'Call Failed,' the screen read. She tried again with the same result.

She swallowed back her panic and decided to try calling the police. Sometimes emergency numbers went through, even when the phone had very little charge left or there wasn't a good signal. She began to tap in the numbers 999, but remembered the number for the police in the U.S. was different, and called 911 instead. She held her breath as she prayed for an operator to answer.

'Call Failed.'

Quinn tried again and again. She pressed herself to the doors in the hope that she might get even a weak signal from the outside, but call after call failed to connect.

She was trapped inside a stone box, and her only mode of communication could only be used to illuminate her surroundings for an hour or so before the battery died. Quinn sat down against the wall closest to the door, wrapped her arms about her legs, and rested her head on her knees. She tried to remain calm, but the panic was rising and bubbling to the surface like lava in a volcano.

Quinn sat up straighter, so as not to put any pressure on her diaphragm, and tried to breathe deeply and slowly. She managed to calm down a fraction, but the dust they'd disturbed had permeated the air and she doubled over in a fit of coughing. Tears ran down her face and she felt lightheaded and nauseated.

The coughing finally subsided and Quinn calmed down enough to check the time on her mobile. It was just past 2:00 p.m., hours until the cemetery closed. Perhaps if she screamed for help someone would hear her, but it was a longshot. There had been few people in the cemetery when she'd arrived with Brett—was it really only a half-hour ago? —and they'd all been milling about the main avenue, taking photos and reading the names on the vaults. There were guided tours of the cemetery, but the Talbot tomb was too far removed from anything of interest, such as the tomb of Voodoo priestess Marie Laveau, a major draw for tourists, or the pyramid-shaped vault that Nicholas Cage had purchased for himself a few years back, planning to make New Orleans the site of his final resting place. There were other attractions, such as the tomb of the pirate Barthelemy Lafon, and the grave of Paul

Morphy, a world chess champion, but they were on the other side of the cemetery. The path to the Talbot vault was so derelict that it was clear no one had ventured that far in a long time.

Quinn turned off the phone to conserve the battery and leaned her head against the cool stone wall. Would anyone even look for her? How long would it take for someone to realize she was missing? If Brett had told Seth she'd gone home, Seth would try to call her, and maybe wait a few days for her to ring him back before trying again. Gabe would call; he rang every day, but would leave a message and wait for her to get back to him. He'd have no reason to suspect anything was wrong and she wasn't just spending time with Seth and Brett. Jason Womack wanted to go over the footage they'd shot in the bayou, but he would hardly come looking for her. He might even go back home and send her a video file in an email to be viewed when she had time.

Quinn's panic mounted as she analyzed her situation. Even if someone realized she was missing, no one would think to look for her in an ancient tomb. She would die here, and so would her baby.

Almost as if it had heard her thoughts, she felt a light kick. Quinn's hand went to her belly.

"Is that you?" she asked.

Another kick. It was feeble, but it was there, a sign of life.

"I'm so sorry I got you into this," Quinn sobbed. "I was such a naïve fool."

She looked at the phone again. It was now nearly three in the afternoon. What if Brett didn't come back? What if he really meant to leave her here? Quinn's thoughts tumbled and tripped over each other, the panic returning in full force as the reality of her situation finally sank in. Would Brett really leave her to die? Would her child never be born? Would Gabe never find out what happened to her and spend the rest of his life wondering and blaming himself for not coming to New Orleans with her? Oh, she should have listened to him. Why had she been so stubborn, so driven? They could have come to New Orleans together after the wedding. During the summer maybe, when Emma had summer holidays. They could have even visited Disney World. The TV advert had said it was the happiest place on Earth, Quinn remembered, as manic laughter bubbled inside her, but came out as a desperate sob.

She probably wouldn't even be lucky enough for some archeologist to discover her remains. Who would look in here, and why? She'd rot here for eternity, with Madeline for company. Two foolish, naïve women who had met their end when they least expected it because they underestimated the depth of their adversaries' fear and hatred.

You must remain calm, Quinn told herself as her pulse raced and she fought to catch her breath. She clasped her hands in front of her and began to pray. She couldn't remember the last time she'd asked God for anything, but this wasn't for her, this was for her baby. Quinn prayed that Brett would come back and let her out, since that was her only realistic hope of rescue. Surely he'd cooled off by now and begun to comprehend the ramifications of what he'd done—or did he feel safe, thinking he'd never get caught?

"Please, God," Quinn prayed. "Help me. Soon," she added as a wave of dizziness washed over her. "I'm not feeling very well."

When her prayer wasn't immediately answered, Quinn wrapped her arms about her legs and rested her head on her knees again. For some reason, sitting in that position brought her comfort.

The minutes ticked by and turned into hours. Her mobile showed it was almost seven o'clock. The cemetery would be closed by now, so there was no chance of anyone finding her until the following day, if they found her at all. The prospect of spending the night in the tomb terrified her, but there was nothing to do but try to rest. Quinn was starving and thirsty. She usually took a bottle of water with her to keep hydrated, but had forgotten the bottle in her hotel room in her excitement. There was nothing in her purse, not even a stick of gum or a mint.

As more hours passed, the air in the tomb grew cold, and the floor was hard and damp. Quinn wished she could lie down, but if she stretched out on the stone floor wearing only her thin T-shirt she'd get even colder. Her mouth was dry, and her stomach growled with hunger. She tried not to give in to despair, but tears slid unbidden down her cheeks and into her mouth. They tasted salty, and for some reason that made her cry harder. She'd never been so scared in her life. Eventually, she exhausted herself, curled into a ball, and slept.

Chapter 48

When Quinn woke, she was cold, stiff, and desperate for a pee. It felt wrong to urinate next to Madeline's remains, but there wasn't much else she could do. She moved closer to the back wall, hoping that the Talbots of yesteryear stowed there in burial bags would forgive her.

She looked at the time on her mobile. It was 7:27 a.m., nearly twelve hours since the last time she'd checked. She tried calling 911 again, but the call failed. How she wished that Brett had forgotten his hold-all in the tomb. A crowbar would have been of great help.

As the horror of her situation sank in anew, Quinn's panic returned in full force. She tried to calm down, but this time the breathing and praying didn't help. Her heart hammered wildly against her ribcage and she felt lightheaded and disoriented. A sharp pain tore through her belly, making her cry out.

"Oh, God, no," Quinn pleaded as the pain intensified. She massaged her belly in a circular motion to try to calm her contracting womb. "Stay with me," she begged the baby. "Please stay with me."

So that we can die together, her mind added. Quinn turned her face up to what would be the heavens and screamed in helpless agony. "Don't let me die here, you heartless bastard!" she yelled. She wasn't sure if she was addressing Brett or God, but it didn't matter. Either one had the power to save her, but she was growing convinced that neither would.

The pain in her abdomen brought her to her senses. It wasn't as sharp as it had been a few minutes ago, but it was there, steadily growing. Quinn felt something warm and moist between her legs. "No," she moaned as she slid her hand down her knickers. Her fingers came away wet and sticky. She brought her hand back up and shone a light on it. Blood.

Quinn screamed again, but this time it wasn't a scream of rage but of anguish, like a wounded animal that knew it was about to die. She had cramps, she was bleeding, and her back ached. She was also dehydrated and hungry. Her body had no energy to fight for the survival of her baby. What did it matter if she lost it? She would be gone in a few days. Without water she couldn't last long. Three days at most. The thought of spending several more days buried alive in her own grave brought on a new flood of tears.

Stop crying, she told herself. *You'll dehydrate faster*. But the tears just came. They were hot and salty, and bitter. She'd seen countless people die in her visions. She'd felt their suffering and heard their thoughts, but although she'd ached with the desire to help them and mourned their loss, she had never understood how it really felt to know that you're doomed, to finally realize there was no hope. No one was sending the cavalry, no one was racing the clock to prevent a tragic outcome. At this moment, she even envied Elise, who'd died in the arms of her lover. And Petra, whose end had been horrific, but quick.

Quinn would die slowly and alone. Had she done something to deserve this fate? She lay on her side, her arms wrapped around her belly. Was this some sort of cosmic retribution? She didn't believe in fate or karma, but she did believe in bad decisions made in haste. She'd been extremely foolish, and now she'd pay the ultimate price.

Quinn shut her eyes. It wasn't as if there was anything to see. She'd been inside the tomb for about eighteen hours. The pain in her belly continued, with contractions coming every few minutes, but the bleeding hadn't gotten worse. Her pulse was racing and she felt nauseous and confused. Quinn began to see bright lights in front of her closed eyelids. They formed into geometric shapes and floated in the darkness, twisting and turning and gyrating in colorful spirals. She reached out to touch one of the bright spheres, but couldn't find it. It seemed to have moved away, higher, out of her reach. She tried again and again, until she was overcome by crippling vertigo that threatened to suck her down into a swirling vortex.

Quinn lifted her head just as a stream of vomit erupted from her belly. She retched again and again, her body heaving in protest. She wiped her mouth with the back of her hand and slumped to the ground, too weak to move away from the pool of vomit. The lights came back, brighter this time, as soon as she shut her eyes. They seemed to go on for hours, frolicking lazily and making Quinn feel weightless and untethered to anything earthly. The contractions grew weaker, but were still there, and the nausea came in waves, but she didn't throw up again. She was depleted, mentally and physically. Her mind drifted, her thoughts mere fragments that made no sense. She entered a state of half-consciousness, for which she was instinctively grateful. It was a buffer between her and reality, and she hoped she would peacefully slip away, too disoriented to comprehend that the end had finally come.

At one point, all the pretty spheres merged into one. They grew brighter and Quinn squeezed her eyes tighter and covered her head with her arms, finding the light too painful to look at. She thought she heard voices, but she had to be hallucinating. Something touched her face and she tried to scream, but the pressure became firmer as she struggled for breath. She couldn't move her head; it was in a vice. The bright lights began to explode behind her eyelids, bringing back the vertigo and the nausea. And then all went dark.

Chapter 49

Quinn's eyes fluttered open and she immediately closed them again. The light was too bright, but so welcome. She tried opening her eyes again, slower this time, giving them time to adjust.

She was in a hospital bed, hooked up to an I.V. drip. A clip on her index finger, meant to monitor her heartrate, pinched hard. There were pins and needles in her right hand. She couldn't move it, as though it were trapped under a heavy object. Quinn slowly turned her head to the right. Even the slightest movement caused nausea and dizziness.

Gabe's head rested on the side of the bed. He was asleep, his cheek pressed against her hand, and his fingers curled around Quinn's. She tried to carefully move her hand, but Gabe immediately woke up. His head shot up, his eyes searching her face until relief gradually replaced the worry in his gaze.

Quinn slowly sat up and allowed Gabe to envelop her in a hug. He was very gentle, but she felt his tightly coiled need to hold her and reassure himself she was all right. Quinn burrowed into him, desperate for his solid warmth. She listened to the steady rhythm of his heart and inhaled his familiar scent as she pressed herself even closer to him, her arms wrapped around his waist. Tears flowed down her cheeks and soaked into the fabric of Gabe's shirt. He stroked her hair and held her close.

"I nearly lost you," he said softly, a catch in his voice. "I nearly lost you both."

Quinn pulled away and looked at him. Now that she saw him more clearly, she noted the dark circles beneath his eyes and the pallor of his skin. His shirt was wrinkled, his jaw darkened by thick stubble. He looked emotionally and physically wrung out.

"Gabe, I'm so sorry. I was so stupid, and so trusting."

"What happened is not your fault. You couldn't have known what Brett intended."

"Who found me? I can't remember a thing," Quinn confessed. "I thought I was going to die." Fresh tears threatened to flow, but she managed to hold them back.

Gabe had just opened his mouth to reply when Dr. Glahn walked into the room. She wore a pristine lab coat and her trendy rimless glasses magnified her kind blue eyes. "Ah, you're awake," she said cheerfully. "You gave us quite a scare, Quinn."

"The baby," Quinn whispered. "Did I lose my baby?" She'd been so relieved to find herself in a hospital with Gabe by her side that she'd momentarily forgotten about the cramping and bleeding she'd experienced inside the tomb. She searched Dr. Glahn's face, desperate for reassurance that she hadn't miscarried.

"The baby is all right, but another few hours in that tomb and you probably would have miscarried. Quinn, we have you on blood pressure medication. Don't worry, it won't harm the little one," she added in response to Quinn's panicked expression. "It was imperative that we lower your blood pressure. It was through the roof. Not surprising after what you've been through."

"What's in the I.V.?" Quinn asked, eyeing the half-empty bag with suspicion.

"Just a glucose solution. You were severely dehydrated after your ordeal. Do you feel up to eating something?"

"Yes, please."

"I'll have the cafeteria send up some breakfast. No caffeine though."

"I'm gasping for a cup of tea. And some toast would be nice." Quinn's stomach felt hollow with hunger. She couldn't remember the last time she'd eaten, but she supposed it must have been breakfast the day Brett locked her in.

"Decaffeinated tea only, I'm afraid. And you need some protein. Eggs will do nicely. Doctor's orders," she said, checking Quinn's chart. "Now, I don't want to worry you, but I just got back the labs for your urine. There was protein in your sample, and combined with the high blood pressure, headaches, and swelling in your extremities, I think it's very likely that you're on the road to developing preeclampsia. This can be very dangerous, for both you and the baby. I need you to see your doctor as soon as you return home. I will give you a copy of your labs to take with you. I want you to rest for the rest of the day."

"When will I be discharged?" Quinn asked. "I want to go home."

Dr. Glahn smiled and shook her head at Quinn's impatience. "I'm keeping you overnight. You are to do nothing but rest, drink lots of fluids, and eat. You are not going anywhere until your blood pressure is stabilized and the swelling in your ankles has gone down."

"I understand. Thank you, Doctor," Quinn replied, unreasonably upset. She knew that Dr. Glahn was doing the right thing, but the thought of spending another few days in New Orleans left her panicked. She would have gladly gotten on a plane this very day, if that were possible, but of course she had to think of the baby, and Gabe. By the looks of him, he needed to rest as much as she did.

"But it's not all doom and gloom," Dr. Glahn announced as she walked toward the door and held it open. "There's someone who desperately wants to see you."

Quinn nearly burst into tears again when Emma exploded into the room, followed by Kathy.

"Quinn, I missed you so much," Emma exclaimed as she tried to hug Quinn. She managed to hug only Quinn's arm because the hospital bed came nearly to her shoulders, but it was enough to make them both feel better. "Daddy said you're ill. Here, you can borrow Mr. Rabbit. He always makes me feel better."

"Thank you, darling." Quinn sniffled. "Mr. Rabbit is exactly what I need, and Mr. Russell," she added, smiling over Emma's head at Gabe.

"I should have never let you go on your own," Gabe said.

"It's not as if you could have stopped me."

"No, but I should have come with you."

"What's done is done. Please don't beat yourself up, Gabe."

"Quinn, can I watch TV?" Emma asked when she saw the television mounted on the wall. She was already bored and looking for a distraction. "They have different programs here, but I like them. I watched *Dora the Explorer* while I was waiting with Kathy."

"Kathy, thank you for looking after her," Gabe said.

"It was the least I could do," Kathy muttered. She avoided looking at Quinn. "Quinn, I'm so sorry for what Brett did. I have no words…"

"What did he do?" Emma demanded. "Was he bad?"

"Yes, he was very bad." Kathy's voice shook with emotion as she met Quinn's gaze over Emma's head. "I don't know what got into him. He's always been so kind, so quiet."

"People do strange things when they feel threatened," Quinn replied. "Where is he?"

"He's at the police station. They are holding him on charges of kidnapping, unlawful imprisonment, and attempted murder. Had you lost the baby… I'm sorry." Kathy broke down and fled the room.

"He could go to prison for years," Gabe said in a low voice, so as not to attract Emma's attention. She was already fixated on *The Mickey Mouse Club*.

357

"He deserves to," Quinn said. "He left me to die. Where's Seth?" she asked, realizing that no one had mentioned her father.

Gabe sighed and looked away for a moment.

"What? What are you not telling me?" Quinn whispered, suddenly scared.

"Seth is also in police custody."

"What? Why?"

"He's been arrested for assault and battery," Gabe replied. "He nearly killed Brett when he finally chased him down. I think he's getting out on bail today. He is desperate to speak to you."

"I'm not ready to speak to him, Gabe," Quinn muttered. She was too tired and weak to deal with a confrontation.

"You don't have to speak to anyone. You will have some breakfast and then Emma and I will leave you to rest. No visitors. Promise?"

Quinn nodded. She wasn't up to talking to anyone, not even her parents. Having to recount what had happened would be too much for her at the moment, and she had to mind her blood pressure. "Will I have to give a statement to the police?"

"Maybe later. I think they have everything they need for now. Ah, here's breakfast."

"Good. I'm ravenous."

Chapter 50

Quinn felt an acute sense of loss as soon as the door closed behind Gabe and Emma. Without Emma's chatter and the squeaky voice of Mickey Mouse, the room was unbearably quiet. They would come back later, but for now Quinn had to follow Dr. Glahn's orders. She removed the lid and faced her breakfast. Scrambled eggs, toast, butter, and a packet of grape jelly. There was also weak tea and a container of orange juice. Despite her hunger, the sight of the food brought back the nausea. For one terrible moment, she was right back in the dark tomb, terrified and alone.

Not alone. The baby gave Quinn a vicious kick and she laughed out loud. "All right, you. I get the message. I'm eating," she said to her belly and picked up a forkful of egg. It wasn't the best breakfast she'd ever had, but it would suffice. Once she began eating, she actually felt better. The nausea receded and the terrible weakness in her limbs began to ebb, replaced by a feeling of wellbeing, or something close to it. Quinn ate as much as she could and pushed the tray away.

The blinds were partially closed, but shafts of sunlight peeked between the plastic slats. *Sunlight.* She'd thought she'd never see it again. Funny how so many things in life could be friend or foe, depending on the situation. When on a dig in the Middle Eastern desert, there were days when Quinn had thought the sun would burn her to cinders and made sure to cover every part of her body before leaving her tent in the morning. There, the sun was a ruthless enemy that took no prisoners. But when she had been locked in that tomb, she'd have given anything for one more glimpse of the light, one more sunrise, and one more chance to look up at the vast blueness of the sky.

Quinn leaned back and closed her eyes against the light that crept along the wall and caressed her face with its gentle fingers. She'd mistaken Brett for a friend. She'd liked and trusted him, and believed they had something in common and would have a link for the rest of their lives, but he had callously left her and her baby to die. He'd have had the deaths of two people on his hands had Gabe not found her in time.

As she sank deeper into the pillows, Quinn wondered if the propensity for violence ran in families. Sybil had shown no remorse after shooting Clara and Madeline. She had been cool and matter-of-fact when she spoke to Joe about the disposal of their remains. Seeing Clara and Madeline as a threat, she had felt justified in doing whatever was necessary to protect her interests. Was that how Brett saw Quinn, as a hindrance to be disposed of? They'd spent hours together walking, talking, and exchanging ideas and stories of their lives. Did he not see her as a human being, a person whose life mattered? Was she nothing more to him than an obstacle to his future? And what sort of future would he have now?

Quinn looked up when there was a soft knock on her door. She thought it might be the hospital porter, come to take her tray away, but instead, Seth stepped carefully into the room, his hands held up as if warding off an attack. "Please, give me a couple of minutes, Quinn. I beg you."

"All right," she replied, although the last thing she wanted to do was talk to Seth. She didn't know what to say. Part of her wanted to rage at him, make accusations, and vent her anger, since she couldn't take it out on Brett. But another part of her felt overwhelming sympathy for him. Brett had been his only child up until a few weeks ago. Brett was his baby, his dream. Perhaps if Brett had assaulted a stranger, or someone who'd physically threatened him, Seth would be able to reason his actions away, but Quinn was Seth's daughter, the mother-to-be of his first grandchild, and Brett's sister. No amount of reasoning could justify what Brett had tried to do. No amount of love could blind a parent to such a crime.

Seth pulled up a chair and sat down heavily. He seemed to have aged twenty years since she'd last seen him. There were bags under his eyes and his knuckles were swollen and bruised.

"Quinn, I have no words," he began. He shook his head in mute denial as his eyes filled with tears. "When I think what might have happened had Gabe not arrived when he did."

"Seth, it wasn't your fault," Quinn replied, and meant it. "Brett knew what he was doing. He planned it. He wasn't sure if he'd go through with it, but the intent was there all along."

"He regrets it deeply."

Quinn pinned Seth with her unyielding gaze. "If he regretted it, he would have come back and let me out. He left me there, and I nearly lost my baby."

Seth hung his head, but not before Quinn saw that he was crying. "It's my fault, Quinn. I was so excited to have found you at this stage of my life. I wouldn't shut up about you. I should have been more sensitive to Brett's feelings and reassured him that my relationship with him wouldn't change, but I was blind to what he was going through."

Quinn regarded Seth carefully. He clearly knew nothing of Brett's gift and didn't understand the real reason for his actions. Of course, money was part of it, but Brett might not have gone so far had he not been threatened with exposure. He couldn't bear for people to know he had Negro blood or reconcile himself to that part of his heritage. Perhaps Brett identified with White Supremacist views, or maybe he was just a raging racist, but whatever his reasons, he couldn't allow the truth to come out.

She opened her mouth to explain the situation to Seth, but changed her mind. He was devastated, and she had no wish to add to his misery by telling him he was descended from a young girl of mixed blood who'd been a product of incest, and the ancestor he admired had committed murder and disposed of her victims in cold blood. Not to mention that both his son and daughter possessed a psychic ability he knew nothing about.

"Seth, you love Brett and you want to find an excuse for what he's done, but there is no excuse."

"Is there anything I can do?" Seth asked, his eyes pleading with Quinn for forgiveness.

"You can give me time."

"Of course. I understand. You can call me day or night if you want to talk. Or send me a text or an email if you are not ready for personal contact," he added.

"I will—in time."

Seth got to his feet, kissed Quinn's forehead, and left the room. He looked like a broken man.

Chapter 51

"Gabe, tell me what happened," Quinn said when he came back a short while later. Through the open door of her room, they could see Emma at the nurses' station, showing off her new doll, which she'd named Dora. The two nurses on duty were charmed by Emma's Scottish accent and kept asking her questions that Emma was more than happy to answer. She had a few questions of her own, specifically about how far it was to Disney World and if she could walk there from New Orleans.

"Are you sure you want to hear it, love?" Gabe asked. "It will only upset you."

Quinn shook her head. "It won't. I want to know how you found me."

"All right, but first, I want you to drink this apple juice." He held up a cup. "You're not consuming enough fluids."

"Oh, so you've joined the ranks of medical professionals now, Dr. Russell?"

Gabe raised one eyebrow in a silent rebuke, making Quinn laugh.

She drank the juice and handed him the empty cup. "Go on, then."

"When Emma and I got to the hotel, we wanted to surprise you, so we went up to your room. You weren't there. I rang you on your mobile, but you didn't pick up, so I left a voicemail, and took Emma out for something to eat since she was tired and hungry. I thought you'd ring me back by the time we were finished. When I hadn't heard back from you after several hours, I returned to the hotel, but you were still out. I thought you might be with your father, so I tracked Seth down at his office. He seemed very surprised to hear from me, since he was under the impression you'd left New Orleans. That's when I began to genuinely worry," Gabe said, taking Quinn's hand in his own.

"How did you find me?" she asked. "No one knew where Brett and I were heading."

"After I spoke to Seth, I asked the concierge to check if your things were still in your room. They were, so I knew you hadn't checked out. I rang Rhys and he put me in touch with the cameraman you'd been working with. He said he'd left you several messages, but hadn't heard back from you. He was about to leave for Charleston, but came right over. He was worried about you. He is a nice bloke."

"But Jason had no idea where I'd gone," Quinn interjected.

"No, he didn't, but he thought I might need his help, since he was familiar with the city and had a vehicle at his disposal. I kept trying your mobile, but it eventually informed me that your mailbox was full, which sent me into a blind panic. I know how fanatical you are about checking your messages."

Quinn smiled in acknowledgement. "Type A personality. Can't help it."

"I know, love."

"So what led you to the cemetery?" she asked.

"I rang the police, but they said you had to be missing for at least twenty-four hours before they could begin treating it as a missing person case. I had no idea exactly how long you'd been gone but, according to the concierge, you'd ordered room service that morning, so it was definitely less than twenty-four hours. The police wouldn't even speak to me until the following day, and I wasn't prepared to wait that long. I was worried sick."

Quinn squeezed Gabe's hand in gratitude. He was the most methodical, logical person she knew. He would have made an excellent detective. In a sense, he was one, because any archeologist had to find the clues and then string them together to form a hypothesis and establish a timeline of events. Gabe had done exactly that, and within a fairly short time.

"I asked the manager to talk to the employees, to see if anyone could recall you leaving the hotel. No one could, but the manager, lovely lady by the way, contacted someone who'd worked the earlier shift and had left for the day. The woman remembered you meeting a young man of Brett's description in the lobby. She overheard you talking about breaking into a tomb. She thought it was a joke, but I know you better than that."

"But she didn't know which tomb," Quinn pointed out.

"No, but Brett did. I contacted Seth again and he went in search of his son, since he couldn't raise him on his mobile. I nearly lost my mind, but Jason kept me company and invited us to stay in his room. The hotel was fully booked, and I just couldn't be bothered to go looking for something at that time of night. Emma was jetlagged and needed to go to bed. And she was frightened."

"They wouldn't let you stay in my room?" Quinn asked, surprised at the priggishness of the hotel staff.

"I didn't want to disturb anything, in case the police would need to search the room," Gabe replied. He might have been mad with worry, but he was still practical as ever, God bless him. "I called Seth again first thing in the morning, but he still hadn't managed to locate Brett. He'd been in touch with his ex-wife and told me of your visit to the hospital."

Gabe's voice sounded hoarse and Quinn knew he was trying to keep it together. She couldn't begin to image the thoughts that must have passed through his head when she'd failed to turn up by morning.

"Seth eventually managed to track down Brett through a friend of his. Brett had turned off his phone and the GPS signal, and took off. He was halfway to Texas by the time Seth caught up with him."

"I saw Seth's knuckles," Quinn remarked.

Gabe nodded. "He beat the truth out of him, then forced him to come back. Seth took him to the police, at which point Brett accused his father of assault and Seth was taken into custody."

Quinn shook her head in disbelief. Not only had Brett left town, proving once and for all that he'd had no intention of coming back for her, but he'd accused his own father of a crime against him when Seth was only trying to save his daughter and grandchild. What an unbelievable prick her brother had turned out to be.

"Kathy Besson came over to the hotel first thing in the morning. She thought I might need help with Emma, which was very kind of her. Jason and I raced to the cemetery as soon as we got the call from Seth. When I saw you lying there, I thought we were too late," Gabe muttered. "You were so white, so still. Jason called an ambulance and the police, and they were there within minutes. Kathy called Dr. Glahn. She met us in the Emergency Room."

"I'm glad it was Seth who ultimately found Brett," Quinn said. Had Gabe laid a hand on Brett, he might have been arrested, and she would never have been rescued.

"Quinn, had I been the one to find Brett, I would have killed him with my bare hands. I would have torn him apart. He's actually safer in custody," Gabe growled.

"He'll go to prison for years if convicted," Quinn speculated. "It will destroy Seth."

"Brett Besson must answer for what he's done."

"Gabe, I want to go home," Quinn pleaded. "Please take me home."

"We can leave as soon as Dr. Glahn gives us the green light," Gabe promised.

"Gabe, I was thinking about the wedding…"

366

"So have I."

"I don't want one."

Gabe lifted his gaze to hers. "Have you changed your mind about marrying me?" He looked stunned, as if he'd just been punched in the gut.

"No, my love," Quinn replied, smiling up at him. "Marrying you is about the only thing I'm sure about at this moment, but I don't want a circus, which it's sure to become given the incredibly dysfunctional nature of all these newly minted relationships. All I want is you, me, and Emma."

"Our parents will never forgive us. All our parents. Well, mostly yours," he joked. "That's half a dozen people at this stage."

"No, they probably won't, but this is about us, and our children. I don't want it to become about jealousy, resentment, unfinished business, or blame. I just want to sneak away and tie the knot."

"We can get married right here, right now. I'm sure they have a chaplain on the premises," Gabe suggested.

"As romantic as that sounds, I'm not getting married in a hospital gown with my bum hanging out."

"There you go complicating things again," he replied, rolling his eyes and making Quinn laugh.

"I want to get married in England, somewhere that's special for both of us."

"And where would that be?" Gabe asked, his interest piqued.

"I know just the place," Quinn replied with a cryptic smile. "You just get the rings and I'll take care of the rest."

"As long as by 'the rest' you mean inviting my mum and your parents. We can't get married without them. It wouldn't be right."

"Okay. You win," she conceded with a smile. "I would have invited them anyway. And of course, we'll need a maid of honor and a best man."

"Pete."

"Jill."

"That's settled then. So, where is this magical place then?" Gabe asked.

"You'll just have to wait and see."

Chapter 52

June 2014

Glastonbury, England

The day dawned rainy and gray, but by dinnertime the clouds had dispersed, leaving the sky a brilliant blue as clear as a looking glass. The inclement weather had driven the tourists away, leaving the site nearly deserted, which was perfect. Quinn stood just outside St. Michael's tower and took in the surrounding countryside that probably hadn't changed much since the time of King Arthur and his Camelot. Glastonbury Tor rose above the hills and valleys, its roofless tower reaching toward the heavens and marking the tallest point of the Isle of Avalon.

The sun began to set, painting the sky in almost violent shades of vermillion, gold, and aubergine. A shaft of blood-red sunlight pierced the archway of the tower and set it aglow, the sun's final act before darkness claimed this mystical place. To Quinn, there was no more fitting spot for two archeologists to make their own history.

"Breathtaking, isn't it?" Gabe said as he came up behind Quinn and wrapped his arms around her, his hands resting on her rounded belly.

"I've no words," she breathed as she watched the sunset.

"Ready?"

"Yes."

Gabe took Quinn by the hand and led her inside the tower where a small group of people had gathered to witness the ceremony. Susan and Roger Allenby, who'd flown in from Spain a fortnight ago, Phoebe Russell, Jill Allenby, and Pete and Brenda McGann were quietly chatting, while Emma danced around in her white frock, the flowers in her hair doing a dance of their own every time she twirled.

Reverend Trent took his place. "If everyone is ready," he said, smiling at the small assembly.

Jill and Pete took their places next to Quinn and Gabe, while the parents stepped back to give the bridal party some space. Brenda stood off to the side, camera at the ready. She'd been appointed the event photographer.

Gabe held out his hand to Emma. She took it and stood in front of Quinn and Gabe, her face alight with wonder.

"Dearly beloved, we are gathered here…" the reverend began.

The setting sun shone on Quinn and Gabe as if they were the only two people in the world, and it felt like a benediction, and a promise of good things to come. Quinn had felt a pang of guilt earlier at leaving the majority of family and friends out of their special day, but now that the moment was upon them, it felt just right. They didn't need endless toasts, drunk groomsmen, or stressed parents. All they needed was each other, their nearest and dearest, and this place, shrouded in mystery and wrapped in layers of legend.

Gabe made his vows and then it was Quinn's turn.

"Quinn Elizabeth Allenby, will you take this man to be your lawfully wedded husband, to love, honor, and cherish till the end of time?" Reverend Trent asked.

"I will," Quinn said, smiling into Gabe's eyes.

"You may now kiss the bride."

Gabe leaned toward her, but Quinn held up her hand and smiled into his eyes. "Not yet. I have one more vow to make."

The reverend looked surprised, but Gabe stood back, relaxed and eager to hear what Quinn had to say.

She turned Emma toward her and put both hands on her small shoulders. "Emma Jane McAllister Russell, I vow to love, honor, and cherish you as my daughter till the end of time. I will never replace the mother you lost, but hopefully, I can be the mother you gain, if that's all right with you."

"It's okay with me." Emma wrapped her arms around Quinn's legs, resting her cheek on Quinn's belly. "You can be my mum."

"Now may I kiss the bride?" Gabe asked. He leaned toward Quinn again, but his left hand rested on Emma's shoulder, including her in the embrace. She lifted her face and watched from beneath as they kissed.

"I now pronounce you husband and wife," the reverend said, closing the prayer book and smiling happily at the bridal couple, his job done.

Quinn and Gabe exited the tower and stood still, watching the last rays of the sun as it dipped below a mist-covered hill. Somewhere a bird sang, but it did nothing to disturb the church-like quiet of the moment.

"How do you feel?" Gabe asked, his arm draped around her, solid and protective.

"Happy. Peaceful. Blessed," Quinn replied. "You?"

"Hungry."

Quinn elbowed Gabe in the ribs and he drew her near and held her close. "I have dreamed of this moment since the day you fell into my arms at that dig and nearly knocked me off my feet. I never imagined it would be on Glastonbury Tor with my daughter serving as a bridesmaid and our baby kicking between us as we shared our first kiss as husband and wife, but this is even more perfect than I could have wished."

"I wouldn't have it any other way," Quinn replied.

371

"Daddy, let's go," Emma whined.

"Yes, let's go," Quinn replied. "We have a wonderful dinner waiting for us at the Pilgrim's Inn."

"Can I stay in your room tonight?" Emma asked, her expression sheepish.

"No, darling. Tonight you will stay with Grandma Phoebe," Gabe replied softly. "Quinn and I need to sleep alone tonight, but tomorrow, we'll go home and you can sleep in our bed if you like."

"All right," Emma conceded. "But Grandma Phoebe snores," she added plaintively.

**

Quinn snuggled closer to Gabe, a sated smile on her face. This was the first time since their return from New Orleans that they'd had absolute privacy, and they had taken full advantage of it, making their wedding night one to remember. After weeks apart, their lovemaking had been urgent and passionate, and very thorough. Quinn's hand slid down beneath the covers.

"Woman, I'm exhausted," Gabe complained. "Is that the way it's going to be from now on?"

"It's your husbandly duty to satisfy me."

"I thought you were satisfied already."

"I think I'd like to be satisfied one more time."

"Well, you asked for it," Gabe growled and rolled on top of her, pushing her legs apart with his knee and sliding into her as she gasped with delight and wrapped her legs around his waist.

Growing up, she'd often felt lonely and unsure of her place in the world, but at that moment, she was exactly where she wanted to be with the one person she wanted to be there with. Tomorrow, they would return to reality, and deal with the prospect of selling their homes and moving to Berwick, Quinn's high-risk pregnancy, and Emma's displeasure at having to be uprooted once again. But tonight was just for them.

Later, after Gabe had fallen asleep, Quinn reached for a glass of water and noticed that there was one voicemail message on her mobile. It was from Rhys.

"Quinn, Legal didn't turn up any of Clara's descendants. There's not enough to go on, so we are in the clear as far as that goes. Also, the powers-that-be don't feel comfortable with revealing your psychic ability on air. They fear it might undermine the integrity of the program and cause a backlash. So, a letter from George to Amelia will miraculously materialize, recounting all that he'd learned from Sybil about Madeline's parentage and demise. It will forestall any awkward questions about how you learned the location of her resting place. And, last but not least, brilliant news, BBC has renewed *Echoes* for a second season. Hope you're on-board. Talk soon."

Epilogue

September 1859
Arabella Plantation, Louisiana

George knocked softly and entered his grandmother's bedroom. She was propped up in bed, reading, as she always did before going to sleep. An oil lamp illuminated her face as she frowned at something happening in the story. During the day Sybil Besson was perfectly groomed and fashionably attired, but now her face was devoid of the powder and rouge she used to brighten her cheeks, and her severe gown had been replaced by a simple cotton nightdress. Her gray hair was plaited, and the braid rested on her shoulder, secured with a blue ribbon.

"George," Sybil said, putting the book down on the counterpane. "Come in."

"I've come to say goodnight," George said. He was still dressed, but had removed his coat and silk cravat, and taken off his shoes.

"Is little Brett all right?" Sybil asked.

"Yes, he's full to the brim and down for the night. I love watching him nurse," George confessed. "I do wish Amelia could have the pleasure of breastfeeding our son, but we'll take what we can get."

"Your grandfather liked watching his boys nurse as well. I almost wish I'd breastfed them myself, just to get him to look at me with such love," she reminisced.

"Grandfather loved you," George replied. "I know he did."

Sybil didn't answer, but looked at George more closely. "Is something troubling you, Georgie?"

"Have you heard from Madeline? Surely she's settled in Paris by now."

"No, I haven't heard anything," Sybil replied, her eyes sliding away from George's anxious face.

George shook his head in dismay. "I just don't understand, Grandmamma. She left without a word. She didn't even take any of her things. I know I behaved badly. I was selfish and careless, but Madeline never gave me a chance to put things right between us. I can understand why she refused to see me while she was with child, but I thought we'd finally have a chance to talk after the baby was born. I would never have forced her to marry Gilbert if she had no wish to. I would have taken care of her and made sure she had a good life. I would have thanked her for my beautiful boy. Doesn't she even want to know how our son is doing?"

"I suppose not."

"Grandmamma, where was Madeline planning to stay? The Monroes are going to France for the winter, so I'll ask them to look her up. I just want to know that she is well, and that she's all right for funds. I know you gave her a large sum, but perhaps she needs more. I can wire her the money if I just have the name of the bank."

Sybil exhaled loudly and looked up at George. Her lips were pressed into a thin line, and she suddenly looked older and grayer. "George, Madeline is gone."

"I know she's gone, but I am worried about her. I want her to know I haven't forsaken her, and she has nothing to fear from Amelia. Amelia holds no grudge against her, not after the precious gift Madeline has given her."

"George, Madeline is dead," Sybil said bluntly.

George's knees went weak and he rested his hand on the corner of a dresser to brace himself. "Dead? But you told me you arranged for her and Mammy to go to Paris."

"I told you that to spare you pain."

"Did she die in childbirth?" George exclaimed. "You should have had Dr. Halbrook attend on her. You should have allowed her to stay here, in comfort. Amelia and I would have stayed away, if it made things easier for Madeline. We would have respected her wishes."

"She didn't die in childbirth, George."

He stared at his grandmother, understanding dawning. "What did you do to her?" he asked, his voice low.

"She would have never relinquished the child. She made threats."

"Please, please tell me you didn't have a hand in her death."

"It was quick and merciful."

"Quick and merciful?" George cried. "She was sixteen. Her life had barely begun. She was your granddaughter."

"George, stop bellyaching about that pathetic half-breed. We're better off without her. I did what had to be done. No God will fault me for cleansing our family of that stain."

George glared at his grandmother. "I always knew you were cruel and unforgiving, but this…. Does Amelia know?"

"Of course not. No one knows except Joe, and he won't tell a soul. Not if he wants to keep his children."

"And Mammy, what have you done to her?"

Sybil let out a bark of laughter. "I fed her to the crocodiles. It was appropriate, I think."

George sank into a chair and buried his face in his hands. He felt ill. This was all his fault. He'd given in to his loneliness and disappointment, and his weakness had resulted in the deaths of

Madeline and Mammy. Somewhere at the back of his mind, he'd suspected his grandmother hadn't told him the truth, but he'd pushed the thought away, too enamored of his son to probe deeper.

"You'd better go now, George. I'm tired," Sybil said as she laid her book on the bedside table and fluffed her pillows. She set aside one pillow to lie down more comfortably.

George got to his feet and approached the bed. "Goodnight, Grandmamma," he said and bent to plant a kiss on his grandmother's cheek. "Sleep well."

Sybil slid down on her pillows. "Turn out the lamp, will you?"

"Of course."

George grabbed the extra pillow and pressed it over Sybil's face. He held it down, ignoring her muffled screams. She clawed at his forearms and kicked wildly, but after a few moments her thrashing subsided, and she eventually went quiet and still. George waited a little while longer before he removed the pillow and set it aside. He looked at his grandmother's face for a long time as silent tears slid down his cheeks.

Tomorrow, he would grant freedom to Zachary, Zane and their families, and give them enough money to start a new life up North. He could never tell them the reason for his generosity, but letting them go was the least he could do, in view of his grandmother's deeds. He would plan a small, private funeral for her and lay her in the Besson tomb, which he would never visit again until it was his turn to join those already there.

George finally got to his feet, turned out the lamp, and walked softly to the door. He went downstairs to the parlor and poured himself a large cognac. Only a few weeks ago he'd learned about Jean's affairs, Corinne's birth, and his uncle's incestuous marriage. He'd finally understood why his grandmother had despised Madeline and never forgave her son, but now there were three murders to add to the Besson legacy. Nothing he could do would atone for what they'd done. His soul was forfeit, and he'd die unforgiven.

The End

The Forsaken

(Echoes from the Past Book 4)

Coming Soon

Notes

I hope you've enjoyed this installment of the *Echoes from the Past* series, and the revelations it brought. I would like to thank Dina and Annette, who've generously allowed me to use their names for two of the characters in this book. It certainly made those characters more real for me, even though they only had minor roles to play. If you think you'd like to be a character in by books, please reach out to me at irina.shapiro@yahoo.com and submit your name. You just might win a walk-on part.

And now, a brief word about book four. Even though Quinn has finally found her real father and discovered the source of her gift, there are still more revelations and cases to come, so please stay tuned for the next book. Quinn is in for quite a surprise, one she never saw coming, but that's all I'm willing to say at the moment.

If you'd like to receive updates and information about new books, please visit me at www.irinashapiro.com or email me at irina.shapiro@yahoo.com. I'm always thrilled to hear from you.

And lastly, if you've enjoyed the book, a review on Amazon or Goodreads would be much appreciated.

Made in the USA
Middletown, DE
21 June 2020

10382460R00224